Sunset Express

Sunset Express

Robert Crais

AN ELVIS COLE NOVEL

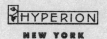

HYPERION

NEW YORK

ISBN 0-7868-8915-2

Original Book Design by Chris Welch

FIRST MASS MARKET EDITION

10 9 8 7 6 5 4 3 2 1

For Leonard Isaacs,
who opened the door,
and
for Kate Wilhelm and Damon Knight,
who invited me in.

Acknowledgments

The author would like to thank Bruce J. Kelton, former Assistant United States Attorney and a managing director of the investigative firm Kroll Associates, for sharing his knowledge of the law and the criminal justice system. Additional thanks go to Det. John Petievich, whose counsel on matters relating to the Los Angeles Police Department in this novel and others has been invaluable. Any errors contained herein are solely the responsibility of the author.

Special thanks go to the world's greatest editor, Leslie Wells.

The author would also like to thank Patricia Crais, Lauren Crais, Robert Miller, Lisa Kitei, Carol Perfumo, Samantha Miller, Brian De Fiore, Marcy Goot, Chris Murphy, Kim Dower, and Jennifer Lang for their support, superior talents, and great efforts on the author's behalf.

Sunset Express

PROLOGUE

The sky above the San Fernando Valley that Saturday morning was a deep blue, washed clean of the dirt and chemical particulates that typically color L.A. air by a breeze that burbled out of the San Gabriel Mountains and over the flat valley floor and across the high ridge of the Santa Monica Mountains. Mulholland Drive snakes along the crest of the Santa Monicas, and, if you were walking along Mulholland as Sandra Bernson and her father were doing that morning, you would have been able to look south almost forty miles across the Los Angeles basin to the tip of the Long Beach Peninsula or north some thirty-five miles across the San Fernando Valley and through the Newhall Pass to the deep purples of the Santa Susana mountains and the peaks surrounding Lake Castaic. It was a day of unusual clarity, the far horizons magnified as if by some rare trick of optical law that might even allow you to see into the lives of the sleeping millions in the valleys below. Sandra Bernson later said that as she watched the small private airplanes floating into and out of Van Nuys Airport in the center of the valley that morning, she imagined them to be flying carpets. On mornings like these, she later said, it was easy to believe in magic.

Sandra was a fifteen-year-old honor student at the prestigious Harvard-Westlake School, and her father, Dave Bernson, was a television writer and producer of moderate success, then working as the supervising producer of a popular series on the Fox Television network. The Bernsons lived in a contemporary home on a small private road off Mulholland Drive in Sherman Oaks, approximately one mile west of Beverly Glen, and they left their home at exactly 6:42 that morning. Both Sandra and Dave were able to tell investigators their exact departure time because it was Dave's habit to call out when their walks began so that they could time themselves. They intended to walk east along Mulholland to Warren Beatty's home approximately one mile east of Beverly Glen, where they planned to reverse course and return. Their typical walk would cover four miles round-trip and take almost exactly fifty minutes. On this particular Saturday, however, they never made it to Beatty's and they didn't complete the walk.

On this Saturday, Sandra Bernson saw the deer.

They proceeded east from their home, climbing one of Mulholland's steeper grades to a high, flat stretch of road abreast Stone Canyon Reservoir. That was Sandra's favorite part of the walk because she could see the valley to the north and the reservoir to the south, and just before they came to Beverly Glen Canyon they would reach the Stone Canyon overlook. The overlook is built into the top of a little knoll there beside Mulholland, with manicured walks and observation points and benches if you want to sit and admire what realtors like to call a 360-degree jetliner view. Sandra remembers that as she and her father reached the top of the overlook she saw the deer creeping up from the valley side of Mulholland, sniffing and listening, and she whispered to her father, "Look, Dad!"

"Mule deer. See the size of his ears? It's a buck, but he's already shed his horns. See the knobs above his eyes?"

The deer heard them. It looked in their direction, its huge ears cocked forward, and then it bounded across Mulholland and the overlook's little parking lot and disappeared. Sandra said, "I wanna see where he goes!"

She slid across the overlook's low wall and ran to the edge of the knoll just as the buck vanished near a cut in the slope that had caught a lot of dead brush and beer cans and newspapers and brown plastic garbage bags. Dave arrived at her side a moment later. Everything caught by the cut looked old and dusty and weathered as if it had been there for a very long time, except for the garbage bags. They looked shiny and new, and Sandra was using them as a landmark to point out to Dave where she had last seen the mule deer when she saw the hand sticking out of the bags. The nail polish was very red and seemed to gleam in the breathtakingly clear morning sun.

It never entered Dave's mind that the hand might be a movie prop or belong to a mannequin; the moment he saw it he knew it was real. It looked real, and it also looked dead. Dave recalls that he considered working his way down to the body, but then says that he remembered things like clues and evidence, and so he led his daughter back to Mulholland where they flagged down a passing Westec private security car. The security cop, a twenty-eight-year-old ex-Marine named Chris Bell, parked his unit and went to see for himself, then returned to his car and reported the find to the Westec offices. In less than eight minutes, two LAPD patrol units arrived on the scene. The uniforms observed the hand protruding from the plastic, but, as had Dave Bernson, decided not to venture down the slope. The uniforms relayed their observations in code by radio, then secured the area to await the arrival of the detectives.

Dave Bernson offered to wait also, but by that time Sandra had to pee really bad, so one of the uniforms drove them home. Forty minutes after Sandra Bernson and her father were returned to their home, and thirty-nine minutes after Sandra began calling her friends just as quickly as she could to tell them about this incredibly gross thing that had just happened, the first detective unit arrived on the scene.

Detective Sergeant Dan "Tommy" Tomsic and Detective-two Angela Rossi were in the first car. Tomsic was a powerfully built man who'd spent a dozen years on the street before making the transfer to detectives. He had almost thirty years on the job, and he viewed the world through suspicious, unblinking eyes. Angela Rossi was thirty-four years old, with twelve years on the job, and had been Tomsic's partner for only five weeks. Rossi spoke her mind, was entirely too confrontational, and, because of this, she had trouble keeping partners. So far Tomsic didn't seem bothered, but that was probably because he ignored her.

Eleven minutes after the first car, the senior detectives arrived on the scene. Detective Sergeant Lincoln Gibbs was a tall, thin African-American with mocha-colored skin, a profoundly receding hairline, and tortoise-shell spectacles. He looked like a college professor, which was a look he cultivated. He had twenty-eight years on the job, less than Tomsic, but more time in grade as a detective sergeant, so Linc Gibbs would be in charge. He arrived with Detective-three Pete Bishop, a twenty-two-year veteran with an M.A. in psychology and five divorces. Bishop rarely spoke, but was known to make copious notes, which he referred to often. He had a measured IQ of 178 and a drinking problem. He was currently in twelve-step.

The four detectives got the story from the uniforms and the Westec cop, then went to the edge of the overlook and stared down at the hand. Gibbs said, "Anybody been down there?"

One of the uniforms said, "No, sir. It's undisturbed."

The detectives searched the ground for anything that might present itself as evidence—scuff marks, drops of blood, footprints, that kind of thing. There were none. They could see the path that the body had followed as it slid down the slope. Scuffs on the soil, broken and bent plants, dislodged rocks. Linc followed the trail with his eyes and figured that the body had been dumped from a point just at the rear of the parking lot. The body was between twelve and fifteen yards down a damned steep slope. Someone would have to go down, and that presented certain problems. You wouldn't want to follow the same path as the body because that might disturb evidence. That meant they'd have to find another route, only everything else was steeper and the drop-off more pronounced. Linc was thinking that it might take mountaineering gear when Angela Rossi said, "I can get down there."

The three male detectives looked at her.

"I've done some rock climbing in Chatsworth and I work terrain like this all the time when I'm backpacking." She pointed out her route. "I can work my way down the slide over there, then traverse back and come up under the body. No sweat."

Dan Tomsic said, "That goddamned soil is like sand. It won't hold your weight."

"It's no sweat, Dan. Really."

Rossi looked like the athletic type, and Gibbs knew that she had run in the last two L.A. marathons. Tomsic sucked down three packs a day and Bishop had the muscle tone of Jell-O. Rossi was also fifteen years younger than the rest of them, and she wanted to go. Gibbs gave his permission, told her to take the camera, and Angela Rossi went back to the car to trade her Max Avante pumps for a busted-out pair of New Balance running shoes. She reappeared a minute later, and Gibbs, Tomsic, and the others watched as she worked her way down to the body. Tomsic frowned as he watched, but Gibbs nodded in approval—Rossi seemed graceful and confident in her movements. Tomsic was praying that she wouldn't lose her balance and break her damned neck—

one slip and she'd flop ass over teapot another sixty or eighty yards down the slope.

Down below, Rossi never once entertained the notion that she might fall. She was feeling absolutely confident and more than a little jazzed that it was she who had taken the lead in recovering the body. If you took the lead you got the promotions, and Rossi made no secret that she wanted to become LAPD's first female chief of detectives. It was a goal she had aggressively pursued since her days at the academy and, though there had been what she called her Big Setback, she still hoped that she could get her career back on track and pull it off.

When Rossi reached the body, she could smell it. The sun was rising and the dark plastic was heating quickly and holding the heat. As water evaporated from the body it collected on the plastic's inner surface, and, Rossi knew, it would be humid and damp inside the bag. The victim's abdomen would swell and the gases of decay would vent. Decomposition had begun.

Linc called down to her, "Try not to move the body. Just take the snaps and peel back the bags."

Rossi used the Polaroid to fix the body's position for the record, then pulled on rubber surgical gloves and touched the wrist, checking for a pulse. She knew that there would be none, but she had to check anyway. The skin was pliant but the muscles beneath were stiff. Rigor.

Rossi couldn't see much, as yet, but the body appeared intact and double-bagged in two dark brown plastic garbage bags. The bags were secured around the body with silver duct tape, but the job appeared to have been done hastily. The bags had parted and the hand had plopped out. Angela Rossi peeled the bags apart to expose the shoulder and head of a blonde Caucasian woman who appeared to be in her early thirties. The woman was clothed in what looked like a pale blue Banana Republic T-shirt that was splattered with blood. The woman's left eye was open but her right eye was closed, and the tip of her tongue protruded between small, perfect teeth. The hair on the back and right side of her head was ropey and matted with blood. Much of the blood was dried, but there was a shiny, wet quality to much of it, also. The skull at that portion of the hair appeared depressed and dark, and brain matter and ridges of white skull were obvious. The woman's nose was straight and her features rectangular and contoured. In life, she would've been pretty. Angela Rossi had an immediate sense that the woman looked familiar.

Tomsic yelled down, "Don't pitch a goddamned tent down there. What's the deal?"

Rossi hated it when he spoke to her that way, but she clenched her jaw and took it. She'd been taking it more and smarting off less since the Big Setback. Anything to resurrect the career. She called back without looking at them. "Caucasian female. Early thirties. Blunt force trauma to the back of the head." She pushed the garbage bag back farther, exposing the victim's head and shoulders. She saw no additional injuries and wanted to peel back the bags even farther, but was concerned that the body would dislodge and tumble down the slope, possibly taking her with it. She took more pictures, then said, "The blood around the wound appears to be tacky, and it's wet in some spots. She hasn't been here long."

Bishop said, "Lividity?"

"A little, but it could be bruising."

Above her, Linc Gibbs was growing impatient with all the conversation. He didn't like Rossi perched on such a steep slope, and he wanted to call in the criminalist. He said, "What about a weapon?" Murderers almost always dumped the murder weapon with the body.

He watched Rossi lean across the body and feel around the bags. She moved out of sight twice, and each time he tasted acid because he thought she'd fallen. Another Tagamet day. He remembers that he was just getting ready to ask her what in hell was taking so long when she said, "Don't see anything, but it could be under the body or in the bag."

Gibbs nodded. "Leave it for the criminalist. Take some more pix and get back up here."

Rossi took the remainder of the roll, then worked her way back up the slope. When she reached the top, the others crowded around to see the pictures. All of the male detectives pulled out reading glasses except for Gibbs, who wore bifocals.

One of the uniformed cops said, "Hey. She looks like somebody."

Rossi said, "I thought so, too."

She didn't look like anyone to Gibbs. "You guys recognize her?"

Bishop was turning the pictures round and round, as if seeing the victim from every possible view was important. All the turning was making Tomsic nauseated. Bishop said, "Her name is Susan Martin."

The Westec cop said, "Holy Christ, you're right. Teddy Martin's wife."

All four detectives looked at him.

The Westec cop said, "They live right over here in Benedict Canyon. It's on my route." Benedict Canyon was less than one mile from the overlook.

Gibbs said, "I'll be damned."

The four detectives later testified that they thought pretty much the same thing at the same time. Teddy Martin meant money and, more important than money, political power, and that meant the case would require special handling. Dan Tomsic remembers thinking that he wished he had called in sick that day so some other asshole would've answered the call. Special cases always meant special trouble, and investigating officers almost always caught the short end of the deal. Teddy Martin was a rich boy who'd made himself even richer; a successful restaurateur and businessman who used his wealth to cultivate friends and social position and notoriety. He was always having dinner with city councilmen and movie stars, and he was always in the newspaper for giving millions of dollars to all the right causes. Tomsic knew the name because Teddy Martin had opened a new theme restaurant with a couple of movie star partners that his wife had been nagging him to take her to. He'd been foot-dragging because he knew it'd cost sixty bucks for a couple of pieces of fish just so the wife could eyeball some second-rate movie props and maybe some closet-fag actor. Tomsic hated guys like Teddy Martin, but he kept it to himself. Guys like Teddy Martin were headline grabbers and almost always phonies, but a phony with the right connections could end your career.

Pete Bishop said, "It's gonna be a headliner. We'd better call the boss."

Gibbs said, "Use your cell phone. You put it on the radio, we'll have media all over us. Tommy, see if there's anything on the wire."

Angela Rossi walked with Tomsic and Bishop back to their units. Fine soil and foxtails had worked down into her running shoes and between her toes, so she sat in the backseat of her radio car and cleaned her feet with a Handiwipe before changing back into her Max Avantes. While she sat in the car, Tomsic and Bishop stood apart from each other in the overlook's parking lot, each talking into their respective cell phones.

By the time Rossi finished cleaning her feet and had rejoined Gibbs at the top of the slope, both Tomsic and Bishop were off their phones. Tomsic said, "Nothing on the board about a Susan Martin."

Bishop said, "I called the boss and notified the coroner. Criminalists are on the way, and the boss is coming out." The boss was the detective captain who oversaw the Westside detectives. When he reached the scene, everyone knew he'd decide whether Gibbs would keep the case or it would be reassigned to someone else. Gibbs knew that because of Mr. Martin's stature, the case would almost certainly be assigned to one of the elite robbery-homicide units downtown. He had no problem with that.

Gibbs said, "Okay, we'd better notify Mr. Martin and

see what he says." He looked at the Westec guy. "You know where they live?"

"Sure. I'll take you over, you want."

Gibbs started for his car. "Okay. Let's go."

Bishop was shaking his head. "We'd better stick around for the boss, Linc."

Tomsic said, "Angie and I'll go."

Angela Rossi later said that if she'd known where it was going to lead, she would have shot Tomsic right there.

Dan Tomsic and Angela Rossi followed the Westec guy east along Mulholland to Benedict, then south down through the canyon into a lush winding world of million-dollar homes and Mercedes convertibles. Most of the homes were new and modern, but the Westec guy pulled off the road in front of a Mediterranean mansion that could have been a hundred years old. A big mortar wall with an ornate iron gate protected the mansion from the street, the wall laced by delicate ivy with tiny, blood-red leaves. The wall was cracked and crumbling beneath the ivy, but you could see the cracks only if you took your time and looked between the vines. A gate phone stood to the left of the drive so you could identify yourself before being buzzed in. Tomsic figured the grounds for four or five acres, and the house beyond for maybe twenty thousand square feet. Tomsic and his wife and four children were squeezed into a twenty-two-hundred-square-foot cracker box in Simi Valley, but those were the breaks. Anyone could be a cop, but it took real talent to serve bad food in an overpriced restaurant.

They were getting out of the car when Angie said, "The gate's open."

The big wrought iron gate was open maybe nine or ten inches. You didn't live behind walls and gates and security cops, then leave the front gate open so that any stray goofball or passing psycho could come inside and make himself at home. Tomsic remembers that his first thought on seeing the open gate was that they would find a body inside.

They went to the gate and pressed the button on the call box twice, but they got no answers. Angie said, "We don't need to wait for a warrant, do we?"

Tomsic said, "Shit." He pushed at the gate and went through.

The Westec guy said, "We can't just walk in, can we?" He looked nervous. "I'll call the office and they can ring the house."

Tomsic ignored him, and Rossi followed Tomsic toward the house.

The drive was hand-laid Mexican pavers and had probably cost more than Tomsic's house, his two cars, and the quarter interest he owned in a Big Bear Lake cabin combined. The mansion itself was built of mortar and rough-hewn wooden beams and was finished with an ancient Spanish tile roof. A healthy growth of ivy covered the ground along the east side of the drive, nestling up to a couple of monstrous podocarpus trees before continuing around a four-car garage. Each car had its own door, and the whole effect was more that of a stable than a garage. A large fountain sat just off the front entry, trickling water.

Tomsic thought that it looked like the kind of house that Errol Flynn might've owned. His wife would love the place, but Tomsic knew that most of the old stars, just like most of the new stars, were perverts and scumbags, and if you knew the things that went on in places like this you wouldn't be so thrilled with being here. Normal people didn't go into the movie business. Movie people were shitbirds with serious emotional problems who kept their secret lives hidden. Just like most lawyers and all politicians. Tomsic completely believed this, probably because everything he'd seen in almost thirty years on the job confirmed it. Of course, Tomsic had never in his thirty years shared what he knew with his wife because he didn't want to rain on her parade. It was easier to let her think he was a grump.

Nothing seemed amiss. No bodies were floating in the fountain and no cars were parked crazily on the front lawn. The massive front door was closed and appeared undamaged. A large ornate knocker hung in the center of the door, but there was also a bell. Tomsic pressed the button, then used the knocker. Loud. The Westec guy came running up behind them. "Hey, take it easy. You're gonna break it." His face was white.

Angie said, "Stay back, okay? We don't know what we have here."

Tomsic glanced at Angie and shook his head. Fuckin' Westec geek, worried about losin' the account. Angie rolled her eyes.

Tomsic slammed at the door two more times without

getting an answer and was starting back to the car when the door opened and Theodore "Teddy" Martin blinked out. Martin was a medium-sized man, a little shorter than average, with pale, delicate skin. He was unshaven and drawn with hollow, red-rimmed eyes. Tomsic says that he would've bet that the guy had spent most of the night blasted on coke or crystal meth. "Mr. Martin?"

Martin nodded, his head snapping up and down. He was wearing baggy gray sweatpants and no shirt. His torso was soft and undeveloped and covered with a thick growth of fine hair. He squinted against the bright morning sun. "Yeah, sure. What do you want?"

Both Tomsic and Angela Rossi later testified that Tomsic badged him and identified himself as a detective with the Los Angeles Police Department. Angela Rossi noted that Teddy Martin never looked at the badge. He kept his eyes on Tomsic and blinked harder as if something were in his eyes. Angela Rossi thought at the time that he might have allergies. Tomsic said, "Mr. Martin, does a woman named Susan Martin live here with you?"

When Tomsic asked the question, Angela Rossi says that Teddy Martin took a single sharp breath and said, "Oh, my Christ, they killed her, didn't they?"

People say the damnedest things.

Tomsic took Rossi aside, gave her his cell phone, and told her to call Gibbs and tell him to get over here. Rossi walked out to the drive and made the call. When she returned to the house, Tomsic and Teddy Martin and the Westec geek were inside, Tomsic and Martin sitting on an antique bench in the entry. Teddy Martin was blubbering like a baby. "I did everything they said. I did everything, and they said they'd let her go. Jesus Christ. Oh, Jesus, tell me this isn't happening."

Tomsic was sitting very close to Martin and his voice was soft. He could make it soft whenever he wanted to calm people. "You're saying she was kidnapped?"

Martin sucked great gulps of air as if he couldn't breathe. "Christ, yes, of course she was kidnapped." He put his face in his hands and wailed. "I did everything they said. I gave them every nickel. They said they'd let her go."

Angela Rossi said, "You gave someone money?"

Martin waved his hands, like a jumble of words were floating around him and he had to grab hold of the ones he wanted to use. "Half a million dollars. Just like they said. I did everything exactly the way they said. They promised they'd let her go. They *promised*."

Tomsic gently took Teddy's wrists and pushed his hands down. He said, "Tell me what happened, Mr. Martin. You want to tell me what happened? Can you do that?"

Martin seemed to regain control of himself and rubbed at his eyes. He said, "I came home Thursday night and she was gone. Then this guy calls and says he's got Susan and he puts her on. I think it was around eight o'clock."

Rossi distinctly remembers asking, "You spoke with her?"

"She was crying. She said she couldn't see anything and then the guy came back and he told me that if I didn't give them the five hundred thousand they'd kill her. I could hear her screaming. I could hear her crying."

Tomsic said, "Did you recognize this man's voice?"

"No. No, I asked him who he was and he said I should call him James X."

Tomsic glanced at Rossi and raised his eyebrows. "James X?"

"He said they were watching the house. He said they would know if I called the police and they would kill her. Oh, Jesus, I was so scared." Teddy Martin stood, taking deep breaths and rubbing his stomach as if it hurt. "He said I should get the money and he would call tomorrow and tell me what to do with it."

Angie said, "Tomorrow was yesterday?"

Martin nodded. "That's right. Friday. I got the money just like he said. All in hundreds. He wanted hundreds. Then I came back here and waited for his call."

Tomsic said, "You just walked into the bank and got five hundred thousand dollars?"

Teddy Martin snapped him an angry look. "Of course not. My business manager arranged it. He cashed bonds. Something like that. He wanted to know why I wanted the money and I told him not to ask."

Rossi saw Tomsic frown. Tomsic prompted Martin to continue. "Okay. So you got the money, then came back here to wait."

Martin nodded again. "I guess it was around four, something like that, when he called. He told me to put the money in a garbage bag and bring it to a parking lot just off Mulholland at the four-o-five. They have a little lot there for people who carpool. He told me that there was a dumpster, and I should put the money into the dumpster, then go home. He said they would give me exactly twelve minutes to get there, and if I was late they'd know I was working with the police and they'd kill Susan. They said I should just drop the money and leave, and that after I was gone they'd pick up the money and count it and if everything was okay they'd let Susan go. They said it probably wouldn't be until nine or ten with the counting." He sat again and started rocking. "I did everything just like they said and I've been waiting all night. I never heard from them again. I never heard from Susan. When you rang the bell I thought you were her." Teddy Martin put his face in his hands and sobbed. "I made it in the twelve minutes. I swear to God I made it. I was driving like a maniac."

Tomsic told Angie to take the cell phone again, call Gibbs, and this time tell him to have someone check the dumpster. She left, and Tomsic stayed with Martin and the Westec guy. Rossi was gone for only four or five minutes, but when she returned she looked burned around the edges. He said, "You get Gibbs?"

She didn't answer the question. Instead, she said, "Dan, may I see you, please?"

Tomsic followed her outside to the ivy alongside the expensive Mexican drive. She took out her pen, pushed aside some leaves, and exposed a ball peen hammer clotted with blond hair and bits of pink matter. Tomsic said, "I'll be damned."

Rossi said, "I was just looking around when I saw it. The handle was sticking up out of the ivy."

Tomsic stared at the hammer for several seconds, noticing that a single black ant was crawling in the pink matter. Tomsic made the same whistling sound that he'd made at the Stone Canyon overlook when he'd seen the body. Angela Rossi then said, "He killed her, didn't he, Dan?"

Lincoln Gibbs and Pete Bishop turned into the drive as she said it. Dan Tomsic, who had a million years on the job and whose opinion as a professional cynic almost everyone valued, glanced at the mansion and said, "The sonofabitch killed her, all right, but now we have to convict him."

"Hey, we've *got* this guy, Dan! He's *ours*!"

Dan Tomsic stared at her with the disdain he reserved for shitbirds, defense attorneys, and card-carrying members of the ACLU. He said, "It's easier to cut off your own goddamned leg than convict a rich man in this state, detective. Haven't you been around long enough to know that?"

It was the last thing that Dan Tomsic said to her that day.

Susan Martin's murder made the evening news, as did the events that followed.

I was able, months later, to piece together the events of that Saturday morning from police reports, participant interviews, court testimony, and newspaper articles, but I couldn't tell you what I was doing when I heard, or where I was or who I was with. It didn't seem important.

I did not think, nor did I have reason to believe, that Susan Martin's murder and everything that grew from it would have such a profound and permanent impact upon my life.

1

Jonathan Green came to my office on a hazy June morning with an entourage of three attorneys, a videographer, and an intense young woman lugging eight hundred pounds of sound recording equipment. The videographer shoved past the attorneys and swung his camera around my office, saying, "This is just what we need, Jonathan! It's real, it's colorful, it's *L.A.!*" He aimed his camera at me past the Mickey Mouse phone and began taping. "Pretend I'm not here."

I frowned at him, and he waved toward the lawyers. "Don't look at me. At *them*. Look at *them*."

I looked at *them*. "What is this?" I was expecting Green and an attorney named Elliot Truly, but not the others. Truly had arranged the meeting.

A man in his mid-forties wearing an immaculately tailored blue Armani suit said, "Mr. Cole? I'm Elliot Truly. This is Jonathan Green. Thanks for seeing us."

I shook hands with Truly first, then Green. Green looked exactly the way he had the two times I'd seen him on *60 Minutes,* once when he defended an abortion rights activist accused of murder in Texas and once when he defended a wealthy textile manufacturer accused of murder in Iowa. The Texas case was popular and the Iowa case wasn't, but both were victories for the defense.

The videographer scrambled backward across the office to fit us into his frame, the woman with the sound gear hustling to stay behind the camera as they captured the moment of our first meeting. Armstrong steps onto the moon; the Arabs and the Israelis sign a peace accord; Jonathan Green meets the private detective. The woman with the sound equipment bumped into my desk and the videographer slammed against the file cabinet. The little figures of Jiminy Cricket on the cabinet fell over and the framed photo of Lucy Chenier tottered. I frowned at him again. "Be careful."

The videographer waved some more. "Don't look at me! *Not at me!* You'll ruin the shot!"

I said, "If you break anything, I'll ruin more than the shot."

Green seemed embarrassed. "This is tiresome, Elliot. We have business here, and I'm afraid we're making a bad impression on Mr. Cole."

Truly touched my arm, trying to mitigate the bad impression. "They're from *Inside News*. They're doing a six-part documentary on Jonathan's involvement in the case."

The woman with the sound equipment nodded. "The inner workings of the Big Green Defense Machine."

I said, "Big Green Defense Machine?"

The videographer stopped taping and looked me up and down as if he found me lacking but wasn't quite sure how. Then it hit him. "Don't you have a gun?" He glanced around the office as if there might be one hanging on a wall hook.

"A gun?"

He looked at Truly. "He should be wearing a gun. One of those things under the arm." He was a small man with furry arms.

Truly frowned. "A shoulder holster?"

The woman nodded. "A hat would be nice. Hats are romantic."

I said, "Truly."

Jonathan Green's face clouded. "I apologize, Mr. Cole. They've been with us for the past week and it's becoming offensive. If it bothers you, I'll ask them to leave."

The videographer grew frantic. "Hey, forget the gun. I was just trying to make it a little more entertaining, that's all." He crouched beside the water cooler and lifted his camera. "You won't even know we're here. I promise."

Truly pursed his lips at me. My call.

I made a little shrug. "The people who come to me usually don't want a record of what we discuss."

Jonathan Green chuckled. "It may come to that, but let's hope not." He went to the French doors that open onto the little balcony, then looked at the picture of Lucy Chenier. "Very pretty. Your wife?"

"A friend."

He nodded, approving. When he nodded, the two lesser attorneys nodded, too. No one had bothered to introduce them, but they didn't seem to mind.

Jonathan Green sat in one of the leather director's

chairs across from my desk and the two lesser attorneys went to the couch. Truly stayed on his feet. The videographer noticed the Pinocchio clock on the wall, then hustled around to the opposite side of my desk so that he could get both me and the clock in frame. The Pinocchio clock has eyes that move side to side as it tocks. Photogenic. Like Green.

Jonathan Green had a firm handshake, clear eyes, and a jawline not dissimilar to Dudley Do-Right's. He was in his early sixties, with graying hair, a beach-club tan, and a voice that was rich and comforting. A minister's voice. He wasn't a handsome man, but there was a sincerity in his eyes that put you at ease. Jonathan Green was reputed to be one of the top five criminal defense attorneys in America, with a success rate in high-profile criminal defense cases of one hundred percent. Like Elliot Truly, Jonathan Green was wearing an impeccably tailored blue Armani suit. So were the lesser attorneys. Maybe they got a bulk discount. I was wearing impeccably tailored black Gap jeans, a linen aloha shirt, and white Reebok sneakers. Green said, "Did Elliot explain why we wanted to see you?"

"You represent Theodore Martin. You need investigators to help in the defense effort." Theodore "Teddy" Martin had been arrested for Susan Martin's murder and was awaiting trial. He had gone through two prior defense attorneys, hadn't been happy with them, and had recently hired Jonathan Green. All the hirings and firings had been covered big time by the local media.

Green nodded. "That's right. Mr. Cole, I've spoken

at length with Teddy and I believe that he's innocent. I want your help in proving it."

I smiled. "*Moi?*"

The videographer edged in closer. I raised a finger at him. Unh-unh-unnh. He edged back.

Truly said, "We've talked to people, Mr. Cole. You've an outstanding reputation for diligence, and your integrity is above reproach."

"How about that." I glanced at the camera and wiggled my eyebrows. The videographer frowned and lowered the lens.

Jonathan Green leaned toward me, all business. "What do you know about the case?"

"I know what everybody knows. I watch the news." You couldn't read the *Times* or watch local television without knowing the business about James X and the five hundred thousand dollars and the dumpster. I'd heard Theodore Martin's sound-bite version of it ten thousand times, but I'd also heard the DA's sound-bite version, too, that Teddy and Susan weren't getting along, that Susan had secretly consulted a divorce attorney and told a friend that she was planning a divorce, and that Teddy had offed her to keep her from walking away with half of his estimated one-hundred-twenty-million-dollar fortune. I said, "From what I hear, the police have a pretty good case."

"They believe they have, yes. But I don't think all the facts are in." Green smiled and laced his fingers across a knee. It was a warm smile, tired and knowing. "Did you know that Teddy and Susan loved to cook?"

I shook my head. That one had slipped right by me.

"Teddy arrived home early that night, and they had no engagements, so the two of them decided to cook something elaborate and fun. They spent the next couple of hours making a pepper-roasted pork tenderloin with wild cherry sauce. Teddy makes the sauce with fresh cherries, only they didn't have any, so he ran out to get some."

Truly took a step toward me and ticked points off his fingers. "We have the receipt and the cashier whom Teddy paid. That's where he was when Susan was kidnapped."

Green spread his hands. "And then there's the question of the money. What happened to the money?"

Truly ticked more fingers. "We have the bank transactions and the business manager. The manager says that Teddy was visibly shaken when he came for the money that Friday morning. He says Teddy was white as a sheet and his hands were shaking."

Green nodded. "Yet the cashier remembers that Teddy was relaxed and happy a dozen hours earlier." Green stood and went back to the balcony. The videographer followed him. At the French doors he turned back to me and spread his hands again. I wondered if he thought he was in court. "And then we have the murder weapon and the crime scene evidence."

Truly ticked more fingers. He had used up one hand and was starting on the next. "There were fingerprints on the hammer, but none of them match Teddy. There were also fingerprints on the garbage bags that Susan was in, but those don't match Teddy, either."

I said, "You think he's innocent because of that?"

Green came back to the director's chair, but this time he didn't sit. He stood behind it, resting his hands on the wooden posts that hold the back. "Mr. Cole, I don't win the number of cases that I do because I'm good. I turn down ten cases every day, cases that would bill millions of dollars, because I will not represent people I believe to be guilty."

The videographer went down to the floor for a low-angle shot, the woman with the sound equipment with him, and I heard him mumble, "Oh, man, this is great."

Green said, "I don't represent drug dealers or child molesters. I only take cases that I believe in, so that every time I walk into court I have the moral high ground."

I leaned back and put my foot on the edge of my desk. "And you believe that Teddy is innocent."

"Yes. Yes, I do." He came around to the front of the chair and tapped his chest. "In here I know he's innocent."

The videographer muttered, "This is fabulous," and scrambled around to keep Jonathan Green in the shot.

Green sat and leaned toward me, elbows on knees. "I don't yet know all the facts. I need people like you to help me with that. But I do know that we've received several calls that are disturbing."

Elliot Truly said, "Have you heard of our tip line?"

"I've seen the ads." Green's office was running television, radio, and print ads offering a reward of one hundred thousand dollars for anything leading to the capture, arrest, and conviction of James X. There was a number you could call.

Green said, "We've received over twenty-six hundred

calls and there are more every day. We try to weed out the cranks as quickly as possible, but the workload is enormous."

I cleared my throat and tried to look professional. "Okay. You need help running these things down."

Green raised his eyebrows. "Yes, but there's more to it than that. Several of the callers have indicated that one of the arresting officers has a history of fabricating cases."

I stared at him. The videographer scrambled back across the office, again running into the cabinet, but this time I did not look. "Which officer?"

Truly said, "The detective who claims to have found the hammer. Angela Rossi."

I looked at Truly. "Claims?"

Jonathan Green, Elliot Truly, and the camera stared at me. No one spoke.

I looked back at Green. "Do you believe that Angela Rossi planted evidence against Teddy Martin?"

Green shifted in the chair and the camera swung back toward him. He looked uncomfortable, as if the subject bothered him. "I don't want to say that, not yet, but I believe that the possibility exists. She was the first to go down to Susan's body, and she went alone."

Truly said, "She had the opportunity to recover the murder weapon and secrete it on her person."

"A full-size ball peen hammer."

Truly smiled. "Where there's a will."

I shook my head. "Why would she take the chance?"

Green said, "Elliot."

Truly leaned toward me, serious. "Rossi was on a fast track up the promotion ladder until she blew a homicide investigation two years ago. She failed to Mirandize a suspect who subsequently confessed, and the suspect walked. She might feel she needs a headline case to resurrect her career, and if she tampered with evidence to make this case, it may not be the first time she's done so." Truly made a little hand move at one of the lesser attorneys, and the lesser attorney slipped a manila envelope from his Gucci case and brought it to me. Truly said, "Rossi arrested a man named LeCedrick Earle five years ago for possessing counterfeit money and attempting to bribe an officer. He's currently serving a six-year sentence at Terminal Island." Terminal Island is the federal facility down in San Pedro. "Earle phoned six days ago and told us that Rossi planted the money." He gestured at the envelope. "He's been saying that he was set up since day one, and sent us a copy of his case file and the various letters of complaint to prove it."

I opened the envelope and fingered through the arrest reports, legal correspondence, and letters of complaint. Terminal Island return address, all right. I said, "All perps claim they're innocent and every cop I know has had charges brought against him. It goes with the job."

Green nodded, reasonably. "Of course, but Mr. Earle's claim seems to have a bit more merit than the others."

Truly said, "A former LAPD officer named Raymond Haig told us about the Earle case, also. Haig was Rossi's partner."

I said, "Haig was her partner at that time?"

"Yes."

"And he said that she planted the goods?"

Truly smiled again. "He wouldn't say that, but he says that he knew her and that she would do anything to further her career. He suggested that we look into it."

I said, "If Earle made the allegation, there would've been an internal police investigation."

The smaller lesser attorney said, "There was, but no charges were filed."

Green said, "Mr. Haig indicated that Detective Rossi has a history of excessive behavior."

I put the envelope down and tapped at the edge of my desk. The videographer crept back to the water cooler and focused on me. I said, "Mr. Green, you should know that my partner, Joe Pike, is a former LAPD officer."

"We're familiar with Mr. Pike."

"I work with LAPD often, and I have many friends there, and in the district attorney's office."

He leaned toward me again, very serious now, sincere. "I'm not looking for a stooge. I have plenty of those, believe me." He tried not to glance at the lesser attorneys but couldn't help himself. "I'm looking for an honest detective who won't just tell me what I want to hear. I want the truth. Without the truth, I have nothing. Do you see?"

I nodded. Maybe I could see why he was one of the world's greatest defense attorneys after all.

Truly said, "What we're discussing with you is only a small part of the larger picture. We have sixteen investigators working with us now, and we'll probably have as many as thirty, but you'll be the only investigator working on this aspect of the case."

The larger lesser attorney said, "We have fourteen attorneys on board, in addition to the investigators."

The smaller lesser attorney's head bobbed. "Not to mention eight forensic specialists and three criminalists." He seemed proud when he said it. Peace through superior firepower.

I made a whistling sound. "The best defense money can buy."

Jonathan Green stayed serious. "As I said, there's plenty of work to go around, and more work every day. Will you help us, Mr. Cole?"

I leaned back, thinking about it, and then I held up the envelope. "And what if I find out that Rossi's okay?"

"Then that's what you find. I owe it to myself and my client to exhaust every possibility. Do you see?"

I said, "Wherever it leads."

"That's exactly right."

"The moral high ground."

"My reputation rests on it."

I watched the Pinocchio clock. I looked at the picture of Lucy Chenier. I nodded. "If Rossi's clean, that's what I'll report."

"I wouldn't have it any other way."

Jonathan Green put out his hand and we shook.

e worked out my fee, Elliot Truly cut me a check, and the Big Green Defense Machine left me to get on with it. I stood in the door as they walked to the elevator, watching the videographer record every moment of the departure. Cindy, the woman who runs the beauty supply distribution office next door, came out of the elevator as they were getting on and saw Jonathan. She stared at him until the doors closed, and then she smiled at me. Incredulous. "Isn't he that guy? The lawyer?"

"Jonathan Green."

"I saw him on *Geraldo*. He's famous."

I held out crossed fingers. "We're like this."

Cindy opened her door, then cocked an eyebrow at me. "I always did think you were cute."

"Big time. I am nothing if not big time."

She laughed and disappeared into her office. That's Cindy.

I went back into my office, closed the door, and looked at the picture of Lucy Chenier. She was sitting in her backyard wearing shorts and hiking boots and an

LSU T-shirt. I had had the picture in my office since Lucy sent it to me a little over three months ago, and I looked at it a lot. Lucy was a lawyer, too, but she hadn't been on *Geraldo*. His loss. I stared at the picture. Something about it wasn't right and, being an astute detective, I deduced that this was because the videographer had bumped the cabinet. It was not too late to rush down the stairs and shoot him, but that would probably be overreacting. Besides, he was part of the Big Green Defense Machine, and teammates shouldn't shoot each other. Jonathan Green might think me small.

I adjusted the picture, then went back to my desk and dialed Lucy's office in Baton Rouge, Louisiana. If Cindy was impressed with Jonathan Green, so might be Lucy Chenier. I am also nothing if not a show-off.

A warm southern voice said, "Ms. Chenier's office." Lucy's assistant, Mrs. Darlene Thomas.

"It's me." I'd phoned quite often in the three months since I'd been in Louisiana, and the calls were becoming more frequent.

"Hello, Mr. Cole. How are we today?"

"We're fine, Darlene. And yourself?" Small talk.

"Very well, thank you. I'm sorry, but she's in court today."

"Oh." Dejected.

Darlene said, "She'll call for her messages, though. I'll tell her that you phoned."

"Tell her that I'm lonely, Darlene."

Darlene laughed. "I'll tell her that Mr. Cole says he's lonely."

"Tell her that I miss her, Darlene. That the longing

grows with every passing moment and has become a weight impossible for me to bear."

Darlene gasped. "Oh *my*, but you do go on!"

I was grinning. Darlene did that to me. "Darlene, have I ever said that you've got a very sexy voice?"

"Get on with you, now! You stop this nonsense before I tell Ms. Chenier!"

We said our good-byes and I called Joe Pike to tell him that we were once more employed. His answering machine picked up on the first ring and beeped. He used to have a one-word message that just said, "Speak," but I guess he felt it was long-winded. Now, there was just the beep. When I asked him how people were supposed to know who they had gotten or what to do, he'd said, "Intelligence test." That Pike is something, isn't he?

I said, "This is the Lone Ranger, calling to inform you that someone has once again been foolish enough to give us money. We're working for Jonathan Green." I hung up. It might be days before I heard from him.

The envelope that Truly left contained a copy of Le-Cedrick Earle's arrest report as well as a formal letter of complaint written by a public defender on Earle's behalf. The arrest report was written by Officer Angela Rossi and stated that Rossi had arrested Mr. Earle at his home after Mr. Earle attempted to bribe his way out of a traffic code violation with eight hundred dollars in counterfeit one-hundred-dollar bills. The letter of complaint alleged that Rossi had planted the counterfeit money on Mr. Earle and that Mr. Earle was innocent of all wrongdoing. The arrest report said little, and the letter of complaint said even less. She said, he said. A single sheet bearing both Angela Rossi's home address and Raymond Haig's business address and phone number was the last entry in the file. A newspaper photograph of Rossi was clipped to the sheet. It was an old photo that showed an attractive woman with a lean, rectangular face and intelligent eyes. She looked determined.

I put everything back into the envelope, then called my friend Eddie Ditko at the *Examiner*. Eddie has been a reporter for about ten million years, and he answered with a voice that was maybe three weeks away from throat cancer. "Ditko."

"Is this Eddie Ditko, the world's finest reporter?"

He made a hacking sound like a cat gakking up a hairball. "Yeah, sure, it says that right here on my Pulitzer. Hold on a minute while I wipe my ass with it." That Eddie. Always with just the right thing to say.

"A guy named LeCedrick Earle was busted on a funny money beef five years ago. He claimed it was a setup by the arresting officer."

"They all claim that. It's a natural law." You see?

"The arresting officer was Angela Rossi."

"I'm hearing Notre Dame." Bells.

"Rossi put the cuffs on Teddy Martin. She found the hammer."

Eddie made the gakking sound again. "You're shitting me."

"Nope."

He wasn't saying anything. Thinking. Sniffing the words and smelling a story. "What's this to you?"

I didn't say anything.

He gave the big sigh, like I was asking for an organ donation. "What do you want?"

"Whatever you've got on the Earle arrest, and anything in your files about Rossi." Ever since the Christopher Commission the *Examiner* kept a database on LAPD officers. The Fourth Estate's version of Big Brother.

"What's this have to do with Teddy Martin?"

I didn't say anything some more.

"Yeah, right. I'll get back to you." Then he said, "You really give me ass cramps."

He hung up without another word. Always the pleasant conversationalist.

I put everything back in the envelope, then locked the office and drove up through Hollywood and the Cahuenga Pass and into the San Fernando Valley. I left the Hollywood Freeway at Barham and drove east along the foot of the Verdugo hills through Burbank into Glendale. Raymond Haig owned a Mr. Rubber Discount Tire franchise in an area of gas stations and falafel stands and flat single-story buildings with shops that sold secondhand clothes and wholesale electronics. A weathered Hispanic guy in a broken straw hat had set up a little *churro* cart outside the tire store, the *churros* hanging in ropes inside the glass cart. The Hispanic guy was decked out in cowboy boots and jeans and a wide leather belt with a gleaming silver buckle inlaid with the image of a Brahma bull. A *vaquero*. A couple of kids with skateboards were holding fistfuls of wax paper and long brown *churros*, and a black dog with a bandana around its neck was sitting between them, looking first at one, then the other. Hopeful.

I parked on the street in front of the *churro* cart, then went into the store. A young Hispanic woman with tired eyes and too much makeup was sitting behind the counter, staring at a little television. I handed her a card. "I need to see Mr. Haig. If you tell him that Elliot Truly sent me, he'll know what it's about."

She took the card and disappeared through a door leading to the service bay, and a couple of minutes later she came back with a tall guy in his late forties. Haig. He was wearing a plaid shirt and a maroon knit tie, and he had a pencil caddy in his shirt pocket. The caddy's plastic flap said *Beamis Shocks*. He came over. "You Cole?"

"That's right. Elliot Truly said that someone from his office spoke to you, and that you'd be willing to answer a few questions about Angela Rossi."

His face split with a sleek smile and he put out his hand. "You bet. Let's go in back and I'll tell you everything you need to know about that rotten bitch Rossi." Nothing like an unbiased opinion.

He led me to a small office cluttered with parts catalogs and product manuals and posters of bikinied young women posing on lug wrench displays. Enlightened. A couple of padded chairs sat opposite his desk for customers, and a Mr. Coffee with a tower of Styrofoam cups sat on a table next to the glass door. "You want a little coffee?"

"No, thanks."

Haig poured a cup for himself and brought it to his

desk. There was a picture of a younger Haig in an LAPD uniform on the desk.

I said, "How long were you on the job?"

"Fifteen bullshit years." Unbiased, all right. "Best move I ever made was getting out and going into business for myself. Yes, sir." He settled in behind the desk, then picked up an unlit cigar and popped it into the side of his mouth. I took out a little pad and a Uniball pen to take notes. He said, "Rossi's the reason I left the goddamned force."

"How so?"

"I didn't want to ride with a woman."

I smiled at him. "You left because you didn't want to ride with a woman."

He pulled the cigar from his mouth and made a move with it. "Hey, you get these women in a car, they're either scared shitless and not worth a damn when things get hairy, or they're out of their minds aggressive and you never know what they're gonna do."

"And Rossi was aggressive?"

"Christ, yes. Always tryin' to be more man than a man." He had some of the coffee, then sucked at the cigar again.

I said, "You were partners when she made the Le-Cedrick Earle arrest?"

"Yep. That's the bust got her into plainclothes. She got a big promotion off that bust." He leaned back, and I noticed that small brown flecks of matter were scattered over the catalogs and desk and floor. I squinted at them and wondered what they were.

I said, "LeCedrick Earle claims that she planted the

money, and Truly says that you agree." I felt something gritty on the arms of the chair and looked. More flecks. Sort of like brown dandruff.

Haig chewed at the cigar, then took it out and examined it. The end was soggy and frayed, and while he looked he absently spit little pieces of tobacco off his tongue. I saw a piece land on an air filter catalog. I saw another piece land on the framed photo of young LAPD Haig. Haig didn't seem to notice, or didn't care. I lifted my elbows from the chair and brushed at my arms. Yuck. Haig shook his head. "Nope. I didn't say that. I said that I wouldn't **put** it past the bitch."

"But you don't know?"

He shrugged and spit more tobacco. "If you read the arrest report you know I wasn't listed as an arresting officer. Rossi went back later without me. That way only one name gets credit for the collar. You see how she was?"

"She cut you out."

Another shrug. "Just her way. When it came to wearin' a uniform she was just passin' through and she made no secret of it. All she used to talk about was gettin' ahead, gettin' that gold shield. She told me she'd do anything to get that gold shield, and that's what I told Truly. I had to listen to that every goddamned day like a goddamned matrah."

"Mantra."

"Whatever."

The Hispanic woman rapped at the glass then stepped into Haig's office. She was holding a clipboard. "Warren wan's you to sign these estimates."

Haig grinned and made a little c'mere gesture. "Lemme see what you've got."

She kept her eyes down when she crossed to him, probably because Haig was making a big deal out of looking at her. A gold wedding band and a large, ornate engagement ring were on her left hand, the stone square and flat and enormous, and probably zircon. The polished gold of the rings looked warm against her brown skin. She said, "Warren says a truck is here with the new tires. He says he needs you to come see." Warren was probably Haig's assistant.

"Yeah. I'll be out in a minute."

Haig took the clipboard and flipped through a couple of pages without really looking at them. He used one hand to flip the pages and the other to feel her right hip. He scratched his name and handed back the board, still with the big grin. "*Gracias,* babe. Lookin' good."

"Warren says he needs you about the new tires." Like Warren had been making a thing and she didn't want to mention it, but felt obligated.

Haig's grin turned brittle. "Tell Warren to hold his water. I'll come when I come. *Comprende?*" He patted her hip again, letting his hand linger.

She took the board and walked out, Haig watching her go. He spit more tobacco, and I thought that if any of the flecks landed on me I might shoot him. Haig glanced at his watch and frowned. Warren.

I said, "Okay, Rossi was ambitious. But did she ever do anything illegal to your knowledge?"

"Not to my knowledge."

"Ever rig an arrest?"

Haig shook his head.

"Plant evidence?"

"Not with me around." Offended.

"You told Truly that you thought Rossi was capable of falsifying evidence. You said that your statement was based upon your experience as her partner. Do you really know anything, Haig, or are you just blowing smoke?"

Haig frowned. "Look, Rossi used to skirt the line all the time. She'd do anything to make a case, go through a window, pop a trunk, jump a fence. I used to say, hey, you ever heard of the search and seizure laws? You ever heard of a warrant?"

"And what would she do when you said that?"

"Look at me like I'm an asshole." He chewed at the cigar some more, then suddenly seemed to realize what he was doing and dropped it into the trash. "Christ, she made me crazy in the car, always running plates, always looking for the collar."

"Sounds like good police work."

"Try livin' with it every day." He glanced at his watch again. "I gotta get going."

"One more thing. You weren't with her when she made the Miranda violation."

"Nah. That was later. I was already off the job and she was a detective-one. Rossi the hot shot, bustin' balls like always."

"Then how do you know about it?"

"I saw her after. Bobby Driskoll's retirement up at the Revolver and Athletic Club." The Revolver and Athletic Club is the Police Academy's bar. "She was goin' on about it, sayin' how rotten it was, sayin' that she was going to do whatever it took to get her career back on track."

"Were there other people around?"

"Hell, yes. Rossi never made a secret about her ambition. 'They can't keep me down.' That's the way she talked. 'All it takes is one big bust and I'm on top again.' Like that."

"But you have no personal knowledge of her having done anything illegal?"

Haig frowned at me. "Any bitch that in-your-face is up to something."

I closed the pad and put it away. Jonathan Green probably wasn't going to like what I had to say about Haig. "Tell me something, Haig. Are you an asshole by choice?"

Haig gave me the hard cop eyes, and then the slick grin came back and he stood. "Yeah, I guess it sounds that way, but there's more to it than her attitude. You see where she lives?"

I didn't know what he meant. "No."

"Go see where she lives."

We walked out to the little showroom together. A guy who was probably Warren was standing with a black guy in a Goodyear shirt, and together they were reading what was probably a delivery manifest. They looked up when we came out and Warren said, "We got those tires."

Haig ignored him. He slipped behind the counter and I went to the door, and neither of us said anything to the other.

The Hispanic woman was behind the counter. Haig moved against her and mumbled something that the rest of us couldn't hear. She didn't look at him, and didn't respond. She stared at the TV, as if by staring hard enough it wouldn't be happening.

I went out into the sun, thinking that maybe I should have shot him anyway.

3

The two kids with their skateboards were gone, but the dog was still sitting by the *churro* cart, watching the *vaquero*. The *vaquero* was still waving his *churro* at the passing cars and looking sad. All the way up from Zacatecas to stand on a corner and sell something that no one except a couple of kids and a dog wanted. A man who had worked with the Brahmas, no less.

I climbed into my car and opened Truly's envelope and looked at Angela Rossi's address, wondering what Haig had meant about seeing where she lived. 724 Clarion Way. I looked up Clarion Way in the Thomas Brothers Guide, found it in Marina del Rey, and thought, "Well, hell."

The Marina wraps around the ocean on a stretch of sand just south of Santa Monica. It's home to sitcom writers and music producers and people who own Carpeteria franchises, maybe, but not cops. The cheapest house in the Marina maybe goes for six hundred thousand, and even the smallest apartments would set you back fifteen hundred a month before utilities. Condos had to start at three hundred grand. Raymond Haig was probably just a raging sexist who had been shown up on the job and was working out on the person who had shown him up, but how did that explain a cop living in the Marina? Of course, there were probably ten million explanations for how Rossi might live there, but I probably wouldn't ferret them out sitting in front of a tire store in Glendale.

The *churro* salesman caught me staring at him and gestured with the *churro*, his eyes somehow embarrassed in their sadness. I climbed out of my car and paid him thirty-five cents for ten inches of fried dough that had been dusted with powdered sugar and cinammon. He thanked me profusely, but he still seemed sad. I guess there's only so much you can do.

I went back to my car and worked my way across the valley floor, then up onto the San Diego Freeway and down through the westside of Los Angeles to the Marina. It was sunny and bright, with the sun still riding a couple of hours above the horizon. The air smelled of the sea and crisp white gulls floated and circled overhead, eyeing McDonald's and Taco Bell parking lots for fast-food leftovers. Women with ponytails raced along the wide boulevards on Rollerblades and shirtless young men pedaled hard on two-thousand-dollar mountain bikes, and everybody had great tans. Aging *vaqueros* selling rubber-hose *churros* weren't in evidence, but maybe I hadn't looked close enough.

I turned down Admiralty Way with its wide green traffic island and drove along the Silver Strand to a short cul-de-sac lined with low-density condominiums partially hidden behind tropical plantings. Clarion Way.

Seven twenty-four was part of a four-unit building at the front of the curve, and even from the street I could see that the units were large and spacious and expensive. Definitely not cop digs. A gated drive led down beneath the building, and a gated walk led along the front of the units. A mail drop was built into the front gate, along with a security phone so that you could call inside to let the residents know you'd come to visit. I circled the cul-de-sac, parked across the street at the curb, and walked back to the mail drop to see if Angela Rossi's name matched the address. No names. I guess the postman was expected to know who lived where.

A thin man with thick glasses and a bulging forehead squinted out at me from behind the gate. "May I help you?"

I gave him one of my better smiles and tried to look reasonable. "Do you know if Keith's home?"

He frowned at me. "Keith?"

I nodded. "That's right. Keith Adams in seven two four. He said he'd wait for me, but no one answers."

He shook his head. "You must have the wrong address. There are only four of us in the building, and no one by that name lives here."

I dug out my wallet, drew a cash receipt from Hughes Market, and frowned at it. "It says seven twenty-four Clarion."

He was shaking his head before I finished. "Maybe there's another Clarion. I know the woman in seven twenty-four. I don't think she's home now." The woman.

"You don't think we could be talking about Keith's

wife, do you?" I peered through the gate. A boy's red bike was leaning against a planter in the entry to seven two four. A plastic hamper filled with Nerfballs stood behind the bike.

He put his hands on his hips, still shaking the head. "Oh, no. It's just Angie and her kids." Angie. You see how it adds up?

I put my wallet away and scratched my head. Klem Kadiddlehopper comes to the big city. "Has she lived here long? Maybe Keith moved." Trying to find out how a cop could afford to live here. Trying to find out if she rented or stayed with a friend or had won the place in a lottery.

"Not long. She moved in two years ago."

"She own it, or does she rent?"

Now he was frowning. Suspicious. "Why don't you leave your number. Maybe the lady knows something about your friend and will call you." The detective presses his luck a tad too hard.

"That's okay. I'm pretty sure I've got Keith's number back at the office."

I thanked him for his time, went back to my car, then drove to a pay phone in a little shopping center at the mouth of the Marina where I called a realtor friend who works in Pacific Palisades. A bright woman's voice said, "Westside Realty, how may I help you?"

I tried to sound like a G-man. "Adrienne Carter, please."

"May I tell her who's calling?"

"Richard Tracy."

"Please hold."

Maybe twenty seconds later another woman's voice came on. "This is Adrienne Carter."

"I'd like to buy the Hearst Castle. Wanna handle the deal?"

Adrienne Carter laughed. "Dick Tracy. Oh, *please.*"

I gave her Angela Rossi's address and asked if she could run an owner-of-record check for me. I told her it was a matter of utmost urgency and the security of the nation depended on her. She said, "I'll bet, *Dick.*" I think I had started something that I was going to regret.

Forty minutes later I made the slow pull up Laurel Canyon into the mountains above Hollywood and the rustic A-frame I have there. It's woodsy where I live, and though I have neighbors, our homes are separated by mature eucalyptus and olive trees that give us shade and lend stability to the steep slopes upon which we live. I bought the place many years ago when it was in disrepair and, over time, have rebuilt and refinished it both alone and with the help of friends.

I parked in the carport, let myself in through the kitchen, and was looking in the refrigerator for something to eat when the cat-door squeaked and the cat who lives with me walked in. I said, "Hey."

The cat is large and black and one ear sits kind of cocked to the side from when he was head-shot with a .22. The flat top of his head is laced with scars and his ears are shredded and lumpy. When he was younger he would often bring me bits of squirrel and bird to share, but he's older now and the gifts are not as frequent. Perhaps he's slowing, or perhaps he's just less generous. He snicked across the floor and sat by his bowl. "Naow."

"I'm hungry, too. Hang on."

I took out leftover chicken that I'd baked with garlic and rosemary, and a half can of tuna. I turned the oven to 350, wrapped the chicken and canned new potatoes together in foil, then put it in the oven to heat. I forked the tuna into the cat's bowl, then set the can next to it so he could lick the juice. He prefers the chicken, but the garlic gives him gas, so I've had to draw the line. He doesn't like me for it, but there you go.

It was eighteen minutes after seven, and I was getting ready to take a shower when the phone rang. Adrienne. I said, "Hi, Adrienne." Elvis Cole, Too Hip Detective, pretends he can read minds.

Lucy Chenier said, "Adrienne?" The Too Hip Detective steps in deep doo-doo.

"A realtor friend," I said. "I'm expecting her to call with some information I need."

"Do tell. Well, heaven forbid I should tie up your line."

I gave her Groucho. "Can't think of anyone I'd rather have tie me up, heh heh."

"Oh, you." I love it when she says 'oh, you.' And then she said, "Hi, Studly."

I felt the smile start deep in my chest and grow large like an expanding bubble, and then I was standing in my kitchen with the phone and Lucy Chenier's presence seemed to fill the house with warmth and light. I said, "I miss you, Luce."

"I miss you, too."

"Hmm."

"Hmm-mm." We often have conversations like this.

I had met Lucy Chenier three months earlier when I was working in Louisiana for an actress named Jodi Taylor. Lucy was Jodi Taylor's lawyer and I was Jodi Taylor's detective, and the attraction, as they say, was immediate. We had called each other regularly since then, and two months ago I had flown back to Louisiana to spend a long weekend with Lucy and her eight-year-old son, Ben. Three weeks after that, Lucy and I had met in Cancun for four days of snorkeling and grilled shrimp and sunburns, and it was harder still to say good-byes when she boarded her plane and I boarded mine. Thereafter, the phoning grew more frequent, and the conversation less necessary, and soon we were in a kind of comfortable/uncomfortable place where the occasional murmur on the other end of the line was enough, but not nearly enough. Over the weeks an increasing part of my day has become the anticipation of the evening's call, when I would sit in my home and Lucy would sit in hers and we would share a few minutes together linked by two thousand miles of fiber-optic satellite relays. It wasn't as nice as actually being with her, but if romance were easy, everyone would do it. I said, "You may be interested in why I am waiting for Adrienne to call."

"I'm sure I don't want to know."

"Do I detect coolness?"

"You detect indifference. They are not the same."

I said, "Ha. We'll see if you feel the same after you hear my news."

She said, "Let me guess. You've changed your name to Jerry Lee Lewis Cole?" You see what passes for humor in Louisiana?

"I'm working with Jonathan Green."

There was a moment's silence, and then Lucy Chenier said, "Is that true, or is this more of the famous Elvis Cole wit?" Not joking, now.

"Hired me today for the Big Green Defense Machine."

Lucy Chenier made a soft whistling sound, then said, "Oh, Elvis. That's wonderful." You see? Impressed. Lucy being impressed made me want to thump my hind leg on the floor and roll over so that she could scratch my belly. She said, "We used to study his cases in law school."

"How about that."

"It must be very exciting."

"He's just another client."

She said, "I have news, too." She sounded happy, like maybe she was smiling when she said it.

"Okay."

"The firm has business to take care of in Long Beach, and they're sending me out. Ben's out of school, so how would you like a couple of freeloading house guests?"

The background noise of the TV and the CNN newscasters was suddenly a million miles away. I said, "I could handle that."

"What?" I guess she hadn't heard me. I guess my voice had come out hoarse and small.

"Hold on a minute and let me check my calendar."

"You rat."

I was smiling. I was smiling so wide that my face felt tight and brittle, as if I smiled any farther my cheeks would crack. "Yes. Yes, I think that would be fine. Are you kidding? That's great."

"I thought so, too."

I said, "I'll be at the airport in an hour."

She laughed. "You can be there in an hour, but Ben and I won't be there until the day after tomorrow. I'm sorry to spring this on you, but I didn't know for sure until this afternoon."

I was too busy smiling to answer.

"I'll call tomorrow and give you the flight information."

"Hey, Luce."

"Hm?"

"I'm really happy about this."

"Me, too, Studly. Oh, you don't know."

We talked for another hour, mostly about where we would go and what we would do and how excited we were that we would see each other again. When my food was warm I sat on the kitchen floor, eating as we talked, and the cat came over and stared at me. Purring. Lucy asked about Green and the Teddy Martin case, and as I told her I listened to the soft country sounds of k.d. lang behind her, and the passing voices of Ben and his best friend as they tumbled through her home. The sounds of Lucy Chenier's life. I told her about the videographer and that Green was shorter and thinner than he looked on television, though still imposing, but after a while our conversation drifted back to us, and to how our tans from Cancun were fading and how much fun we'd had drinking blue iced cocktails and eating the fresh *ceviche* that the hotel chefs would make at the beach, and then after a while the conversation was over.

Lucy blew me a kiss and hung up and I lay back on the kitchen floor with the phone on my stomach, grinning at the ceiling. The cat stopped purring, and came closer to stare into my face. He looked concerned. Maybe he didn't know I was grinning. Maybe he thought I was dying of some sort of hideous facial stricture. Is that possible? Death by grinning. I said, "She's coming to see us."

He hopped up onto my chest and sniffed at my chin and began to buzz again. The certainty of love.

Later, I washed the dishes and shut the lights and went up to bed. I lay there for a very long time, but sleep wouldn't come. I could only think of Lucy, and of seeing her, and as I thought the grin seemed to grow. Perhaps the grin would grow so wide that it would crash through the sides of the house and slop down across the mountain and just keep expanding until it became The Grin That Ate L.A. Of course, if that happened, the grin would eat LAX and Lucy couldn't land. Then where would I be?

At a little after two that morning, I went downstairs to the guest room and stripped the bed and put on fresh linen and then dusted and vacuumed and cleaned the guest bath. I figured I could borrow a camper's cot from Joe Pike; Ben could use the cot and Lucy could have the bed.

At sixteen minutes before four, I went out onto the deck and stared down at the lights in the canyon below. A family of coyotes who live around Franklin Reservoir

were singing, and a great desert owl who lived in the
eucalyptus trees made his hooting call. I breathed the
cool night air and listened to the coyotes and the owl,
and I thought how fine it was that so much of my being
could have so suddenly become focused on an airplane's
time of arrival.

I did not sleep, but I did not mind.

4

By nine o'clock the next morning I had gained some measure of control over the sappy grin and was once more feeling focused, productive, and ready to swing into investigative action. Sappy grins are fine in your personal life but somehow seem less than professional when one is representing the Big Green Defense Machine. Credibility, as they say, is everything.

By eight-forty I had shaved, showered, and phoned Terminal Island to arrange an interview with LeCedrick Earle. I was eating a breakfast of nonfat yogurt and sliced bananas when Eddie Ditko called and said, "Hold on a sec while I fire up a smoke." First thing out of his mouth.

"Top of the morning to you, too, Edward."

There was the sound of the strike and a little pause like maybe Eddie was sucking up half of the earth's pollutant supply, and then a burst of coughing that sounded wet and phlegmy. He said, "Christ, I'm passing blood."

So much for breakfast. I pushed the bowl away and said, "Are you all right?"

"Think I'm gonna drop a goddamned lung." He croaked it out between coughs.

"You want to call back?"

The coughs settled to a phlegmy wheezing. "Nah, nah, I'm fine." When he got his breathing under control, he said, "Whadda they make these things outta nowadays, fiberglass? Ya gotta rip the filters off to get any taste."

"Jesus Christ, Eddie."

Eddie Ditko said, "Listen, I made a few calls and got some stuff for you."

"Okay."

"Rossi looks like a pretty sharp gal." Gal. "Divorced. Got a couple of little boys. Her ex is some kind of middle manager at Water and Power."

"All right." I was making notes. I had been thinking that she might've married well and gotten the expensive house in the divorce, but middle managers at Water and Power aren't known for their bank accounts.

"She was top of her class at the academy and moved right up the promotion ladder once she got into uniform. She responded to more calls, worked more hours, and made more arrests than all but three other officers with her time in grade. That's probably where the marriage went."

I was still writing.

"The LeCedrick Earle bust is what led to the gold shield, and everybody kind of figured that Rossi had a shot at being the first female chief of detectives until the Miranda thing. You blow a murder-one case because you failed to Mirandize a suspect, and that's it for you. She lost a grade in rank and received a letter of censure. That pretty much killed her career."

I was nodding as I wrote. Everything he said was confirming both Haig and Truly. "What happened with the Miranda?"

"Two idiots armed with machetes robbed a Burito King in Silverlake and hacked three people to death. Rossi spotted a car matching the getaway vehicle and collared one of the suspects after a high-speed chase. She was jazzed from the pursuit and forgot to give the guy his warning before he confessed and implicated his accomplice. They hadda let both idiots walk, and Rossi took the heat for it. You see?"

"Man. Did she dispute the Miranda?"

"Nope. She blew it and she admitted it. How about that?" Like he was surprised that someone would take responsibility for their actions. "I can fax you this stuff, you want."

"Thanks, Eddie. What about Earle?"

"Another genius. Rossi tags the guy for a taillight violation and he slides across a C-note with his license, which he saw some moron do in a Dirty Harry movie. Rossi recognizes the Franklin's a fake and tells him it'll cost him a lot more than that, so he brings her back to his house where he pulls out a stash and says she can have all she wants. She says thank you very much and let's go to jail."

"That's her side of it."

Eddie laughed. "Yeah, sure. Your man LeCedrick is what we call a career-type criminal. Prior to the funny-money arrest, he'd been in and out of the system half a dozen times, mostly dope and burglary charges, including two prior associations with a guy named Waylon Mustapha. Mustapha makes his living by selling down funny money for points." Selling for points is when you discount the face value of the counterfeit money to sell it in quantity. Sort of like being a broker. "My guy at the PD says that the bills they recovered when Rossi made the collar matched up with the goods Mustapha handles."

I tapped the pen against the pad, frowning. "Just because LeCedrick was a creep most times doesn't mean he was a creep *that* time."

Eddie laughed harder. "Keep dreaming."

I said, "You hear anything that would indicate she might be willing to fudge a case?"

"You talk to his mother?"

"Whose mother?"

"Earle's mother was in the house when Rossi made the collar. She saw the whole thing."

"Anything in the file?"

"*Nada*. IA would've talked to her, though. 'Course, whether they listened is a different matter."

"Do you have her address, Eddie?"

He did, and he gave it to me. It was the same address in Olympic Park as that listed on LeCedrick Earle's arrest report. I hung up, then phoned information for Louise Earle's number and called her. I still needed to see LeCedrick, but maybe I could see her first. Maybe she had something to offer that might bolster his version of events, or clarify it. I let the phone ring ten times but got no answer. Guess I'd have to see LeCedrick *sans* clarity.

I hung up again, washed the dishes, then climbed into my car and made the long drive south to see LeCedrick Earle.

The harbor town of San Pedro lies on the water at the southeast point of the Palos Verdes peninsula, sixty miles south of Los Angeles. It's pretty much a straight shot down the San Diego Freeway across a rolling flat fuzz of low buildings and single-family homes, past Inglewood and Hawthorne and Gardena to Torrance, and then yet farther south on the Harbor Freeway to the water. The Port of Los Angeles is down there, with the gleaming white cruise ships that come and go and the great *Queen Mary* that forever stays and the U. S. Federal Correctional Facility at Terminal Island.

Terminal Island is on the western side of the harbor, and the facility itself is on the outermost end of the island. The *Queen Mary* is next door, as are the berths for the cruise ships, but neither can be seen from the prison. From the prison, you could only see open water, and the water looked very much like iron. Sort of like the bars of the cells.

I crossed a land bridge to the island and followed the signs to the prison, and pretty soon I passed through a high chain-link gate and parked at the administration building. A tall link fence topped by concertina wire surrounded the prison, which was new and modern and clean. A guard tower overlooked the grounds, but it was new and modern and clean, too. No gun ports. No swivel-mounted machine guns. No snarling guard dogs or barrel-chested yard-bulls sapping prisoners into line. All of the guards wore blue blazers and ties, and none of them carried guns. They carried walkie-talkies, instead. Modern justice.

I went inside to the reception desk, identified myself, and told the guard that I had an appointment to see LeCedrick Earle. The guard was a clean-cut guy in his early thirties. He found my name in his log, then turned it around for me. "Sign here, please. Are you armed?"

"Nope."

He flipped through a large loose-leaf book until he found Earle's name, then used his phone to tell someone that he wanted prisoner number E2847 brought out. When he was finished he smiled at me and said, "Someone will be right out for you. Wait by the sally port."

A couple of minutes later a second guard brought me through the sally port to a glass-walled interview room. A neat new table sat in the middle of the floor with four comfortable chairs around it. A second glass door was behind the table, and there was a nice gray berber carpet. The air smelled of Airwick. If it weren't for the guards peering in at you and the wire in the glass, you'd never know you were in a prison. Portrait of the Big House as corporate America.

Thirty seconds later the same guard opened the rear door and an African-American guy in his late twenties came in and squinted at me. "You that guy come about Rossi?"

The guard said, "Buzz me when you're done and I'll come get him." The guard had bored eyes and spoke to me as if Earle wasn't there and hadn't said anything.

"Sure. Thanks."

The guard left, locking the door.

LeCedrick Earle was maybe an inch shorter than me, with dark glossy skin and a shaved head. He was wearing a prison-issue orange jumpsuit and Keds. I said, "That's right. I work for an attorney named Jonathan Green."

"You a lawyer?"

"Nope. I'm a private investigator."

Earle shrugged. "I saw that ad in the paper and called. I talked to some guy say he was a lawyer."

"The ad was about information leading to the arrest of James X for the murder of Susan Martin." Truly had filled me in before he'd left the office. "You know anything about that?"

He dropped into the near chair, put his feet on the table, and crossed his arms. Showing smug. "Don't give a damn about that. I know about Rossi. I read in the paper she one of the cops arrest Teddy Martin. She put the fuck on me, I figure she maybe put the fuck on him, too."

"You don't care about the reward?"

"Fuck the reward." Giving me righteous. Giving me can-you-believe-this? "Can't a brother just wanna do his civic duty?"

"I read your arrest report, and I read the letter of complaint your lawyer filed against her. What happened with that?"

"Shit, what you think happened? They didn't do a goddamned thing. Say it's my word against hers."

"Your mother was there."

All the show and the exaggeration flicked away. His

eyes darkened and his face seemed to knot. "Yes, well, she don't know nothing. Just a crazy old lady scared of the police."

I said, "Okay, so the arrest report is wrong and Rossi is lying."

"Goddamned right. Bitch set me up."

"She says that you tried to buy your way out of a traffic violation with a fake C-note."

"Bullshit. That money was real."

"You really tried to buy your way out with a C?"

"Man, I had so many outstanding warrants I was scared she was gonna run me in. *That's* what I was tryin' to avoid."

"So what happened?"

He uncrossed his arms and leaned forward. "I pass her the note and she laughs. She says she don't come that cheap and I say it's all I got. She says I guess we gonna get locked down, then won't we? I'm gettin' the Hershey squirts cause of all the warrants, so I say I got a few hundred stashed at the house. She says let's see it, and that's when we go home."

"She followed you to your house to get more money."

"Oh, yeah. That part's true."

"Okay."

"So we get there and go inside and I got the money back in my room, not much, a few hundred, but it's real. I worked for that cash."

"Okay."

"We go back to my room to get the money and the next thing I know the gun's coming out and she's screamin' at me to get on the floor an' I'm squirtin' for real 'cause I think the crazy bitch gonna shoot me and so I go down and she snaps on the cuffs and then she takes this little bag of cash from under her jacket and that's the shit."

"The funny money?"

He was nodding. "I say, what's that? I say, whatchu think you doin'? She say shut the fuck up. Oh, man, next thing I know more cars are pullin' up and she's tellin' them other cops that the flash cash is mine and now I'm in here. How you like that shit?"

I stared at LeCedrick Earle and LeCedrick Earle stared back. His eyes did not waver. He said, "Well?"

"Well what?"

"Just thinking."

"Thinkin' what?"

"Wondering about you and Waylon Mustapha."

He waved his hand. "That's just bullshit bad luck." He waved the hand some more. "Waylon grow up down the street from me. Waylon and me know each other since kindergarten and blow a little smoke together, that's all. I can't help it I know Waylon. I know guys who killed people, an' I ain't no murderer."

"The money Rossi booked into evidence matched with paper that Waylon deals."

LeCedrick crossed his arms and grinned. "Half the funny money on the street come from Waylon. She probably got it from the goddamned evidence room. She mighta even bought it from Waylon his own damn self."

"Okay." I stared at him some more.

LeCedrick Earle started to fidget. "Now what you

lookin' at? You don't believe me, jus' say so, callin' me a liar." He got up and walked in a little circle.

I said, "I'm going to write down everything you've said. I'm going to check it out. I'm going to pass it along to Jonathan Green. You sure you don't want a piece of the money?"

"Fuck the money. I just wanna get out of here."

I nodded.

He jabbed a finger at me. "I'm tellin' you and God and everyone else that bitch set me up. You check it out, you see. Bet she set up this Teddy Martin, too."

I said, "Something about what you're saying bothers me, LeCedrick. You want to help me with something?"

His eyes narrowed. Suspicious. "What?"

"If she wanted to set you up, she didn't need to go to your house. All she had to do is bust you on the street and say she found the money under the front seat."

"Damn bitch is crazy! Who know how a goddamn crazy bitch think?" He threw up both hands, then came back to the table and slapped the buzzer for the guards. "Shit on this. I shoulda known you asshole muthuhfuck-uhs wouldn't believe me. Fuck you and fuck her, too. I guess a brother just has to rot in here."

The guard came and took LeCedrick Earle back to his cell.

5

As I tooled north back to Los Angeles I tried to keep an open mind. Just because someone looks like a liar and acts like a liar doesn't mean that he is a liar. It doesn't even mean he's a liar when his story is full of holes. Even the truth has been known to have holes. Of course, when his story doesn't make sense it becomes a little more difficult to swallow. I could see Angela Rossi's side of it, but not LeCedrick Earle's. Rossi's report said that she followed Earle to his house because he only had the single hundred-dollar bill on his person and she knew that he could plead innocent to a knowledge of its being counterfeit; she reasoned that if he had more at home as he stated, he couldn't reasonably deny knowledge and the intent to defraud, and the arrest would stick. LeCedrick Earle said that she followed him to his home where she produced a hidden amount of counterfeit money and made the arrest. He opined that she might've done this so that there would be no witnesses, yet Mrs. Louise Earle had been there and Rossi apparently consummated the arrest. Rossi's version made sense and LeCedrick Earle's didn't.

Still, people sometimes do strange things for strange reasons, and I decided to see what Mrs. Louise Earle had to offer. I expected that she would support her son's claims, but in the doing perhaps she would add something to give them greater credence.

I opened Truly's envelope, shook out my notes, and looked up her address. It would be polite to pull off the freeway and call again to see if she was at home, but when people know you're coming they often find reasons to leave. I decided to risk it.

Forty-five minutes later I dropped off the Harbor Freeway onto Martin Luther King Boulevard, and five minutes after that I found my way to Olympic Park.

Olympic Park is a downscale residential area just north of USC and Exposition Park and the Natural History Museum, not far from downtown L.A. The Coliseum is nearby, along with the L.A. Sports Arena, and on game nights the surrounding residential streets are jammed belly to butt with parked cars and pushcarts and hawkers selling souvenirs and iced drinks.

Louise Earle lived in a stucco bungalow on Twenty-fifth Street, four blocks south of the freeway, within walking distance of USC. The houses and the yards are small and the drives are narrow, but the properties are neat and clean, and the Earle home was painted a happy yellow with about a million multicolored flowers blooming on her porch in about a million clay pots and wooden planters. Flowers hung from the eaves and filled the porch and two large wrought iron baker's racks. There were so many flowers on the porch that you had to walk along a narrow path to make your way to the door. It probably took her two hours a day just to water the things.

A six-year-old Buick Skylark was parked in the drive and an air conditioner was humming in a side window. I parked at the curb opposite her house, then went up the drive past the Buick and through the jungle of flowers to her door. The Buick's engine was still ticking. Recent arrival. A little metal plaque under the doorbell said WELCOME. I rang the bell.

The door opened and a thin woman in her early sixties looked at me. She was wearing a simple print dress in a flowered pattern and comfortable canvas shoes and her gray hair had been pulled into a bun. Neat. I said, "Mrs. Earle?"

She smiled at me. "Yes?"

I gave her my card. "Mrs. Earle, my name is Elvis Cole. I'm an investigator looking into your son's arrest. May I ask you a few questions?"

She frowned, but she might've been squinting at the sun. "Are you from the police?"

"No, ma'am. I'm private." I told her that I was working for an attorney named Jonathan Green, and though Green did not represent LeCedrick, the events of his arrest might have a bearing on another case.

She shifted in the door, uncomfortable and unsure about what I might want. "LeCedrick is at Terminal Island."

"I know. I understand that you witnessed his arrest, and I have some questions about that." Something moved in the house behind her.

"Well, I guess it would be all right." Reluctant. She

glanced back into the house, then stepped aside and opened the door. "Why don't you come in so we don't let all the cool air out."

I stepped in and she closed the door.

A short, slight gentleman was standing in the living room. He had wavy marcelled hair and he was wearing a brown summer-weight suit that had probably been new twenty years ago. His hair was more gray than not, and his skin was the color of fine cocoa parchment. He was holding a small bouquet of zinnias. I made him for his late sixties, but I could've been off five years either way.

Louise Earle said, "This is my friend, Walter Lawrence. He just dropped in, and now he'll have to be leaving. Won't you, Mr. Lawrence?" She said it more to Mr. Lawrence than to me, and he didn't seem to like it very much.

Mr. Lawrence frowned, clearly disappointed. "I suppose I could come back later."

Louise Earle said, "And I suppose you could just phone later and see whether or not a person is busy before you drop around, now couldn't you?"

Mr. Lawrence ground about four inches of enamel off his teeth, but he managed a grim smile anyway. He wasn't liking this one bit. "I suppose."

She nodded approvingly, then took the flowers. "Now you just let me get these lovely flowers in some water and we'll speak later." She cradled the flowers and encouraged him toward the door.

Mr. Lawrence stood very straight when he walked, trying to get as much height as he could. He mumbled something to her that I couldn't hear, frowned at me as he passed, and then Louise Earle shut the door. A couple of heartbeats later the Skylark backed out of the drive. I said, "Ah, romance."

Louise Earle laughed, and the laugh made her fifteen years younger. "May I offer you coffee, Mr. Cole, or something cool to drink?"

"Coffee would be fine, Mrs. Earle. Thank you."

She took the flowers back to her kitchen, calling over her shoulder. "Please make yourself comfortable."

I sat on a well-worn cloth couch with a handmade slipcover and needlepoint throw pillows. An overstuffed chair made an L with the couch and the couch and the chair were angled around an inexpensive coffee table, and all of it looked across the room at a cherry wood armoire. The armoire was open and its shelves were lined with tiny vases and knickknacks and family photographs, some of which were of LeCedrick. LeCedrick as a teenager. LeCedrick as a child. LeCedrick before choosing a life of crime. He seemed like a happy child with a bright smile. Her home was neat and cared for and smelled of the flowers.

Mrs. Earle appeared a few moments later with two cups of coffee, walking carefully so as not to slosh. She said, "That business with LeCedrick was several years ago. Why are you interested in that now?"

"I'm investigating the officer who arrested him."

"Oh, yes. I remember her." She put the cups on the table, then offered one to me. "Would you care for milk or sugar?"

"No, ma'am. Then you were present during the arrest?"

She nodded again. "Oh, yes. The police came to see me about that. They came back three or four times. Those affairs people."

"Internal Affairs?"

"Mm-hm." She sipped at her coffee. It was so hot that swirls of steam followed the contours of her face and fogged her glasses.

"You know LeCedrick is disputing the arrest."

"Of course, I know."

"LeCedrick claimed at the time of his arrest, and still claims, that Officer Rossi planted counterfeit bills in order to make the arrest."

Mrs. Earle nodded, but it was noncommittal, like she was waiting to hear more.

"Is that what you told the Internal Affairs people?"

Mrs. Louise Earle gave a deep sigh and the mask of noncommittal detachment melted away into eyes that were tired and pained. "I know he says that, and I'll tell you just what I told those affairs people."

I leaned toward her.

"You can't believe a thing that child says."

I blinked at her.

She put down the coffee and waved toward the armoire. "I was standing right there when LeCedrick and that officer came in. I saw every little thing that happened." Louise Earle closed her tired eyes, as if by closing them she could see it all again, just like she'd told the affairs people. "The officer stood right there, holding her hat and telling me about her day. I remember that she was holding her hat because I thought how polite that was, to hold her hat like that. I didn't know she'd come to arrest him."

"She didn't go back to his room?" LeCedrick had said that Rossi had gone back to his room.

"Oh, no. She just came in and stood there, talking with me the whole time. I was certainly angry when she arrested the boy, but she was very nice about it." Very nice about it. I could see Jonathan Green when I related this. I could see his color drain, his eyes bulge. I wondered if he would pass out and Truly and I would have to administer CPR.

"LeCedrick claims that she accompanied him to his room. He says that she had a bag under her jacket containing the counterfeit bills."

"It was summer. What would anyone be doing with a jacket in summer?" Louise Earle shook her head, and now there was a sadness to her. She crossed her hands in her lap. "Mr. Cole, you listen to LeCedrick and you'd think he was just the most innocent thing, but that just isn't the way it is. LeCedrick will lie at the drop of a hat, and always has."

I sighed. So much for LeCedrick Earle.

Louise Earle said, "Make no mistake about it. I love that child and it grieves me no end he's in jail, but he's said exactly the same thing every other time he's been arrested. It's always somebody else's fault. It's always the police out to get him. Like that."

I nodded. "Yes, ma'am."

"If you're lookin' for me to say that boy is innocent, I can't. If you're lookin' for me to speak against that lady officer, I can't do that, either." She looked stern when she said it.

"No, ma'am. I'm not looking for that."

"He wanted me to lie for him back then, and I wouldn't. He wanted me to cover for him, and make excuses, and I said no. I said, LeCedrick, you have to learn to stop makin' excuses, you have to learn to be a man." Her voice wavered and she stopped. She picked up the coffee, sipped, then said, "It's cost me greatly, but it's for him. Something has to shock some sense into that boy."

"Yes, ma'am."

"He hasn't spoken to me since the trial. He said he'd never speak to me again."

"I'm sorry, Mrs. Earle." I didn't know what else to say. I felt awkward and ashamed that I'd come into her life and driven off Mr. Lawrence and made her relive something that was clearly so painful.

"I tried to raise that boy right. I loved that boy as much as any mother could, and tried to show a good example, but he just went wrong." Her eyes grew pink and a single tear worked its way down her cheek. "Maybe that was where I went wrong. Maybe I held him too close and excused too little. Is it possible to love someone too much?"

I looked at her, and then I looked at the furniture and the pictures, and then back at her weary eyes and the weight they carried. "I don't think there can ever be too much love, Mrs. Earle."

She seemed to consider that, and then she put her coffee down again. "Has this helped you?"

"Yes, ma'am. It has." Jonathan Green wouldn't think so, but there you go.

She stood, and it was clear that she wanted me to leave. "If you don't mind, then, I should clip those zinnias and get them in water."

"Yes, ma'am. I'm sorry I interrupted you and Mr. Lawrence."

The tiny smile came back, though it wasn't as strong as before. "Yes, well, it'll take more than a little interruption to discourage that man."

"Men are like that, Mrs. Earle. We find something worthwhile, we stay with it."

The tired eyes crinkled and suddenly the younger self was there again. "Oh, you get on with you, now."

She walked me to the door and I went out into the sun and got on with me.

6

The early afternoon heat shimmered off the sidewalks and cars and surrounding roofs in a kind of urban illusion of life's silver lining. It was just before two on the second day of my investigation into Angela Rossi and the doors of investigative possibility were rapidly closing, and with every closed door Angela Rossi looked better and the people making claims against her looked worse. Louise Earle was credible, cogent, in full command of her faculties, and did not seem to be a person who would miss seeing a cop carrying a bag of funny money through her living room. Of course, maybe Angela Rossi was a master of misdirection and had secreted the money behind her back. She might've shouted, "Look over there!" and run to LeCedrick's room and planted the cash when Louise turned to look. Perhaps my investigative task for the afternoon should be finding out whether or not Angela Rossi was an amateur magician.

Or maybe not. Three teenaged girls with long skinny legs and halter tops came out of the house across the street and went to an ancient Volkswagen Beetle parked in their drive. They were lugging beach towels and bottles of Evian water, and everybody wore thongs. Off to the beach. Maybe I should offer to go with them and protect them from the thugs at the beach. Maybe we could discuss my findings. On the other hand, Lucy Chenier was arriving tomorrow, and maybe I should snap out of it before I found myself in really deep doo-doo. *C'est la vie.*

When I reached the sidewalk a tall, muscular black guy appeared beside my car. As he reached the car a heavy white guy in his early fifties climbed out of a blue sedan parked across the street and started toward me. The black guy was in impeccably pressed designer jeans and a tight knit shirt that showed his muscles, and the white guy was in a rumpled light gray winter-weight suit. A million degrees, and he's wearing winter weight. Cops. A woman's voice said, "Excuse me, sir. May I have a word with you?" Polite, and kind of cheery.

The cheery woman was coming toward me from the adjoining yard as if she had been standing at the corner of the house there, waiting. She was maybe five-eight, and dark the way you're dark when you spend a lot of time in the sun running and working out and playing sports. I made her for her early- to mid-thirties, but the lines around her eyes and mouth were deep. Probably from all the sun. She was wearing designer jeans like the black guy and Reebok court shoes and a loose linen top that she would probably cover with a linen sport coat if it weren't so hot. Stylish and attractive, even with the Browning 9mm clipped to her right hip. She badged me with an LAPD detective shield as she approached, still cheery with the smile, and I recognized her just before she said, "Mr. Cole, my name is Angela Rossi. The detective in the gray suit would like to ask you a few questions."

She glanced at the guy in the bad suit and I followed her look just as she knew I would, and when I did she stepped close and threw an overhand with a black leather sap, trying for the side of my head. Sucker shot. I picked up her move and tried to twist out of the way, but she was good and fast and I caught most of the sap on my right cheek with a blossom of pain. The guy in the suit yelled, "Hey!" and the black guy grunted, "Shit!" like they were surprised, too. Rossi followed the sap with a hard knee, but it caught me in the thigh instead of the groin, and then the older guy was there, wedging himself between us, forcing her away and saying, "Dammit, Rossi, you want another beef in your file? Is that what you want?"

I wobbled, but kept my feet and let the older guy move her back.

The black guy hustled up behind me and his hands went to my wrists, pulling my arms behind me. The three girls ran up onto their porch and watched from the door, one of them with her hand to her mouth. My right cheek felt like someone had popped a firecracker under the skin and my eyes were watering. I didn't want to double over, but I couldn't exactly stand up straight either. It's hard to look tough when you're thinking that maybe you'll vomit. Especially when you've been suckered with an eye-fake. Maybe Rossi was a master of misdirection after all.

Angela Rossi jabbed her finger at me, saying, "This

shitbird came to my *home!* What were you doing at my *home,* you creep?" She wasn't smiling, now. Her face was etched and drawn, and she looked as if she wanted to rip out my eyes.

The older guy pushed her hand down and shoved her further away. "Dammit, Rossi. Step back."

The black guy locked my right arm above the elbow, walked me to a white Cressida, and pushed me down across the trunk. The skin of the car was so hot from the sun it felt like a branding iron. I said, "Are you guys really cops or is this *America's Funniest Home Videos?*"

The black guy ignored me. He went through my pockets and down my pants, and then he said, "He's clean, Tommy."

Rossi stopped all the squirming and trying to get at me. The older guy came over and badged me, too. "I'm Detective Tomsic, and you're being investigated for stalking a Los Angeles police officer. Do you understand that?"

The teenage girl with her hand to her mouth disappeared inside the house. The other two stayed on the porch, watching. A couple of faces appeared in the windows, and I said, "Hey, look, Tomsic. I think they've got a video camera."

Tomsic said, "Good. Let'm watch."

"Maybe they got the sap on tape. You think?" Saps are classified as dangerous weapons. They are illegal to carry, sort of like rocket launchers and samurai swords.

Rossi said, "What were you doing at my home?" She was breathing hard, but she was well back on the sidewalk and she probably wasn't going to hit me again.

"ID and license are in my wallet. I'm a private investigator." The black guy tossed my wallet to Tomsic.

Rossi said, "We know who you are, shitbird. Tell me why you came to my house."

"I was investigating a lead that you were living beyond your means."

"Why?"

"It's what I do. Investigate."

The third girl returned from her house to join her two friends, but Tomsic didn't seem overly concerned. He was going through the wallet like he had all the time in the world. "He's our boy, all right. California PI license. Elvis Cole." He looked at me. "You've got a license to carry here. Where's the piece?"

"Under the seat."

The black guy laughed. "You left it under the seat?"

"I was talking to a woman in her sixties. Who would I shoot?"

The black guy said, "I hear you." He went to my Corvette without having to ask which car was mine. They'd probably followed me. Rossi's neighbor had probably copied my tag number and they'd run the plates and picked me up at my house or maybe even on the way to Terminal Island.

Rossi frowned at Louise Earle's place. "You investigating the LeCedrick Earle thing?"

"Earle claims you planted the cash."

"That's bullshit."

I nodded. "I had to check it out."

She put her right hand on her right hip, just above the Browning. "Who are you working for?"

"Jonathan Green. In the matter of Teddy Martin."

Tomsic said, "Well, fuck me."

The black guy stood out of the Corvette, grinning. "You on the Martin defense? Whadda they call it, the Big Green Defense Machine?" Like he wanted to laugh.

I looked back at Rossi. "People are making accusations that may be relevant to the defense effort, and I'm checking them out. So far you look pretty good."

She looked surprised. "What accusations? Teddy Martin killed that woman."

I made a little shrug. "If you planted evidence once, the theory is that you'd plant it again. Some people called Green and told him that you've got a history of doing anything it takes to jump your career. Green hired me to see if there's anything to it."

Angela Rossi squared herself and took a step toward me. Tomsic shook his head. "Angie."

Rossi took another step closer and the black guy came back to stand with Tomsic between us. Like the two of them were scared of what she might do. She said, "Green's a shithog and so are you."

Tomsic said, "Take it easy, Angie."

Rossi shoved at Tomsic. "Hey, I don't have to take this shit! Assholes coming into my life and trying to put this on me!"

I said, "No one's trying to put anything on you. I just want the facts. No one's looking to axe you."

Rossi jabbed her finger at me, but spoke to Tomsic. "This guy's in *my life*, Dan!"

Tomsic said, "Chill out, will you? This stuff happens. I've been investigated nine thousand times."

I said, "Look, Rossi, it's like I said. I've been through most of it and you're looking good. This is a legal investigation, and if you check out clean I'll report that to Green and that'll be the end of it."

Tomsic said, "You hear that? Clean." Like we were both on the same team, now, trying to keep her calm. Maybe Haig had been right about her being a nut case. Tomsic was acting as if he was scared what might happen if she lost control of herself. He turned back to me. "You understand why we dropped on you, right? Your nosing around her house."

"No problem." My cheek was throbbing and the skin around my eye was starting to stretch, but there was no problem. Sure.

A black and white LAPD radio car turned onto the block and came at us with its light bar flashing, probably responding to a call from the three girls. The radio car roared in to a sliding stop with a couple of uniforms unloading even before the car stopped rocking. An Asian guy in his mid-forties was driving with an Hispanic guy in his late-twenties along for the ride. Tomsic said, "Fuckin' great. A cheering section." He nodded toward the black guy, then the uniforms. "Robert, chill out these guys, okay?"

Robert badged the uniforms and trotted over. The Asian guy had a couple of stripes on his sleeve and was built like he'd spent the last twenty years in the LAPD's weight room. His name tag read SAMURA. Robert met Samura first and spoke to him in low tones as they walked back to us. When Samura heard my name he looked at me. "You're Cole?"

"Unh-hunh."

He looked at Tomsic. "This guy works with Joe Pike."

Robert and Tomsic stared at me. So did Rossi. Robert said, "No shit?"

I spread my hands. "Somebody has to."

Tomsic's face went red and he wasn't so friendly any more, like he and I were no longer on the same team. "*The* Joe Pike?"

"How many you know?"

His jaw worked, and he said, "The Joe Pike I know can kiss my goddamned ass." When Joe left the PD it hadn't gone well.

I smiled at him. "I'll give you his number. You can tell him yourself."

A little tick started in Tomsic's left eye. "Maybe we should march your butt in, after all. Dig around and see if you're in violation of your license."

I rolled my eyes. "Oh, please, Tomsic. Spare me."

The tick fluttered into a rapid-fire blink, but then he stepped back and looked embarrassed. Samura pretended not to notice. "We got a robbery in progress call. What's the deal?"

Tomsic filled him in, telling him about my nosing around Rossi's home, telling him about Teddy Martin and Jonathan Green and Rossi's role in the Martin arrest. Samura listened, but didn't seem particularly interested. You spend enough years on the street, you're not even interested if a nuke goes off.

When Tomsic was finished, Samura said, "Cole has a good rep. I know guys who've worked with him." He squinted at me, then took off his hat and wiped his face.

It had to be a million degrees, standing in the sun. "You remember a guy named Terry Ito?"

"Sure." I'd worked with Ito four or five years back.

Samura put his hat back on and looked at Tomsic. "You don't have to sweat it. Ito thinks that this guy's the cat's ass."

I said, "Terry has a way with words, all right."

Robert said, "We didn't know who the guy was and he was poking around an officer. You know how it is."

"Sure." Samura squared his hat, then nodded toward his radio car. His partner drifted away. Samura started after him, then turned back and looked me over. "I'd never heard Terry Ito say a good thing about anybody. Terry know you work with Joe Pike?"

"Yes."

Samura cracked the world's smallest grin, then went back to his car and drove away. The three girls were still gaggled at their front door, but most of the other faces had disappeared from the windows. You've seen one crime scene, you've seen'm all.

Tomsic looked at Rossi. "Okay. We know who this guy is and what he's doing. You okay with it?"

She made a grudging shrug.

Tomsic looked back to me. "How about you? You gonna file a beef because of the sap?"

"Barely touched me."

Robert laughed. "Yeah. Look at you."

Tomsic said, "Okay, then. Everybody knows where it stands." He nudged Rossi. "We don't have to like it, we just have to know where it stands."

Rossi said, "One thing."

I looked at her.

"You're doing a job, and I can live with that. Investigate all you want, but stay the hell away from my home. If you come around my home again, I'll break you down. If you even look at my kids, I'll kill you on the spot."

Tomsic said, "Jésus Christ, Angie, knock that shit off. Sayin' shit like that is what gets you in deep."

She raised a neutral hand. "Just laying it out."

I said, "You're looking good, Rossi. Don't sweat it."

"Yeah, sure." She stared at me for another couple of seconds, but she didn't look relaxed and she didn't look as if she believed it was over. She was breathing hard, and the crinkled skin around her eyes was jumping and fluttering as if tiny butterflies were trapped there, trying to get out. Then something that looked like it might've been a smile flickered at the corners of her mouth and she said, "Tell Joe that Rossi says hi."

Angela Rossi turned away without another word, crossed the street, and slid into the passenger side of Tomsic's dark blue G-ride. Tomsic joined her, and Robert got into a tan Explorer. In a couple of minutes they were gone. Even the three girls were gone, vanished in their Volkswagen for a belated trip to the beach.

I stood there for a time, alone except for the dull ache in the side of my face, and then I got into my car and drove to my office.

7

I stopped at a 7-Eleven to buy ice for my eye. A Pakistani gentleman was behind the counter, watching a miniature TV. He was watching an episode of *COPS*, and he viewed me with suspicion as I paid.

I told him what the ice was for and asked if I could use the bathroom to look at myself, but he said that the bathroom was for employees only. I asked if he had a little mirror that I could borrow, but he said no again. He sneaked a look toward the door as if he wanted me to leave, as if whatever wraith of urban violence had assaulted me might suddenly be visited upon him and his store. Guess I couldn't blame the guy. You look at enough episodes of *COPS*, and pretty soon you're thinking that life is a war zone.

I thanked him for the ice, then went out to the car and looked at my eye in the rearview mirror. A neat little mouse was riding high on my right cheek and was already starting to color. Great. I wrapped a handful of ice in my handkerchief and drove back to my office with one hand. Nothing like bucking rush hour traffic with a faceful of ice.

It was just after five when I reached my building and turned down the ramp into the building's garage. A line of cars was on its way out, but most of the garage was already empty. Cindy's Mazda was missing, and so were the cars belonging to the people who worked at the insurance company across the hall from my office. I left my car in its spot, walked up to the lobby, then took the elevator to my floor. Lights off, doors locked, empty. Empty was good. Maybe if Los Angeles had been empty I would've been able to spot two carloads of cops tailing me around half the city.

I let myself into my office, popped on the lights, and found Joe Pike sitting at my desk. I said, "You could've turned on the lights, Joe. We're not broke."

Pike cocked his head to the side, looking at my eye. "Is that a pimple?"

"Ha-ha." That Pike is a riot. A real comedian, that guy.

Joe Pike is six foot one, with long ropey muscles, dark hair cut short, and bright red arrows tattooed on the outside of each deltoid. He got the tattoos in a faraway place long before it was stylish for rock stars and TV actors and Gen X rave queens to flash skin art. The arrows point forward, and are not a fashion statement. They are a statement of being. Pike was wearing a gray sweatshirt with the sleeves cut off and Levi's and dark pilot's glasses. Even at night he wears the glasses. For all I know he sleeps in them.

I went to a little mirror I have on the wall and looked at the eye. The side of my face hurt like hell, but the ice was working; the swelling had stopped. "Your friend

Angela Rossi hit me with a six-ounce sap. Suckered me with an eye move."

"I know."

I looked at him. "How do you know?"

He got up, took two Falstaffs from the little fridge, and handed one to me. If you listened as hard as you could, you still wouldn't hear him move. "Angie called and told me. She wanted to know what we were doing."

"She called you."

He popped the tab on his Falstaff and had some. "I've been here a while. Lucy called. I didn't know she was coming out."

"Tomorrow."

"I left her flight information on your desk." Pike took his beer to the couch. "Why are we working for Theodore Martin?"

"We're not. We're working for Jonathan Green." I told him about Haig and his allegations that Rossi would fabricate evidence to boost her career. I told him about LeCedrick Earl and his allegations that Rossi had done just that. "Green hired us to look into the allegations. I told him that we would report what we found, even if it hurt his case. He said okay."

"Lawyers are lizard people." Life is simple for Pike.

"Lucy's a lawyer."

Pike's head shifted a quarter of an inch. "Not Lucy."

I said again, "Angela Rossi called you."

He stared at me with impenetrable black lenses. Two months before I'd had canvas Roman shades installed on the French doors to cut the western exposure in the afternoon, and when the shades were down the office filled with a beautiful gold light. They were down now, and Pike was bathed in the light. It made his dark glasses glow. "We worked Rampart Division together. She was coming on when I was going out." Pike had spent three years riding in a radio car for LAPD. "I knew Haig. Haig was an asshole. I knew Rossi, too. I didn't ride in a car with her, but she seemed like a straight shooter."

"Okay."

"That what you find?"

I took my ice and my Falstaff and went to my desk. I saw the notepaper with Lucy's flight information. Pike's printing was meticulously neat, but so small it was almost impossible to read. "She's aggressive, ambitious, and no one likes her much, but there's no evidence that she dumped LeCedrick Earle or anyone else. Haig comes across like a crank, and Earle's own mother said that her son is a liar."

Pike nodded.

"The only thing that doesn't fit is her house. Two years ago she bought a condo in the Marina that had to go for four hundred thousand dollars. I've got a call in to Adrienne Martin."

"Forget the house. Her mother left her an apartment building in Long Beach. When Rossi sold it she had to roll the cash into another property or get hit with the capital gains."

I stared at him.

"We were close."

"I see."

"Very close." Still hidden behind the black lenses.

I stared at him some more, and then I nodded. "I

guess that's it, then. No crime, no graft, no corruption. Jonathan won't like it, but there it is." There hadn't been much to check and it hadn't taken long, but it rarely does when everything is aboveboard.

"She's a sharp cop, Elvis. It's a tough game for a woman, tougher still if the woman is better than the boys and lets them know it."

I smiled at him. "She doesn't seem like the retiring type."

He canted his head a couple of degrees. "She had a real shot at being the first female chief of detectives. She still might, even with the Miranda beef."

"High praise coming from you."

Pike shrugged.

I said, "Joe, are you soft on this woman?"

Pike finished his beer, then got up and placed the empty carefully into the wastebasket. "I admire her, Elvis. In much the same way I admire you."

I didn't know what to say to that, so I said, "Since you admire me so much, I've got a favor to ask."

He waited.

"Lucy and Ben are coming, and I've got the two-seater. Can I borrow your Jeep to pick them up?"

Pike stood motionless. The Jeep was in immaculate condition, and Pike kept it flawless. You could shave in the fender. You could eat off the engine block.

I said, "I'll wash it before I give it back. If someone dents it I'll shoot them."

Pike's head swiveled one-half a degree. I think he was stricken. "Why don't I come with you to pick them up?"

"Joe." It was like pulling teeth.

He still wasn't happy about it, but he finally nodded. Once.

I said, "I'll draft the report on Rossi tonight. I'll call Truly and tell him that I'm going to turn it in tomorrow, and he'll probably want to see me. You want to go along?"

Pike said, "No." Lizard people.

"Just thought I'd ask."

Pike went to the door, then looked back at me, and gestured to his right eye. "That's going to look nice for Lucy."

"Thanks, Joe."

"Good to see Angie hasn't lost her touch." His mouth twitched a single time and he left. Pike never smiles or laughs, but sometimes you'll get the twitch. Mr. Hilarity.

I had the rest of my beer, then phoned Elliot Truly. When Truly came on the line, I said, "I've concluded the investigation into Angela Rossi. I'm going to write the report tonight."

He didn't say anything for a second. "So soon?"

"I'm fast, Truly. Cases solved in no time flat or your money back."

Truly said, "Well, hell." Like he was disappointed it hadn't taken longer, like he was maybe thinking that I had given the job short shrift. "What did you find?"

"She's clean. Earle is a liar and Haig is a crank with a grudge. There's absolutely no evidence that Rossi's ever been anything other than a good cop."

Another silence. "You'd better come in. Jonathan will want to talk about it." You see?

"I have guests coming in from out of town at five tomorrow evening."

I could hear him fumbling with something. "We're going to have a staff meeting here tomorrow morning at nine. Can you make that?"

"I'll be there."

It took less than twenty minutes to write the report, and then I drove home listening to k. d. lang. k. d. lang was Lucy's favorite, and as I drove I found that I was thinking less about Jonathan Green and Angela Rossi, and more about Lucy Chenier. I thought that I might clean the house and make a shopping list. The house was already clean and it was too late to shop, but that didn't matter. My work was done and Lucy was coming, and what could be better than that? Anticipation is everything.

When I got home, Pike's Jeep was waiting in the drive, freshly washed, immaculate and gleaming. I found a note under the windshield that said, *Give my love to Lucy, and please drive carefully.*

That Pike is something, isn't he?

8

At twenty minutes before nine the next morning I worked my way down the mountain along Laurel Canyon to Sunset, then turned west toward Jonathan Green's office.

Most prominent attorneys in Los Angeles will black-jack their mothers to find office space in Beverly Hills or Century City, both of which are considered prestige addresses for the legal community. Jonathan Green's office was on Sunset Boulevard in an ornate four-story Spanish office building across from the Mondrian Hotel. I guess if you're Jonathan Green, any place you happen to be is a prestige address.

The building was older, with an established landscape of royal palms and bougainvillea, and state-of-the-art security equipment discreetly hidden from public view. A tasteful sign built into the front of the building simply said THE LAW OFFICES OF JONATHAN GREEN. The parking garage was gated, and the gate wouldn't open until a gentleman wearing a red blazer strolled out to my car and asked my name. He was exceedingly polite, and possessed of a bulge in the line of his jacket beneath his left arm. The bulge, like the sign and the security equipment, was also discreet.

I left my car in the garage, then followed the guard's directions past a Spanish tile fountain in the lobby to the elevators, and then to the top floor. Another blazered gentleman smiled at me in the lobby, and a third just happened to be on the elevator. Both were polite and both, like the guard in the parking garage, had the corded necks of men who spent a lot of their time honing confrontational skills. Corded necks are a dead giveaway.

When the elevator opened, Elliot Truly was waiting for me. I guess the parking guard must've called. I said, "Some security."

He stared at my eye.

"Cut myself shaving."

Truly realized he was staring and looked away. "Yes, well, I guess that happens."

I followed him past the floor receptionist and along a glass hall. "Why all the spooks?"

"Many of Jonathan's cases are unpopular, as you might imagine. You'd be surprised at the number of people who don't believe that defendants are entitled to the best possible defense."

"No kidding."

Men and women in business suits hurried in both directions, some carrying files, others long yellow legal pads, still others small Styrofoam cups of what I took to be coffee. Nine in the morning, and everyone looked tense. I guess tension is a way of life when you're trying to give people the best possible defense. Especially at five hundred dollars an hour.

I said, "Are all of these people working for Teddy Martin?"

"Oh, no. The firm is involved in over two hundred active cases."

"Mm."

"Jonathan only involves himself in the more, ah, trying cases." He gave me a sly smile.

I nodded.

He looked at me. " 'Trying.' "

"I got it."

Truly looked disappointed. "Oh." Lawyer humor.

We turned down another hall and then into a conference room about the size of Rhode Island. A breakfast buffet had been set up at one end of the room with coffee and mineral water and enough lox and bagels to sink the *Lexington*. Six men and three women were crowded around the buffet, talking in soft whispers. Everyone had coffee, but no one was eating. Probably too tense. Truly said, "Would you like something to eat?"

"Just coffee." Elvis Cole, at one with the team.

"Let me introduce you. Jonathan will be along in a moment."

We got the coffee, and Elliot Truly introduced me. Everyone in the room was an attorney except me. While the introductions were under way, yet more attorneys arrived. I stopped counting at fourteen. The large lesser attorney came in, followed by the small lesser attorney, both of whom were wearing beige linen Armani suits. So was Elliot Truly. I said, "Beige."

Truly said, "Pardon me?"

"Nothing." Jonathan Green would be wearing beige, too. You could bet your house on it.

Thirty seconds later Jonathan Green came in wearing a beige linen Armani. You see? I said, "Shucks."

Truly glanced at me and whispered, "What?" Now that Jonathan was here I guess we would whisper.

"No videographer. I was hoping for more air time."

Truly blinked at me, then seemed to get it. "Oh, right. Ha-ha." Ha-ha. We're just a riot at nine A.M.

Another man came in behind Jonathan. He was a little shorter than me, but his arms were as long as backhoe shovels and his shoulders so wide they looked like they had been built of steel frame girders. The arms and the shoulders didn't go with the rest of him, as if they had once belonged to King Kong or Mighty Joe Young or some other large mammal, and now this guy was using them. He was carrying a manila envelope.

Green smiled when he saw me and offered his hand. "Thank you for coming. This is Stan Kerris, our chief of security. Stan, this is Mr. Cole." Stan Kerris was the guy with the shoulders. He had a monstrously high forehead, sort of like a Klingon's, and eyes that looked at you but gave you nothing, like windows to an empty room.

Truly said, "Let's get started."

Jonathan Green took his seat at the head of the table with Stan Kerris sitting next to him. The two lesser attorneys elbowed each other to sit nearby. Like the lesser attorneys, everyone else tried to jockey as close to Jonathan Green as possible. Truly sat next to me. When everyone was down, Green crossed his legs, and smiled at me. "So. Elliot tells me that you've found no corroborating evidence to Mr. Earle's claims."

"That's right."

"And the same for Mr. Haig?" He raised his eyebrows in a question.

"That's right. I spoke with Haig and with Earle, then with Earle's mother. I did a cursory background check on Earle, and reviewed the Internal Affairs investigation into the funny money bust. IA found that Rossi made a quality bust."

Truly was shaking his head. "What does that mean? Of course, they would say that."

"No, Mr. Truly. They wouldn't. LAPD takes these things seriously." I looked at Green. "I concur."

Green laced his fingers across a knee and settled back. "Please tell us why."

At least seven of the assembled attorneys copied what I said. I started with Raymond Haig and worked my way through Eddie Ditko and Rossi's condo and my interviews with both LeCedrick Earle and Louise Earle. I told them about LeCedrick's past record, including his close association with Waylon Mustapha, and I described in detail how Louise Earle's version of events matched with Rossi's police report. I spoke for close to twenty minutes, and for twenty minutes pens scratched on legal pads and Jonathan Green sat unmoving. His eyes narrowed a couple of times, but mostly he watched me as if he could absorb the details without effort and assimilate them. Or maybe he was just bored.

When I finished Kerris said, "Anything we can use in the Miranda?"

"What do you mean, use?"

Truly smiled. "Was there anything in her action indicative of malice aforethought or a willingness to commit an illegal act?"

I took the reports that Eddie Ditko had faxed me from my file and passed them to Truly. I told them about the guys with the machetes. I described what had happened at the Burrito King. "They let both these guys walk and Rossi took the heat for it. I don't think there was much forethought to blowing out her career at the end of a high-speed chase because of an adrenaline rush."

Truly smiled again and shrugged at Kerris. "Guess not."

Jonathan Green said, "You're sure about these things?"

"Yes, sir. There is no evidence that this woman has ever done anything illegal or even improper other than the Miranda beef, and she stood up for that one. She wouldn't have had to set up LeCedrick Earle. He's a career criminal."

Green nodded. "Then you don't believe that she could've planted the hammer on Theodore's property?"

"No, sir."

"We should abandon this as a legal theory?"

"That would be my opinion, yes, sir."

Jonathan Green nodded again, then stared at the far wall for what seemed like several minutes. No one moved, and no one spoke. All of the other attorneys stared at Jonathan as if he might suddenly utter some dictum and they would have to act on it. Apprehensive.

I looked at my watch. It was nine forty-two, and the staring continued. Maybe Jonathan Green had lapsed into a trance and no one knew it. Maybe he would continue to stare all day and I'd still be sitting here when Lucy and Ben landed at LAX. I drummed my fingers on the table and Elliot Truly looked horrified. I guess it just wasn't done.

Jonathan Green suddenly spread his hands, then placed them on the table and leaned forward. "Well, that's that. Better to know now than embarrass ourselves in court. You've done an outstanding job, Mr. Cole. Thank you."

The other attorneys breathed as one and broke into large smiles, saying what an outstanding job I'd done.

Green swiveled toward Truly and said, "It was one theory, and there's still plenty of ground to cover. We'll just have to roll up our sleeves and try harder." Green swiveled back to me and leaned forward again, absolutely serious. "I remain convinced of Teddy's innocence, and I'm determined to work all the harder to prove it."

The fourteen other attorneys around the big table nodded, and I guess I could understand why. Green seemed to bring it out in you. I wanted to nod, too.

Jonathan Green said, "Mr. Cole, I know you were hired for this specific part of our investigation, but it's very important to me that people of your caliber work with the team."

Elliot Truly said, "Here, here." Really.

Green gestured toward Kerris. "We've been absolutely overwhelmed with people calling our hotline, haven't we, Stan?"

Kerris nodded, but the nod conveyed nothing, sort of like his eyes. "We've gotten several hundred calls from people claiming to have information about the kidnapping. We can dismiss some based on the phone interview, but most have to be checked. We're dividing these things up among our investigators."

Green said, "Stan, give him the envelope, please."

Kerris pushed the envelope down along the table to me. I opened it. Eight single-sheet interview forms were inside.

Jonathan said, "Each sheet contains the name, phone number, and address of a person claiming to have information about Susan Martin's murder. If you could see your way clear to staying with us on this and checking these people out, we would appreciate it."

I looked at the sheets. I slipped them back into the envelope. "I have guests coming into town."

Truly shrugged. "There isn't a rush with this, Cole. Sure, sooner is better than later, but you know the justice system."

"Okay."

Green broke into a wide smile. "Well, that's just great. That's fabulous."

The assembled attorneys told me how great it was.

I glanced at my watch, thinking I could knock off three or four interviews before Lucy's plane. The more I finished before Lucy's plane, the more time I'd have for her.

Truly said, "We don't know anything about these people. As Stan said, our screeners were able to rule out the obvious cranks, but you never know. We want you to use your best judgment to determine if they have anything of merit to offer."

"Judgment. Okay." I looked at my watch again. "I've got it."

Truly spread his hands. "And when you're done with those, of course, there's more."

The lesser attorneys chuckled and someone said, "A *lot* more." Even Jonathan Green chuckled at that one.

Green stood and everyone stood with him, and I was hoping I hadn't been too obvious with all the watch-glancing. Jonathan came around the table and offered his hand again, and this time when we shook he held it. He said, "I want you to know that I appreciate the good, fast work you've done, Mr. Cole. It's important to me, and it's important to Teddy, also. I spoke with him yesterday and told him that you're on the team. You're going to like Teddy, Mr. Cole. Everyone does."

"I'll look forward."

"Good hunting." He tried to let go of my hand, but this time I held onto him, not realizing that I had. In that instant he smiled warmly and I let go.

Jonathan Green swept out in a wave, Kerris beside him and the lesser attorneys in his wake, jostling each other to better their positions.

t was a little before ten when I followed the trail of security men down to my car, then zipped to the Virgin Megastore, bought the new k.d. lang and a collection of Louisiana hits called *Cajun Party*, then sat in the Megastore's parking structure and went through the envelope of hotline tipsters. I had almost seven hours until Lucy's plane; plenty of time for the world's fastest detective to do his marketing and work his way through a significant number of interviews, especially if he attacked his investigatorial responsibilities in a methodical and professional manner.

I organized the twenty statement forms by location and decided to start with those people who were closest and work outward.

I went back into the Virgin, got change from a pretty young woman with a pin through her nose, then found a pay phone on Sunset Boulevard to arrange the interviews. A homeless man with a shopping cart filled with neatly folded cardboard squares was seated beneath the phone, but he graciously moved aside when I told him I needed to make some calls. He said, "Please feel free. It is, after all, a public instrument." He was wearing spats.

I fed in a quarter and dialed Mr. C. Bertrand Rujillio, who lived less than five minutes away. A man with a soft, raspy voice answered on the fourth ring and said, "Who is this?"

"My name is Cole, for the law firm of Jonathan Green. I'm calling for Mr. C. Bertrand Rujillio, please."

There was a pause, and then the rasp came back. "Do you have the money?"

"Is this Mr. Rujillio?"

Another pause, softer. "The money?"

"If you mean the reward, that won't be paid unless the information you provide leads to the arrest and conviction of Ms. Martin's murderer." Truly said that the phone bank operators had explained all this. Truly said I wouldn't have to worry about it. "I need to take your statement, Mr. Rujillio. Can we arrange that?"

The pause again, and this time the line went dead. I stared at the phone for a couple of seconds, then hung up and scratched C. Bertrand Rujillio's name off the list.

The homeless man said, "No luck?"

I shook my head.

Of the next three calls, two reached answering machines and one went unanswered. Nobody home. I said, "Damn."

The homeless man said, "Four out of four is poor luck."

"It can't last forever."

"Will you have many more calls?"

"A couple."

He sighed and looked away.

Two more calls and two more answering machines and all the nearby people were done. So much for efficiency. So much for my plan of starting in close and working out. I said, "Well, hell."

The homeless man said, "Tell me about it."

I looked at him. "I had a plan, but no one's home."

He made a sympathetic shrug, then spread his hands. "Flexibility, my friend. Flexibility is the key to all happiness. Remember that."

I told him that I would and shuffled through the witness forms and decided to hell with starting close. I called Floyd M. Thomas in Chatsworth. Chatsworth was a good forty minutes away. Floyd M. Thomas answered on the third ring in a fast, nervous voice and told me that he had been expecting my call and that he would be happy to see me. I hung up. The homeless man said, "You see? When we force events we corrupt them. Your flexibility allowed events to unfold in a way that pleases you. We know this as synchronicity."

"You're a very wise man. Thank you."

He spread his hands. "To possess great wisdom obliges one to share it. Enjoy."

I drove to Chatsworth.

Floyd Thomas lived in a studio apartment on the second floor of a ten-unit garden apartment just off Nordhoff. Scaffolding was rigged around the front and sides of the place, and Hispanic men in baggy pants were chipping away cracked stucco. Earthquake repairs. Thomas himself was a thin, hunched man in his early fifties who opened his door only wide enough to peer out at me with one eye. When he opened the door a cloud of moist heat oozed out around him like a fog. I slipped in a card. "Elvis Cole. I called you about the Martin murder."

He looked at the card without taking it. "Oh, yes. Floyd Thomas saw that. Floyd Thomas saw exactly what happened." Floyd Thomas. Don't you love it when they speak of themselves in the third person.

"That's great, Mr. Thomas. I'll need to take your statement."

He unlocked four chains and opened the door just wide enough for me to enter. If it was in the high nineties outside, Thomas's apartment must've been a hundred ten with at least three industrial-strength humidifiers pumping out jets of water vapor. Stacks of newspapers and magazines and periodicals sprouted around the room like some out-of-control toadstool jungle, and everything smelled of mildew and body odor. I said, "Hot in here."

"Floyd Thomas chills easily." Sweat leaked down out of his scalp and along the contours of his face and made his thin shirt cling to his skin. Thirty seconds inside his apartment, and I was beginning to sweat, too.

"So what did you see, Mr. Thomas?" I dug out the form and prepared to take notes.

He said, "We were over the Encino Reservoir. They were in a long black convertible. A Mercury, I think."

I looked at him without writing. "Over the Encino Reservoir?"

He nodded. "That's right. I saw them with a woman

in their car, and I'm sure it was her. She was struggling."
His eyes shifted side to side as he spoke.

I put down the pen. "How were you over the reservoir?"

His eyes narrowed and he looked suspicious. "They'd taken me up in the orb to adjust the chips."

"The orb?" I said. "The chips?"

He pulled back his upper lips so that his gums were exposed. "They force chips into my gums that no one can see. They won't even show up on X-rays." He made a tiny laugh. Hee-hee. Like that.

I said, "You believe you saw Susan Martin in a black Mercury convertible when you were up in the orb."

He nodded again. "There were three men in black and they had the woman. Black suits, black ties, black hats, dark glasses. She had seen the orb and the men in black had to make sure she was silenced. They work for the government, don't you know."

"Of course."

"When will I get the reward?"

"We'll let you know, Mr. Thomas."

I thanked Floyd Thomas for his time, then drove to a nearby 7-Eleven and made five more calls, which resulted in three more interviews. Mr. Walter S. Warren of Van Nuys was a retired general contractor who was convinced that his younger brother, Phil, was behind the kidnapping. He revealed that Phil had once eaten in Teddy Martin's Santa Monica restaurant, had cracked a tooth while enjoying the steak tartare, and had promised to "get that prick" for what had happened to his tooth. Ms. Victoria Bonell, also of Van Nuys, was an extremely thin woman who shared her ranch-style home with seven pug dogs and nine million fleas. Ms. Bonell described an elaborate scenario in which "lipstick lesbians" and "power dykes" were behind Susan Martin's murder, information she had overheard while having her hair colored at a place called Rosa's. I dutifully noted these things, then went to see Mrs. Lewis P. Reese of Sherman Oaks, who offered me tea and finger cakes, and who clearly knew nothing of Teddy Martin, Susan Martin, or the kidnapping. She was elderly and lonely, and I stayed twenty minutes longer than necessary, chatting about her dead husband. The detective does his good turn.

I left Mrs. Reese at twenty minutes after two, bloated on tea cakes, itching from fleas, and smelling of Floyd C. Thomas's pod-person environment. I thought that if I was going to make any more calls maybe they should be to Jonathan. Maybe I should ask him if he really wanted to spend his money having me interview these people?

I stopped at a Ralph's market, bought Tide, Downy Fabric Softener, two Long Island ducklings, enough salad ingredients for a family of nine, and was home by ten minutes after three. The airline told me that Lucy's flight was expected to arrive on time. I put the ducks into a large pot, covered them with water to thaw, and put the pot in the refrigerator. I showered, shaved, put on fresh clothes, and made a last-minute check of the house. Spotless. Pristine. Free from embarrassing dust bunnies.

I took Pike's Jeep, pushed back down the hill and made my way to LAX, arriving at the gate twenty-eight minutes early. I took a seat across from an older woman with brittle white hair and pleasant eyes. I nodded hello and she nodded back. She said, "I'll bet she's very pretty."

"Who?"

"The one you're waiting for. You should see the smile on your face." Know-it-all.

The gate grew crowded and, with the growing crowd, I began to feel anxious and goofy. Then the plane was down and my heart was hammering and it was hard to breath. I said, "Snap out of it, dummy. Try to get a grip."

The older woman laughed, and a man holding a two-year-old moved away.

I saw Lucy first, emerging from the jetway behind three elderly gentlemen, and I wanted to yell, "Hey, Luce!" and jump up and down.

Lucy Chenier is five feet five, with amber green eyes and auburn hair rich with golden highlights from all the time she spends in the sun. She was wearing black shorts and a white long-sleeved shirt with the sleeves rolled and white Reebok tennis shoes, and she was carrying a gray canvas shoulder bag that probably weighed nine thousand pounds and her Gucci briefcase. When she saw me she tried to wave but her hands were full with the bags. Ben yelled, "Hey, there's Elvis!" and then I shouldered past two Marines and Lucy was hugging me and I was hugging her back, and then she stepped away and said, "Oh, your poor eye!"

"You look so good, Luce. You don't know."

We gave each other a long kiss, and then I hugged

Ben, too. Ben Chenier had grown maybe four inches in the three months since I'd last seen him. "You're taller."

He beamed. "Four six and a quarter. I'm getting close to five feet."

"Wow."

I took the shoulder bag and we moved with the flow of arrivals down to baggage claim, Lucy and I holding hands and Ben ranging ahead of us, burning off eight-year-old-boy energy. Lucy's hand felt dry and warm and natural in mine, and as we moved along the white tiled corridors they told me about their flight (uneventful) and how Ben was spending his summer (a week at Camp Avondale with his Cub Scout pack) and about Lucy's business in Long Beach (amicably renegotiating a six-year-old divorce settlement involving complex corporate holdings). As we talked there was a growing feeling that these were not just two people with whom I would spend time, but two people I was allowing into my life. It was a thought that made me smile, and Lucy said, "What?"

"Just thinking how glad I am that you guys are here."

She squeezed my hand.

When their luggage arrived we loaded it into the Jeep and followed LaTijera out of the airport northeast up through the city. It was rush hour, and the going was slow, but going slow didn't seem to matter. Ben said, "We're going to your house?"

"That's right. I live in the hills above West Hollywood."

"Where are we gonna sleep?"

Lucy and I traded a smile. "I've got a guest room.

There's a bed for your mom, and a camper's cot for you."

"What's your house like?"

Lucy said, "You'll see when we get there, Ben."

I smiled at him in the rearview. "It's perched on the side of a mountain and it's surrounded by trees. A friend said that it reminds her of a tree house."

Ben said, "Cool."

Lucy raised an eyebrow and looked at me. "What friend?"

I said, "That was years ago."

"Mm-hmm."

We made great time through the Slauson Pass, then climbed north through the Fairfax District past CBS and finally up Laurel Canyon and into the mountains, and then we were home. The summer sun was still high in the west as we turned into the carport and got out, and Lucy said, "Oh, this is just wonderful!" You could smell the eucalyptus and the pine and, high above us, the two red-tailed hawks who lived in the canyon floated on rising thermals. I said, "You guys hungry?"

Ben said, "Yeah!"

Lucy said, "Starving, but I want to take a bath first."

I showed them in through the kitchen and led them past the entry and across the living room and, as we walked, I watched Lucy's eyes flick over the kitchen counters and the refrigerator with its Spider-Man magnets and the bar built into the dining room wall and the stone hearth in the living room and the bookcases and pictures; trying to take in as much of my life in those few seconds as she could. She caught me watching her and gave me a smile of approval. "I like."

I showed them their room and bath, then brought them out onto the deck. Ben said, "Oh, wow," and raced around the handrail, looking down. It's about a twenty-foot drop.

Lucy said, "Elvis, it's beautiful."

"This canyon merges with Nichols Canyon, which opens out into the basin. The little bit of city you see is part of Hollywood. Tomorrow morning we'll take the road below us down to the Budget Rent-a-Car."

She turned back to the house and lowered her voice. "And where does the master sleep?"

I grinned and pulled her close. "The stairs off the living room lead to the master's quarters."

She pushed away, then leaned against the rail and crossed her arms. It was a pretty good pose. "Perhaps a bit later I'll get a chance to inspect the premises."

I shrugged, but even pretending to be disinterested was somehow impossible. My voice came out hoarse and broken. "If you're good, perhaps I'll let you."

She let a smile curl out from under the world's longest eyelashes and lowered her voice still more and let the southern accent come thick. "Oh, Studly, Ah intend to be very, very bad."

The air seemed to spark with a kind of electric heat and then Ben raced back from the side of the house. "Elvis, can I go down the hill?"

"Up to your mom, pal."

Lucy looked over the rail. "Is it safe?"

"Sure. It's a gentle slope. The people who live over

there have a couple of boys, and they play all along the ridges."

Lucy didn't look convinced, but you could tell she was going to give in. "Well, okay, but stay close to the house."

Ben ran around the side of the house again, and this time we could hear him crashing down through the dried grass and into the trees. Lucy looked at me and I looked back, but now she was giving me serious. "So. Are you going to tell me about the eye, or do I have to keep wondering?"

"A police officer named Angela Rossi popped me with a sap."

Lucy sighed and shook her head. "Other women date doctors or businessmen. I have to fall for someone who gets into street fights."

"It wasn't much of a fight. She suckered me." I told her about what Green had hired me to do, and how I had done it, and how I had come to get the eye.

Lucy listened, interested more in the parts about Jonathan Green, and frowning when I told her how Rossi had eye-faked me. "She caught you off guard. You underestimated her because she was a woman."

"If I said that it would be taking something away from her. I didn't underestimate her; she was just good enough to sucker me with an eye-fake."

Lucy gave me one of her gentle smiles, then touched the mouse. "You're such a sweetie."

I nodded.

She came close and went up on her toes and kissed it.

"I need to make some calls about tomorrow, and I want to take that bath. May I use your phone?"

"Sure." I brushed at her hair, then stroked her upper arms. "You don't have to ask, okay? Whatever you want to do while you're here, just do it. Ben, too."

She went up on her toes and kissed me again. "Keep an eye on Ben?"

"The good eye or the bad eye?"

"Funny."

While Lucy was making her calls I fired the grill, then split the ducks and rubbed them with lemon juice and garlic and pepper. Lucy phoned two attorneys to arrange her next day's meeting, and then she called Jodi Taylor. Jodi was filming her series, *Songbird*, and had invited Ben to spend the day with her on the set. When Lucy was off the phone and in the bath I checked on Ben and, when the coals were right, put the four duck halves on the grill and covered them. I was back in the kitchen working on tarragon rice and salad when the cat door clacked and the cat walked in. He froze in the center of the kitchen floor and growled.

I said, "Knock that off."

He moved through the kitchen, stopping every couple of steps, his cat nose working and the growl soft in his chest. I said, "We're going to have guests for a few days, and if you bite or scratch either one of them it will go hard for you."

His eyes narrowed and he looked at me. I said, "I mean it."

He sprinted back through his door. There are some things you just can't talk to him about.

I checked on Ben again, then finished with the salad and set the table and put on the new k. d. lang. Lucy reappeared in fresh shorts and wet, slicked-back hair, wrapping her arms around me from behind and sharing her warmth. She said, "Everything is just perfect."

"Not yet," I said. "But soon."

We called in Ben and ate, and little by little we moved through the evening, talking about and planning our coming days, Lucy and I gently touching as we talked, each touch a way of sharing something larger than a simple tactile experience, and after a while even the excitement of the adventure couldn't keep Ben going and Lucy finally whispered, "He's sleeping."

"Need help getting him to bed?"

"No. I'll get him on his feet and he'll walk."

When their door was closed I shut all the lights save one, then went upstairs and took off my clothes. The house was still, and I thought that I could smell her the way, I supposed, the cat had. But maybe that was my imagination.

I lay in the dark for what seemed forever, and then I heard the door below open and the sound of her on the stairs, and I thought how very lucky I was that she had come, and that I was the one whom she had come to see.

10

The sun was bright and hot on the sheets, and I woke smelling coffee and hearing *Bewitched* on the television, Elizabeth Montgomery saying, "But Darren is a wonderful man, Mother," and Agnes Moorehead saying, "That's the problem, dear. He's a *man*, and you deserve so much more."

When I went downstairs, Lucy and Ben were up and dressed, Ben on the couch watching television, and Lucy at the dining room table, sipping coffee. She was wearing a pale yellow pants suit and her Gucci briefcase was open, with papers spread on the table beside her. Preparing for business. I said, "Hey. There are people in my house."

Lucy smiled. "We tried to be quiet."

"You were. I didn't hear a thing." She held out her hand, fingers spread, and I laced my fingers through hers.

She said, "Mm."

I wiggled my eyebrows, then made a shifty look back toward the stairs. "Mm-mm."

Lucy took back her hand. "No time, my dear. Jodi's

going to pick up Ben on her way in to the studio, then you have to take me to the Budget office. She should be here soon."

"Great." We were grinning at each other with great loopy grins that probably looked silly. "Did you sleep all right?"

Lucy managed a straight face. "Very well, thank you. And yourself?"

I pretended to stifle a yawn. "A little restless. I feel drained this morning."

Lucy raised her eyebrows. "Imagine that. Perhaps you need more rest."

Ben looked at us from the couch, confused. "You don't look tired to me."

Lucy and I grinned, and Ben looked even more confused. "What did I say?"

Lucy said, "I got directions to my meeting, so all we need to do is pick up the car. You shower and dress, and I'll make breakfast. Deal?"

"Deal."

I did and she did, and we were finishing coffee and toasted banana bread and scrambled eggs when Jodi Taylor's black-on-black Beemer tooled up and stopped across the drive. I pushed open the kitchen door and gave her a kiss as she entered. "What, no limo for the star?"

Jodi Taylor tugged at my shirt and said, "I'll buy a stretch if you'll come for a ride, handsome." Then she winked at Lucy and said, "Oops, sorry. I see he's already taken."

I gave her the eyebrows. "Taken, yes, but perhaps available for rent."

Lucy said, "In that case she should buy a hearse. Better to lay out the body."

Jodi laughed. "Grr-owl. These southern belles are *very* territorial."

"Possessive," Lucy said. "The word is possessive."

Lucy and Jodi hugged, and Ben ran in from the living room. Like Lucy, Jodi Taylor was from Louisiana, though, unlike Lucy, you couldn't hear it in her voice. She was maybe an inch taller than Lucy, with hazel eyes and dusky red hair and a kind of natural beauty that made her accessible and real to thirty million people every week. Supermarket beauty, they called it. The kind and quality of beauty that let you believe that you might bump into her in the market, buying Pampers or Diet Coke. *Songbird* had been renewed for a second full season, and Jodi Taylor had just begun production on the new episodes. She was happy and confident in returning to work, and was at ease with herself in a way that she hadn't been three months ago. Lucy said, "Jodi, you look wonderful."

Jodi smiled shyly. "Thanks to you two."

I had seen Jodi from time to time in the three months since I'd helped her, but Lucy hadn't, and they chatted and worked out the details of Ben's day while I cleared the table, loaded the dishwasher, then went upstairs to gather together my file of tipsters. I considered bringing along a can of bug repellent for the day's assignment, but decided against it. Too hard to force the can into my holster.

When I went back downstairs, Jodi and Lucy were standing together, grinning. Jodi said, "You're working for Jonathan Green? My, my." Impressed.

I spread my hands. "He's just another client, ladies." Mr. Modest.

Lucy put her hands on her hips. "No, he's not. He's Jonathan Green."

I spread my hands again. They're carrying on like this, and I'm battling fleas and talking to people who think they've got chips in their gums.

Lucy made her voice low and breathy. "He positively *dominates* a court room. And his presence is so *commanding*."

Jodi Taylor slinked over to me and toyed with my collar. "Could you arrange a personal introduction?"

Lucy said, "Would he autograph my law school diploma? Would he do that for lil' ol' me?"

Jodi purred, "I've got something else he could autograph."

Girl humor.

Jodi and Ben finally left for the studio, and then I brought Lucy down to the Budget office, working our way along the back canyon road in silence. Lucy was staring out of the car, and I thought that she might be watching the alien scenery and the strange mountain houses, but she wasn't. She said, "What I said about possessive. I was joking." Her voice was soft, and when she said it she didn't look at me.

"Sure."

Her hands were in her lap and her briefcase was on the floor beneath her legs. She said, "Elvis?"

"Hm?"

Another pause. Longer. "Do you see anyone else?"

I looked at her, but she still wasn't looking at me. I went back to the road.

Lucy said, "I mean, it's none of my business. We've never talked about other people."

I nodded. I looked at her again, but she still was focused outside. "I went out twice in the month after I came back from Louisiana. Once with a woman I'd seen several times before, and once with a waitress I met in the Valley, and both times went poorly."

"Oh." She didn't sound disappointed.

"I was with them, but I was thinking of you. Then you and I started talking about going to Cancun. I haven't been out with anyone since then. I don't want to go out with anyone else." I was looking more at her than the road, which isn't smart in the hills.

Lucy Chenier looked at me, then nodded once and turned back to the window.

I said, "Have you been seeing anyone?"

She shook her head. "No."

I thought about it and what it meant. "Good."

Without looking at me, she put out her hand. I took it. We drove like that the rest of the way to the Budget office, where I dropped her off and began another exciting day in the employ of the Big Green Defense Machine.

11

After I dropped Lucy off I stopped at a diner on Hollywood Boulevard and made more calls. Of the remaining names on my list, two were in El Monte, one in San Marino, and one was in Pasadena, all of which were on the eastern rim of the Los Angeles sprawl.

I called a Mr. James Lester first. A woman answered, sounding young and whiny, and told me that he was sleeping. She said that he didn't have to go in until noon, so he always slept late. I told her that I would be in their area later, and how about I call back then. She said, "Mister, I don't give a rat's ass what you do." Nothing like starting off your work day with a bang.

No one was home on my next call, and then I phoned Ms. Mary Mason of San Marino. A woman with a low, breathy voice answered on the third ring. She identified herself as Mistress Maggie Mason and told me that Mary was her sister. When I told her why I was calling she said that Mary would be available shortly and gave me directions to their home. One for three.

Mary Mason lived on Winston Drive in a stately well-kept home set back from the street. It was an older place, built of heavy stone and stucco. I rang the bell three times, knocked twice, and was just getting ready to leave when the door opened and a tall, statuesque woman in a black leather teddy, net stockings, and six-inch platform shoes stepped out. A twined cobra was tattooed on her right thigh. She said, "May I help you?" She had long black hair pulled back tight against her head.

"Are you Mary Mason?"

She smiled nicely. It was a friendly smile, relaxed and personable. "No, I'm her sister, Maggie. I spoke with you earlier."

"Ah."

"Come in and I'll get Mary."

The living room was tastefully decorated with minimalist Italian furniture, a spherical saltwater aquarium, and custom bookshelves lining three walls. The bookshelves were African teak and must've cost a fortune. Maggie Mason said, "Wait right here and I'll get her." She was bright and cheery, not unlike a Girl Scout troop leader from Nebraska.

I waited. The house was so quiet that I could hear neither street noise nor passing cars nor the sound of Maggie Mason getting her sister. I looked at the books. Short fiction by Raymond Carver and Joan Didion. Asian philosophy by T'sun T'su and Koji Toyoda. Crime novels by James Ellroy and Jim Thompson. Science fiction by Olaf Stapledon and Jack Finney. Eclectic and impressive. I had finished reading the titles on one wall and was starting on a second when Mary and Maggie Mason returned. Twins. Both were tall, but where Maggie was dressed in the teddy and the fishnet, Mary wore a smartly tailored business suit and conservative low-heeled pumps. Her face was very white and her lips were liquid red and her black hair was cropped short and oiled to severe perfection. I said, "Mary Mason?"

Mary Mason sat next to the aquarium, crossed one gleaming leg over the other, and said, "Four payments. I want the first payment now, another when there's an arrest, the third on arraignment, and the final on the first day of the trial. That's the only way I'll do business."

I said, "Business?"

Her sister smiled politely. "If you'll excuse me, I have something to take care of." She left without waiting for either of us to respond.

Mary Mason leaned toward me. "I hear things." She arched her eyebrows, which, like the rest of her, were perfect. "I know the identity of James X. I can help Teddy Martin."

I gave her the same news that I'd given Floyd Thomas, that there would be no money until a conviction.

Mary Mason said, "Bullshit." When she said it, a muffled *crack* came from the back of the house.

I looked past her. "What was that?"

Mary Mason leaned closer and put her hand on my knee. "Pay something as a sign of good faith. Five thousand dollars, and I'll give you a physical description. How about that?" There was another dull *crack* and then a whimpering sound.

I looked past her again. "I can't do that, Ms. Mason."

She squeezed the knee. "Three thousand, then. Teddy Martin can afford it." She ran her tongue along glistening lips, and then a man in the rear of the house moaned

something about being called a dog. The voice was muffled and far away, and I thought that maybe I'd heard
him wrong. Then the man howled.

"Thanks for your time, Ms. Mason." I walked out,
wondering if it were too late to change professions.

It was twenty-eight minutes after ten when I left the
Mason twins and dropped south out of San Marino to
San Gabriel. I pulled into a strip mall, made two more
calls, and on each of the calls got an answering machine.
That meant I was back to James Lester, who may or may
not be awake. I called his number again anyway, and this
time a man answered. I said, "Mr. Lester?"

A woman was shouting in the background. Lester
shouted back at her, "Just shut the fuck up, goddammit," and then he came on the line. "Yeah?"

"Mr. James Lester?"

"Who wants to know?" One of those.

I told him who I was and what I wanted.

"You're the guy from the lawyer, right?"

"That's right."

"Okay, sure. C'mon over."

I went over.

El Monte, California, is a mostly industrial area north
of the Puente Hills and south of Santa Anita, with small
working-class neighborhoods to the south and west.
James and Jonna Lester lived in a poorly kept bungalow
on a narrow street just west of the San Gabriel River in
an area of postwar low-income housing. The lawn was
patchy and yellow from lack of water, as if the Lesters
had given up against the desert and the desert was re-

claiming their yard. Everything looked dusty and old, as if there were no future here, only a past.

I left my car on the street, walked up across the dead yard, and a guy I took to be James Lester opened the door. He was average-sized in dark gray cotton work pants, dirty white socks, and a dingy undershirt. His hair was cut short on the sides and on top, but had been left long and shaggy in back, and he looked at me with a squint. He was thin, with knobby, grease-embedded hands and pale skin sporting Bic-pen tattoos on his arms and shoulders and chest. Work farm stuff. I made him for thirty, but he could've been younger. He said, "You're the guy called. You're from the lawyer, right?" A quarter to eleven in the morning and he smelled of beer.

"That's right."

I followed him into a poorly furnished living room that wasn't in any better shape than the yard. Stacks of magazines and newspapers and comic books were piled around on the furniture, and no one had dusted since 1942. A tattered poster of the Silver Surfer was thumb-tacked to the wall, four darts growing out of the Silver Surfer's chest. Lester dropped into a battered, over-stuffed chair and pulled on a workboot. An open can of Hamm's was on the floor by the boots. "I gotta get ready for work. You wanna brewscalero?"

"Pass."

"Your loss, dude. I can't get going without it."

A barefoot woman with a swollen, discolored lip came out of the kitchen carrying a sandwich in a paper towel. She was wearing baggy shorts and a loose top and her skin was very white, as if she didn't get out in the sun much. She dropped the sandwich on a little table next to the chair as if she didn't give a damn whether he ate it or not. She looked sixteen, but she was probably older.

I smiled and said, "I believe we spoke earlier."

She said, "Well, whoop-de-doo."

James Lester pulled hard at his bootlaces. "I need another brewscalero, Jonna. Go get it."

Jonna Lester shot a hard look at her husband's back, then stomped back into the kitchen. Pouty.

James said, "She don't do nothing but run around with her friends all day while I'm bustin' my ass. That's why it's such a sty in here. That's why it's a goddamned shithole." They didn't have air conditioning. A couple of ancient electric fans blew hot air around the room, one of the fans making a slow, monotonous *chinging* sound. Jonna Lester came back with a fresh Hamm's, put it down next to the sandwich, then stomped out again. I hadn't been in their house for thirty seconds and already my neck was starting to ache.

I said, "I'm here to follow up the call you made about Susan Martin's kidnapping and murder."

Lester finished tying the first boot, then started on the second. "Sure. That guy I spoke to on the phone, he said someone would come talk to me about it. That's you, I guess."

"I guess." Mr. Lucky.

He looked over and grinned when he saw my eye. "Hey, you and Jonna kinda match, doncha?" He laughed after he said it, huh-yuk, huh-yuk, huh-yuk. Like Jughead.

I stared at him.

James Lester killed what was left of the first Hamm's, then popped the tab on the second. "I think I met the guys who did it."

"Okay."

He took another pull on the Hamm's, then had some of the sandwich. When he bit into the sandwich he jumped up and opened the sandwich as if he'd just bitten into a turd. "Goddammit, Jonna, what in hell is this?"

"That's your potted meat!" Yelling from the kitchen.

"Where's the fuckin' mayonnaise?"

"We're out. I gotta get some."

"Where's the *little pickles?*" Now he was whining worse than her.

"I'm gonna go get some, all right?" Screaming, now. "*Do you think I'm your fuckin' slave?*"

His face went sullen and his breathing grew loud. He had more of the Hamm's. He had more of the Hamm's again. My neck was hurting so bad I thought it would go into spasm.

"Tell me what you know, James."

He stayed with the loud breathing a little longer, then closed the sandwich and took another bite. You'd think it was killing him, having to eat his sandwich without the mayonnaise and the little pickles.

I said, "James."

He went on with his mouth full. "A week before it's on the news about her gettin' killed I stop in this place for a couple of brewscaleros. There's these two guys, one of the guys, he was wearing a Shell station shirt had the name 'Steve' sewn over the pocket."

"Okay." I wrote *Shell station* on my notepad. I wrote *Steve*.

"We were talkin' about how shitty it was, havin' to work for a livin', and this guy, he gives me the big wink and says he's got her whipped. I'm all, whaddaya mean you got'r whipped? He goes, hey, a guy with the 'nads could snatch one of these rich Beverly Hills bitches and score enough fast cash to retire in style."

I said, "Steve said that?"

"Unh-hunh." He stuffed the rest of the sandwich in his mouth and washed it down. "I tell'm that sounds like a fast track to the gas chamber to me, but he goes, all you need is a layout of the house and a slick way in and out, stuff like that." He swallowed hard and let out a gassy belch.

"The other guy say anything?"

"Nope. Just sat there drinkin'."

"What'd they look like?"

"Steve was kinda tall and skinny, with light hair. I'm not sure about the other guy. Shorter. Darker."

A phone rang in the kitchen and we could hear Jonna Lester answer. James's face clouded and he yelled, "That better not be one'a your cunt friends!"

She yelled back, "Fuck you!"

I said, "James."

He turned the cloud my way.

"'Cunt' is an ugly word."

He squinted at me as if he wasn't sure what I'd said, and then he shook his head. "All she does is yack with her friends. All she does is run around the mall while I'm bustin' my ass." Like that should explain it.

I said, "Steve and the dark guy say anything else?"

He sucked at his teeth, getting rid of the last bits of the sandwich. "I hadda pee so I went to the head. When I come back they was gone."

I stared at him, thinking about it. Seven interviews so far, and his was the only one that seemed to be worth checking out. It would probably add up to nothing, but you never know until you know. "You remember the bar?"

"Sure. It was a place called the Hangar over on Mission Boulevard. I go there sometimes."

I wrote it down. *The Hangar.*

"Last thing the guy says before I go to the head, he says he knows just who to grab, too. He says she's a one-way ticket to Easy Street."

"Steve said that?"

"Yeah. Steve."

"He say a name?"

"Unh-unh."

Jonna Lester reappeared wearing strap sandles and carrying a small purse. She'd made her face, but the lip still looked puffy. He said, "Where the fuck do you think you're going?"

She pouted the lips at him, giving him attitude. "I gotta go to the store. I got things to buy."

"You think you're gonna run around with your cunt friends while I'm bustin' my ass? You think you're gonna spend my dough in some fuckin' mall?"

"We're outta mayonnaise. We're outta those little pickles."

He jumped up and grabbed her right arm. "You're gonna stay here and clean this fuckin' rathole, that's what you're gonna do!"

I stood.

She tried to twist away from him, screaming, "You piece of shit! I'm not your fuckin' slave!" She pounded at him with her left fist, pretty good shots that nailed him on the head and face and chest until he was able to grab her left arm, too.

"James." The ache in my neck had moved up to my scalp. Never a good sign.

She said, "You're hurtin' me, you asshole!"

"James. Leave go of her."

James Lester said, "Fuck you. This is my house. This is my wife. She's gonna do what I say or I'll give'r a fat lip!"

I held up my right index finger. "Watch the finger, James. I want to show you something."

His eyes went to the finger, like maybe it was a trick, only he couldn't figure out what the trick might be.

"Are you watching my finger?"

"Suck my ass." She was watching my right finger, too.

I hit him flush on the nose with a left.

He yelled, "Ow!" and grabbed at his face with both hands. He stumbled back and tripped over the little side table. Jonna Lester leaned over him, wiggled her butt, and yelled, "Ha-ha, *asshole!*" Some wife.

James Lester was on his back, eyes watering, blinking at me. He said, "You piece of shit. You wait'll I get up!"

I put my notes in the manila envelope, then went to the door. Lucy was probably in the midst of her negotiation right now. Ben was probably watching Jodi Taylor shoot a scene right now. The world was turning on its axis right now.

I said, "Thanks for the statement, James. If anything comes of it we'll be in touch about the reward."

"You better not jew me out of that reward! I'm gonna call the cops, you hear? I'm gonna have you *arrested!*"

I left them to their lives and walked out into the sun. You want to do the right thing, but sometimes there is no right thing to be done.

Another day, another moron. And to think, some people have to work for a living.

12

The Hangar was a small, bright hole-in-the-fence-type bar wedged between a place that sold balsa-wood rocket kits and another place that repaired appliances. They were doing a pretty good lunch business when I got there, selling chili tacos and grilled sausages to people swilling down schooners of beer. Both of the bartenders were women in their fifties, and neither of them knew a blond guy named Steve who worked for Shell. I didn't expect that they would, but you never know. The older of the two women called me 'sweetie.' The younger of the two didn't like it very much. Jealous.

I bought a grilled sausage with kraut, a schooner of Miller, and asked if they'd mind letting me use their phone book. The older one didn't, but the younger one warned me not to walk out with it. I assured them that I wouldn't. The younger one told me to be careful not to spill anything on it. The older one asked the younger one why she always had to make such a big thing, and the younger one said what if I ruined it? I assured them that I'd buy them a new phone book if I ruined the loaner. The older one said, "Oh, don't you give it another thought, sweetie," and the younger one went down to the far end of the bar and sulked.

Half the schooner later I had addresses for the nine Shell service stations located in the El Monte/Baldwin Park/West Covina area. I finished the sausage, thanked the older one for her help, and made the round of the Shell stations. At each stop I spoke to the manager or assistant manager, identified myself, and asked if a tall blond guy named Steve had worked there anytime in the past six months. At the first four stations I visited, the answer was no, but at the fifth station the manager said, "You mean Pritzik?"

"Who's Pritzik?"

"We had a fellow named Steve Pritzik." The manager was a Persian gentleman named Mr. Pavlavi. He was short and round and stood in the shade of his maintenance center with his arms crossed. His maintenance center, like the rest of his service station, was polished and gleaming.

I said, "Was he tall?"

"Oh, yes. Very tall."

"Was he blond?"

"Oh, yes. Very blond."

I said, "Mr. Pavlavi, is he employed here now?" Just because a tall blond guy named Steve worked here didn't mean it was the *same* tall blond Steve. Maybe it was just a coincidence.

Pavlavi frowned. "Not in a very long while. He quit, you know. One day here, the next day not, never to return." He sighed as if such things are the stuff of life, to be expected and therefore no great cause for anxiety or resentment.

"About how long ago was that?"

"Well," he said. "Let us see."

He led me into the air conditioned office and took a ledger from his desk. The ledger was filled with page after page of handwriting that, like the service station, was immaculate. "Pritzik was last here exactly one hundred two days ago."

"Hm." Steve Pritzik had last been in four days before Susan Martin's murder.

"I owe him forty-eight dollars and sixteen cents, but he has not been in to collect. I will keep it for exactly one year, then give it to charity."

"Mr. Pavlavi, would you have an address on Pritzik?"

He did, and he gave it to me.

Steve Pritzik lived in one of a cluster of six small duplex cottages in an older neighborhood at the base of the Puente Hills, not far from the Pomona Freeway. The duplexes were single-story stucco and clapboard buildings stepping up the side of the hill and overgrown with original planting fruit trees and ivy and climbing roses.

I parked at the curb, then made my way up broken cement steps, looking for Pritzik's address. The steps were narrow, and the heavy growth of ivy and roses made them feel still more narrow. Pritzik's apartment was the western half of the third duplex up from the street. Each side of the cottage had its own little porch, separated by a couple of ancient orange trees and a trellis of roses. The eastern porch was neat and clean and decorated by a small cactus garden. Pritzik's porch was dirty and unadorned, and his mailbox was heavy with letters and flyers. I rang the bell and could hear it inside, but no one answered. I listened harder. Nothing. I went to the mailbox and fingered through gas and phone and electric bills. They weren't addressed to Steve Pritzik; they were addressed to a Mr. Elton Richards. Hmm. I walked around the orange trees and up onto the adjoining porch and rang the bell. You could hear music inside. Alanis Morissette.

A woman in her late twenties opened the door. "Yes?" She had long dark hair and great floppy bangs and she was wearing cutoff jeans under an oversized man's T-shirt. The T-shirt was blotched with small smears of color. So were her hands.

I gave her the card and introduced myself. "I'm trying to find a guy named Steve Pritzik. I think he lives or used to live next door."

She read the card and grinned. "Are you really a private eye?"

"Pretty amazing, huh?"

She grinned wider and nodded. "Cool."

"You know Pritzik?"

She offered the card back, but I raised a hand, telling her to keep it. "I don't think so. Elton lives next door."

"Is Elton tall and blond?"

"Oh, no. He's short and kinda dark." Ah. She rolled her eyes. "He's such a creep. He's always hitting on me, so I try to avoid him."

"I was just over there, and it looks like Elton hasn't been around." I told her about the mail.

She pushed her hands in her pockets. "You know,

now that I think about it, I haven't seen him in a while. I haven't heard his TV or anything."

"You think he might've moved?"

"I don't know."

"Can you give me a guess how long he's been gone?"

She scrunched her face, thinking. "Couple of months, maybe."

"Between three and four months?"

She waffled her hand. "He's just such a creep I try to duck him. Sorry."

I said, "You ever see a tall blond guy hanging around with him?"

She frowned.

"Maybe four months ago."

She was swaying with Alanis, then she kind of cocked her head. "You know, I think maybe there was a guy like that. Elton had such scuzzy friends." She nodded, then, starting to see it. "Yeah. There was this blond guy." She nodded harder, the image pulling into focus. "Oh, yuck, what an asshole. He sees me on the street and follows me up the walk one day. He asks me if I want to go inside and fuck, just like that. Oh, yuck. I think he worked at a gas station or something."

I nodded.

"All of Elton's friends were like that. Real lowlifes." She suddenly put out her hand. "I'm Tyler, by the way."

"Hi, Tyler." We shook, and I gave her the big smile. "Can I ask you something?"

"Sure." She smiled back, anxious to hear what I was going to ask. Alanis was really tearing it up inside.

"I'm thinking about popping Elton's door and sneaking in to look around. You wouldn't call the police if I did that, would you?"

Her smiled grew wider as I said it. "No way! Could I come, too?"

I shook my head. "Then if we're caught, we're both in trouble, you see?"

She looked disappointed. Behind her, Alanis stopped singing and Tyler pulled a hand out of her pocket long enough to brush at the bangs. They were pretty incredible. "You really know how to pick locks and stuff?"

"I'm a full-service professional, Tyler."

She stared at me for a few seconds and then she crossed her arms. She looked out from under her bangs at me. "And just what kind of service do you provide?"

"I've got a girlfriend. Sorry."

Tyler stared at me from under the bangs for another couple of seconds, then uncrossed her arms and looked at my card again. "Yeah, well. If I ever need anything detected, maybe I'll call."

"How about the cops?"

Tyler made a zipping move across her lips.

I gave her the big smile again, then went next door, slipped the lock, and let myself into Elton Richards' half of the house. It was dim from the drawn shades, and I flipped the light switch but the lights stayed dark. I guess the power company had killed the juice. I said, "Mr. Richards?"

No answer. Next door, I could hear Alanis start again, faint and far away.

The house smelled musty. A ratty couch was against the wall under a Green Day poster, fronted by a coffee table made of a couple of 2 by 10 planks lying on cinder-blocks and cornered by someone's secondhand lawn chair. A black streamline phone waited on the planks. A pretty good Hitachi electronics stack was against the opposite wall, and a beat-up Zenith television with a coat hanger antenna was on the floor, and everything was covered with a light patina of undisturbed dust.

I crossed into the kitchen and turned on the tap. No water. I went back to the living room, used my handkerchief, and lifted the phone. No tone. I guess Elton Richards had ignored his bills long enough for the power and water and **phon**e companies to turn everything off. Say, about four months.

I stood in the living room by the phone and thought about it. James Lester had met a short dark man and a tall blond man named Steve in a bar about a week before Susan Martin's kidnapping and murder. Steve speaks of snatching a rich woman as a means of attaining the better things in life, and maybe the two are connected, but maybe not. Four months after the fact, I identify a possible Steve and trace him to this address which, in fact, is apparently owned by a shorter, darker man named Elton Richards. Maybe they are the same two men, but maybe not. Maybe tall blond guys named Steve just naturally have short dark friends.

Two small bedrooms bracketed the bath. I searched each thoroughly, looking for receipts or ticket stubs or anything else that might provide a clue as to when and where Elton Richards and Steve Pritzik went. There was nothing. I went into the bathroom and checked behind and beneath the toilet and in the water tank. I pulled the medicine cabinet out of the wall. I checked in the little wooden cabinet beneath the lavatory. *Nada*. I went back into the living room and pulled the cushions off the couch and found a single 9 by 12 manila envelope. It was the kind of envelope you get in the mail from those sweepstakes companies declaring that you've just won ten million dollars, and it was addressed to Mr. Elton Richards. The end of the envelope had been scissored open, then retaped. I pushed my car keys under the tape, opened the envelope, and looked inside. Then I sat down.

I took deep rhythmic breaths, flooding my blood with oxygen and forcing myself to calm. Pranayamic breathing, they call it.

I looked in the envelope again, then tilted it so that the contents spilled out onto the couch. Inside there were seven separate photographs of Susan Martin and Teddy Martin, and two hand-drawn maps. One map was the floorplan of a very large house. The other was a street map showing the layout of someone's neighborhood and a house on Benedict Canyon Road. It was Teddy Martin's neighborhood, and it was Teddy Martin's house.

13

I went to my car for the new Canon Auto Focus I keep in the glove box. I made sure I had film and that the flash worked, and then I took a pair of disposable plastic gloves and went back into the house. I put on the gloves, then photographed everything as I had found it, making sure I had clear shots of the handdrawn maps as well as the photos. When I was done, I left everything lying on the couch, then went next door and asked Tyler if I could use her phone.

I called Truly first, who listened quietly until I was finished, then said, "I'll notify Jonathan and we'll get there as quickly as we can. Don't let anyone else in the residence." He cupped the phone, and I could hear muffled voices. Then he came back. "We'll notifiy the police, too. Cooperate with them when they arrive, but keep an eye on them. Watch that they don't destroy the evidence."

"Truly, they won't do anything like that."

He said, "Ha."

When I hung up, Tyler was leaning against the back of her couch, arms crossed, a long paintbrush in one hand. Her home smelled of fresh jasmine tea and acrylic paint, and was decorated with oversized sunflower sculptures that she'd made from cardboard and wire. "You really think that this creep next door had something to do with Susan Martin's murder?"

"Maybe."

"I thought her husband did it. That restaurant guy."

"You never know."

"They said on TV that he did."

"That's TV."

She shook her head. "L.A. is so perverted."

The first black and white arrived eighteen minutes later. The senior officer was a guy named Hernandez, and his partner was a younger African-American woman named Flutey. I went out to meet them carrying a glass of Tyler's jasmine iced tea. Hernandez said, "You Cole?"

"Yep." I told him what we had.

He nodded. "Okay. Flutey, get the tape from the car and let's seal it, okay? I'll check inside and around back."

Flutey went for the tape, and Hernandez looked at me. "Where you gonna be?"

"I'll hang around out here unless you want company."

Tyler called from the porch. "Would you and the other officer like some iced tea?"

Hernandez smiled at her. "That'd be real nice, miss. Thank you." Tyler ducked back inside. Hernandez stared after her. Portrait of the crime scene as a social occasion.

Two detectives from the L.A. County Sheriff's Office arrived, followed almost immediately by a criminalist van. The lead detective was a heavyset guy with thinning hair named Don Phillips. A DA's car came next, off-loading a thin woman named Sherman, a bald guy named Stu Miller, and an intense African-American guy in dark glasses named Warren Bidwell. Sherman was the Assistant Deputy DA charged with prosecuting the Teddy Martin case. Miller and Bidwell worked for her.

All three of them slipped under the tape and went into Richards' duplex, then Miller and Sherman slipped out again and came over to me. Tyler gave them a bright smile and pushed aside her bangs. "Would either of you like iced tea?"

Sherman said, "No." She squinted at me. "I'm Anna Sherman from the district attorney's office and this is Stu Miller. Would you come inside, please?"

"Sure."

Tyler said, "Can I come, too?"

Anna Sherman said, "No."

I shrugged at Tyler and followed them.

Inside, Sherman said, "Okay. Walk me through what happened."

I told them about getting the address from Pavlavi and finding the duplex deserted and popping the lock to let myself in. I told them about finding the envelope under the couch cushions and opening the envelope. Sherman stopped me. "You touched the envelope?"

"That's right."

The criminalist said, "What about the contents?"

I shook my head. "Edges only. When I saw what I had I slid the stuff out onto the couch. I used my knuckles to separate the pages first time through. When I photographed the material I was wearing gloves."

Bidwell was glowering so hard his body was making little jerks and lurches and I wondered if he knew he was doing it. He said, "I want those photographs."

I shook my head. "I don't think so."

Bidwell lurched harder. "You don't? Are you a sworn officer? You have a search warrant or any authority to break into a private residence?"

I looked at Sherman. "You want me to continue or should I call my lawyer?"

Sherman closed her eyes and shook her head. "Not now, Warren."

The yard and the walk outside grew crowded with cops and media people and rubberneckers from the neighborhood drawn by gathering news vans. Between questions I watched the on-air television talent fan out among the cops. A woman I'd seen a thousand times on the local NBC affiliate was talking with her camera operator when the camera operator saw me standing in the window and pointed me out. The reporter said something and the operator trained his camera on me. The reporter ducked past Flutey and hurried over to the window. She was all frosted hair and intelligent eyes. "Are you the detective who found the kidnappers?"

I gave her Bill Dana. "My name José Jimenez."

She waved her camera operator closer. "Look, we know that two men named Elton Richards and Steve Pritzik lived here and we'd like an on-camera statement." The camera operator held the camera over his head, trying to scan the room.

Don Phillips saw the camera coming through the window and said, "Jesus Christ!" He pushed in front of me, then leaned out the window and yelled at a uniformed sergeant. "Clear the area, for Christ's sake. Seal it off from the street back." The sergeant hustled away, and Phillips looked at me. "Are you trying to be cute?"

I spread my hands. "Trying has nothing to do with it."

The uniforms were pushing the press and gawkers along the walk when a ripple spread up from the street and across the crowd as if someone had amped a jolt of electricity through the air. Heads turned and voices rose, and the TV people surged toward the street. Phillips said, "Now what?"

Jonathan Green and Elliot Truly and the videographer from *Inside News* were working their way through the crowd. The videographer's sound tech was trying her best to move people out of their way, but it was hard going until Hernandez and Flutey and a couple of other uniforms lent a hand. Anna Sherman came to the window, then gathered Bidwell and Miller for a whispered conference. When Green and the others pushed their way through the front door past the uniformed sergeant, Phillips said, "Where in hell do you think you're going?"

Anna Sherman came over and smiled tightly. "Let them pass, detective." She offered her hand. "Hello, Mr. Green."

"Ms. Sherman." Jonathan Green smiled at me. "Congratulations, son. I think you've made my day." The videographer bumped into Phillips as he tried to get the shot, and Phillips shoved him away. Hard. The videographer said, "Hey."

Anna Sherman said, "Detective Phillips, this is Jonathan Green. Mr. Green represents Theodore Martin."

Phillips said, "How about that."

Jonathan and Truly went to the couch and leaned over the papers without touching them. Phillips said, "Don't touch anything. We haven't printed them yet."

Truly was grinning wildly and shaking his head. "This is wonderful. Would you look at this? This is absolutely fabulous." He grinned at me and then he grinned at Sherman, only Sherman didn't return it.

Green said, "Mr. Cole, are these the same documents you found when you entered this residence?" He said it loudly so that everyone in the room could hear.

"Yes."

Green motioned to videographer. "Would you get a close up of this, please?"

The videographer almost tripped over himself getting there. Bidwell said, "Who *is* this dork?"

Truly said, "They're from *Inside News*. They're doing a documentary on Jonathan."

Bidwell said, "Oh, for God's sake," and shook his head.

As the videographer panned the evidence, Jonathan looked back at me. "There are no new documents, and none of the documents you found are now missing?"

"Of course not."

The videographer panned up to Jonathan, and Jonathan said, "Mr. Cole photographed the documents found in this envelope before the police were summoned. That photographic record constitutes an accurate accounting of exactly what was here before the police took possession of the evidence. We intend to compare those photographs with these to see if the evidence has been tampered with."

Phillips went red. "Hey, what the fuck?"

Anna Sherman told him to shut up. She said that if Phillips couldn't control himself he should go outside.

Phillips said, "I know what he's saying and I don't like it. I run a clean house, goddammit." He was purple.

Sherman said something to Bidwell and Bidwell led Phillips out.

They had me go through it again, Jonathan Green and Elliot Truly asking questions and the videographer and the sound tech recording me. Anna Sherman listened with her arms crossed, occasionally digging her heel into the floor and rocking her foot, and, like Green and Truly, occasionally asking more questions. Bidwell and Phillips came back, but this time Phillips kept his mouth shut and glowered at us from the corner. When I was done, Jonathan Green looked at Sherman again and said, "We'll want these documents preserved, and we'll want to examine them as soon as practicable. We'll want the results of your fingerprint analysis, and then, of course, we'll want to do our own."

Anna Sherman's jaw was tight. "Of course."

"Do you have anything more for Mr. Cole?"

The criminalist said, "I asked Cole for permission to take his prints. He said okay."

Green nodded. "Please do it now in our presence." The criminalist broke out his fingerprint kit and had me sit on one of the dinette chairs. He took my prints quickly and professionally, then gave me a Handiwipe to clean off the ink. The videographer recorded every moment. I said, "Don't you ever run out of tape?"

The sound tech laughed.

Green walked back to the couch, again examined the papers without touching them, then looked back at Sherman. "You realize what we have here, don't you, Anna?" The patient father.

Anna Sherman did not respond. The pouty daughter.

Jonathan Green smiled. "If you don't, Ms. Sherman, I'm sure the district attorney will. Tell him I'll expect his call soon, if you would."

Her jaw flexed.

Green said, "I think we can go, Elliot. Mr. Cole's had a long and fruitful day. I expect he wants to go home."

Phillips coughed loudly from his corner of the room, but the cough soundly suspiciously like, "Fuck you."

I followed them out. The street at the end of the walk was jammed with media people and broadcast vans and uniformed cops trying to clear a path. Hernandez and Flutie flanked Jonathan and we crossed under the tape, and the media people surged around us, pushing their cameras and microphones at Jonathan and shouting their questions. There were so many broadcast vans that it looked as if we were in a forest of transmitters, each spindly stack pointing at the same invisible satellite 22,500 miles above in geosynchronous orbit, like so many coyotes crying at the moon. I said, "This is nuts."

Truly yelled in my ear so that I could hear him. "It hasn't even begun."

The woman with the frosted hair jammed her microphone past Hernandez and shouted, "Jonathan, can you tell us what was found?"

"I'm sorry. That information should come from the district attorney's office."

She yelled, "Is it true that a plan of Teddy Martin's house was found?"

"I'm sorry." We were working our way toward Jonathan Green's Rolls-Royce.

A short man who himself had been an attorney before becoming a broadcast journalist shouted, "Jonathan? Is it true that evidence found in the house exculpates Theodore Martin in the murder of his wife?"

Jonathan smiled benignly. "I've seen the evidence that Mr. Cole found, and I'll be in consultation with the district attorney's office sometime in the next few days. Now, if you'll excuse me."

More questions exploded at us from a dozen directions, and they were all about Mr. Cole.

I didn't think Jonathan was going to answer, but he stopped and put his hand on my shoulder and said, "This is Mr. Elvis Cole of the Elvis Cole Detective Agency, and I believe that his discovery is going to be the breakthrough that we need. I can't tell you how proud I am of this young man, and how impressed I am with the caliber of his work."

I said, "Gee."

The microphones shifted toward me as one and the questions came so fast and loud that the words blended into white noise. I was pretty sure that no one heard me say, "Gee." I may have said it twice.

Green said, "All we can say at this time is that we

received a tip through our hotline, and Mr. Cole followed it to this conclusion." He squeezed my shoulder again as if I were his son and I'd just made Eagle Scout. "What we have here is the result of good, solid detective work, and I suspect that when all is said and done Mr. Cole will be the hero of this little drama."

Truly added, "And Teddy Martin the victim."

Jonathan slid into his Rolls-Royce, and then Truly and the two uniforms walked me to my car. The press stayed with us, jostling and shoving and keeping up with the questions. We had to push a fat guy and two women away from my car to get the door open. Flutie lost her hat. Truly said, "Screen your calls. If anyone gets through to you, refer them to our office. Jonathan is the only one who deals with the press. Do you have a problem with that?"

"No."

"It should die down in a few days."

"And if it doesn't?"

Truly shrugged. "Enjoy the idolatry. You earned it, my friend. You really came through for us."

A tall thin guy from one of the national networks yelled, "Hey, Sherlock Holmes! Are you really that good or did you just get lucky?"

I said, "Some idol."

Truly laughed and I climbed into my car and drove away. Slowly. I almost ran over a cameraman.

14

I pulled into the carport at two minutes after six that evening. The TV was on, and Lucy and Ben were at the dining table, Lucy still in her business suit and Ben wearing a *Songbird* T-shirt. The cat was nowhere to be found, but that was probably just as well. If he'd been home, Lucy and Ben would probably need stitches.

Lucy smiled when she saw me and said, "It's the world's greatest detective. Congratulations, Sherlock."

Ben jumped up and clapped. "We saw you on television!"

I said, "How do you know it was me? Maybe it was an imposter."

Lucy crossed her arms and considered me. "Now that you mention it, the man on television was devastatingly handsome and darkly mysterious."

I said, "Oh. That was me."

Lucy was beaming. "We just turned on the news and there you were. You and Jonathan Green. Was it exciting?"

"Being with Jonathan?"

"No, silly! They said you made some kind of breakthrough that might turn the case around. Jonathan said that you were the finest investigator he's ever worked with."

I tried to look blasé and stifled a yawn. "Oh, that."

She punched me in the arm. "Be serious."

I gave her a kiss. "There were so many reporters I thought I'd have to shoot my way out." I gave her a second kiss and then a nuzzle. "Enough about me. How was your day?"

"It was good. We'll meet again the day after tomorrow, then perhaps once more, so there's plenty of time to play." She was surrounded by tourist brochures and tour books with Post-Its and a list of things to see and do.

I looked at her list. They wanted to see my office and visit both Disneyland and Universal Studios and take in a Dodgers game and eat a hot dog at Pink's on LaBrea in Hollywood. They wanted to ride the roller coasters at Magic Mountain and go to Malibu and spend a day at the beach. They wanted to see the Venice boardwalk and Beverly Hills and Rodeo Drive. They wanted to see Griffith Observatory, where James Dean had his famous knife fight in *Rebel Without a Cause*, and the Hollywood sign. They wanted to see Ronald Colman's house. I said, "Ronald Colman?"

Lucy said, "Of course, silly. We can't miss that." She was marking yet more things as I watched. She would finger through the tour books and refer to notes and frown as she juggled alternatives and weighed options and planned the Great L.A. Adventure. She glanced at me, then went back to the Frommer's, then came back to me again. She said, "What are you smiling at?"

"How I Spent My Summer Vacation."

She closed the Frommer's on a finger and looked miserable. "There's so much."

"Too much. You're never going to do all that in the few days that you have."

She put down the Frommer's. "What are your suggestions?"

"Visit more often."

She smiled and patted my hand. "What are your suggestions for *now?*"

"For now, how about dinner at Spago? For tomorrow, how about the Universal tour with lunch at the Universal City Walk, then either Beverly Hills and Rodeo Drive or Malibu and dinner at the beach?"

She looked longingly at the Frommer's. "Couldn't we squeeze in Ronald Colman?"

I leaned close and lowered my voice so that Ben couldn't hear. "We could, but that would fill the forty-five minutes I've alloted for lovemaking." I stepped back and spread my hands. "Your call."

She frowned and drummed the table. "We didn't need forty-five minutes last time." Everyone's a comedian.

She shrugged and frowned like it was the trade-off of the century. "Okay. Forget Ronald Colman."

Ben said, "Hey! You're on TV again!"

Lucy grabbed my hand. "Oh, look!"

I looked as the local anchor said that there had been a "surprise development today" in the Theodore Martin murder investigation that might "derail the prosecution's case." They cut to a clip of Elton Richards's duplex and the frosty-haired remote reporter took over. You could see me talking with Hernandez and Flutey in the background. Ben and Lucy both yelled, "*There you are!*"

The reporter told us that a private investigator working for the Big Green Defense Machine had followed a tip to evidence that implicated two El Monte men in the kidnapping/murder of Susan Martin. She referred to notes and said, "We've learned that the two men are Stephen Pritzik and Elton Richards, both of whom have lengthy criminal records." The image shifted to grainy mugshots of Pritzik and Richards. Pritzik looked narrow and mean; Richards looked stupid. Lucy said, "Oh, those guys are choice."

The reporter said, "Sources close to the investigation tell us that the evidence found here today provides a direct link between these men and Susan Martin's kidnapping." They cut to a clip of me and Jonathan Green standing by Jonathan's Rolls-Royce, Jonathan with his hand on my shoulder, saying that I had found the breakthrough that the defense has needed. Both Lucy and Ben cheered again when Jonathan said it, and Lucy hooked her finger in my belt loop. I thought that I looked like a turnip head.

The anchor reappeared, said that the two men were being sought for questioning, then shifted to a story about sweatshops in East L.A.

I said, "Shucks. He didn't put in the part where Jonathan said I would be the hero of the case."

Lucy tugged at my belt loop. "So what did you find?"

I told her about the map and the pictures. Lucy wasn't smiling now. She looked grave, and then she shook her head. "Wow."

I nodded.

"Do you think you'll be able to come out and play with us tomorrow?"

"I'll call Jonathan in the morning. I'll have to follow up on Pritzik and Richards, but it shouldn't take all day. Maybe just half a day."

We stared at each other.

She held out her hand, and I took it. She said, "It's okay, Studly. I understand."

"I'll grab a shower and we'll eat."

I phoned Spago for a reservation, then showered, changed, and when I came back down she was grinning. I said, "What?"

Grinning wider. "Nothing."

"What?"

"Just a little surprise. Let's go."

It was almost eight by the time we made it down the mountain, and the sky was deep purple edging into darkness. The Sunset Strip was alive with middle-aged hipsters driving Porsches to show off for women twenty years younger and goateed Val Dudes chasing the Christian Slater look and young women sporting navel rings set fire by the neon. The sidewalks outside of clubs like the Viper Room and the House of Blues and the Roxy were jammed with people, some of whom wanted to get in but most of whom were content to make the concrete scene out front, laughing and goofing and tossing back test-tube shooters of red dye number six vodka. Ben said,

"Mom, look! There's a man with a bone through his nose."

I said, "Welcome to Planet Los Angeles."

Lucy shook her head and smiled. "Well, it isn't Baton Rouge, is it?"

"Wait'll you see Melrose."

"It's fun, though. Sort of like Mardi Gras three hundred sixty-five nights a year."

"Yeah," I said. "L.A. is okay that way."

She turned back to me. Serious. "Do you like living here?"

"If I didn't, I wouldn't."

She stared at me for a moment, then she nodded and turned back toward the window. "Yes, I guess you wouldn't."

We pulled into Spago and let the valet have the car. Lucy suggested that I wear my Groucho Marx nose as a disguise to prevent adoring fans from mobbing me, but I pointed out that then everyone might think I was Groucho Marx and I would be mobbed anyway. I decided to risk going as myself.

We went upstairs for very nice Caesar salads and duck sausage pizza and a pretty good merlot. Johnny Depp was there with several friends, and so were three of the cast members of *Beverly Hills 90210*. No one stared at me and no one asked for my autograph and no one took my picture. Everyone was looking at Johnny Depp. Even the *90210* people. Disappointing, but maybe the people who go to Spago don't watch the news.

Lucy said, "Perhaps you should've worn the Groucho after all."

"Perhaps."

She patted my arm. "Don't feel bad, sweetie. They would recognize you if all these *faux* celebrities weren't here."

"Yeah." I sneered. "Johnny Depp."

Throughout the meal Lucy would grin with the knowledge of her secret, and I would ask, "What?" and she would say, "You'll see." Then everyone stopped looking at Johnny Depp and turned toward the door. Lucy grinned wider, and I looked, too.

Joe came over, gliding across the floor as the room parted for him. Tall men in sleeveless sweatshirts and dark glasses and brilliant red tattoos tend to stand out in Spago. Even Johnny Depp was looking.

Lucy stood to greet him. "Hi, Joseph."

Joe kissed Lucy's cheek, hugged her, then shook Ben's hand. "You ready, sport?"

"Yeah!"

I said, "What's going on?"

Joe swiveled my way, and you could tell he was amused. You could see that he was positively dying, even though his face showed nothing. "Peter Nelsen's down in the car. Peter and I are taking Big Ben to a screening of Peter's new movie." Peter Alan Nelsen is the third most successful movie director in the world. Once he was a client, but now he's a friend.

I looked at Lucy.

Joe said, "We won't be back until late."

I looked back at Joe.

"Very late."

Lucy gave Ben a hug. "You guys have fun."

Joe's mouth gave the twitch, and then he and Ben were gone.

I looked back at Lucy, and she said, "Alone time is very important."

"You called him while I was in the shower?"

"Uh-huh."

"I knew there was something I liked about you."

She sipped her wine. "I think that there's something you like very much about me."

We enjoyed a slow, noisy dessert with Lucy and I playing footsie under the table. We spoke in greater detail about her day and mine, and I told her about the Mason twins and the Pug Woman and the man who claimed to have seen Susan Martin's kidnapping from the Orb. I didn't often speak of my work, but it seemed natural with Lucy, and as we talked we laughed and goofed about Orb people and stroked each other's hands and arms and fingers. The time passed with the slow, warm feel of dripping honey, and finally Lucy wrapped my feet with hers and said, "Maybe we should go."

We left Spago at 10:35, and when we got home Lucy went into her room and I put Janis Ian on the CD player, then poured a merlot that would go nicely with the one we'd had at Spago.

When Lucy came out she had changed into shorts and a cropped T-shirt that said *Tank Girl* and silver evening slippers with four-inch heels. The lights were low and Janis was singing. Lucy did a slow pirouette. "Is the world's greatest detective tired after his long and successful day?"

I watched the pirouette. I watched the way the warm

light caught her back and hair and the long, smooth line of her legs and the sexy counterpoint of the formal evening slippers to the shorts and T-shirt. "He was, but now he feels a growing revitalization."

"Ah. Is that what's growing?"

"One way to look at it." I held out the merlot and Lucy took a sip. I said, "Nice shoes."

Lucy brushed against me, swaying to the music. The merlot left a sweet, rich taste in my mouth that I liked a lot. She said, "You'll probably be on the news again at eleven. Shall we turn on the TV and see?"

I shook my head. "Seeing me once is plenty. Besides, something else is already turned on."

"Ah."

"I think I'm ready for the rest of my surprise."

She took my hand and tugged me toward the big glass doors. Outside, the sky was clear, and would be filled with stars.

I said, "The deck?"

She let her hair fall across one eye. "I thought your middle name was Adventure."

"So it is."

I followed her out, and what I found there tasted better than any wine, and was more beautiful than the stars.

15

Lucy and Ben woke giggling and excited and filled
with plans. As they readied for their day, I phoned
Elliot Truly at his office. "It's Cole. Has there been word
on Pritzik or Richards?"

"Not yet, but there'll be something soon." He
sounded distracted.

"I was thinking that I'd go back to Richards's place
and talk to some of the neighbors, but the police will be
there and they won't like it. Maybe Jonathan could talk
to Sherman and smooth the way in the spirit of cooperation."

Truly didn't say anything for a moment. "Why do
you want to go back there?"

"To try to get a lead on Pritzik and Richards."

"Forget it. We're talking with the cops. We've got Kerris on it. Take the day off and relax." I could hear voices
behind him.

"It's a cold trail already, Elliot. We shouldn't let it get
any colder."

"Look, you just said that the entire area will be swarm-
ing with cops. We've got a staff meeting here in a couple

of minutes to try to figure out what to do next. Jonathan's trying to get a meeting with the DA."

"What does that have to do with finding Pritzik and Richards?"

"Take the day off, enjoy yourself, and I'll get back to you."

"You want me to do nothing."

"Yeah. What could be better than that?" He hung up, and I stared at the phone.

Lucy said, "What's wrong?"

I looked at the phone some more and then I put it down. "Not a thing. I get to spend the day with you. What could be better than that?"

Their excitement was contagious. We made a fast breakfast of sliced fruit and cottage cheese and toast, and then we dressed in shorts and light shirts and baseball caps for the always popular Ralph Cramden look. I considered bringing my Dan Wesson .38 caliber revolver, but thought it unsightly strapped over my flowered shirt. Besides, blue steel wheel guns aren't exactly requisite tourist attire in southern California. Florida maybe, but not yet California.

It was early, so we decided to see my office first, then head for the Universal tour. We took Lucy's rented Taurus down Laurel Canyon, then along Sunset toward the office. The sky was free of haze and smog, and more blue than white because of it. A great V of gulls floated above West Hollywood, heading toward the sea, and the streets were busy with cars sporting out-of-state license plates and people with camcorders and young Middle Eastern guys selling maps to the stars' homes. Summer had come to the City of Angels.

When we turned onto Santa Monica. one block up from my office, we saw two television news vans parked at the curb in front of my building. I said, "Uh-oh."

Lucy said, "Do you think they're here for you?"

"I don't know." Maybe they were here for Cindy. Maybe they wanted to do a story about hot new beauty supply products.

"You don't want to speak to them?"

Jonathan's the only person on the team who talks to the press."

I pulled past the vans. A very attractive young Asian-American woman was on the sidewalk talking to a guy holding a Minicam, and a guy who looked like a surfer in a sport coat was smoking with a scruffy woman in a work shirt. I pulled to the curb on the next block, asked Lucy for her cell phone, and called Cindy's office. Cindy answered on the first ring and said, "Wow, are you ever the big deal."

"Have they been upstairs?"

"All morning. They knock on your door and when you don't answer they come to me or the insurance people and ask about your hours." The insurance people had the office across the hall. "That was a great picture in the paper."

"I'm in the paper?"

"You haven't seen it?"

"Uh-uh." Mr. With-it. Mr. Hip L.A. Private Eye with his fingers on the pulse.

"Oh, man, you look so cool. And I saw you on TV, too. I saw you *twice*." Even Cindy was excited.

"Is anyone upstairs now?"

"Yeah. There's a guy sitting in the hall. I think he's from a radio station."

I thanked her and handed back Lucy's phone. Lucy was looking at me. "They're upstairs?"

I nodded. "You mind if we don't go up? I'll show you guys my office another time."

She patted my leg and put away her phone. "Another time is fine, Studly. I want to see my man in the paper."

We stopped at a Sav-on drugstore where we bought the *Times*, the *Examiner*, and the *Daily News*, then stood in the parking lot, reading. Elton Richards, Steve Pritzik, and the discovery I'd made in Richards's duplex were front page news in all three papers. A picture of me with Jonathan Green was on page one of both the *Examiner* and the *Daily News* and on page three of the *Times*. Guess the people at the *Times* had higher standards. Lucy said, "Oh, Elvis. This is so exciting."

I said, "Um."

"Aren't you proud?"

"It's kinda neat, I guess." I held up the paper next to my face and frowned. "Do I look like Moe Howard?"

Lucy compared me to the picture, then nodded. "Yes. Yes, I think you do."

A round man with thick glasses and a nervous tic walked past, staring. He went to a brown Cressida, still staring, then called out, "Hey, are you that guy?"

I folded the paper and tossed it in the car.

"I read about what you did. I saw you on the news. That was good work."

I gave a little wave. "Thanks."

He said, "These cops here in L.A. suck, don't they?"

I frowned at him. "Some of my best friends are cops."

He made a nasal, braying laugh, then climbed into his car and drove away.

I opened the door for Lucy and we drove east across West Hollywood and Hollywood, and then up through the Cahuenga Pass to Universal Studios. We parked in one of the big parking structures with about twelve million other tourists, then followed along with what seemed an endless stream of people to the ticket kiosks and then into yet more lines that led to the trams. It made me feel like a lemming.

We rode the trams around the Universal back lot and took goofy pictures of ourselves posing with giant toothpaste tubes and rode little cars past screeching dinosaurs and gargantuan gorillas, and then Lucy said, "I feel the urge to spend."

I looked at her. "Spend?"

Ben made as if he was horrified. "Not that, Mom! Not that! Try to control it!"

Lucy's eyes narrowed in concentration and her gaze went blank. "The shopping gene is beyond all control. Souvenirs. *I must have souvenirs!*"

It was horrible to behold. Lucy bought; I carried. Three T-shirts, two sweatshirts, and a snow-shaker paperweight later, we had exhausted the selection in the upper park and trekked down to CityWalk in search of more booty. The CityWalk is a large, open-air mall with shops, bookstores, restaurants, and other fine places to spend your money. Some people have described the CityWalk as an urban version of Disney's Main Street U.S.A., but I've always thought of it as a G-rated take on *Blade Runner*. Only without the rain.

It was just before noon when we got there, and, like the park above, the CityWalk was thick with tour groups from Asia and visitors from around the country. We walked the length of the CityWalk, browsing in the shops and watching the people, Lucy and I holding hands while Ben ranged around us. It felt good to be not working and good to be with Lucy. I said, "Do you think you can rein in your spending spree long enough to eat?"

She looked at me the way the cat does when I take his bowl before he's finished.

"I may not be able to carry this stuff much longer without an infusion of calories."

"You'll manage."

"We may have to hire porters."

"It's only money."

"We may have to stop spending."

She made a big sigh and rolled her eyes. "Modern men are such wimps."

I leaned close to her ear. "That's not what you said last night on the deck."

Lucy laughed and hugged my arm tight, biting my shoulder through the shirt. "O.K., Studly, your wish is my command. Where would you like to eat?"

"You said that last night, too."

She dug her thumb in my ribs and said, "Shh! Ben!"

"He didn't hear. C'mon. There's a Puck's ahead. We can eat there."

"Puck's! Oh, goody!"

We went to Wolfgang Puck's and stood in line for a table. Everyone around us was from Iowa or Canada or Japan, and no one seemed to have seen the news or read the paper or, if they had, didn't care. There was plenty of outdoor seating, and the people at the tables were enjoying salads and sandwiches.

We worked our way up the line to a pretty blonde hostess who told us that it would be just another minute when I caught an overweight guy staring at me. He was sitting at one of the tables, eating shredded chicken salad and reading a *Times*. He looked from me to the paper, then back to me. He stopped a passing waitress, showed her the paper, then they both looked at me. I turned so that I was facing the opposite direction. Lucy said, "Those people are looking at you."

"Great."

"I think they recognize you."

"I know."

"He's pointing at you."

The Korean couple behind us looked at me, too. I guess they saw the pointing. I smiled and nodded at them, and they smiled back.

Lucy said, "Ohmigod, he's showing the paper to the people at the next table."

I touched the hostess's arm. "Do you think you could find us a table, please. Inside or out. First available."

"Let me check." She disappeared into the restaurant.

Lucy said, "Maybe we should run for it."

"Very funny."

"We could leave. I don't mind."

"No. You want Puck's, we're going to eat at Puck's."

An older couple behind the Korean people craned around to see what all the looking and pointing was about. The woman looked from me to the people with the newspaper, then back to me. She said something to her husband and he shrugged. I turned the other way, and now the heavy man with the newspaper was locked in conversation with a table of six people, all of whom were twisted around in their seats to see me. I said, "This is nuts."

Lucy was smiling.

I said, "This isn't funny."

The woman behind the Korean couple said, "Excuse me. Are you somebody?"

I said, "No."

She smiled at me. "You're an actor, aren't you? You're on that show."

Lucy began one of those silent laughs where your face goes red and you're trying not to but can't help yourself.

I said, "I'm not. Really."

"Then why is everybody looking at you?"

"It's a long story."

The woman gave me huffy. "Well, it's not very friendly of you, if you ask me, snubbing your public like this."

Lucy leaned toward the woman. "He can be just horrible, can't he? I talk to him about it all the time."

I stared at her.

The woman said, "Well, you should. It's so unkind."

Lucy gave me a little push. "Why don't you give her an autograph."

I stared harder. "You're some kind of riot, you know that?"

Lucy nodded. Brightly.

The woman said, "Oh, that would be just so nice." She gestured to her husband. "Merle, we have a pen, don't we?" She shoved a pen and a souvenir napkin from Jodi Maroni's sausage kitchen at me to sign. The Korean couple were talking in Korean to each other, the man searching frantically through a shoulder bag.

I took the napkin and leaned close to Lucy. "I'm going to get you for this."

She turned away so no one could see her breaking up. "Oh, I really, really hope you do."

Ben said, "Mom? Why are these people looking at Elvis?"

The older woman's eyes grew large. "You're *Elvis?*"

The Korean woman held out an autograph book and the Korean man began taking pictures. Two teenaged girls who were seated behind the party of six saw me signing the Jodi Maroni napkin and came over, and then two younger guys from the table of six followed. A tall, thin man across the restaurant stood up at his table and aimed his video camera at me. His wife stood with him. An Hispanic couple passing on the CityWalk stopped to see what was going on, and then three young women who looked like they'd come up to the CityWalk on their lunch hour stopped, too. A woman with very loose upper arms pointed at me and told her friend, "Oh, I just love his movies, don't you?" She said it loudly.

The heavy man with the newspaper who had started it got up and walked away. Lucy and Ben were walking away, too. Quickly. Off to ruin someone else's life, no doubt.

The crowd grew. I signed twenty-two autographs in four minutes, and they were the longest four minutes of my life. I finally begged off by announcing that as much as I enjoyed meeting them, the President required my counsel and so I must leave. When I said it the woman with the loose arms said, "I didn't know he was in politics, too!"

When I finally found Lucy and Ben they were well along the CityWalk, grinning and walking fast away from me.

I said, "Lucille Chenier, you can run but you can't hide." I said it loud enough for them to hear.

Lucy and Ben laughed, and then they ran.

16

After another $182.64 in souvenirs, postcards, and gifts, Lucy called Baton Rouge to check her messages. I was hoping that there might be word on Pritzik or Richards, so I phoned my office, also. Sixteen messages were waiting for me. Of the sixteen, seven were from newspeople asking for interviews and five were from friends who had seen me on the news. Of the remaining four calls, two were hang-ups and two were from Elliot Truly. On the first hang-up a woman's voice said, "Oh, shit," and on the second the same voice said, "Just eat me!" The voice was muffled and irritated. Truly's secretary left the first message from his office, asking me to return the call. Truly himself left the second message, saying, "Cole? Cole, if you're there, pick up. This is important." I guess Truly was irritated, too. Maybe I bring it out in people.

I returned Truly's call. When he came on the line he said, "Thank Christ! I've been trying to reach you all day. Where have you been?" He sounded frantic.

"You told me to take the day off, remember?"

"Yeah, well, we don't want you to do that anymore.

Channel Eight wants to interview you on the evening news and Jonathan thinks it would be a good idea."

I said, "Go on television?"

"It's maybe three minutes on the four o'clock newscast, and Jonathan wants you to do it."

"Truly, I made plans. I've got guests from out of town."

"Look, the team talked about this today and we want the press to have access to you. Either we're going to control the media or the district attorney's office will, and we'd rather it be us. Openness is important. Honesty is everything. That's all we have going for us."

I was sorry that I had returned his call.

"They want to know how some guy all by himself beat the entire LAPD at their own game."

"I didn't beat anybody. I followed a tip and got lucky." Lucy had finished her call and was looking at me.

"Right. That's why you scored the breakthrough while eight thousand blue suits were sopping up coffee and donuts."

"I didn't beat anyone, Truly." He was getting on my nerves with that.

"All you have to do is sit there and be likable. People like you; you're a likable guy. That's all they care about. It's TV."

I cupped the receiver and told Lucy, "They want me to give a television interview this afternoon, and it'll interfere with going to Beverly Hills."

Lucy smiled and rubbed my arm. "If you have to you have to. We'll do Beverly Hills after."

"It'll cut into your shopping time. Are you sure?"

She smiled again. "We'll come watch you get interviewed. It'll be fun."

Truly said, "What did you say?"

"Relax, Elliot. I'll do it."

Truly said, "It's almost three now and they want you at Channel Eight by four-thirty. Grab a pencil and let me tell you where to go."

Truly gave me the directions. Lucy, Ben, and I drove home, changed, then made our way back down the mountain to Channel Eight's broadcast studio just east of Western in Hollywood. KROK-TV. *Personal News from Us to You—We take it personally!*

We parked in the lot beside the building, then walked in the front entrance to a receptionist seated in a bulletproof glass booth. The lobby was walled off from the rest of the building with more heavy glass, and there was a big door next to the receptionist that she would have to buzz open to let you enter. I wondered if anyone had ever tried to shoot their way in. *Put me on the news or die!* You never know.

I told her who I was and why I was there, and a few minutes later a woman in her early forties appeared and opened the door from the inside. She said, "Hi. I'm Kara Sykes, the news director. Are you Mr. Cole?"

"That's right. This is Lucy Chenier and her son, Ben. They're with me." I was holding Lucy's hand.

Kara Sykes held the door. "That's fine. You'll go on

in a few minutes, so we don't have much time. Please come this way."

We followed her down a long hall, then through a newsroom filled with desks and production people and onto the news set. A man and a woman were seated at the anchor desk, facing cameras fitted with TelePromp-Ters. A floor director was standing between the cameras with his hand touching the TelePrompTer that the man was reading from. There were places at the anchor desk for a sportscaster and a weatherperson, but those seats were empty. The set was built so that the anchors were seated with their backs to the newsroom so the audience could see that the Channel Eight news team was bring-ing them personal news personally. Kara whispered, "Lyle Stodge and Marcy Bernside are the five o'clock anchors. Lyle is going to interview you."

"Okay." Lyle Stodge was a rugged-looking guy in his early fifties, just going gray at the temples. Marcy Bern-side was a profoundly attractive woman in her late thir-ties with dark hair, expressive eyes, and a wholesome, girl-next-door smile.

Kara said, "Have you done a live interview before?"

"No."

"It's no big deal. Just speak directly to Lyle. Don't look at the camera."

"Okay."

"I spoke with Jonathan, so I know how important this is. Everyone here is on your side."

"My side?"

"Just relax and enjoy it. You're the man of the hour."

Lucy squeezed my hand and whispered, "I guess they heard how you were mobbed at Universal."

Lucy's a riot, isn't she?

Lyle finished reading a story about illegal Taiwanese aliens found working in a sweatshop in Gardena, and Marcy began reading a story about Pritzik and Richards. She said that the police and the FBI had expanded their search into seven states, and that there was a growing though unofficial belief that Pritzik was, in fact, James X.

The floor director raised his hand, made a circling gesture, and Marcy Bernside said that Channel Eight's Personal News Team would return in just one minute. The director raised both hands, then announced, "In commercial. We're clear."

Marcy Bernside shouted, "*Fuck!* Who blew the feed to my *fucking* ear phone?" She twisted around to glare at the newsroom. "Come on, Stuart. What're you assholes doing back there? Jesus *Christ!*" So much for wholesome.

Kara pulled my arm and said, "Showtime."

She hustled me to the anchor desk and had me sit in the sportscaster's vacant seat while the camera operators repositioned for a two-shot of me and Lyle. I could see Lyle's lines frozen on the TelePrompTer, waiting for the commercial to end. The floor director clipped a tiny microphone inside the lapel of my sport coat, then ran the wire under my jacket and plugged it into a larger cable that had been lying on the floor. Kara introduced me to Lyle Stodge who said, "I'm glad that you could join us. You're quite a guy."

I said, "Will anyone notice if I make faces at the camera?"

Lyle Stodge shuffled loose yellow legal sheets. "Don't worry about anything. I've done this ten thousand times, and I can make anyone look good. Even you." I looked at Lucy and Lucy laughed. I looked back at Lyle Stodge and he winked. Another comedian.

A makeup person was adjusting Marcy Bernside's hair. Marcy was singing to herself and moving to the song as if she were alone in her home. She was singing the Z.Z. Topp song, *Legs*. Nervous energy.

The floor director said, "Ten seconds." He raised his hand above Lyle's camera. Lyle straightened his jacket and leaned toward the camera. The makeup person left the set. Lyle said, "Would you stop with the goddamned singing, for Christ's sake?"

Marcy Bernside gave him the finger and kept singing.

"Three, two, one—" The floor director touched the TelePrompTer and Lyle's script scrolled upward. Lyle made his patented crinkly-eyed smile at the camera. "As we reported at the top of the hour, a private investigator working for the Big Green Defense Machine has made a startling discovery that may shed new light on the Theodore Martin murder investigation. He joins us now in a Channel Eight Personal News exclusive, bringing *you* the people who *make the news*." Lyle turned the pleased smile toward me. "Mr. Elvis Cole, thank you for joining us in a Channel Eight Personal News exclusive."

"Thanks, Lyle. It's good to be here." Mr. Sincerity.

Lyle laced his fingers and leaned toward me, getting down to serious journalistic business. "How is it that one man working alone was able to uncover these things when the entire Los Angeles police department working for three months couldn't?"

"I followed a tip that Jonathan Green's office received on the hotline. If LAPD would've gotten the tip, they would've made the same discoveries, and probably sooner."

Lyle chuckled good-naturedly. "Sounds like you're being modest to me." The chuckle vanished and Lyle turned serious again, cocking an eyebrow to let everyone know just how serious he was. "Tell us, was it dangerous?"

"It's just meeting people and asking questions, Lyle. It's no more dangerous than crossing the street."

Lyle made the chuckle again, then twisted around to smile at Marcy Bernside. "Marce, I'll tell you, I've never met the real McCoy who liked to blow his own horn, have you?"

Marcy Bernside said, "Never, Lyle. Real men let their deeds speak for themselves."

Lyle twisted back to me. "Theodore Martin has proclaimed his innocence from the beginning. Many people are now saying that your discovery proves him right."

"It's another piece of the puzzle."

Lyle leaned toward me, serious and professional. "Many people are also saying that the LAPD botched this investigation, and now they're unwilling to admit their mistake."

"LAPD is the finest police force in the nation, Lyle."

Lyle nodded as if I'd just laid out the Unified Field Theory. "Well, sir, we've checked into *your* background and learned that *you* certainly have an excellent reputation, even among members of the police department and the district attorney's office."

"Those guys. Did they really say that?"

Lyle nodded gravely. "Personal News Eight is told that this isn't your first high-profile case. Apparently, you've worked in a confidential capacity for some very high-profile celebrities."

"I never discuss my clients, Lyle. That's why it's called 'confidential.'"

Lyle squinted approvingly. "A man of integrity." He gave an encouraging smile. "Most of us see private eyes on television or in movies but never get a chance to meet the real thing. Tell me, is it as exciting as it seems?"

"No."

Lyle laughed. They paid him seven hundred thousand dollars a year for that laugh, and I wondered if he practiced it. "Looks like you're a truthful man, as well. How does it feel to be compared to that famous, fictional Los Angeles detective, Raymond Marlowe?"

Marcy said, "Philip Marlowe."

Lyle looked confused and twisted to look at her again. I guess she'd said her bit and he hadn't expected her to speak again. "What was that, Marce?"

"Raymond *Chandler* created *Philip* Marlowe."

Lyle laughed again, but this time the laugh was strained. Guess you weren't supposed to correct the anchor while you were on the air. He twisted back to the camera and said, "Well, it looks as if Los Angeles has found its very own Sherlock Homes, and, unfortunately, that's all the time we have for this segment." Lyle Stodge offered his hand to me, and we shook as if he had just awarded me the Congressional Medal of Honor. "Mr. Cole, it's been my privilege to meet you. Congratulations, and thank you for taking the time to talk with us."

"Thanks, Lyle. It's been personal."

The floor director raised both hands. "In promo. We're clear."

Lyle Stodge glared at Marcy Bernside. "You fucking cunt! Don't you ever do that to me again on air!"

Marcy Bernside gave him the finger again. "It's Holmes, moron. Sherlock *Holmes*. With an *L*."

"Oh, yeah, right. Sure."

Kara Sykes unclipped my lapel mike and helped me off the set. No one gave me a second glance.

We followed Kara Sykes back to the lobby, then left the building and walked to the car. Lucy hugged my arm. "That was almost as much fun as Beverly Hills."

"Un."

She stepped back and looked at me. She cocked her head. "Are you okay, Studly?"

I said, "Luce?"

"Mm?"

"If Truly wants me to do another of these, I'm going to shoot him to death. Will you represent me?"

She smiled sweetly. "Oh, you know that I will, hon. You shoot him all you like."

"Thanks, Luce."

17

Lucy, Ben, and I spent the next two days seeing Disneyland and Malibu and the Griffith Observatory. We saw Ronald Colman's house. We shopped in Beverly Hills. I called Jonathan's office twice each day, asking to speak with either Jonathan or Truly, but neither was ever available. Busy, they said. In meetings. No one returned my calls.

I stayed away from my office because of the press. The answering machine was flooded with so many interview requests that I deleted them without playing them. The eat-me lady called back twice.

Elliot Truly's assistant phoned to arrange three more television interviews and two appearances on local talk radio. It's important to Jonathan, she said. We need our side of it known, she said. I asked her about Pritzik and Richards. I said that I wanted to know what was going on. She said that she would talk to Jonathan and get back to me. She didn't.

News reports questioning LAPD's investigative techniques appeared with greater frequency. A summer marine layer moved in, filling the morning sky with an oppressive layer of dark clouds. Sometimes they burned off by noon, but not always.

On the morning of the third day, Peter Alan Nelsen took Ben to spend the day on the set of his new movie and Lucy was dressing for her second meeting when the phone rang and Elliot Truly said, "We're meeting with Teddy Martin at ten this morning in the Men's Central Jail. Teddy wants to meet you, and Jonathan would like you there. Can you make it?"

I said, "What in hell is going on, Truly? How come no one returns my calls?"

"You're not the only investigator we have on this, Cole. We've been swamped. Jonathan's working sixteen hours a day."

"I'm an investigator. I investigate. If you don't want me to investigate anymore, fine." I was feeling sullen and petulant. Mr. Maturity.

Truly said, "Look, talk about it with Jonathan at the jail. One other thing. Jonathan's having a get-together at his home tonight, people who've been behind Teddy through this thing, some press people, like that. Jonathan personally asked me to invite you. You can bring a date if you want."

I cupped the phone and looked at Lucy. She was standing in the kitchen, dressed and Guccied and ready for business, eating peach yogurt. "Would you like to go to a party at Jonathan Green's house tonight?"

Lucy blinked at me and the spoon froze between cup and mouth. "Are you serious?"

"Truly just asked."

She shook her head, the spoon forgotten. "I don't have anything to wear to meet Jonathan Green."

I uncupped the phone. "Forget it, Truly. We can't make it."

The yogurt cup hit the floor and Lucy grabbed my arm. "I didn't say that! I'll get something!"

"My mistake, Truly. We'll be there."

Truly said, "Great. I'll see you at the jail. Ten o'clock."

I smiled at Lucy. "How about that? You'll get to meet Jonathan."

Her eyes were glazed and distant. "Ohmigod, what am I going to wear?"

"Wear what you have on. You look great."

She shook her head. "You don't understand. I'm going to meet Jonathan Green."

I said, "You've got time. Go to your meeting, then go into Beverly Hills. You'll find something."

Lucy looked miserable. "I wouldn't know where to go. It could take *days*."

"Call Jodi. Jodi can tell you."

Lucy's eyes widened and she latched onto my arm again. "That's right. Jodi can save me!" I guess these things are relative.

Lucy set about arranging her salvation, and I drove down to my office. I hadn't been there in three days and wanted to check my mail and return calls. There weren't any news vans parked at the curb. Maybe my fifteen minutes of fame was over. Live in hope.

I locked the door in the outer office, then answered mail. Most of the mail was bills, but even World Famous Private Eyes have to pay their Visa charges. When the bills were done I was getting ready to return calls when the phone rang and I answered, "Elvis Cole Detective Agency. Please leave a message at the sound of the beep. Beep." The detective as Natural Born Wit.

There was a pause, and then a muffled woman's voice said, "You're not a machine." The eat-me lady.

"Who is this?"

"That weevil-dicked fuck James Lester is fulla shit. You find out about Stuart Langolier in Santa Barbara." She was speaking through cloth, but I'd heard the voice before.

"El-ay-gee-oh . . ." Spelling it. "No, wait . . . Capital el-ay-*en*-gee-oh-el-eye-ee-are."

I said, "Jonna?"

There was another pause, and then Jonna Lester hung up. I listened to the dial tone for several seconds, then called an investigator friend of mine named Toni Abatemarco who works at a large agency in Santa Barbara. Toni had worked as an investigator since the day she was old enough to get the license, and had hammered out twelve-hour days for years, building her small agency into one of Santa Barbara's finest. Then she met a guy, fell head over heels, and decided that she wanted a small herd of children. She sold the small agency to a larger outfit, had four little girls, and now worked three days a week for the organization that had bought her. She loved investigating, she loved being a mom, and the little girls often accompanied her to the office. They would probably grow up to be investigators, also.

I gave Toni the name, asked her to see what she could find, and then I went to jail.

The Men's Central Jail is an anonymous building behind Central Station, less than ten minutes from the Criminal Courts Building in downtown L.A. I parked in a neat, modern underground parking structure, then walked up steps to a very nice plaza. Nicely dressed people were sipping *lattes* and strolling about the plaza, and no one seemed to mind that the plaza adjoined a place housing felons and gangbangers and the wild men of an otherwise civil society. Perhaps because this is L.A. and the jail is so nice. There's a fountain in the plaza, and it's very nice, too.

Truly was waiting for me in the jail lobby. "Jonathan and the others are in with Teddy. Come on. I've checked us in."

"I'm carrying a gun."

"Okay. Sure." Like Terminal Island, you can't bring guns into the interview room or the holding areas.

We crossed the lobby past the deputies at the information desk to the gun locker, then went through the metal detector and flashed our IDs at the security gate. The guard there sits behind bulletproof glass and controls the metal doors that let you into or out of the interview area. He's the last guard that you'll see in the jail who has guns. He has shotguns, pistols, tasers, and CS gas. Preparation is everything.

The guard threw switches and the metal door crawled to the side. We stepped through into a room like a gray airlock, and then the door closed. When the door behind us was closed, the door in front of us opened and we stepped through into a large room sporting two long tables lined by metal stools. The tables were narrow and dark, sort of like public-school cafeteria tables, only with low vertical partitions running lengthwise down their centers. Inmates in orange jumpsuits sat on stools along the inside of each table, staring across at the attorneys who sat opposite them. The vertical partition was supposed to make it hard for illegal contraband or weapons to be passed from one to another. Sometimes it worked. Another deputy sat behind glass in the far corner, keeping track of who came and who left and making sure that no one was stabbed to death. Sometimes that worked, too.

Everyday dirtbags had to sit in the big room at the long tables and talk about their cases with no privacy, but high-profile defendants like Teddy Martin rated a private interview room. I followed Truly along a short hall, then into a room that was not dissimilar to the one in which I had seen LeCedrick Earle at Terminal Island, only older and uglier and smelling of urine.

Jonathan Green said, "Here he is now."

The interview room was small and crowded. Stan Kerris, Green's chief of security, was leaning against the glass with his Fred Munster arms crossed. Jonathan Green was seated at a work table with one of the lesser attorneys and Teddy Martin. I had never met Teddy Martin before, but I knew him from his picture. Teddy Martin had a round, boyish face, a steeply receding hairline, and pale, soft skin. Theodore Martin looked like someone's younger brother grown older; a kind of nonguy who just happened to have built six family-owned hot dog stands into an empire. Truly said, "Elvis Cole, this is Teddy Martin. Teddy, the man."

Teddy Martin came around the table and offered his hand. He said, "I don't know what to say except thank you." His eyes were wide and kind of frantic. "I did not kill my wife. I loved her, Cole. I tried to save her, do you see? They're blaming this thing on me, and it feels like you're the first one who's done anything to help me."

"I'm glad we could finally meet." He gripped my hand with both of his and pumped hard, as if hanging onto me was the most important thing in his life.

Green said, "Theodore."

Teddy Martin seemed to realize what he was doing and flushed. "Sorry." He let go and went back to the table.

I said, "Why did you have me come down here?"

Green patted Teddy on the shoulder, much the way that he had patted me. "Twofold. Teddy very much wanted to meet you, and I've arranged a press conference to take place in the plaza. The core of the team will be there, and I'd like you to be there, too."

I looked at Kerris. The empty eyes were unimpressed. "Press conferences are fine, Jonathan, but what about the investigation? I've called you guys five times, and nobody returns my calls."

Jonathan Green's face stiffened ever so slightly, as if he wasn't used to being questioned and didn't like it.

Truly said, "We're swamped. I told you."

Jonathan waved his hand, cutting off Truly. "What would you like to do?"

"Follow up Pritzik and Richards. Run down more hotline tips."

Kerris shifted against the glass. "I've got other people

on Pritzik and Richards. I can give you all the hotline tips you want."

Jonathan made the hand wave again. "Let's not waste Mr. Cole's time with that." He left Teddy and sat on the edge of the table.

I said, "The police and the feds are looking for Pritzik and Richards. We can launch a collaborative effort with them. The cops aren't our enemy."

Jonathan spread his hands. "If you want to work with the police, fine. If it helps us free Teddy any sooner, that's all to the good."

I looked from Jonathan to Kerris to Truly. They were staring at me. The lesser attorney was staring at me, too. I said, "There's something else. A woman I believe to be Jonna Lester called me. She said that James Lester was lying. She said that I should check into someone named Stuart Langolier."

Jonathan nodded. "By all means." He looked at his watch. "We really should be going now. Can't keep our friends in the press waiting."

We said our good-byes to Theodore Martin, and walked out. Jonathan walked beside me. When we were out the door and down the hall, Jonathan said, "A proper criminal defense effort is an enormous managerial task, akin to staging the Normandy invasion or launching the Gulf War. All the pieces will come together. Trust me on that."

I nodded.

"Elliot tells me you'll be joining our little soiree this evening."

"That's right. Thanks for inviting me."

"I understand you have a lady friend."

"She's an attorney, also. She's excited about meeting you."

"Well, who can blame her?" Jonathan made a little laugh. "Ha-ha." I glanced at Truly and Truly was nodding. Serious.

Jonathan said, "We'll discuss the team's progress and direction. I want you to be a part of that meeting. I don't want you to feel left out."

I said, "You don't have to handle me, Jonathan."

"I know that, son. I respect you."

I recovered my gun, then we stepped out into the plaza and a wall of people and cameras and microphones surged forward and enveloped us. I thought that maybe this wasn't the jail anymore and maybe I wasn't me. Maybe I'd stepped through Calvin and Hobb's transmogrifier and I was no longer a detective and Green was no longer a lawyer. Maybe we had just discovered life on Titan. Maybe we had found the cure for AIDS and were about to tell the world. Why else would so many people be here shouting questions?

Jonathan went to the microphones. "We're not here to answer questions, but I want to make a short statement." He spoke in his normal voice, and the crowd shushed itself to hear him.

Jonathan's expression turned somber, and then he looked at me and again rested his hand on my shoulder. He said, "As you all know, three days ago Mr. Cole found important evidence that both the police department and the district attorney's office failed to uncover, evidence that we believe supports our client's claim of innocence. Both the police department and the district attorney's office promised to evaluate this evidence, and act on it, but they have not." He let go of my shoulder, and the somber expression turned fierce. "We demand that the police stop their footdragging and issue immediate arrest warrents for Stephen Pritzik and Elton Richards. Concurrently with this, and in consideration of the state's weakened case, I hereby request that the district attorney stop this injustice, admit the failure of his investigation, and dismiss all charges against Theodore Martin. In lieu of that, we have filed a motion with the bench to set bail so that Mr. Martin might be released."

Reporters in the back were tossing out questions as the reporters in front pushed their microphones even closer.

Jonathan's voice grew, and the fierce expression became outraged. He grabbed my shoulder again, and all the grabbing was making me uncomfortable. "The tyranny of evil men cannot be hidden from the light of truth! We have not only uncovered evidence of a specific crime, but also of gross incompetence, negligence, and a police department all too willing to obfuscate the truth in an attempt to hide their own shortcomings." Still cameras were clicking and videocameras were panning, and they seemed to be panning toward me.

I said, "What's he talking about?"

Truly nudged me. "Jonathan knows what he's doing."

Green bellowed, "We do not rest. We continue to investigate. And, ladies and gentlemen, we are about to blow the lid off the evil and the desire for personal gain that underlies this tragic and wrongful prosecution!"

Jonathan abruptly turned away from the microphones,

and a wall of sound came from the press. They surged around us and shouted their questions, and just as abruptly Kerris and maybe a dozen of his security guys appeared from nowhere and surrounded us in a kind of flying wedge. Truly was smiling. I grabbed his jacket and shouted to make myself heard. "What's he talking about, Truly? What just happened here?"

Truly laughed. "The truth happened, Cole. Don't worry about it. We'll see you at the party."

Kerris's people worked us across the plaza and down to the parking structure. I moved with the crush of bodies the way a leaf is carried by the wind, a part of an unseen world, yet not.

18

I drove back to the house feeling hollow and uncertain, and spent the rest of the afternoon waiting for Lucy to return from her shopping excursion with Jodi Taylor.

Darlene called at ten minutes after three and said, "Good afternoon, Mr. Cole. How are we today?"

"We're fine, Darlene. And yourself?" I wondered if she had seen the press conference.

"Would Ms. Chenier be about?" I guess not.

"I expect her return shortly, Darlene. May I take a message?"

Darlene hesitated, and seemed confused. I have never known Darlene to sound confused. "Oh, no message. Please ask her to call."

"I don't expect her for another hour or so, Darlene, and it's already after five, your time. Is tomorrow okay?" Baton Rouge was two hours ahead of us.

"She could call me at home."

"Is everything all right, Darlene?"

"Everything is fine, Mr. Cole. Please have a good evening."

We hung up, and maybe five minutes later the cat

door clacked and I heard him in the kitchen. I got up from the couch and found him standing just inside his door, motionless, tiny nose twitching as he tested the air. I said, "It's just us."

He stared at me for maybe forty seconds, then crept to the living room and tested the air again. I said, "How about some tuna?" He hadn't been home in almost four days, and I had missed him.

I opened a small can of Bumble Bee Fancy White, sat on the floor, and put it down beside me. He loves Bumble Bee Fancy White. It's his most favorite thing. That and field mice. "Well?"

You could see him catch the scent. You could see his eyes widen and his nose shift gears and his ears perk. He looked at the can, took two steps toward me, then squinted back toward the living room. He made his little growl.

"Lucy and Ben aren't here, but they will be. You'd best get used to it and get over this attitude you have."

He stopped the growling and came over but did not touch the tuna. I stroked his back, but he did not purr. "I know, buddy. I feel a little bit disrupted, too."

He head-bumped me, then trotted out of the kitchen and up the stairs, heading for the safety of my loft, moving fast in case Lucy or Ben was lying in wait. I had to shake my head, but at least he was home. You take your progress where you find it.

I checked my office messages at 3:45. Thirteen more interview requests were jamming the machine, but there was also a message from Toni Abatemarco, saying she had something on Stuart Langolier. I called her back and said, "What's the word, Toni?"

"I'm showing seven arrests over a five-year period, starting when he was sixteen for grand theft, auto. We've got a couple more GTAs, one count of fencing stolen auto parts, and an armed robbery. Real working-class doofball stuff."

"That's it?" I was thinking about Jonna Lester. I was wondering what Stuart Langolier had to do with James Lester.

"His most recent arrest was eight years ago. Nothing after that. I can fax this stuff to you if you want."

"Sure." I gave her the number. "Is there a James Lester listed as an accomplice or a known associate?"

"Hang on and lemme see." I waited. "Nope. I don't see one."

I thought about it some more. "How about a phone number or address listed for Langolier?" I thought I might call him. I thought I might ask him why Jonna Lester had brought him into this.

"There is, but it's eight years old, so I double-checked with information. There is no Stuart Langolier listed or unlisted in Santa Barbara, or anywhere in Ventura county."

"How about an attorney?" His docket sheet would list his attorney of record. I could call the attorney and see if they had a current address.

She said, "Sure. He had a public defender named Elliot Truly."

I was poised to write it down, but I didn't. I said,

"Stuart Langolier was represented by a public defender named Elliot Truly."

"That's right. You want his number?"

"No, babe. I think I have it." I thanked Toni for the good work, told her to say hi to her husband, Frank, and then I hung up.

I stood in my kitchen, staring at the canyon through the glass doors for a time, and then I dialed Truly's number. "Mr. Truly's office."

"This is Elvis Cole. Is Truly in?"

"I'm sorry. Could I take a message?"

"How about Jonathan?"

"I'm afraid they can't be disturbed."

I hung up again.

I showered and changed and was just getting ready to run down to my office when Lucy got back. I wanted to check the fax. I wanted to have the facts with me when I confronted Truly at the party and asked him what in hell was going on. Lucy came in flushed and excited and beaming, carrying a shopping bag with shoes and a long plastic dress bag. She said, "I want to show you! It's absolutely gorgeous and they took up the hem right there while we waited and it's just perfect!"

Her smile made me smile. "You would look perfect in anything."

"Yes, but I'll look even better in this."

I reached to peek into the bag, but she held it away. "Don't peek. I want you to see me with it on."

"How about I see you without it on, then with it on, so I can decide which way I like you better. Sort of like before and after."

She smiled. "If you're as smart as I think you are, you'll rave about me both ways."

I pulled her close. "I'll rave, but smart has nothing to do with it."

She kissed my nose. "I'm having such fun."

"Me, too, Luce. I'm glad you guys are here."

We kissed again, and then I told her that Darlene had called and said that Lucy should phone her at home.

Lucy frowned. "She said to call her at home?"

"Unh-hunh. I asked if there was a problem, but she said no."

Now Lucy wasn't smiling. She seemed somehow distant and distracted.

"Lucy?"

She smiled again, but now it was forced. She stepped back. "I'd better call Darlene and see. Why don't you go along to the office and I'll show you the dress when you get back?"

"You sure?"

She was already moving toward her room. "I'm sure it's business and it could take a while. I'll model the dress when you get back."

She disappeared into the guest room and closed the door.

I said, "Okay."

The marine layer had burned off but it was bright and hot as I drove down to my office. We get these inversion layers, and the air stops moving and grows milky from the exhaust of five million cars. A thin haze was forming to the east. I was surprised that Jonathan Green would allow an inversion layer on a day when he was going to have a party. Might cast a pall on the entire affair.

I parked in my spot, walked up the four flights to my floor, and saw that my door was open. I stepped in and found Dan Tomsic sitting on the couch. He looked large and heavy, and his eyes were closed. I glanced at the fax. Something had printed out in its basket. I looked back at Tomsic. "I could've sworn that I locked the door."

Tomsic opened his eyes but didn't move. His arms were spread along the back of the couch, and he appeared neither surprised nor concerned. "You did, but what's that to a couple of guys like us?"

I stared at him.

"I'm trying to figure you out, Cole. I ask around and everyone says that you're solid, but now there's this shit with Pritzik and Richards, and the double-dealing with Rossi."

I shook my head. "What are you talking about?"

"The press conference. You and Green looked real sweet standing out there on the plaza. A couple of liars."

"I don't know what you're talking about, and I don't know what Jonathan was talking about, either. All I know is that no one seems to be doing very much about Pritzik and Richards."

Tomsic frowned, like maybe he was confused, and then the frown became a nasty smile. "You don't know, do you?"

"Know what, Tomsic?"

"Pritzik and Richards are dead. They died together in an auto accident three weeks ago in Tempe, Arizona."

"So what's the big secret? All you had to do was let us know."

Now the smile dropped away like a gold-digger's interest. "We didn't find out until last night. We called Green's office and notified him at five minutes after nine this morning."

I stared at him. I opened my mouth, then closed it.

Tomsic stood and walked past me to the door. "That's some asshole you're working for. He knew that they were dead even when he was making a big speech about how we weren't doing enough to find them. Foot-dragging, he said. Covering up."

I said, "Were either Pritzik or Richards ever represented by Elliot Truly?"

Tomsic squinted at me. "How in hell should I know?"

I glanced at the fax again.

Tomsic came very close to me. "Shitting on the department is one thing, but Rossi's personal. You said she was clear. You said she was out of it."

"She is, Dan."

"That's not what Green's saying on the news. They're saying she planted the hammer. They're saying she set him up and that they've got proof. You call that being out of it?"

I didn't know what to say.

Tomsic turned back to the door, then raised a single finger, like a teacher instructing a pupil. "My first name is for my friends. You don't rate." He lowered the finger. "Jonathan Green is willing to destroy a good detective's life to save a piece of shit murderer. That makes him a piece of shit, and you're a piece of shit, too."

"Don't mince words, Dan. Tell me what you really think."

Dan Tomsic kept the flat cop eyes on me for another lifetime, and then he left.

My heart was hammering and my head felt swollen. I collected the pages from the fax, then turned on the little Sony TV and found the four o'clock news. The frosty-haired reporter was saying that Pritzik and Richards had plowed into a culvert, saying that they had been drinking, saying we might never know if Pritzik had in fact been James X.

The chiseled male anchor came on, and they cut to a live shot of Jonathan on the sidewalk outside his office. Jonathan and Truly and the lesser attorneys were accusing Angela Rossi of planting the murder weapon, and they were demanding a full investigation, not only of Rossi but of the LAPD command that was protecting her. Jonathan said that his team had uncovered proof that Rossi had tampered with evidence on other occasions, and then Stan Kerris brought out Mrs. Louise Earle. When I saw Mrs. Earle I leaned forward and the swollen feeling spread to my neck and my shoulders. Jonathan introduced her, saying that she had come forward through the efforts of Elvis Cole. He reminded everyone that Elvis Cole was the fine young detective who had made the breakthrough about Pritzik and Richards. He said that what Mrs. Earle was about to say was even more shocking. The camera closed on Mrs. Louise Earle, and she said that Detective Angela Rossi had planted counterfeit money on her son, LeCedrick, and then arrested him. She said that Rossi had threatened to have him killed in prison if she said anything. Mrs. Earle was crying when she said it, and Jonathan Green put his arm around her shoulders to comfort her.

I watched the news for another ten minutes and then I turned off the television. I said, "What in hell is going on here?"

No one answered.

I took a deep breath, let it out, then leaned back in my chair and wondered if I could feel any more out of the loop. I could, and in about twelve seconds I did.

I paged through the faxes until I came to Stuart Langolier's D-55 booking page from the Ventura County Sheriff's office. The booking page showed Stuart Paul Langolier's fingerprints in two rows of five along the bottom of the page, and his front- and side-view mug shots above the prints. The fax quality was poor and the prints had come through mostly as black smudges, but the mug shots were clear enough.

It was eight years ago and the hairstyle was different, but Stuart Langolier wasn't just Stuart Langolier. He was also James Lester, onetime client of Elliot Truly.

I gathered together the faxes, locked my office, and went home to pick up Lucy.

It was going to be a hell of a party.

19

It was just after six when I got back to the house. I let myself in through the kitchen and saw Lucy on the deck. She was standing at the rail, and she was wearing a white silk slip dress with spaghetti straps that left her shoulders and back bare. The silk was without embroidery or detail, and seemed to glow in the lowering sun.

I said, "Simple. Elegant. Utterly devastating."

She turned and smiled, but the smile seemed strained. "Ben called. Peter's going to bring him home after dinner."

"Great."

"You were gone a long time."

"Angela Rossi's partner was waiting for me. Have you seen the news?"

"No."

I turned on the local station, but now they were talking about a fruit fly infestation in Orange County. I changed channels twice, but other things were happening in the world. "They've got a woman I interviewed saying that Rossi framed her son."

"Congratulations." She didn't understand.

"That isn't what she told me. Rossi didn't frame anyone. I cleared her, and that's what I reported to Jonathan."

"I'm sure it's just a misunderstanding. These things happen." She said it, but it was as if she wasn't really there.

I turned off the television and looked at her. "Is everything okay with Darlene?"

"Of course." She glanced away, then made a little shrug. "Just something at the office."

I looked closer. "You sure?"

Lucy stiffened ever so slightly. "Shouldn't you get ready, or are we not going?"

"Luce, he made it sound like I uncovered this woman. He made it sound like I turned up something that implicates Angela Rossi." I said it carefully.

"Perhaps you're just being sensitive." Cool.

I took a step back and went upstairs and put on a jacket and tie. The cat watched me from the closet. Hiding. I said, "Don't say a word."

He didn't.

I folded the fax from Santa Barbara and put it into my inside jacket pocket, and then we went out to the car. I said, "Would you like the top up or down?" Thinking of her hair.

"It doesn't matter."

I left the top down.

I said, "If there's a problem, I wish we could talk about it."

She looked out the window. "Please don't start one of those conversations."

I nodded.

Lucy relaxed as we moved along Mulholland and down Coldwater, and by the time we gave the car to a valet she was smiling again and holding my hand. She said, "There're so many people."

Jonathan Green lived in an expensive home on a corner lot just north of Sunset in Coldwater Canyon. It was an older, established area of great red pines and curving drives and ranch-style estates that looked not unlike the Ponderosa. A small army of valets was trotting along the walks, and the curbs were already lined with cars and limousines and an awful lot of people who looked as if they'd just stepped out of the Academy Players Directory.

Jonathan's front entry was open, and, as we approached, we could see that his home was crowded. I said, "Prepare to be stared at."

She glanced at me. "Why?"

"You'll be the most beautiful woman there."

She hooked her arm through mine.

"In the most beautiful dress."

She squeezed my arm. I'm such a charmer.

A news crew from Channel Eight had lights set up on Jonathan's front lawn and was interviewing a well-known figure who had starred in a hit television series in the early seventies, and who now ran a major studio. Lucy said, "Isn't he somebody?"

"Yep." He was well known for his efforts as an active fund raiser for private social programs and had received humanitarian-of-the-year awards twice, in large part because Teddy Martin had contributed heavily to his causes. He was less well known for the violent, hair-trigger temper that he has frequently shown toward the young men whom he supplies with heroin.

As we passed, he was telling the reporter, "I've known from the beginning that Teddy is innocent, and this proves it. Teddy has been a force for good in our community for years. He's stood by us, and now it's our turn to stand by him. I can't understand why the district attorney has this vendetta." Other reporters were spread through the crowd, interviewing other supporters.

The entry was wide and long and opened onto a great room that flowed outside through a line of French doors. The floors were Spanish tile and the decor was western, with plenty of rich woods and bookshelves and oil paintings of cattle and horses. An original Russell hung over a great stone fireplace. Behind the French doors were a pool and a pool house and, still farther back, a tennis court. Maybe a half-dozen of Kerris's security people were standing around, trying to be unobtrusive and not having a lot of luck at it. The grounds were lush and dramatically lit, and waiters and waitresses moved through the crowd, offering wine and canapés. Maybe three hundred people were drifting through the house and around the pool. Lucy said, "This is beautiful."

I nodded. "Crime pays."

"Oh. There's Jonathan."

Green was near the fireplace, talking with a couple of men in dark suits and a together-looking woman in her late fifties. One of the men was tall and thin, with little round spectacles and a great forehead and bulging Adam's apple. Intense. As we approached, he said,

"LAPD has an entrenched white male racist attitude that is impervious to change. I'm telling you that the time is right to simply abolish them."

The together woman said, "That's a non-issue, Willis. Angela Rossi is a white female."

Willis jabbed the air. Agitated. "And as such must subjugate herself to the dominant white male racist attitudes that surround her. Don't you see that?"

The together woman said, "But LAPD is over fifty percent women and minority now, and the percentage is inceasing."

Willis's eyes bulged. "But is it increasing fast enough to save us? My God, we're living in a virtual police state! If it could happen to Teddy, it could happen to any of us!"

Jonathan saw me and offered his hand, looking not altogether unhappy to shut Willis off. "Everyone, I'd like to introduce Elvis Cole, an integral member of the team."

Willis's eyes lit up and he grabbed my hand. "Great to meet you. You're the one who nailed that fascist bitch."

The together woman drew a deep breath and Lucy said, "Please don't refer to any women by that word in my presence." She said it politely.

Willis stepped back and held up his hands. "Oh, hey, I apologize. Really. But these cops have just gone over the line, and I'm so frustrated."

The together woman said, "You're such a hog."

Jonathan introduced us. The woman was Tracy Mannos, the station manager from Channel Eight. Willis was a writer for a local alternative weekly, the *L. A. Freak*.

When Green was finished introducing me, I introduced Lucy. She said, "It's a pleasure, Mr. Green."

He smiled warmly and took her hand. "Please call me Jonathan. I understand that you're an attorney."

She nodded. "I practice civil law, but your cases have been inspirational. Especially the Williams case in nineteen seventy-two." He was still holding her hand.

"That's a lovely accent. Where are you from?" He patted her hand.

"Louisiana."

"Well, perhaps we'll have the pleasure of working together some time."

He patted her hand again, and I said, "Jonathan, I'd like to see you."

As I said it, Kerris appeared behind Jonathan and whispered something. Jonathan stared at me as Kerris spoke, and then Jonathan nodded at me. "I have to see the others for a moment. Why don't you come along?"

I left Lucy with Tracy Mannos and followed Jonathan through his house to an office that was the size of my living room. Elliot Truly was there, along with the larger of the lesser attorneys and two men who looked vaguely familiar. One of them was tall and hard and African-American. When Kerris closed the door, I said, "Jonathan, I saw the statement you made this afternoon. What's going on with Louise Earle?"

Jonathan spread his hands. "I'm sorry. I don't know what you mean."

"She's changed her story. She didn't implicate Rossi when I talked to her."

Kerris said, "Guess you got it wrong." He had drifted

to the wall behind Jonathan so he could lean. Every time I saw him he was leaning. Guess it wore the guy out carrying all those shoulders and arms.

"I cleared Rossi, and now you're attacking her. You made it sound like I'm behind it."

No one said anything for a moment, and then Jonathan spread his hands. "Angela Rossi found the murder weapon when she went down the slope to Susan's body. She hid it on her person, then planted it on Teddy's property in order to frame him for Susan's murder. She was hoping that if she was credited with solving such a high-profile case, her career would be resuscitated." He smiled at me. "It's as simple as that."

I looked at Truly and Kerris and the two other guys. "That's nuts."

Kerris crossed the arms. He was so wide that maybe he was twins who didn't quite separate. "What's your problem? Everyone thinks you're a hero."

I stared at him. "What's going on?"

Jonathan shook his head.

"How'd you get Mrs. Earle to change her story?"

Jonathan smiled the way you smile when you're incredulous. "Excuse me. Are you accusing me of tampering with evidence?"

Kerris said, "Good thing for us that I double-checked your work. Here everyone thinks that you're some kind of top-dog investigator, and the truth is you suck."

Jonathan frowned. "Please, Stan. There's no need to be insulting."

Kerris kept the empty eyes my way. "He sucks. I'm with the woman five minutes and she breaks down, telling me she's terrified, telling me she's wanted someone to help her for damn near six years because those cops framed her son, then threatened her into keeping her mouth shut."

Everyone was so still that they might have been a fresco. Elliot Truly had a kind of idiot half-grin. He glanced away when I looked at him. I said, "James Lester is a fraud."

Truly was shaking his head before I finished. "That's not true. I should've said something about him when you mentioned Langolier at the jail, but I didn't know how Jonathan wanted to handle it."

Jonathan glared at him.

I took the fax from my pocket and tossed it at Jonathan. "James Lester is an alias. James Lester is a convicted felon named Stuart Langolier. Truly knew him."

Jonathan didn't touch the fax. "This is my fault. You're used to working on small cases and this is a large case, and I should've briefed you on our meetings. Then you wouldn't think we're keeping things from you."

Truly shrugged and looked apologetic. "Look, I didn't realize that Lester was Langolier until I saw his picture in the paper, okay? As soon as I knew I notified Jonathan. We called the district attorney's office and filed a brief about it this afternoon."

Kerris said, "There's a reason they call it 'coincidence.'"

I said, "No secrets?"

Jonathan shook his head. "I'm sorry that I've left you out of the loop. An effort like this is such a large undertaking."

"Like the Gulf War."

"That's right. There are no secrets here."

I said, "What about the lies here? You knew Pritzik and Richards were dead when you attacked the police this morning."

Jonathan frowned as if I were a child he had once thought backward but now stubborn. "I'm disappointed, Elvis. Clearly, you don't understand a team effort, or my obligations as a defense attorney."

Truly shook his head. "What a spoilsport. This case has made you a celebrity."

I said, "Spoilsport?"

Kerris said, "How about 'prick?'"

I looked at him, and Kerris shifted away from the wall. Jonathan said, "No, Stan."

I smiled at him. "Kerris, anytime you want to go for it, I'm available."

Jonathan said, "No, Stan."

Kerris settled against the wall again, and still the empty eyes did not move. The black guy was grinning at me. So was the other idiot.

I looked back at Jonathan Green. "You're right, Jonathan. I don't appreciate it. I quit."

Jonathan said, "I'm sorry to hear that, but under the circumstances I understand."

Kerris said, "You want I should walk him out?"

I said, "Kerris, if you walk me out you won't make it to the door."

Kerris said, "Oo."

I walked out of the office and slammed the door and stood in the crowded living room until my pulse slowed and my ears stopped ringing. The room was so crowded and so noisy that no one heard the door slam. Foiled again. I wandered around for twenty minutes before I found Lucy and Tracy Mannos talking by the pool. Willis and the other guy were nowhere in sight. Just as well for Willis. I said, "Excuse me." My face felt tight, and obvious. "Luce, could I see you please?"

Tracy Mannos handed Lucy a card. "It's been fun, Ms. Chenier. Call me when you get the chance."

Lucy smiled at her, then Tracy Mannos walked away. Lucy said, "Interesting woman."

"I'm glad you're having a good time."

She looked at me. "What's wrong?"

"I am no longer a member of the Big Green Defense Machine. It would probably be appropriate for us to leave."

Lucy stared at me. "What happened?"

"I quit."

We got the car from the valets and found our way back to Coldwater and climbed the mountain to Mulholland. "I'm sorry that we have to leave this way. I know you were excited about meeting Jonathan."

"I don't care about Jonathan. Are you all right?"

I told her about Truly and Lester. I told her again about Mrs. Earle, and about Jonathan making the misleading statement about Pritzik and Richards. I said, "I don't get it. The guy's Jonathan Green. He's an All-World attorney. What does he think he's doing, behaving in this manner?"

She looked at me. "He probably thinks he's doing his job."

I shook my head.

"It's his job to attack the prosecution's case. That's how he creates reasonable doubt."

"Is it his job to lie?"

"No, but you're assuming it's a lie. Reasonable people can disagree and have opposing interpretations of the facts. It's Jonathan's job to present an interpretation that's favorable to his client. It would be malpractice for him to do otherwise." When she said it she was stiff and testy, and it felt like we were having a confrontation.

I said, "What's wrong?"

"Nothing's wrong."

"Are you mad that we had to leave the party?"

"Why are you staying with this? I told you that nothing is wrong."

"Fine."

"Fine."

I turned on k. d. lang. k. d. sang, but I'm not sure either Lucy or I listened. Neither of us spoke.

Peter Alan Nelsen's black Range Rover was parked off the road across from my house, waiting. I said, "Looks like they're home."

Lucy still didn't speak.

We parked and went inside. Peter and Ben were on the couch watching a laser disc of *When Worlds Collide*. The house smelled of popcorn. Peter yelled, "Hide the babes, Ben! It's the police!" Peter always yells things like that.

Ben said, "Hi, Mom. You shoulda seen the neat stuff on Peter's set!"

"You can tell me in the morning, sweetie."

Lucy walked across the living room and into the guest room and shut the door. Ben and Peter looked at me. I said, "I guess she's tired."

Peter said, "Oh, yeah. Looks that way to me."

I frowned at him, and then I stalked up to the loft.

Another fun evening in Tinsel City.

20

Sometime before sunrise the cat's door made its sound, then, a few minutes later, made its sound again. Come and gone.

When the eastern sky was lit gold and the great glass steeple opposite my loft with filled with copper I pulled on gym shorts and slipped down the stairs. The door to the guest room was closed. I went out onto the deck and breathed the cool morning air and did twelve sun salutes from the hatha yoga as the finches and the sparrows and two mockingbirds watched. The canyon was still and quiet and just beginning to fill with light. I did one hundred push-ups and one hundred sit-ups, enjoying the rhythm of the count and the feeling of accomplishment that came with the exertion and the sweat.

The cat climbed onto the deck and watched me from the corner of the house. He didn't look happy.

I worked through the stronger asanas, starting with the half locust, then the full, and then the scorpion and the peacock. The air warmed and the sweat began to flow more freely, and then I saw Ben standing in the glass doors, his face thoughtful. I said, "You're up early."

He nodded. Upset about last night, maybe.

"Come on out."

Ben came out. He was wearing baggy pajama bottoms and a white T-shirt. When he came out the cat lowered his ears and growled. Ben said, "He doesn't like me."

"It's not you. He doesn't like anyone."

"He likes you."

I nodded. "Yeah. He likes me and Joe, pretty much, but he doesn't care for other people. I've never known why."

The low gutter of his growl spiraled up into his war cry and I grew worried he might charge. I'd seen him charge, and it wasn't pretty. I said, "Knock it off." Loud.

The growling stopped.

"That's better."

His ears stayed down, but at least he didn't leave.

Ben crossed the deck to the rail, keeping one eye on the cat, and looked out at the canyon. He put his weight on the rail, then leaned out. He said, "Hawks."

Two redtail hawks were gliding low over the canyon. "They're redtails. They nest up the canyon."

He bounced on the rail. "I think I heard coyotes last night. Was that coyotes?"

"Yep. A family lives by the reservoir."

He bounced faster, then edged along the rail and bounced more. Nervous. I guess he hadn't come out just to look at the hawks. "Your mom and I are going to work things out, Ben. It's okay."

The bouncing stopped and he gave me the same eyes that he'd given me when we'd first met, eight-going-on-nine and taking care of his mom. "She was crying."

I drew a deep breath. I squinted at the canyon, then looked back at him. "Is she crying now?"

He shook his head. "I think she's sleeping."

"She's upset about something, but I'm not sure what."

The bouncing was over, but he still looked uncomfortable.

"She say anything?"

He looked down at the deck, and seemed even more uncomfortable.

"She seemed okay until Darlene called." I watched him. "After Darlene, she seemed kind of upset."

Ben looked at the cat. The cat's ears were up now, and he seemed calm. Ben said, "She's fighting with my dad." Fighting.

"Ah."

"My dad didn't want us staying here. He said we should be in a hotel."

"I see." The hawks reappeared, higher now, following the air back toward their nest. The female had something in her talons. "Are you okay with this, Ben?"

He shrugged without looking at me.

I went to the rail and leaned next to him. "It's tough when your parents are fighting. You get caught in the middle and no matter what you do, you always feel like you're letting one of them down."

Ben said, "She really likes you."

"I really like her. I like you, too. I'm glad you guys are here."

He didn't seem moved by that, but there you go.

I took a breath and went to the center of the deck and worked through a simple *kata* from the *tae kwon do* called the Crane. You do a lot of bending and your arms pinwheel a lot and you spin, but it isn't difficult. Ben watched me. I did the Crane slowly, moving from one end of the deck to the other, and taking great care in my movements, sort of like with the *tai chi*. When I reached the end of the deck, I turned and did it again, back to the other side, only much faster, moving at three-quarter speed. Ben said, "What's that?"

"Ballet."

Ben grinned. "Nunh-unh." He stopped leaning over the rail and crossed his arms. "Is that karate?"

"Korean karate. It's called *tae kwon do*." I went through it again. Left to right, right to left.

He said, "They do that on *Power Rangers*. They beat up monsters."

"Well, it's a fighting skill, but only if you look at it that way. That's a choice you make. You could also choose to look at it as a way to make yourself stronger and more flexible and healthy. It's also fun." I did it again and watched him watch me. "Want me to show you how?"

He came over and I showed him. I modeled the postures and adjusted his position and walked him through the moves. "Don't try to hurry. Slow is better."

"Okay."

We did the Crane. After the Crane I showed him the Tiger. Ben took off his T-shirt and tossed it aside. Sweating. We worked through the *katas* together as the sun floated up from the eastern ridge and the air warmed, and then I saw Lucy watching us from the door. I smiled. "Morning."

"Hi."

Ben said, "Look at this, Mom! This is called the Crane. It's a *tae kwon do kata*. Watch."

Ben worked his way through, and as he did, Lucy put her hand to the glass, fingers spread, and I put my hand to hers. She said, "Joe's on the phone."

Ben said, "Mom, you're not watching!"

I went in and found the phone on the counter. "Now what?"

Pike said, "Put on Channel Five."

I put it on and went back to the phone. The morning anchor was recapping yesterday's report on Green's accusations, and again ran the clip where Green made it look like I had been the one who turned up Mrs. LeCedrick Earle. I said, "We quit last night. We're no longer working for the Big Green Defense Machine."

Pike grunted. "Keep watching."

The anchor said that LAPD had announced a full investigation into Angela Rossi. The anchor said that Rossi had been suspended pending the outcome. I felt a dropaway feeling in my stomach and said, "Oh, man."

Pike said, "I tried calling her, but the phone's off the hook."

"How about I pick you up?"

He hung up without answering. Lucy had come inside, and Ben was still on the deck. I said, "We've got to go see about Rossi."

Lucy nodded. "I thought you might. I've got the meeting later in Long Beach. I'll take Ben."

"Sure."

She started away, then turned back. "I liked seeing you together with him."

I smiled, but I didn't say anything. I wanted to ask what was going on with her former husband, but I didn't want to press her. I wanted to be supportive, but sometimes support can be oppressive. Maybe it would work itself out. Maybe, too, it was none of my business. I decided to give her some room. Giving them room is often the better part of valor, especially when you're trying not to make things worse.

I showered and dressed, and then I drove down to Culver City and found Joe waiting at the curb. Pike slid into the right front seat and closed the door without a word. He buckled the seat belt and still didn't say anything. I guess he was angry, too.

It was a few minutes after nine when we drove to the beach, then turned south to the Marina and slowed at the mouth of Angela Rossi's cul-de-sac. We would've turned onto her street, but we couldn't because of the news vans jamming the cul-de-sac and spilling out onto Admiralty Way. Knots of reporters and camera people were clustered on the sidewalks and in the street, and a couple of women who were probably Rossi's neighbors were arguing with a short, stocky guy in a sport coat. Apparently, his van was blocking their drive. Apparently, they wanted the reporters to lay off Rossi and get out of their neighborhood. Pike said, "Look at this crap."

We parked across Admiralty and walked back. A beefy reporter sitting in a Blazer did a double-take when we passed, then hurried after us, asking if he could have a word. He reached Pike first and Pike seemed to give a lurch, and then the reporter sat down on the street hard, going "Omph!"

Pike didn't lose a step. "No comment."

I guess some interviews are harder than others.

We walked past the reporters to the front gate. The thin man with the glasses and an older woman were telling an attractive red-haired reporter that they weren't going to let her in, when the thin man recognized me and shook his finger at me. "It's you. You lied to me when you were here. You weren't looking for anyone named Keith!"

I said, "Would you please tell Detective Rossi that Joe Pike and I would like to see her?"

The red-haired reporter turned and yelled for her camera operator to hurry up. She yelled that she wanted a shot of this.

The thin man kept shaking his finger. "You're a prick. You should be ashamed of yourself."

Joe Pike stepped to the gate and murmured something that I couldn't hear. Pike didn't seem threatening now. He seemed gentle and calming. The woman went to Rossi's front door. I guess she was the thin man's wife.

The red-haired reporter's camera operator hustled up behind us and began taping. The reporter asked if I had any additional information implicating or incriminating Angela Rossi. She asked if I was here to get a statement from Rossi or to follow up a line of inquiry. I kept my back to her. I stared at the hamper filled with Nerf balls. I stared at the red bike.

The thin man's wife came back and let us through the gate. The red-haired reporter tried to push through, but the wife shoved her back, yelling, "Don't you dare!" The thin man wasn't happy that I was coming in.

Joe Pike rapped at the door once, then opened it, and we stepped through into Angela Rossi's life.

It was a nice place, roomy and spacious, though the furnishings weren't expensive, just a sofa and love seat arranged in an L, and a BarcaLounger. I guess she'd put all of the money into buying the place and hadn't had a lot left over for furniture. A woman and a man were standing behind the love seat, and another woman was sitting on the couch, and two little boys were sitting on the floor, the smaller sitting in the larger's lap. I guess the boys belonged to Rossi. I guess the adults were friends or family come to lend support. Off-duty cops, maybe, but maybe not. Everyone in the room was looking at me. Even the boys.

Angela Rossi was standing by the sofa with her arms crossed. Her cheeks looked hollow and her eyes were dark and haunted. I said, "I wanted to tell you that I didn't have anything to do with this. I told Green that you were clean. He told me that he bought it. I don't know what happened."

"Okay. Thanks." Like she was numb.

Joe said, "Angie."

She shook her head. "I didn't do those things. I didn't frame that guy."

Joe said, "I know."

Angela Rossi looked confused. "I don't know why she's lying. She seemed like such a nice woman."

I said, "We'll talk to her. We'll get this straightened out."

Angela Rossi said, "It won't matter. I'm done with the job."

Joe stiffened and shook his head once. "Don't say that, Angela. You're not."

"So what kind of career will I have when it's over?" She walked past us to the window and peeked out. "I can't believe that all these people have nothing better to do." She looked back. "Can you?"

All of them kept staring. I wanted to say something, but I didn't know what to say. My eye still hurt where she'd hit me, and I was thinking that maybe she ought to hit me again. "I'm sorry."

"Forget it." She shrugged, no big deal.

Joe said, "We'll help you fight it."

"Nothing to help. I've decided to resign."

Joe leaned forward. His dark lenses seemed to blaze. "Don't resign. You're too good to resign."

She said, "Oh, Joe."

Pike was leaning so far forward he seemed to sway.

"They've taken everything away, but that's okay. I just have to survive this, and I know I can." She smiled when she said it, as if she were at peace with all of this.

Joe said, "What's wrong with you?" His voice was so soft I could barely hear him.

Angela Rossi's left eye began to flutter, then grew wet, and I had the sense that if she were fine china there would be a webwork of spider-silk cracks spreading beneath her surface. She held up her right hand and said, "Please go now."

Pike nodded, and I started to say something else, but then she turned the hand to me, and I nodded, too.

21

We left Angela Rossi's and walked out to the car. The whiny reporter who had once been a lawyer saw us first and ran toward us, shouting, "They've come out! They've come out!" The rest of the reporters stayed back, shifting their feet and keeping their distance. Pike raised a palm at the whiny reporter, and he stopped, too. I guess word had spread, or maybe it was in our faces.

We drove slowly, neither of us speaking, and worked our way out of the Marina, up through Venice, and along the beach. It was automatic driving, going through the motions without conscious thought or direction, movement without destination or design. Pike hunkered low in the passenger's seat, his face dark in the bright sun, his dark lenses somehow molten and angry. It is not good to see Joe Pike angry. Better to see a male lion charge at close quarters. Better to hear someone scream, *"Incoming!"* I said, "Where do you want to go?"

His head swiveled sideways maybe half an inch.

"How about we just drive?"

His head moved up, then down. Maybe half an inch.

"Okay. We'll drive."

We followed Ocean Avenue up through Venice and along the bluff above the beach, Pike as still as an undisturbed lake. We stopped for a light on Ocean Park, and I watched the joggers and bikers and smiling young women with deep tans who dotted the bike paths along the bluff. Everyone was smiling. Happy people having a great time on a beautiful day. What could be better than that? Of course, they could be happy because they hadn't just come from Angela Rossi's house. It's always easy to smile when you haven't helped destroy an innocent person's life.

The light turned green, and a red Toyota pickup filled with surfers and surf boards blew their horn behind us. The driver yelled for us to get out of the way, and Joe Pike floated up out of his seat and twisted around, and when he did the honking stopped and the Toyota jammed into reverse and sped away at high speed. Backwards.

I said, "Well. I guess we'd better talk about this before we kill somebody."

Pike frowned. His arms were knotted and tight, and the veins in his forearms were large. His dark glasses caught the bright sun, looking hot enough to sear flesh. The red arrow tattoos on his deltoids were as bright as arterial blood. I wondered if the idiots in the Toyota knew how close they'd come.

I said, "It isn't just Angela Rossi, is it?"

Pike's head moved from side to side one time.

"You don't like the cops we know thinking that we're part of this. You don't like people thinking that you and

I believe this garbage or had a part in destroying an innocent woman's life."

Pike's head moved again. Just a bit. Just the smallest of moves.

"But that's the way it looks."

Pike's jaw rippled with tension.

We went to a Thai place a few blocks up from the beach. It was still shy of noon when we parked at the curb and went in. Early. It's a tiny place with beat-up Formica tables, and it was empty except for two women sitting at the single window table. The young guy who greeted us said we could sit where we liked. An older woman who was probably his grandmother was sitting at the table nearest the kitchen, snapping the stems off an enormous pile of snow peas and watching a miniature Hitachi television. She smiled and nodded, and I smiled back. I have never been in their restaurant when she was not snapping peas. We took a table near her, ordered two Thai beers, squid pad thai, vegetable fried rice, and seafood curry. The little woman was watching the midday news as she worked. Something about the Middle East.

The beer came and I said, "Joe, I'm thinking that there is something larger here than an attorney's zealous defense of his client." The master of understatement.

Pike cocked his head toward me.

I told him about the connection between James Lester and Elliot Truly, and about Lester's record. "Lester could be for real, and his tie to Truly could be a coincidence, but maybe it isn't. Pritzik and Richards were killed before Lester called the hotline."

"Are you thinking he knew that?"

"Say he knew them better than he let on. Say he knew that they had gone to Arizona and were dead, and figured that they would be the perfect crash-test dummies to take the heat for Susan Martin's murder. Lester may have done a little homework and planted the evidence himself to take a shot at the reward."

"Or Truly might have helped him."

I nodded. "Just thinking out loud."

"Because you have no proof." The veins in his arms weren't as prominent, and his tattoos had lost their glow. The danger of thermonuclear meltdown was passing.

I shook my head. "No. Lester could be on the level, even though he's a creep."

"What about the woman?"

"Louise Earle is different. Kerris went to see her, and now she's changed her story. I don't buy that she was lying to me, and I don't buy that Rossi held a gun to her head and made her lie six years ago. Rossi wouldn't have done that, and Louise Earle wouldn't have lied about it."

"If she wasn't lying then, she's lying now."

"Yes. But why?" The waiter brought our food, and the smells of mint and garlic and curry were strong. He set out the dishes and said, "We make spicy. Like always."

"Great."

When the waiter was gone, Pike said, "Because the law is war, and to defeat the prosecution Green must do two things. He must float a viable theory for what happened to Susan Martin, and he must discredit the prosecution's theory."

"Okay."

"Lester gives him the alternative theory. The business with Rossi gives him a way to discredit the prosecution's evidence."

"If Rossi framed LeCedrick Earle, she's also framing Teddy Martin."

Pike nodded. "Yes." Pike twisted toward the Hitachi and said, "Listen."

Jonathan Green was on the noon news. The lead story was Elliot Truly's connection to James Lester, also known as Stuart Langolier. Green was announcing that James Lester had revealed to a defense investigator that he had once been known as Stuart Langolier and, under that name, had once been represented by Elliot Truly. Green said that it was his understanding that Mr. Truly had no recollection of Mr. Lester as a client and added that the defense team had immediately notified the district attorney's office to mitigate the appearance of a conflict and to allow them the opportunity for a complete investigation. I said, "He's doing just what he said."

Pike grunted. "Covering his ass."

The little woman noticed that we were watching the TV and turned the Hitachi so that it would be easier for us to see.

The news anchor shifted the story to the charges against Angela Rossi and cut to the same tape of Louise Earle that I'd seen last night, Mrs. Earle crying as she charged that Angela Rossi had framed her son, saying that the police had made her lie before, saying that they had threatened her. The tears looked real. Her pain looked real. Jonathan Green was standing next to her.

Elliot Truly was standing behind them. Everyone looked oh-so-concerned.

Pike turned away. "I can't look at this."

I stared at the Hitachi. I watched Green and I watched Louise Earle, and it just didn't make sense. "If what we're thinking about Lester and Louise Earle is true, why would a guy like Jonathan Green risk who he is and what he does?"

"Because he's an asshole." The world according to Pike.

I said, "Lizard people."

Pike's glasses gleamed. "We can talk about this forever, but the only way we're going to find out what's going on with these people is to ask them."

The young waiter was watching us. He didn't like it that we hadn't touched the food, and he looked concerned. He said something to the little woman. She frowned at us and seemed to share his concern.

The waiter came over and wanted to know if anything was wrong. Pike looked at him and stood. "Probably. But if there is we'll fix it."

We picked up the Santa Monica Freeway and drove to Louise Earle's home in Olympic Park. We knocked twice, and rang the bell three times, but she didn't answer. Pike said, "I'll look in back."

Pike disappeared around the side of the house. The day was bright, and the same three girls were across the street, whiling away their summer on their porch. I waved and they waved back. Getting to be old friends. Pike reappeared from the opposite side. "She's not home."

"Then let's see Lester."

We climbed back onto the freeway and worked our way east past Pasadena to La Puente and James Lester's house.

Lester's home was unchanged from the last time I was there. The yard was still dead, the Fairlane was still rusted, and everything was still covered with fine gray sand. We parked at the curb and walked across the gray soil to the house. The front door was open, and music was coming from the house. The George Baker Selection doing "Little Green Bag." When we got closer, Pike said, "Smell it?"

"Yep." The sweet rope smell of hashish was coming from the house.

When we reached the door we didn't have to knock. Jonna Lester was sitting on the couch, sucking hard on a glass pipe, the little electric fans arcing back and forth as they scattered her hash smoke. She was wearing a Michigan State University T-shirt and short-shorts and the clear plastic clogs. Her left eye was red and blue and swollen almost closed, and the bottoms of the clogs were crudded with something dark, as if she'd stepped through mud. She smiled stupidly when she saw me and waved the pipe at her eye. "Helps with the pain. You wanna smoke a bowl?"

I opened the screen door and we went in. There was another smell in the room, just beneath the dope. I tilted her face to better see the eye. "James do this?"

She pulled away from me and waved the pipe again. "It'll be the last time, yessireebob." She took another pull on the pipe.

"We need to see him."

Jonna Lester giggled. "He's in the bathroom. It's his favorite room in the house. He always said that." She giggled again.

"Would you tell him we want to see him, please?" The other smell felt wet and old, like melons that had gone soft with age.

Jonna Lester sank back on the couch. "This is such a cool song."

Joe Pike walked over to the radio and turned it off. Jonna Lester screwed up her face and said, "Hey!"

I called, "James?"

Jonna Lester pushed to her feet and angrily waved toward the back of the house. "He's back there, you wanna see the sonofabitch so bad. C'mon, I'll show ya."

Pike and I looked at each other, and then Pike took out his .357 Python and held it down along his leg. We followed her out of the living room and across a square little hall to the bathroom. It was an old bathroom, built sometime back in the fifties, with a buckled linoleum floor and corroded fixtures and a brittle glass shower door, the kind that can hurt you bad if you fall through it. Jonna Lester stopped in the door and waved the hash pipe. "Here he is. Talk to the sonofabitch all you want."

I said, "Oh, man."

James Lester was lying through the broken shower door, half in the tub and half out, impaled on half a dozen jagged glass spikes. His head was almost severed, and the walls and the tub and the buckled linoleum were sprayed with gouts of dark red blood that looked not unlike wings raised toward heaven.

We had wanted to ask James Lester about Pritzik and Richards and the fabrication of evidence, but now he wasn't around to answer our questions. Neither were Pritzik and Richards.

Funny how that works. Isn't it?

22

I got as close to the body as I could without stepping in blood. Jonna Lester's footprints were already on the linoleum from an earlier visit, but there didn't seem to be any other marks or tracks or signs of passage. There was a single small window at the far end of the bathroom above the toilet, open for the air. The window's screen was dirty and torn, but was hooked from the inside and appeared undisturbed. Metallic black flies bumped against the screen, drawn by the blood. I said, "Did you touch anything?"

She said, "Yee-uck! I ain't touchin' that mess."

"Your footprints are on the floor. There's dried blood on your shoes."

Jonna Lester took another pull on the hash pipe. The hash nut must've gone out, because she frowned at the pipe and poked the bowl. "I hadda turn off the water." One of the black flies worked its way through the screen and droned low across the slick floor. You could see its reflection in the blood.

"The water in the sink was running?"

"Yeah."

James Lester was wearing pants and the work boots, but no shirt. Both legs and one arm were crumpled in a kind of K on the floor, with the other arm and the upper half of his body hanging through the glass into the tub. There was water on the linoleum around the base of the sink where it had spilled over and mixed with James's blood. A bar of soap and a Bic razor and a can of Edge shaving cream were on the sink, which was splashed with water, like maybe he had been getting ready for work and turned and slipped and gone head first through the glass. I said, "What happened, Jonna?"

She shook her head. "I spent the night with my friend Dorrie, and he was like this when I came home. I guess he fell." She made a big deal out of showing me her eye. "The prick did this to me yesterday. You see what he did?" She shook her head and her lips went *wubba-wubba-wubba* like a cartoon character. "Oh, man, doesn't that smell just make you wanna vomit?"

She went back into the living room, and we followed her. She tried stoking the pipe again, and I pulled it away from her. "Hey, whatcha doin'?!"

"He's dead, Jonna. A material witness in a murder case who stands to collect a hundred thousand dollar reward doesn't just fall through a shower door."

Jonna Lester slapped at me and tried to push me away. "We had this big fight yesterday and I hadda get outta here! I don't know what happened!"

"Was he expecting anyone?"

"I don't know!"

"Did he mention anyone to you, like maybe he was concerned?"

She put her hands over her ears. "I don't know I don't know I don't know!" Shouting.

I stepped back, breathing hard, and let her calm. I looked at Pike and Pike shrugged. I took a breath, let it out, then sat next to her. I said, "Okay, Jonna, what did you guys fight about?" Calm.

"We fought because he's an asshole!"

"Was it because you blew the whistle to me about James being Stuart Langolier?"

She froze for a moment, and then she squinted at me. Suspicious. "I don't know what you're talking about."

"C'mon, Jonna. I recognized your voice. Why'd you tip me about James's real name?"

She slumped back on the couch and stuck out her lower lip. Sulking. "James Lester was his real name. He changed it legally to get a fresh start when he gave up his life of crime."

I said, "Jonna."

"I did it to fuck him." Her voice was soft and petulant.

"Why?"

" 'Cause he was gonna cut me out. I know it."

"How do you know it?"

" 'Cause he said that when he got the big payday he was gonna blow me off and get a Bud Lite girl." Her eyes were welling in a delicate balance at the edge of tears. The point of her chin trembled.

Pike walked away. He has little tolerance for the vagaries of the human condition.

I said, "Jonna? What else do you know?"

"What do you mean?" She rubbed at her eyes. When she touched the bruised eye she winced.

"He may not have been telling the truth. He might have made up the story about meeting Pritzik in a bar. I think maybe he planted the things I found in order to collect the reward, or someone else planted them and James was in on it."

She shrugged, even more sulky. "I dunno."

"Did he know Pritzik and Richards? Did he tell you how he was going to set this up?"

She suddenly sat up, loud and animated. "Hey, I'm still gonna get the reward money, ain't I? I mean, I get it now that he's dead, right?"

Pike said, "Forget the reward. You'll be lucky if you don't go to jail." Pike, the Intimidator.

Jonna Lester's eyes filled again and this time the tears leaked down her cheeks. "Well, that's no fair." No fair.

I said, "Tell me about Pritzik and Richards."

She shook her head. "I don't think he knew them. I mean, he *coulda*, but I don't think so."

"Why not?"

Shrug. "'Cause he didn't have any friends. Just this guy from the video store and Clarence at the transmission shop. Clarence is a Mexican."

I glanced at Pike, but Pike was staring out the front door. Intimidating the neighborhood. I said, "Maybe he mentioned a buddy who worked at a Shell Station or an ex-con he would have drinks with."

She shook her head. "He just went out with Clarence. I know 'cause I followed him."

"You followed him." The detective using advanced interrogation techniques.

She made the kind-of shrug again. "When he started all that talk about gettin' a Bud Lite girl I got worried he might be doin' more than drinkin' when he went out."

"And all he ever did was go out with Clarence?"

Her head bobbed. "Uh-huh."

"How many times did you follow him?"

"Eight or nine." She thought about it. "Maybe ten."

I described Pritzik and Richards. "You ever see him with guys like that?"

Another head shake. "Nuh-uh. James and Clarence would just sit there and drink, and sometimes play video games." Another big fly cruised through the room, this time passing between us before heading toward the bathroom. Jonna Lester watched it, realized where it was going, and made a face. "Oh, yuck."

Pike followed the fly, and closed the bathroom.

I walked over to the front door, stared out at the hot earth, then went back to James Lester's chair and sat. Maybe James hadn't known Pritzik and Richards. It was still possible that he had, but if he hadn't then he wouldn't have been able to fake the evidence. He wouldn't have known they were dead. He wouldn't have known where to plant it. Maybe James had been telling the truth. Of course, maybe his dive through the shower glass was an accident, too.

Jonna Lester got the hey-waitaminute-! look again, then frowned as if she was trying to see shadows within shadows and not having a lot of luck with it. She wiggled her finger in the air and said, "I take it back! There was another guy I saw him with."

I stared at her.

"This time that I followed him, he went to the Mayfair Market over here and talked to this guy."

Pike crossed his arms and looked at me. Well, well.

"A guy in the Mayfair?"

"A guy in the parking lot. I thought he was going to the store, but he just parked there in the lot and went over to this other car. James just kinda squatted by the driver and talked through the window, and then this guy gives him a bag and James left."

"The man in the car gave him a bag?"

"Mm-mm. Like a Mayfair bag. Brown paper."

"When did this happen?"

Her lips made a tight line. Her eyebrows jumped up and down. Time sense distorted by all the hash. "A long time ago. Two or three weeks."

I looked at Pike again, and Pike's mouth twitched. It could've been after Pritzik and Richards were killed and before James Lester phoned the hotline. Maybe we were getting somewhere.

I said, "What did the guy look like, Jonna?"

"Like a guy. I was behind them and he didn't get out."

Pike said, "What kind of car was it?"

"I don't know anything about cars. It was little."

"What color?"

She frowned. "Dark blue. No, waitaminute. I think it was black. A little black car." She was nodding like she could see it.

I said, "Did James ever mention someone named Elliot Truly to you?"

She shook her head. "Who's that?"

"Truly was James's lawyer in San Diego."

She shook her head again. "Nuh-uh."

I looked around their living room. I dug through the comic books and monster truck magazines, and looked under the couch. I finally found four days' worth of the *Los Angeles Times* at the bottom of a plastic trash can in the kitchen. I found the one with my picture and brought it out to her. You could see Elliot Truly clearly behind me and Jonathan Green. I pointed at Truly. "Was this the man in the car?"

Jonna Lester shook her head. "Oh, no. He didn't look anything like that."

I pointed at Green. "Him?"

"Oh, no. Not him, either."

I glanced at Pike and Pike shrugged. He said, "Could've been anybody about anything. Doesn't have to relate to this. Maybe he was buying the hash."

Jonna Lester's pout had come back, and now it was rimmed with petulance. "Look, I've been trying to help, haven't I? All those news people said it looked like we were gonna get the reward, and I think we still should. I mean, even though he's dead he's still due the reward, and that means I should have it, right?"

I stared at her.

"Well, it's only right. You're only guessing that he made it up, and even if he did you can't prove it. I don't think he made it up at all. I think he was telling the truth, even if he was a lyin' no good sonofabitch."

I said, "Jonna, in about two minutes you're going to call the police. Do yourself a favor and don't tell them how much you should get the cash."

The pout edged over into full-blown petulance. "Well, why not?"

Pike said, "Because with all the remorse you're showing, they'll think you killed him for the money. You don't want them to think that, do you?"

Jonna Lester slapped hard at the couch, then threw the glass pipe to the floor. She stamped both feet. Mad. "Life really sucks."

"That's true," I said. "But think of it this way."

She squinted at me, and I glanced toward the bathroom.

"Death sucks worse."

23

Jonna Lester dialed 911, identified herself, and told them that she'd found her husband dead of an apparent bathtub accident. Jonna related the facts as I outlined them, and the operator said that the paramedics were on their way.

I made Jonna dump her hash down the disposal and spray Lysol to kill the smell. Flushing it down the toilet would've been better, but I didn't want anyone in the bathroom. Evidence. I had her wash her mouth with bourbon; if she acted goofy or giggly, they'd smell the booze and figure her for a drunk. The paramedics arrived first, then the police. A uniformed sergeant named Belflower shook his head when we told him who James Lester was and said, "Hell of a thing, ain't it? Guy stands to collect a hundred grand and he gets his neck slit from slipping on a bar of Ivory."

I said, "You think?"

He frowned at me. "You don't?"

We stared at each other until he went out to his squad car and called the detectives. Pike and I stayed until the police were satisfied that Jonna Lester had found the body on her own and that we had stumbled in later, and then they said we could go.

We stopped at an Arco station two blocks away where I used the pay phone to call a friend of mine who works at the Medical Examiner's office. I told him that James might've had help falling through the glass, and I asked if he might share his findings after the autopsy. He said that such a thing might be possible if I was able to share four first-base-side tickets to a Dodgers game. I said, "I don't have first-base-side tickets to the Dodgers."

My friend didn't say anything.

"But maybe I can find some."

My friend hung up, promising to call.

I dropped Pike off, and it was twenty minutes before seven when I arrived home.

Lucy's rental was wedged on the far left side of the carport, silent and cool in the deepening air. The far ridge was rimmed with copper and bronze, and honeysuckle was just beginning to lace in and around the musky scent of the eucalyptus. I stood at the edge of the carport and breathed deep. I could smell the grease and the oil and the road scents of my Stingray mixing with the smells of the mountain. I could feel the heat of its engine, and hear the dings and pops of the cooling metal. The house was quiet. A horned owl glided across the road and down along the slope, disappearing past the edge of my home. Insects swirled over the canyon, erased by the dark blur of bats. I stood there, enjoying the cooling air and the night creatures just beginning to stir and twilight in the mountains. Home is the detective, home for the night. Sandbagged, unemployed, and feeling more than a little suspicious.

I let myself in through the kitchen. Lucy was on the couch in the living room, reading *Los Angeles Magazine*. Ben was on the deck, sitting crosslegged in one of the deck chairs, reading Robert A. Heinlein's *Have Spacesuit, Will Travel*. There wasn't much light, and he would have to come in soon. I said, "Another strange day in Oz, Lucille."

Lucy closed the magazine on a finger and smiled, but the smile was small and uncertain. "We got back around four."

"Sorry I'm so late."

"It's okay." She made a little shrug, and in that moment I wondered how much of the tension from last night was still with us.

"Are you two starving?"

Lucy made the uncertain smile again as if she recognized the tension and was trying to soften it. "I made Ben a snack a little while ago, but we could eat."

"How about I make spaghetti?"

"Oh, that would be nice."

I went into the kitchen, popped open a Falstaff, and took a package of venison sausage from the freezer. I filled a large pot with enough water for the spaghetti, dropped in the sausage, then put on the heat. I heard the glass doors slide open and Ben yelled hi. I yelled hi back. I heard Lucy tell Ben that dinner would be ready soon and that he should take a bath. I heard the guest room door close and water run. The sounds of other people in my house.

I drank most of the Falstaff, then examined the cat's tray. Crumbs of dry food speckled the paper towel around his food bowl and a hair floated in his water. He'd probably slipped down the stairs during the day when no one was home, eaten, then made his escape. I tossed the old food and water, put out fresh, and wished that he was here.

I finished the Falstaff, then opened a bottle of Pinot grigio, poured two glasses, and brought one to Lucy. She was still reading the magazine, so I put the wine on the table near her. I said, "I meant to get home sooner, but Rossi's in pretty bad shape, and the day just sort of grew from there." I didn't tell her about James Lester. Lester would bring us back to Green, and I didn't want to go there. "I was hoping that we'd have more time together."

Lucy's face grew sad and she covered my hand with hers. "Oh, Studly, I know you can't be with us every moment. It's okay."

"It doesn't seem okay."

Lucy stared past me and the sadness grew deeper. She wet the corner of her mouth as if she were going to say something, then shook her head as if changing her mind. "There's a lot going on right now, Elvis, but it doesn't have anything to do with us."

"Can we talk about it?"

She wet the corner of her mouth again, but she still didn't look back at me. She was staring at a point in midspace as if there was a third presence in the room, floating in space and demanding the weight of her attention. "I'd really rather not. Not now."

I nodded. "Okay. Up to you."

She looked back at me and made the little smile again, and now it was clearly forced. "Let me help you cook. Would that be okay?"

"Sure."

We went into the kitchen and collected things for the spaghetti sauce and talked about her day. We chopped mushrooms and onions and green peppers, and opened cans of tomatoes and jars of oregano and basil, and talked as we did it, but the talking was empty and forced, the way it might be if there was a distance between us and we had to shout to make ourselves heard. I asked how her meetings had gone and she said fine. I asked if she was finished with the negotiation, and she said that a final meeting tomorrow would do it. Ben came in and parked on one of the counter stools, but he seemed to sense the tension and said little. After a time, he went into the living room and turned on my Macintosh and went on-line.

We had just put the spaghetti in boiling water and were setting the table when the doorbell rang. I said, "If it's a reporter, I'm going to shoot him."

It was Joe Pike and Angela Rossi. Rossi looked ragged and uncertain, and there were great hollow smudges beneath her eyes. Lucy stared soundlessly from the kitchen, and Rossi glanced from her to me. "I hope you don't mind."

"Of course not." I introduced them.

Angela Rossi glanced at Lucy again, and in that moment there was something very female in the room, as if Rossi somehow sensed the tension and felt that she was not so much invading my space but Lucy's. She said, "I'm sorry." To Lucy, not to me.

Lucy said, "We were going to eat soon. Would you like to join us?" She was holding the sauce spoon over the pan, frozen in mid-stir.

Rossi said, "No. Thank you. I can't stay very long." She smiled at Ben. "I have children."

"Of course." Lucy put the sauce spoon on the counter, then excused herself and took Ben out onto the deck.

We watched the glass doors slide shut, and Rossi looked even more uncomfortable. "Looks like I've come at a bad time."

"Forget it."

Pike moved behind her. He hadn't yet spoken, and probably wouldn't.

Angela Rossi looked at the floor, then looked at me, as if her energy reserves were so depleted she had to conserve what little remained. She said, "Joe told me about Lester. He told me what you've been trying to do."

I nodded.

"I lost it this morning and I want to apologize. You're caught in this, too, just like me."

"Yes, but it's worse for you."

"Maybe." She looked at the floor again, then looked back. "I want you to know that I didn't lie to you. I want you to know that everything I told you was the truth. LeCedrick Earle is lying, and so is his mother. I didn't do those things."

"I believe you, detective."

When I said it her breath gave and her eyes filled and

her face collapsed, but in that same instant she caught herself and rebuilt the calm cop exterior: her breathing steadied, her eyes dried, her face calmed. It wasn't easy to recreate herself that way, but I imagined that she'd had plenty of practice over the years and that, as with every other professional police officer that I'd known, it had become a necessary survival skill. She had allowed a window to her heart to open, then had slammed it shut the way you take a covered pan off the fire when it begins to boil over, removing the heat so that you don't lose the contents. "I'm suspended. I've been ordered to stay away from all official police business or activities pending an IA investigation. The district attorney's office is also investigating me."

"I know."

"The people I work with, there's only so much they can do."

I knew that, too. If Tomsic or the others did anything to find out what was going on, they'd be pounded for obstructing justice and probably accused of trying to cover up Rossi's alleged crimes.

She looked at Joe. "You guys offered to help. Joe said that the offer still stands."

"Of course." I glanced at Lucy on the deck. She and Ben were at the rail. Ben was pointing at something far down the canyon and yakking, but Lucy seemed neither to hear him nor to see. As if the other presence were out there, too, and drawing her attention. I felt my own eyes fill, but, like Angela Rossi, I also knew the tricks of survival. "We're not going to walk away, Angie. We're not going to leave you hanging."

Angela Rossi looked at me for a time, first in one eye and then the other, and then she glanced again at Lucy and Ben. "I'm sorry I intruded."

"Don't worry about it."

She put out her hand. We shook, and then Angela Rossi left my home.

Joe Pike stood in the entry, staring out onto the deck, as if he, too, could somehow sense the tension. Maybe I should just put up a huge sign: DOMESTIC PROBLEM. I said, "What?"

Pike stared a moment longer, then turned and followed Angela Rossi, leaving me in the shadows.

I went back into the kitchen, stirred the sauce, then turned off the heat. The spaghetti was limp and swollen. I poured it in the colander, rinsed it, and let it drain.

I could see Lucy and Ben in the light at the rail, haloed by a swirl of flying insects, Lucy still there but not there, Ben now quiet. The cat door made its *clack-clack* behind me, and the cat crept in. He moved cautiously, pausing between steps, sniffing the air. I smiled at him. "It's okay, bud. They're outside."

He blinked at me, but you could tell he was suspicious. He crept to the dining area, still testing the air, then came back and stood by my feet. I broke off a piece of the venison sausage, sucked off the tomato sauce, then blew on it until it was cool. I offered it to him, and as he ate it I stroked him. His fur was flecked with dust and bits of plant matter, and felt cool from the night air. White hairs were beginning to show through the black, and I wondered how old he was. We had been together a long time.

When he was finished he looked up at me, and I smiled. I picked him up and held him close, and after a time he purred. I said, "Life is complicated, isn't it?"

He licked my cheek, then bit my jaw, but he didn't bite hard.

After a time he hopped down and made his way through the house. He moved slowly, staring toward the deck for a very long time before finally bolting up the stairs and into my bedroom.

I told Lucy and Ben that dinner was ready. We ate, and not long after that we doused the lights and went to bed.

Since Lucy did not come upstairs that night, the cat slept well.

24

he next day Lucy and Ben planned to spend the morning in Beverly Hills, then make the drive to Long Beach for what Lucy hoped would be the final meeting of her negotiation. They were leaving the day after tomorrow.

We made banana pancakes and eggs and coffee, and ate together, but Lucy still seemed pained and distracted as she readied to leave. I found that I was thinking more about her and less about me, but neither of us seemed to be making much progress toward a resolution. Of course, maybe this was because we had so far successfully avoided talking, and maybe the time for talk-avoidance had passed. The ducking of communication rarely leads to a resolution. I said, "What time do you guys expect to be home?"

"Sixish." Lucy was replacing her files in her briefcase. "I don't expect that anything will hang us up in Long Beach."

"Good. I'm going to take us someplace special for dinner."

She smiled at me. The soft smile. "Where?"

"Surprise."

We held each other's gaze for the first time that morning, and then Lucy put out her hand. Her skin was warm and soft, and touching her made me tingle. "A surprise would be nice."

"Leave everything to me." Elvis Cole, Master of the Universe, turns on the ol' charm.

They left the house at ten minutes before nine, and then I phoned my friend at the coroner's office. The autopsy of James Lester had been completed, and when I asked after the cause of death, he said, "The guy took a header through the glass, and he was still alive when he made the fall. You want to know just what was severed and how?"

"Not necessary. Was there an indication that he might've had help going through the glass?"

"You mean, like, did someone beat the hell out of him first, then push him through?"

"That's one way to put it." I could hear papers rustling in the background, and laughter. Someone sharing a big joke to start the day at the morgue.

"Nah. No sign of blunt-force trauma. No bruising, cuts, or scrapes that would indicate a physical altercation."

"Hm." So maybe it wasn't murder. Maybe James Lester was just clumsy.

"But we did find one thing that was odd." Maybe James Lester wasn't just clumsy after all. "There's a pattern of subcutaneous capillary rupture over the carotid area on his neck."

"That sounds like bruising."

"It's not the kind of bruising you'd ever see, and it wasn't caused by impact trauma."

"So no one hit him."

"You see stuff like this when someone vomits or has a coughing fit. Coughing can do stuff like that. You'd be surprised what coughing can do." These medical examiners.

I was thinking about the carotid artery, and I was trying to imagine a type of force that might rupture microcapillaries without creating an impact bruise. "Are you saying that he was strangled?"

"Nah. Bruising would be severe."

"Could he have been strangled in a way to avoid the bruising?"

He thought about it. "I guess he could've been strangled with something soft, like a towel, or maybe choked out, like with a police choke hold. That might show a rupture pattern like this."

"So he could've been choked out, then tossed through the glass."

"Hey, you're saying it, I'm not. We're just speculating."

"But it's possible."

"It's possible the guy swallowed wrong, started coughing, then lost his balance and went through the glass."

I didn't say anything.

"But, yeah, he could've been choked out, too."

I hung up, then called Mrs. Louise Earle. Her answering machine answered, and I said, "Mrs. Earle, this is Elvis Cole. If you're there, would you pick up, please?

We need to talk." I was hoping to catch her before she started her day. I was hoping to convince her to see me.

No one picked up.

"Mrs. Earle, if Angela Rossi or any other police officer threatened you, I wish you would've told me. I'd sure like to hear about it, now."

Still no answer.

I hung up, then once more made the drive to Olympic Park. If I couldn't get her on the phone, I would try to see her in person. If she wasn't home, I would wait. What better way for an unemployed detective to fill his day?

The streets were still heavy with morning traffic, and the day was bright and hot, but a marine cloud cover had rolled across the basin that made the light seem sourceless and somehow disorienting and had charged the air with a kind of vague dampness. It was as if the sun had vanished and the landscape was lit by a weird kind of indirect lighting that made Los Angeles take on a 1950s tract-home fluorescent reality.

I parked two houses down from Louise Earle's, walked back, and rang her bell exactly as I had done yesterday. Still no answer. I stepped through the dozens of plants and peeked through the gap between the curtains of the same front window. What I could see of the room appeared unchanged from yesterday. Hmm. It was twenty-five minutes after nine, and I stood at the edge of Louise Earle's porch and wondered what I should do. The neighborhood looked calm and ordinary; maybe Louise Earle had simply run to the market and would soon be back. Of course, even it she wasn't back soon, it didn't matter a whole hell of a lot. Such are the joys of unemployment.

I went out to my car, put up the roof to cut the sun, and waited. It was hot, and, as the sun rose, it grew hotter. Sweat leaked out of my hairline, and my shirt stuck to my chest and back. A couple of Hispanic kids pedaled by on mountain bikes, both kids sucking on Big Gulps. A thin brown dog trotted behind them, the dog's tongue hanging from its mouth. The dog looked hot, too, and was probably wishing one of the kids would drop his drink. A Carrier Air Conditioning van pulled into a drive on the next block. Probably making an emergency call. An elderly man came down the sidewalk a few minutes later, covering his head with a *Daily News* the way you would if it was raining and you were trying to stay dry.

Two of the three girls showed up in their Volkswagen Beetle, pulled into their friend's drive, and honked. Guess it was too hot to go to the door. The third girl came out with her bag and an orange beach towel and jumped into the Beetle. As they drove away, they waved, and I waved back. Guess the third girl had noticed me when she was watching for her friends. People came and went, and when they did they raced between air conditioned cars and air conditioned homes at a dead run. No one stayed in the heat any longer than they had to, except, of course, for displaced private eyes working on a slow case of dehydration.

Louise Earle still had not returned two hours and twenty-one minutes later, when a very thin white woman wearing an enormous sun hat emerged from the house next door and crossed her yard to Louise Earle's porch. I made her for her late seventies, but she might've been older. She rang the bell, then peered through Louise Earle's window just as I had done. She tromped around to the side of the house, came back with a watering can, and began watering the plants. I got out of the car and went up to her. "Pardon me, ma'am, but Mrs. Earle doesn't wish to be disturbed." The detective resorts to subterfuge.

She stopped the watering and squinted at me. "And who are you?"

I showed her my license. You show them a license and everything looks official. "The news people were bothering her, so I've been hired to keep them away."

She made a little sniff and continued with the watering. Guess she didn't give too much of a damn whether I was official or not. "Well, my name is Mrs. Eleanor Harris and I can assure you that Louise Earle does not consider me a bother. We've been friends for forty years."

I nodded, trying to seem understanding. "Then you must've seen how awful the news people were."

The stern look softened and she resumed the watering. "Aren't they always, though. You watch the way these people on television act and you wonder how they can live with themselves. All that smug attitude." She made a little shiver. "That Geraldo Rivera. That horrible little man on Channel Two. Ugh." She shook her head in disgust and the stern look came back. "You should've been here yesterday. Yesterday is when people were trying to bother her."

"They were?"

She squinted harder. "You know, one of them looked an awful lot like you."

"I came by yesterday to introduce myself, but she wasn't home. I came with my partner, a tall man with dark glasses."

The squint relaxed, and she nodded. "Well, you and your partner weren't the only ones. There were others. One of them even tried to get into her house."

I looked at her. "Who tried to get into her house, Mrs. Harris?"

"Some man." Great. "I remember him because he came three different times. You and your friend came the once. All the different press people came the once."

"What did he look like?"

She made a waving motion. "He was pretty big. You'd better watch out."

"Big." I put my hand a couple of inches above my head. "Like this?"

"Well, not tall, so much. But wide. Much wider than you." She gave me a just-between-you-and-me look. "His arms were so long he looked like a monkey."
Kerris.

"And he was here three times."

She was nodding. "The first time was before you and your friend, then he came back in the afternoon and once more at dusk. When he was here in the afternoon he tried the door and he went around back. He was back there for quite a while, and for all I know he got in. For all I know he did all manner of horrible things in there." She made the little shudder again, equating all manner of horrible things with Geraldo Rivera and the little man on Channel Two. "It's a good thing Louise went away."

"No one told me that she'd gone away."

Mrs. Harris continued with the watering. "Well, no one told me, either, and that is highly unusual. We've been friends for forty years and I always water her plants when she's away. We watch out for each other. Older people have to."

I looked more closely at the plants. Some of the leaves were wilting and the soil was dry and beginning to crack. "Do you know where I can find her?"

Mrs. Harris continued with the watering and did not answer.

I said, "Mrs. Harris, I can't keep people away from her if I'm here and she's somewhere else. Do you see?"

The water can wavered, and then Mrs. Harris looked around at the drying plants and seemed lost. She shook her head. "She always calls when she goes away. Why wouldn't she call?"

I waited.

Mrs. Harris said, "I saw her leave and it just wasn't like her, let me tell you. It was the day before yesterday, the evening after all those horrible people were here, and she just walked away."

I thought about it. "Could she have gone to visit Mr. Lawrence?"

"Not walking. Mr. Lawrence would always come in the car."

"Do you know where Mr. Lawrence lives?" I thought I might drive over.

"I'm afraid I don't. I saw her from the window,

dressed very nicely and carrying her bag, walking right up this street, and in all this heat, too." She made her lips into a thin, wrinkled line. She was holding the can with both hands, and both hands were twisting on the handle. "I came out and called after her. I said, 'Louise, it's too hot for all of that, you'll catch a stroke,' but I guess she didn't hear." The thin lips were pressing together. Worried. "People our age are very sensitive to this heat."

"Yes, ma'am. And she didn't call."

Mrs. Harris looked at me with wet, frightened eyes. "You don't think she's mad at me, do you? We've been friends for forty years, and I just don't know what I'd do if she was mad at me."

"No, ma'am. I don't think she's mad." I was wondering why she might be in such a hurry that she would just walk away.

"But why wouldn't she call? I always water her plants."

"I don't know, Mrs. Harris. Maybe she was just trying to get away from the press. You know how horrible they are."

Her eyes brightened a bit, drawing a little hope. "Yes. Yes, I'm sure that must be it."

"I'm sure she'll be back soon."

The ancient eyes finally smiled, and she turned back to the plants. "When you find her, you'll keep them away from her, won't you? It must be awful, having people like that around."

"Yes, ma'am. I'll take good care."

I helped Mrs. Harris water the remainder of Louise

Earle's plants, and then I went back to my car, wondering why Kerris had come three times, and wondering if his coming around had had anything to do with her going away. If he had come here three times, that meant he very much wanted to see Louise Earle. Three times was a pattern, and if the pattern maintained, he might return again today. Of course, he might not, but I still didn't have a whole lot else to do.

I went back to my car, drove four blocks to a 7-Eleven, bought two large bottles of chilled Evian water, then drove back to Louise Earle's, parked on the next block behind the Carrier van so that Eleanor Harris couldn't watch me, and continued to wait.

Exactly twelve minutes after I pulled up behind the van and turned off my car, Stan Kerris returned, but did not stop. He was driving a Mercedes SL300, and this time he slowly cruised the block, peering at Louise Earle's house, maybe hoping to see if she was home. I copied his tag number, then pulled out the little Canon and took four quick snaps just as he turned the corner.

The Mercedes was small and black, and I was hoping that Jonna Lester would recognize it.

25

I drove south to a Fast-Foto in a minimall on Jefferson Boulevard about six blocks west of USC. A Persian kid was alone in the place, working at the photo processing machine. He said, "I'll be with you in a moment."

"I don't have a moment. I'll pay you twenty bucks if you stop what you're doing and take care of me now."

He eyed me like maybe I was pulling his leg, but he got up and came to the counter. I put the film on the counter between us. "There are only four exposures on the roll. I've got to make a call. If they're done when I get back, you get the twenty."

He wet his lips. "What size?"

"Whatever's fastest."

I used a pay phone in the parking lot to call Angela Rossi at home. She didn't answer her phone; her machine got it. Screening. "Detective Rossi, it's Elvis Cole. I think I might have something."

She picked up before I finished saying it. She sounded tired, but then she probably hadn't slept last night.

I told her where I was and what I was doing and what I had seen. I said, "Do you want a piece of it?"

"Yes." She said it without hesitation and without fear, the way someone would say it when they were still in the game.

"I have to show the pictures to Jonna Lester, first. Call Joe. Have Tomsic call Anna Sherman in the DA's office. If this is going where I think, everything will begin to happen very quickly."

"I'll be ready."

"I'll bet you will."

I hung up, then called Jonna Lester. She answered on the second ring, and I told her that I was on my way to see her.

She said, "But me and Dorrie was just goin' to the mall!"

"Go to the mall after. This is important, Jonna. *Please.*" The detective stoops to begging.

"Oh, all right." Long and drawn out and whiny. "Dorrie wants to meet you. I told her you were really cute." Then she giggled.

I hung up and closed my eyes, thinking that only twenty-four hours ago she'd found her husband impaled on glass. Man. I called the information operator last, and asked if they had a listing for Mr. Walter Lawrence. They did not.

The Persian kid was waiting at the counter when I went back inside. He had the four shots waiting, too. Fast-Foto, all right. He said, "That's all you wanted?" You could see the Mercedes clearly in three of the four pictures. You could see Kerris clearly enough to recognize him.

"That's all."

I paid him for the developing, gave him the extra twenty, then drove hard to the freeway and made my way across town to Jonna Lester. She and her friend, Dorrie, were waiting for me in a cloud of hash smoke so thick that I tried not to breathe. Jonna Lester giggled. "Y'see. I tol' you he was cute."

Dorrie giggled, too.

Dorrie looked so much like Jonna that they might've been clones. Same shorts, same top, same clear plastic clogs and dark blue nail polish. Same gum. Dorrie sat on the couch and grinned at me with wide, vacant eyes while I showed the pictures to Jonna. I said, "Have you ever seen this car?"

She nodded and popped her gum. "Oh, yeah. That's the guy James went to see." She didn't even have to think about it.

"The man at the Mayfair?"

"Uh-huh."

"The man who gave James a large paper bag?"

"Yup."

Dorrie said, "You wanna get high an' fuck?"

I went to the phone without asking and called Angela Rossi, who answered on the first ring. "A man named Stan Kerris met with James Lester twenty-three days ago, eight days before Lester phoned the hotline. Stan Kerris works for Jonathan Green. I think we can build a case that these guys have fabricated evidence and set you up."

Angela Rossi said, "That sonofabitch."

"Yes."

26

We agreed to meet on the second floor of Greenblatt's Delicatessen at the eastern end of the Sunset Strip at three that afternoon.

Angela Rossi was pacing in the parking lot behind Greenblatt's when I pulled up at two minutes before three. Rossi was wearing black Levi's and a blue cotton T-shirt and metallic blue Persol sunglasses. She was pacing with her arms crossed and her head down, and when she stopped to wait for me, she scuffed at the fine gravel on the tarmac with her shoes. I said, "Didn't you think I'd show?"

Rossi shook her head. "Too wired to sit. I think I'm going to vomit."

"Is Sherman here?"

"Yeah. She's not happy about it, and she's not happy about me being here."

I followed Rossi in past the deli counter and up the stairs to the dining room. This late in the afternoon Greenblatt's was mostly empty. Earlier, the upstairs dining room had probably been filled with wannabe television writers and ninety-year-old regulars and Sunset

Strip habitués, but not now. Now, the only civilians were a couple of young guys with mushroom cuts and an African-American woman sitting alone with *People* magazine. Everybody else was cops.

Linc Gibbs, Pete Bishop, Dan Tomsic, and Anna Sherman were sitting at a table as far from everyone else as possible. Gibbs had coffee, and Bishop and Tomsic had iced tea. Anna Sherman didn't have anything, and she was seated with her back to the restaurant, probably because she was concerned about being recognized. Tomsic said, "Here they are."

Gibbs and Bishop turned, but Anna Sherman didn't. I hadn't met Gibbs and Bishop before. Tomsic introduced us, but before he was finished, Anna Sherman said, "I want to make it clear that the only reason I'm here is because Linc and I have a history, and he's asked me to listen. I make no claims that anything said here is off the record. Is that clear?"

Tomsic scowled. "It's great you're on the right side in this."

Linc said, "Dan."

Tomsic crossed his arms and leaned back, his mouth a hard slash. Nothing like having everyone work to the same end.

Linc Gibbs hooked a thumb toward me. "As I understand it, we're here to discuss possible criminal wrongdoing on the part of the attorneys involved in Teddy Martin's defense. Is that it?"

"Yes. I believe that Jonathan Green or agents working on his behalf fabricated the James Lester evidence. I believe that Lester was in on it. I suspect that they also coerced Louise Earle into changing her story, but that's only a suspicion. I haven't been able to locate Mrs. Earle to ask her about it."

Anna Sherman pooched her lips into a knot. She was leaning forward on her elbows, arms crossed.

Gibbs said, "I thought you were working for these people."

"I quit yesterday."

Anna Sherman raised her eyebrows, saying let's hear it.

I said, "James Lester's real name was Stuart Langolier. Eight years ago, he was represented on a grand theft beef in Santa Barbara by Elliot Truly. That's prior association."

Sherman looked impatient. "Green's office notified us about that. It's even been on the news."

"James Lester's original call to Green's hotline was logged eleven days ago. Eighteen days ago, Jonna Lester followed James to a Mayfair Market where she saw him meet this man." I handed her the three snapshots that I'd taken of the black Mercedes. She looked at them.

Linc Gibbs frowned. "Looks familiar."

"Stan Kerris. He's the chief investigator for Green's office. She saw Kerris and Lester speak, then Kerris passed a shopping bag to Lester, who drove away."

Tomsic said, "Man."

Anna Sherman glanced at me, and Pete Bishop made a tiny smile. Gibbs held out a hand, and Sherman passed him the first of the three pictures, then the second. She stared at the third. "Jonna Lester identified him?"

"Yes. Green hired me to check out the allegations

against Detective Rossi, then run down a series of tips he'd received via the reward hotline, one of which was from James Lester. I checked out Louise Earle and the allegations, and Rossi came up clean. I reported that to Jonathan Green, and he seemed to accept it."

Sherman chewed at the inside of her cheek as if she was thinking about leaving.

I tapped the photo she was still holding. "I took these photographs this morning outside Louise Earle's home. A neighbor saw Kerris visit Louise Earle's home three times yesterday, and I saw him there today. When I spoke with Mrs. Earle a week ago, everything she told me confirmed Rossi's version of her son's arrest and the subsequent LAPD investigation. Now she's suddenly changed her story and Kerris is living on her porch. First Lester, now Louise Earle. I think there's a connection."

Sherman passed the final photograph to Lincoln Gibbs and began ticking her right index fingernail on the table. "All right. What else do you have?"

"When the James Lester story hit the news, I wanted to stay after Pritzik and Richards, which would've been the natural thing to do, but Green had me work a dog and pony with the press. I now believe that it was a media manipulation to make Louise Earle's changing her story more credible to the public."

Bishop said, "I thought you were the guy who got her to change her story."

I shook my head. "That's part of the big lie. I saw her one time, and at that time everything she said confirmed Rossi's story. Three days later Stan Kerris pays her a visit and everything changes, and the next thing I know

Green holds a press conference and says that I've turned up evidence to prove Rossi rotten. The wonder boy who showed up the cops and found James Lester now ferrets out the truth from the intimidated mother. You see?"

Anna Sherman continued ticking the nail. She stared at the table and made her mouth the small knot again. Then she looked up and shook her head. "All of you must be out of your minds."

Tomsic threw up his hands. "What does *that* mean?"

The two kids with the mushroom cuts and the African-American woman looked over, and Lincoln Gibbs zapped Tomsic with a look that must've come from the days before he started affecting the professor image, flashing street eyes, mess-with-me-and-I'll-choke-your-eyes out.

Tomsic settled back.

Sherman said, "It means that if my office or the LAPD launched an investigation into Jonathan Green at this time based on this kind of bullshit evidence it would be a public relations nightmare."

Gibbs said, "This is worth something, Anna. You know it is. You can't just ignore it."

She leaned toward him, ticking off the points. "I spoke with Jonna Lester and I know her to be a hash head. Jonna Lester doesn't know if it was eighteen days ago or twenty-eight or just eight, which is exactly what Stan Kerris would say *if* he admitted to having met James Lester, which he almost certainly won't." She ticked another point. "Then, if he did admit to such a meeting, he would say that it was a preliminary interview conducted prior to Mr. Cole's being assigned the follow-up, and, in case you've forgotten, Mr. Lester isn't around to dispute that statement."

I said, "Did you review Lester's autopsy report?"

"There was no sign of foul play."

"That isn't quite correct. Someone who was good could've choked out Lester, then put him through the glass."

Sherman's nostrils flared and she closed her eyes. "Could have."

"I know you can't go to court with that one, Sherman, but it fits with the theory. You really think Lester just happened to cut his own throat?"

Tomsic said, "Subpoena Lester's phone records, and pull Green's records, too. See who was calling who and when they were talking."

Sherman made a hissing sound.

Angela Rossi said, "No one's forgotten about Pritzik and Richards, either."

Anna Sherman shook her head. "You people are talking about accusing an attorney of Jonathan Green's stature of fabricating evidence without any substantive proof to back it up. With even less proof, you want me to accuse him of murder. Ask yourself this: why would Jonathan Green risk his career and his reputation and his freedom to falsify evidence for one client? The press is going to ask that, and you don't have an answer because it doesn't make sense." She glanced from cop to cop, finally coming back to me. It was exactly what I had asked Pike. "All you have are some unseemly coincidences and the testimony of a hash head. Jonathan Green will charge us with harassment, and he will bring us before the state bar, and I, for one, am tired of getting my ass handed to me in the *L. A. Times* every day."

I said, "Is that it?"

She nodded.

I looked at Rossi. I looked back at Anna Sherman. I said, "Getting our asses kicked in the press is how we define truth in the American legal system?"

Anna Sherman stood. "My boss is being pressured to drop the charges against Teddy Martin. I've been fighting him on it because I want to see this through, but I don't think he has the balls. I think he'll give in because he has arrived at his own personal definition of justice. He defines it as political survival." Anna Sherman didn't say anything more for a time, then she looked directly at Rossi. "I'm sorry, but this meeting is now over." She tucked her purse under her arm and walked out.

Tomsic slapped the formica hard, and Bishop made a soft whistling sound through his teeth. Angela Rossi had pushed her fists between her legs onto her chair and gently rocked. Finally, Bishop said, "So where are we, Linc?"

Lincoln Gibbs took a breath. "You heard her. The district attorney's office is not interested in pursuing this investigation."

Tomsic said, "That's bullshit." He jabbed the finger at me. "Cole's onto something! These bastards are over the line!"

Gibbs made his voice harder. "They will not pursue this line, Sergeant. That's the end of it."

Tomsic wasn't letting it go. Now he was waving both hands. "So Green can do whatever? He can murder people? He can rob banks? We just say, oh, we'll look bad if we do something?"

Lincoln Gibbs's nostrils were wide and hard and you could hear him breathe. But then the breathing calmed and he looked at Rossi. Sad. "Sometimes we have the worst job in the world. High-priced, sleazebag shysters make millions getting off murderers and dope dealers and the dregs of this society, but they are wrong, and we are right. And if we have to take some bullets along the way, then we take'm." He reached across the table and squeezed Angie's arm. "Goes with the job."

Tomsic said, "That's bullshit."

Linc Gibbs nodded. "Of course it's bullshit, Sergeant, but it's where we are." He looked at me. "Thanks, Cole. It didn't pan out, but we owe you for the effort."

Bishop got up, then Gibbs. Gibbs told Tomsic to come with them, and he told Angela Rossi he thought she should probably go home. He told her not to worry. He said that they weren't going to let it go, and that they would keep digging into the LeCedrick Earle thing and that they wouldn't abandon her. She nodded and got up and went with them, but she looked abandoned to me. Of course, maybe it was just my imagination.

I sat alone at the empty table for another three minutes, wondering what to do next and having no great surges of inspiration. I think I was feeling abandoned, too, but I probably wasn't feeling as abandoned as Angela Rossi.

I went down the stairs and out the back of Greenblatt's to my car. Anna Sherman was sitting in the passenger seat, waiting for me. A bead of sweat worked its way down along her temple and her cheek. She said, "It's hotter than hell out here."

I stared at her. "Yes. It is."

She ran her fingers along the dash. She tapped the shift lever. "This is a classic, isn't it?"

"Yeah."

"It's a Corvette?"

"Yeah. A Stingray." I looked where she was looking. I touched where she was touching. "I wanted one when I was a kid, and a few years ago I had the opportunity to buy this one, so I did. I couldn't afford it, but I bought it anyway."

She nodded. "I should do something like that. Something crazy." She ran her fingers along the console. "When was it made?"

"Nineteen sixty-six."

"God. I was ten years old." She looked older.

I wanted to start the engine and turn on the air conditioner, but I didn't.

Anna Sherman said, "Three months ago an attorney named Lucas Worley was arrested in a drug sting in Santa Monica. He wasn't the target. He just happened to be there." She tapped my glove box. "I put his address in here."

I waited.

"Worley has a heroin problem. He'll buy a kilo every now and then, then cut it and sell it to his friends to cover his costs. Worley was a junior litigator in Green's office."

I smiled. "Was."

"Green had the case handled to minimize bad publicity for his firm, so Worley was able to cop a first offense probation plea."

"Is Worley still with the firm?"

She shook her head. "Resigned. I guess that was part of the deal." She finally looked at me. It was the first time she'd looked at me since I got into the car. "Worley was a tort litigator. That means he worked in Green's contract department. He would've had access to retainer agreements and to the contracts that Green had with his clients."

"Is he employed?"

She made a little dismissive shrug. "Probably dealing full time, but I don't know."

"So you think there's something to this."

She touched the dash again, watching her fingers move along the gentle lines. "You always follow the money." She shook her head and made a little smile. "I've been doing this for twelve years. I've prosecuted hundreds of cases, and I have learned that people do crime for only two reasons: sex and money. There are no other motives."

"What about power and revenge?"

"That's just sex and money under aliases." The tiny smile again. "If you're right, and if Jonathan Green is willing to break the law, then he's doing it for sex or money."

I was starting to like Anna Sherman. I was starting to like her just fine. "Do you think Worley will cooperate?"

She shrugged. "Lucas Worley is a piece of shit. He sells dope because he likes it. He likes the people, he likes the scene. He says that it's a step up from practicing law." She looked tired. "Maybe he's right."

I said, "Hey."

She looked at me.

"I'll tell you what I told Rossi. Don't give up. The good part of the system outweighs the bad. We just have to fix the bad."

Anna Sherman got out of the car, closed the door, then looked in at me. She said, "This conversation never happened. If you say it did, and if you say I gave you Worley, I'll deny it and sue you for slander. Is that clear?"

"Clear."

She walked away without another word. I opened the glove box and found a plain white sheet of notepaper with Lucas Worley's address written in anonymous block letters.

27

I stopped for roses. I bought a dozen red long-stems, plus a single daisy, then went to a wine shop I know for a bottle of Dom Perignon and an ounce of Beluga caviar. While the clerk was bagging the champagne I used their phone to make a reservation at Musso & Frank for eight o'clock. When I was off the phone, the clerk grinned at me. "Special date?"

"Very special."

He laughed. "Are there any other kind?" Cynic.

I drove home hard, hoping that I would get there before Lucy and Ben. I did. I put the flowers in the refrigerator and the Dom Perignon and three flute glasses in the freezer. The Dom Perignon was cold, but I wanted it colder. I hard-boiled an egg, minced an onion, then minced the egg. I put the egg, the onion, and some capers in three little Japanese serving plates, covered them with Saran Wrap, then arranged the plates on a matching tray with the caviar and put the tray in the refrigerator next to the flowers. I put out Carr's Table Water Crackers, then phoned Joe Pike and told him about Lucas

Worley. Pike said, "You think he might know something?"

"I think he might, or, if he doesn't, he might be able to help us find someone who does."

How do you want to play it?"

I told him.

Joe was silent for a time, then said, "How about we bring in Ray Depente? Ray would be effective on a guy like Worley."

"You think?"

"Ray could get a corpse to talk."

I told him that would be fine. I told him that I would meet them outside Worley's place early tomorrow, and when I was done, Joe said, "Is it going any better with Lucy?"

"Not yet, but soon. I'm about to turn on the charm."

"Why don't you try working it out, instead." Mr. Sensitive.

I hung up, then ran upstairs to finish getting ready. I shaved, showered, put on a jacket and tie, then ran downstairs and took the Dom Perignon out of the freezer. I wanted it cold, not frozen.

When Lucy and Ben pulled into the carport I was waiting at the door when they came through with shopping bags from Saks and Bottega Veneta and Giorgio and Pierre Deux. Lucy looked tired until she saw me, and then she looked surprised. I held out the flowers. "My God, you're beautiful."

Ben smiled so wide I thought his face would turn inside out.

Lucy looked at the flowers. She glanced at me and then the flowers again, and then back to me. Her hands were still full of shopping bags. "Oh, a daisy."

I put the shopping bags on the dining room table, then opened the Dom Perignon. I poured apple juice for Ben. "We have champagne. We have caviar. Then we will have dinner at Musso & Frank."

She said, "The restaurant in Hollywood?"

"Dashiell Hammett fell in love with Lillian Hellman there." I gave her a glass of the Dom Perignon. "It was a love that changed their lives, and endured for as long as they lived."

Lucy seemed embarrassed. "You're being so nice."

I said, "Ben. Would you give your mother and me a moment alone, please?"

Ben giggled. "You want me to amscray?"

"Yes, Ben, I want you to amscray."

Ben amscrayed into the living room. When the TV came on and Agent Mulder started talking about something that ate five human livers every thirty years, I took the flowers from Lucy and put them aside. I put aside her champagne glass, too, and held her upper arms and looked into her eyes. "You have two more nights in Los Angeles. I want those nights to be easy for you. It's okay with me if you'd like to move to a hotel."

Lucy stared at me for ten heartbeats, then shook her head. "I'm exactly where I want to be."

"I know that you're having trouble with your ex-husband. I know that he has a problem with you and Ben staying here. I want you to know that I'll support you in anything you want to do."

Lucy sighed, and glanced toward the living room. "Ben."

"Don't blame Ben. I am a detective, Lucille. I know all and see all."

"Darlene."

"Does it matter?"

She sighed again, then leaned forward to rest her forehead against my chest. "Oh, Studly, there is so much going on right now. I'm sorry."

I put my arms around her and held her. "You don't have anything to be sorry for."

She looked up and her eyes were rimmed red and wet. "I feel like I've ruined our time together."

"You haven't."

"I've let him intrude, and that's not fair to you or to me. I didn't tell you, and that is not the quality of honesty that I want in our relationship."

"You were trying to protect me."

She stepped back and looked into my eyes as if she were searching for something faraway and hard to see, something that she feared might change even as she saw it. "There's so much going on right now. You just don't know." She took a breath, then let it out. "I really need to talk about this."

"Then let's talk."

She took my hand and led me out onto the deck into the cooling night air, with the last breath of day fading in the west. She held my right hand in both of hers and said, "There are things you need to know."

"I don't need to know anything about you, Lucille."

"I'm not going to tell you deep dark secrets about myself. I don't *have* any secrets."

"Shucks." Trying to lighten the moment with a little humor.

Lucy frowned and looked away. "These are things I need to say as much to help me get them straight as for you to be aware of what's going on. Do you see that?"

"Okay."

She looked back. "There are things happening between me and my ex-husband that I should've told you about, but didn't."

I nodded, letting her talk.

"Not because they're secret or because I wanted to keep anything from you, but because I resent the intrusion and did not want these things to impact upon our time together. I did not want *him* to share this time with us." The other presence. "But I let him get to me, and he has intruded and that is not fair to either me or to you and I apologize."

I started to tell her that she didn't have to apologize, but she raised a hand, stopping me.

I sighed. "Okay. I accept."

"I'm not asking for advice. I'm an adult, I'm an attorney, and I will handle this. Okay?"

I nodded.

"I mean, God, I'm paid to advise other people, am I not?"

I nodded again. Getting a lot of nod practice tonight.

She said, "Richard has moved back to Baton Rouge." Richard was her ex-husband. He'd been living in Shreveport for the past three years, and, in the time that I'd known Lucy, she'd mentioned him exactly twice. He, too, was an attorney. "I've encouraged Ben to develop a relationship with his father, but Richard has taken it beyond that. He phones me at my office; he drops around my house unannounced; he invites himself to outings that I've planned with Ben; he's resurrected his friendship with a lot of the people at my firm. He has systematically reinserted himself into my life, and I do not like it."

"You feel invaded."

She made a brief, flickering smile. "Studly, I feel like Normandy Beach."

I said, "Joe likes you. Joe would probably fly down and have a talk with him."

The smile flickered again and, for just a moment, Lucy laughed. The tension was easing. "Perhaps it will come to that." The laugh and the smile faded then, and she said, "When he found out that Ben and I were going to stay here, with you, instead of a hotel, he became abusive. He criticized my judgment and told me that I was setting a bad example for Ben and demanded that I leave Ben with him."

I said, "Luce?"

She looked at me.

I opened my mouth but did not speak. My mouth felt dry and there was a kind of faraway ringing and my fingers and legs suddenly went cold. There are those times when intellect fails us. There are those moments when the modern man fades to a shadow and something from the brain stem reasserts itself, and in that moment the joking is gone and we frighten ourselves with our dark potential. I said, quite normally, quite conversationally, "What do you mean, abusive? Did he touch you?"

She shook her head, and then she placed both palms on my chest. "Oh, no. No, Elvis. And if he had I promise you fully that I would've had him arrested so fast he would've had whiplash."

I nodded again, but now the nods weren't funny. My fingers and legs began to tingle with returning blood.

She said, "I thought it was past, but it isn't. That's why Darlene called. He's been phoning the office and leaving messages on my machine at home, and then I got upset even more that I had let him get me upset in the first place. Do you see?"

My breathing had evened out and the ringing was gone. I nodded. "He pushed your buttons."

"Yes."

"He exerted a kind of power over you that you thought was behind you."

She said, "I'm so sorry you thought it was you, or that you had something to do with this. Oh, sweetie, it wasn't you at all. It was me."

"It's okay, Luce. It's really okay."

She rubbed my chest again and stared up at me because there was more. "Everything is complicated because I haven't been happy at the firm or with where I am in my life, and I don't know what I'm going to do about it."

I looked at her, and my heart began to thud.

"It started before I met you. It started even before Richard moved back."

I looked at her some more, and the night air was suddenly sparkling with a kind of expectant electricity.

"I don't know if I want to stay at the firm. I don't even know if I want to stay in Baton Rouge." She shook her head, glancing past me at Ben, glancing out at the warm house lights in the canyon. She finally looked back at me. "Do you know what I'm saying?"

"Would you consider coming out here?" My heart was thudding so loudly I wondered if the people across the canyon could hear it.

"I don't know." She took a deep breath and rubbed my chest again. "I guess I just needed to tell you that I don't know." She tried to make a joke. "Damn, and I thought I was too young for menopause."

I nodded.

"I'm feeling kind of stupid right now. It just seemed important to tell you."

I touched her lips. I kissed her, with the center of my heart. "I love you, Lucille. Rotten ex-husband or no. Long distance relationship or no. Do you know that?"

Her eyes grew wet again, and she ran her hand along the line of my shoulder. She touched my tie. "You look so nice."

I smiled.

"You went to so much trouble with the champagne and caviar."

I said, "Would you like to go eat? We still have time." They would hold the reservation. I was sure I could talk them into holding the reservation.

She took a breath, then let it out and carefully looked up at me. "What I would like to do is stay home with my two guys. What I would like is to order a pizza and drink your wonderful champagne and play Clue."

I grinned. "You want to play Clue?"

She was suddenly very serious. "I just want to be with you, Elvis. I just want to relax and enjoy being here. Do you know?"

I kissed her fingers. "I know."

I took off my jacket and tie, and we ordered Domino's pizza. We made a large Italian salad with pepperocinis and garbanzo beans and fresh garlic while we waited for the pie. When the pizza came, we drank the Dom Perignon and ate the pizza between bites of Beluga caviar mixed with capers and minced onion, and played Clue until very late that night. There was a smile on Lucy's face that did not leave, and made the room feel light and warm and explosive with energy. Ben laughed so hard that he blew soda through his nose.

It was as if the other presence was no longer with us, as if by exposing the other it vanished the way a shadow will when exposed to light.

We played until very late, and when Ben went to bed, Lucy and I finished the last of the champagne, and then she followed me upstairs into a night filled with warmth and love and laughter.

he next morning I left the house as the eastern sky bloomed with the onrushing sun and drove to Lucas Worley's condominium on a one-way street just off Gretna Green Way in Brentwood. Gretna Green is a connecting street between Sunset Boulevard and San Vicente, lined with apartment houses and condominium complexes and some very nice single-family homes, but in the dim time just before sunrise the traffic was sparse and the neighborhood still. It was a wonderful time of the day for lurking.

Worley's condo was set between the street and a service alley in a lush green setting. They were nice condos, large and airy and stylishly ideal for former on-the-rise young attorneys turned dope dealers. I slow-cruised the street first, then turned down the alley and idled past the rear. Each condominium had a double carport at its back protected by an overhead wrought iron door, and Worley's was filled with a gunmetal blue Porsche 911 sporting a vanity plate. The vanity plate read EZLIVN. Guess the loss of his day job hadn't inhibited his lifestyle.

When I reached the end of the alley, Joe Pike and Ray

Depente materialized out of the murk and drifted silently to my car. Ray was wearing a black suit over a white shirt with a thin black bow tie. I said, "When did you go Muslim?"

Ray looked at himself and smiled. "Joe said you wanted scary. You tell me anything a white boy's more scared of than a Muslim with a hardon?"

Ray Depente was an inch taller than Joe, but slimmer, with mocha skin and gray-flecked hair and the ramrod-straight bearing of a career Marine, which he had been. For the better part of twenty-two years Ray Depente had taught unarmed combat at Camp Pendleton, in Oceanside, California, before retiring to open a karate school in South Central Los Angeles. Now, he taught children the art of self-respect for ten cents a lesson, and instructed Hollywood actors how to look tough on screen for five hundred dollars an hour. The one paid for the other.

Ray extended his hand and we shook as he said, "Haven't seen you in a while, my friend. Better get your butt down to my place before you get out of shape."

"Too many tough guys down there, Ray. Some actor might beat me up."

Ray smiled wider. "Way I hear things been going for you, I guess it could happen." The smile fell away. "We got a plan for Mr. Dope Dealer, or are we just gonna stand around in the dark waitin' to be discovered?" The eastern sky was cooling from pink to violet to blue. Traffic was picking up out on Gretna, and we could hear garbage trucks and cars pulling out of driveways as people left for work. Pretty soon housekeepers would be trudging past to their day work.

Joe tilted his head toward the Porsche. "Worley's been inside since eight-thirty last night."

"Is he alone?"

"Yes."

I said, "He's got to leave sooner or later. When he leaves we'll go in the house and find his stash. We find the stash, we'll have some leverage."

Ray said, "What if he doesn't have a stash?"

I shrugged. "Then we'll live with him until he scores."

Ray stared at the Porsche. "Joe said this guy was a lawyer."

"Yep. Until he got caught with the dope."

Ray looked at the nice car and the nice condo and shook his head. "Asshole."

Joe and Ray vanished back into the thinning shadows, and I pulled out of the alley and down the little street to Gretna Green. I parked beneath a Moroccan gumball tree with an easy eyes-forward view of Lucas Worley's street and waited while the air slowly filled with a mist of brightening light and early morning commuter traffic increased and the city began its day.

At twelve minutes after nine that morning the 911 nosed out onto Gretna and turned south, heading for San Vicente. Worley was a pudgy guy with tight curly hair cut short and close-set eyes and a stud in his left ear. He was wearing a tattered dark gray sweatshirt with no sleeves, and his arms were thin and hairy. Probably just running out for coffee.

I left the Corvette, trotted across Gretna and down

along the little street to Worley's condo, where Pike and Ray were waiting at the front door. Pike already had the door open.

Lucas Worley's condominium was all high-angled ceilings and stark white walls and rented furniture of the too low, too wide, and too ugly variety. A fabric and plastic ficus sat in the L of two full-sized sofas, and a big-screen TV filled one wall. A stack of stereo equipment ran along the adjoining wall with what looked to be a couple of thousand CDs scattered over the floor and the furniture and on top of the big screen. I guess neatness wasn't one of Lucas Worley's strengths. Framed movie posters from *Easy Rider* and *To Live and Die in L.A.* hung above the fireplace opposite mediocre lithographs of Jimi Hendrix and Madonna, and the effect was sort of like a nebbish's fantasy of how a high-end life-in-the-fast-lane hipster would live. He even had a lava lamp. Ray said, "Would you look at this?"

A framed Harvard Law School diploma was leaning against the lava lamp.

Ray was shaking his head. Incredulous. "The kids I work with down in South Central bust their asses just to get a high school diploma so they can get away from this shit, and here this fool is with a goddamned ticket from Harvard Law."

I said, "He won't be gone long, Ray. We've got to find the stash."

Ray moved away from the diploma. He glanced back at it twice and sighed as if he'd seen something so incomprehensible that understanding would forever be denied.

I started for the stairs. "I'll take the second floor. You guys search down here."

Pike said, "Don't bother. It's in the tree." Pike was circling the ficus.

I stopped at the base of the stairs. "What do you mean, it's in the tree? How would you know that?"

"Because it's where a lightweight would put it." Pike grabbed the ficus and yanked it up hard. The ficus came out of its pot, and there was the dope stash. Like Pike had sensed it.

Ray and I stared at each other. We stared at Pike. Ray said, "Nawwww."

Pike made a little shrug.

Ray said, "You're pulling our legs. You saw him foolin' in there through the window last night."

Pike angled the flat lenses at Ray. "You think?"

You never know with Pike.

The ficus had covered two Baggies of white powder, one Baggie of brown powder, a metric scale, and assorted drug sales paraphernalia. I told Joe and Ray what I wanted them to do, and when, and then they left. I stayed. I took the dope out of the planter and put it in a neat pile on the coffee table, then replaced the ficus, looked through the scattered CDs until I found something that I liked, put it in the changer, turned on the music, and sat on the couch to wait. The Police. *Reggatta De Blanc.*

Forty-two minutes later, keys worked the lock, the door swung open, and Lucas Worley came halfway through the door before seeing me. He was carrying a newspaper and a Starbucks cup. He looked surprised, but he hadn't yet seen the dope on the table. "What the fuck is this? Who are you?"

"Come inside and close the door, Luke. Can I call you Luke? Or is it Lucas? Lucas seems pretentious." He was a little bit taller than he had looked in the car. His eyes were bright and sharp, and he spoke quickly. You could tell he was used to talking. You could tell he was used to saying bright things and having them appreciated, and you could tell that he thought he was brighter than he really was. Probably where the smugness came from.

He said, "Maybe I'm confused. Isn't this my house? Isn't that my sofa? The only thing that doesn't seem to belong here is you." Showing attitude.

"Look at me, Luke. Do you recognize me?"

"Sure. On television. You're the detective who's working with Jonathan." He closed the door. He was moving slowly. Wary, but trying to be oh-so-cool about it. "How's Jonathan?"

I smiled at him. "Funny you should ask, Luke. Jonathan is why I'm here."

That's when he saw the Baggies. He stared at them for most of an eternity, and then he said, "What's that?" Like he'd never seen them before.

"Here's the deal, Luke. You used to work in Jonathan's contracts department, and I want to know everything there is to know about Jonathan and his relationship to Teddy Martin. You're going to tell me what you know, and then you're going to get me into his office so that I can see for myself. Are we on the same page with that?"

He shook his head as if I'd spoken Somali. "Are you high? I don't know you. Get out of here."

I leaned back and spread my arms along the back of the couch so that my jacket would open and he could see the Dan Wesson.

"Look, I'm not doing anything for you. I'm going to call Jonathan right now. I'm going to tell him what's going on."

"Oh, you'll go along, Luke. Trust me." I pointed at the Baggies with my foot. "You've been a bad boy."

He smiled like he'd decided exactly how he was going to play it out and he knew he could beat me because he was smarter than me. "Is this how you're going to get me to do what you want? You're going to call the police? You figure you can have me bounced for violating proba- tion?"

I shook my head. "No way, Luke. We don't need the police."

He smiled wider and moved past me, going to the phone. "Tell you what. I'll call them for you." He picked up the phone and waved it, showing me just how in control he thought he was. "Because when they get here and pull us in, I promise you that I can beat this nine ways from Monday in court." Waving the phone at the dope. "That's not mine. You're here, you planted it, and you're trying to extort me to screw Jonathan because of the Martin case. Man, Jonathan will have a field day with that one. I can see it now."

I looked disappointed. "You didn't listen, Luke. I'm not going to call the cops. I've already made my call."

Worley frowned and looked uncertain. "Who'd you call?"

Someone knocked at the door.

Lucas Worley suddenly didn't look so sure of himself. "Don't you think you should get that?"

He didn't look at the door. "Who is it?"

Someone knocked again.

I said, "I kinda figured that you wouldn't cooperate, and that if I tried setting you up with the police that you'd find a way to beat it, so I called a guy I know named Gerald DiVega. You know DiVega?"

His mouth formed into a little O, like the name was ringing a bell but he couldn't quite be sure of it.

I went to the door. "Gerald DiVega sells drugs to westside hipsters like yourself. For many years he sold drugs on the streets, like so many other gentlemen of free enterprise, but in the past few years he's chosen to cultivate a more upscale clientele: movie and TV people, music people, lawyers and doctors, the very same people you're selling to with your little pissant business." I opened the door and Ray and Joe stepped in. They were both wearing sunglasses and looking somber. Ray reached under his jacket and drew out a Colt .45 Government model. Joe Pike took out his Python. I said, "This is Mr. X and this is Mr. Y. Mr. D sent them because he doesn't like you cutting in on his clientele."

Ray Depente said, "This the muthuhfuckuh?" He took a black tube from his jacket pocket and screwed it onto the muzzle of the .45 as he said it.

"That's him."

Lucas Worley's eyes went wide, and he took one step

back. "Hey. What is this? What's going on?" Smug was gone. Arrogance had vanished.

Ray and Joe crossed the room like two large, sinuous sharks gliding toward a blood spoor. Ray moved between Worley and the stairs, and Joe moved in from the other side and grabbed Worley's throat hard and rode him down on the couch. When Joe grabbed him, Lucas made a gurgling sound. I said, "I guess you should've called the cops when you had the chance, Luke."

Ray waved the .45 at me. "You can split now, you want. Mr. DiVega says thanks."

"Can't I stay?"

Ray shrugged like it was nothing to him. "Either way."

Lucas Worley's eyes were bulging and his face changed from red to purple. He was clawing at Joe's one hand with both of his, but it was like a child trying to bend steel bars.

Ray jacked a round into the .45, then put the muzzle of the suppressor against Worley's cheek and held out his other hand to shield himself from the blood-splatter that would surely follow and Lucas Worley thrashed and moaned and his bowels and bladder went loose at the same time. Guess the real world wasn't seeming like *Easy Rider* anymore. Guess it wasn't like a movie or a television program. Not much glamor in messing your shorts.

I said, "You guys don't shoot him, yet."

Lucas Worley's eyes rolled toward me.

I walked over and squatted by him to look into the rolling eyes. I said, "I helped Mr. DiVega out a couple of years back, and he owes me. He knows that I want

something from you, and he's willing to play this however I want. You see?"

Lucas Worley was trying to shake his head, trying to
say he wasn't trying to cut in on anyone's trade and
wouldn't do it anymore if only they'd let him live. Of
course, since Joe was strangling him, we couldn't quite
make out the words.

"These gentlemen have orders to kill you unless I tell
them not to."

Ray said, "Kill yo' ass dead." I frowned at Ray over
the top of Worley's head, and Ray shrugged. Overacting.

I said, "So what's it going to be, Luke? You going to
help me out with Jonathan Green, or do I walk out the
door and make these guys happy?"

Lucas Worley gurgled some more.

I said, "I didn't understand you, Luke."

Joe released some of the pressure, and Lucas Worley
croaked, "Anything. I'll do anything."

Ray Depente pressed the gun in harder and looked
angry. "Shit. You mean we don't get to kill the little
muthuhfuckuh?"

"Not yet. But maybe later."

Ray squinted down at the rolling eyes, then withdrew
the gun and stepped back. Joe let Worley go and also
stepped away. Ray said, "You got a pass this time, dips-
hit. But Mr. DiVega be on your ass now, you understand?"

Lucas Worley was frozen on the couch like a squirrel
in front of an onrushing car.

Ray said, "You just retired from the dope dealin' business, didn't you?"

Worley nodded.

Ray said, "You're giving Mr. DiVega your word, and you know what will happen if you break your word, don't you?"

Worley nodded again. I think he was too terrified to speak.

Ray looked at the framed Harvard Law School diploma and shook his head. "Dumb muthuhfuckuh. You oughta be ashamed of yourself."

He put away the .45, then he and Joe Pike walked over to the bar and made themselves a drink.

I said, "I told you that you'd see it my way, Luke. Now go wash off and change your clothes. We've got some work to do."

29

When Lucas Worley was in the shower I looked at Ray Depente. " 'Kill yo' ass dead'?"

"I thought it was very effective."

Joe Pike shook his head. "Samuel L. Jackson."

Ray frowned. "Since when did you become Sir Laurence Olivier?"

Pike's mouth twitched, and he went over to browse through Worley's CDs.

By the time we got Worley out of the shower and dressed and sitting in the living room, it was two-forty that afternoon. Joe and Ray were back in character, Joe standing behind the couch like an ominous shadow, Ray watching ESPN on the big-screen. I said, "Luke, do you have a gun here in your house?"

He was sitting on the couch with his hands in his lap and his hair wet and spikey. He still looked scared, but now he wasn't looking panicked. "Yeah. Up in the nightstand."

Joe drifted up the stairs.

"That the only one, Luke? You wouldn't have any surprises tucked away, would you?"

He shook his head, eyes jumping with the certain knowledge that surprises would get him killed. "That's all. I swear."

"Are you expecting anyone?"

"No."

"No one dropping around to pick up a little smack? No girlfriends? No repairmen?"

"No. Honest." A dope-dealing ex-attorney saying *honest*.

"Okay. I am now going to tell you exactly what I want, and you're going to tell me how to do it. Okay?"

He looked worried. "If I can."

Ray whirled away from the big-screen, loud and angry and snapping, "What did you say?"

Lucas Worley jumped as if he'd been slapped. "I'll tell you how. Sure. Whatever you want."

Ray's eyes narrowed, and he turned back to the big-screen, mumbling.

Joe Pike came back down the stairs with a pistol. "Glock nine."

"Anything else?"

"Nope." He sat by Ray.

I said, "Okay, Luke. Here's my problem. I suspect that your mentor, Mr. Green, is suborning testimony. I think he may even be involved in murder, only I can't figure out why a man in his position and of his stature would risk his ass by so doing. Do you understand that?"

Worley wasn't just looking at me; he was watching my lips move, careful to get every word. He blinked when he realized that I'd quit speaking, then shook his head. "Of course, he wouldn't. That's dumb."

"That's what everyone says."

"It's true. If he's caught he'd be throwing away his career."

I smiled at him. "Sort of like you."

Lucas Worley swallowed, then shrugged. Like he was embarrassed. "Yeah, but I was just a lawyer, and I never liked it much. He's Jonathan Green. He *loves* it."

"Well, you're going to help me find out if it's dumb or not. Would Jonathan enter into a verbal agreement with a client?"

Worley grinned. "You've got to be kidding."

"Okay, so everything would be written."

"Absolutely. But no one is going to admit to a crime on paper. You're not going to find a paper that says 'I will do murder for X dollars.'" He was smiling at the thought of it. "Such a contract isn't enforceable, anyway. You couldn't sue somebody because they didn't perform an illegal act. You'd be incriminating yourself in conspiracy."

"So Jonathan wouldn't put anything in writing that he couldn't support in a civil action."

"Not a chance. No lawyer would." He spread his hands. "Look, you're not going to find anything incriminating there. I promise you. Jonathan isn't that stupid."

"That's not your concern. Your job is to get me access to all the contracts between Teddy and Jonathan. That is the sum total of your value to me." I nodded toward Joe and Ray. "You know that much, don't you?"

The worried look came back. "Hey, I said that I would. We can't just walk in there in the middle of the day. There're people."

"When do the people go home?"

"The office closes at six, but some of them stay late. Christ, we used to work until ten, eleven at night. Sometimes later."

Joe said, "How many people?"

"A few. It's a big office."

I said, "But most of the people go at six?"

"Yeah. There shouldn't be more than eight or nine there later than that."

"You have a card key to get in?"

"Oh, yeah. I kept it."

"How about the elevator to Jonathan's floor?"

"The card key accesses the parking garage, the elevator, everything."

I thought about it. "How long would it take you to get into the files?"

Lucas Worley stared at me about six seconds too long. "I dunno. It could take a while."

Ray Depente pushed up from his seat and drew out the .45 and stalked over like he'd just hit the red line on the biggest bunch of bullshit he'd ever heard. "I'm killin' this fuckwad right goddamned now! Weasely muthuh-fuckin' bullshit, take a while my ass!"

Worley threw himself to the side and covered his head, screaming, "*Twominutes! Icandoitintwominutes, sweartochrist! It'sallondiskandIcangeteverycontractinthe-goddamnedoffice!*"

Ray stood over him, breathing hard and pointing the big .45. Across the room I could see Pike shake his head as he flipped through a magazine. *Modern Living*. Ray smirked and went back to his seat.

I said, "That's better, Luke. I think you and I are going to work this out just fine."

We had Worley describe the layout of the contracts department, and how we could get in and get out, and then we settled in for the afternoon. Pike left for a time, then returned with a small blue gym bag.

We listened to Lucas Worley's CD collection until five forty-five that evening, and then the four of us wedged into Worley's Porsche and drove to Green's building on Sunset. We bypassed the public parking entrance and used Worley's card key to access tenant parking. It was fourteen minutes after six when we worked our way beneath the building, and Worley said, "You see all these cars? There're still plenty of people working."

We found an empty spot as far in the back as possible, pulled in, cut the engine, and waited. Secretaries and office workers and blue-coated security people and attorneys of one stripe or another trickled out of the elevators and, little by little, the offices above us emptied. By seven-forty the trickle had dried and there were only six cars left, every one of which Worley recognized. He said, "The 420 belongs to Deke Kelly and the white Jag belongs to Sharon Lewis. They both work in Contracts. The little Stanza over there works in Contracts, also; I forget the kid's name. He was new. Sharon's assistant."

Pike said, "Contracts is on the third floor."

"That's right. Just like I said." We'd had him describe it five times. He'd even drawn a little map.

I said, "And Jonathan is on the fourth."

Worley nodded. "Yeah, but we won't have to go up

there. All we have to do is go to Contracts. They have everything in their computers."

"What if Jonathan wanted something kept secret?"

Worley shook his head. "We can still access it from Contracts. The whole office is on the same computer net. Jesus, I should know. I helped design the system."

I looked at Pike and Pike shrugged. "Whenever."

Worley looked worried. "But what about the people up there?"

"What about them?"

Worley was looking even more worried. "You aren't going to kill them, are you?"

Ray glared at him. "That up to you. You get outta line, we be killin' people now till next Tuesday."

Pike looked at me and I rolled my eyes. Jesus, what a ham.

I pushed Worley out of the car and we walked in a tight group to the elevator, Pike with the gym bag, Ray with a hand on Worley's shoulder. Our footsteps were loud and gritty. "You said two minutes, and that's all you're going to have, Luke. Don't mess up."

Lucas Worley didn't answer. His eyes were blinking fast, and he kept wetting and rewetting his lips. Fear.

We got into the elevator and rode up to the third floor. If the doors opened and someone we recognized got on, I planned to say that I had come to see Truly and Jonathan and brazen it out, but when the doors opened on the third floor, the reception area was empty. The cleaning crews wouldn't be in until nine. The door to Contracts was on the left side of reception, opposite a pair of rest rooms. Joe checked the men's room and Ray the women's. They both reappeared, shaking their heads. Clear. Pike opened the gym bag and pulled out a single gray cylinder. Worley said, "What's that?"

I pushed him toward Ray without answering. "Okay, Luke. Here we go." Ray pulled him to the men's room.

I pulled the fire alarm at the same time that Joe Pike used Worley's card key to open the door to Contracts, then yanked the fuse on the smoke canister and tossed it through the door. He held the door long enough to yell, "We have a fire in the building! Please use the main stairs and go to the street!" The main stairs fed into the ground floor lobby and were off the reception area. There were utility stairs in the rear of the Contracts department that would lead down to parking. That's how we planned to get out.

Joe let the door close, and then he and I followed Ray and Worley into the bathroom and pressed against the door. We heard voices and curses and a woman's nervous laughter, and then I said, "That's it, Luke. Showtime."

I dragged Worley out, and we used the card key to open the door again as Pike turned off the alarm. I pushed Worley through white smoke and said, "That's a minute, forty-five. The clock is running."

Joe and Ray scrambled in behind us, Joe taking a dousing blanket from the gym bag and pulling on heavy gloves to recover the smoke canister. Leave no evidence. They stayed at the door and Worley led me into an office. He said, "This used to be mine. Sharon must've taken it." A Macintosh computer was up and running on the desk, as if she'd been in the middle of something when we pulled the alarm. I said, "Ninety seconds.

They'll be asking each other what happened. They'll be wondering why the alarm stopped and wondering if they should come take a look."

Worley closed the files that were on-screen and opened others. A case log heading that read MARTIN, THEO-DORE appeared on the screen along with a list of topics. He grinned and slapped the desk. "Y'see. Fuckin' magic. It's all right here." Like we were on the same team, now. Like he'd forgotten that we'd had to put a gun to his head.

"Print it and open Green's personal file."

Worley frowned. "Whaddaya mean, personal file?"

"Letters, bills, work product, anything that has his name on it." I went to the door and looked at Pike. The canister was out, but a heavy mist of white was spreading through the office as the smoke settled. I said, "C'mon, Luke. Sixty seconds."

Worley frowned harder. "Faster if I disk it." He could tell I didn't know what he was talking about. "I'll just dupe it onto a disk. It's faster than printing."

"Do it."

Ray stepped into the door. "We've got voices on the other side of the door."

Worley slapped in a disk. He punched buttons.

I said, "You'd better not be screwing with me, Luke."

"Jesus Christ, I'm almost done." His eyes were big again. "Okay, *now*! We've got it! That's everything!"

He ejected the disk, and we hurried through the smoke in the outer office to the rear stairs and took them down to the parking level. I was sweating hard, thinking we might meet a blue coat or a maintenance man taking the back way up, but we didn't. Luck.

We crossed the parking garage and got into the Porsche and drove back to Lucas Worley's condominium. It was dark when we got there. No one had thrown up a road block to stop us, and a phalanx of police cars hadn't chased us in hot pursuit. I'd never seen a phalanx before, but I was happy to avoid the experience. I said, "You did okay, Luke, but there's one other thing."

He looked at me. The four of us were still in the Porsche, sitting there in his carport.

I said, "You're going to keep your mouth shut about this. You're not going to tell your buddies. You're not going to brag to your girlfriend. We clear on that?" I was pretty sure that he would, eventually, but I wanted some time.

Ray said, "DiVega still wants this fuckuh dead."

I ignored Ray. "We together on this, Luke?"

Lucas Worley's head bobbed. "I won't breathe a word. I swear to Christ."

I held up the disk. "I'm going to check this stuff, and if it isn't complete, or if I figure you've screwed me, I'm going to call DiVega. We together on that, too?"

Luke flicked from Ray to Joe to Ray again. Ray was glaring at him. "Man, I copied *everything*. If it was there, you've got it. I *swear*."

Ray said, "DiVega said we should do what you say, but I know he don't like it."

I looked at him, making a big deal out of the look so that Worley would see. "Tell Mr. DiVega that we're even now. Tell him I said thanks."

Ray turned back to Luke and punched him once in the forehead, lightly.

Worley said, "*Ow!*"

Ray said, "You ever buy any more dope, we'll hear about it. You ever sell dope again, we'll be back. What happened here won't matter a damn. You understand, Mr. Harvard Law?"

Worley's head snapped up and down like it was on a spring. "Hey, I'm retired. You tell Mr. DiVega. I swear."

Ray and Joe and I climbed out of the Porsche, left Lucas Worley sitting in his carport, and walked out to the street and back to our cars. Ray said, "Is this guy DiVega for real?"

"Nope. I made it up."

Ray nodded. "I was trying to scare the little dip. Maybe wake him up."

"I know."

"That little sonofabitch will be dealing again inside the month."

"You can bet on it."

Ray thought about it. "If this fool goes back to dealing he's gonna meet a real Mr. DiVega sooner or later."

"They always do." We stopped at my car and shook hands. "Thanks, Ray. I appreciate the help."

Ray was staring back toward Worley's condominium, looking more than a little sad. "Think of the waste. Goddamned Harvard."

"Yep."

Ray Depente took a deep breath, let it out, and then walked on to his car. I guess he just couldn't understand how someone could turn his back on so much opportunity. I guess he'd be thinking about it most of the night.

Pike and I watched him leave, and then we drove back to my house.

30

We drove directly to my home, me in my car, Joe following in his Jeep, anxious to see if we had anything that Anna Sherman could use. It was eight-twenty when we arrived, and Lucy and Ben were snuggled together on my couch, watching what looked to be a Discovery Channel program about African plains game. The cat was watching the TV, too, but from the edge of the loft. He still didn't like Lucy and Ben much, but at least he wasn't growling.

Ben said, "They're home! Hi, Joe."

Joe said, "Hey, bud. You want to show me how to boot up this Macintosh?"

"Sure." Ben jumped up and the two of them went to the Mac. The cat stopped watching the television and started watching Joe. He began kneading his paws, but he still did not come down.

Lucy held up her hand, and I took it. She said, "I'm still not going to ask where you've been or what you've been doing."

I kissed her nose. "Damnedest thing. Joe and I found a computer disk on the street. We suspect that it contains contracts and business agreements between Jonathan Green and Theodore Martin." I held it up and showed her.

Lucy closed her eyes and slumped back miserably on the couch. "God. For sure I don't want to know."

"Of course, we won't know where it leads until we review what's here, and it would probably help to have an attorney decipher the stuff."

Lucy buried her face in her hands. "I'll be disbarred. I'll go to jail."

Joe said, "We're ready."

I went over to the Mac. "Yeah, you're right, Luce. Better stay over there out of the way."

Lucy jumped up and hurried around the couch to join us. "Oh, hell. It won't hurt to peek over your shoulder."

We fed the disk into the computer and opened the files. The list of available documents pertaining to Teddy Martin's representation was lengthy. Lucy leaned past me and tapped her nail on the screen. She had put on her reading glasses. "Most of this probably has to do with billing. You want the retainer agreement."

I looked at Lucy. "I thought you wanted no part in this."

She took a half-step back and showed her palms. "You're right. Forget I said anything."

I turned back to the screen.

Lucy said, "But you still want the retainer agreement."

Ben went back to the couch. We found the retainer agreement files and opened them. There were three documents, the original agreement plus two amendments.

The original agreement called for a flat fee of five hundred thousand dollars for Green to represent Teddy from the date of the agreement through final appeal, plus all expenses and costs related to the defense. The five hundred thousand was to be deposited into an escrow account of Jonathan Green's choosing and dispensed in equal parts between signing, pretrial hearing start date, pretrial finish date, main trial start date, and main trial finish date, with the ongoing balance payable on demand should the case be dismissed for any reason. I looked at Lucy and she shrugged. "Looks pretty ordinary."

Pike's face was dark. "Five hundred grand. Ordinary."

I said, "Yeah. But these guys work for it."

Lucy knuckled me in the ribs, and then we opened the amendments. Lucy made a soft, whistling sound, and said, "I guess the price of justice went up."

The first amendment transferred the functional ownership of the entirety of Theodore Martin's business holdings, known corporately as Teddy Jay Enterprises, Inc., as well as Theodore Martin's personal property, into twenty-six different escrow accounts under the control of the Law Offices of Jonathan Green. The list of property and assets went on for pages and included fourteen specific restaurants, the real property associated with same, Teddy's Benedict Canyon mansion, plus homes, apartment buildings, and commercial property in Palm Springs, Honolulu, Denver, and Dallas. Approximate values had been given to each holding, and the total valuation was listed as one hundred twenty million dollars. I said, "Is this legal?"

Lucy scrolled through the document, lips parted, the

screen reflected in her glasses. "Free enterprise, Studly. It looks like the parties renegotiated Green's fee for services, and who cares if it's akin to hyenas feeding on the bones of the dead?"

I looked back at the screen and shook my head. There were retirement accounts and bonds and stock portfolios. "Jesus Christ, Green's getting *everything*."

She continued scrolling. "Appears so." Then her breath caught and the scrolling stopped. "This is odd."

"What?"

She touched the final paragraph of the amendment. "These things are in escrow, but they're payable to Green only in the event that the charges against Teddy are dropped, or that he is acquitted." She shook her head. "This just isn't done. No attorney would predicate payment on the outcome of a case."

Pike said, "This one did."

I nodded. "Sex and money. A hundred twenty million is an awful lot of motivation."

Pike leaned back, and the left corner of his mouth twitched. "Enough to use James Lester to plant phony evidence, and enough to convince Louise Earle to change her story so that the press and the public doubt Angela Rossi's honesty."

I frowned. "I can see it with Lester, but you're not going to buy Mrs. Earle. They had to threaten her in some way, and I'm wondering if maybe they've increased the threat."

Lucy stepped away from the Mac and took off her glasses. "I agree that you could argue motivation now, but there is nothing illegal about this agreement. It's simply unusual. It could also be argued that Jonathan is willing to take the chance on an outcome-based payment because the funds are so large. The very thing that makes it unusual also makes it reasonable."

"You don't think Anna Sherman would be interested?"

Lucy spread her hands. "I'm sure that she would be interested, but what could she do? The California Bar certainly has no grounds for an investigation, and, unless there were some corroborating grounds for an investigation, neither does she." She gestured at the Mac. "Besides, she couldn't show this to anyone. It was illegally obtained."

I said, "Hey, we found it."

Lucy put on her glasses again and leaned past me to the keyboard. "Let's see the final amendment."

The final amendment was less than a page. It simply deleted four personal accounts and a vacation home in Brazil from the second amendment and contained an order releasing the accounts and home from escrow, returning them to Teddy Martin's control. Lucy said, "Mm."

"What?"

She shook her head and took off her glasses again. I guess, "Mm," meant nothing.

She said, "I'm sorry. It's still a stretch."

I looked at Pike, but Pike only shrugged.

I scrolled back through the original contract, then through the amendments. I considered the dates. "Okay, how about this. The first agreement is legitimate. Teddy hires the best lawyer he can, and that's Green. He's thinking that if anyone can get him off, it's Jonathan."

Lucy pulled over one of the kitchen stools and sat. "Okay."

"But as the blood evidence comes in from the police and FBI laboratories, and the investigation proceeds, things aren't looking so good. Maybe Jonathan goes to him and says that they should negotiate a plea. Teddy freaks. He's a spoiled, arrogant, egomaniac and he can't imagine not beating this thing. I don't know who mentions it first, maybe Jonathan, maybe Teddy, but someone floats the notion that there has to be a way to beat this thing, and if such a way were found it would be worth everything that Teddy Martin owns. One of them says it, and the other thinks about it, and then they agree. Maybe the actual plan is never discussed. Maybe the words are never spoken, but they both know what they're talking about and the amendment is drawn, and then things begin to happen. Truly suggests James Lester; Kerris contacts Lester; Lester calls the tip line; I get put on the job. You see?"

Joe shifted in his seat. "Reality begins changing."

Lucy crossed her arms and leaned forward. "Are you saying that Jonathan stays away from it?"

"Sure. He's got Truly. He's got Kerris. He's hidden by layers of people. Jonathan Green's experience is that he has the ability to face twelve people and persuade them to accept the facts as he describes them. More often than not, the reality he constructs is false, but his entire experience is that he is able to convince a jury that this false interpretation is real."

Lucy sighed. "That's what makes a great defense attorney."

"And Jonathan Green is one of the best. He's very good at it, he's very careful, and he leaves no direct evidence to link him to any crime."

Lucy was nodding. "But if what you're saying is true, and he created Lester as a witness, why would he have him killed? Lester was the one link who tied Pritzik and Richard to Susan's kidnapping, and could testify to that end."

Joe said, "Green knew that we'd begun to suspect him of manufacturing evidence. Maybe he decided to eliminate Lester because he was scared that Lester would give him up."

I shrugged. "Or maybe Lester realized what he had. Maybe he went back to Green and threatened to spill the beans. Maybe that's what he was talking about when he told Jonna about a big payoff coming in. Maybe he wasn't talking about the hundred thousand dollar reward, maybe he was talking about whatever he could get by extorting Jonathan Green, only when he made the move and tried to put a gun to Jonathan's head, Jonathan took care of the problem."

Lucy didn't look convinced. "Or maybe he just slipped on a bar of soap." She frowned at the look that I gave her. "Hey, bad luck happens."

I stared at her some more, and then I looked back at the Macintosh. Nothing on the screen had changed. Nothing had presented itself that irrefutably linked Jonathan Green to any wrongdoing. "That's what makes this guy so good, I guess. Everything can be explained. None of it leads anywhere else."

Joe said, "No. It all leads back to the money, and Green doesn't get the money unless Teddy beats the rap."

Lucy was staring at the computer again, the temple of her glasses against her teeth. She said, "Unless they aren't planning to get to trial."

I shook my head. "There's no way that the district attorney will drop these charges."

Lucy reopened the final amendment, the one that released accounts and property back to Teddy, and put on the glasses again. "A house in Brazil. A little less than ten million dollars in various holdings." She stepped back and took off the glasses. "We have no extradition with Brazil. Why would Green release the money and the house? Teddy had already agreed to them as part of his fee."

Pike said, "Bail. They're pushing hard for bail."

Lucy was nodding, clicking at her teeth again with her glasses. "I'll bet he's going to run. If he was willing to give up everything he owns to beat the charge, he's willing to leave it behind. Do you see?"

"Sure." Maybe I should just sit with Ben and watch television. Let Lucy and Joe figure it out.

Lucy said, "Maybe they've amended their agreement again, only this time not on paper. Maybe now it's payable on bail."

I was nodding, too. Mr. Getting-on-Board. Mr. Getting-with-the-Program. "Why wouldn't it be on paper?"

Pike said, "Because payment on bail would indicate a foreknowledge of flight."

I stared at him.

Lucy said, "Joe's right. You two are in the picture and you're making trouble. Lester was a problem, and that's more trouble. Maybe Teddy and Jonathan are getting so pressed that they're willing to take the chance on each other."

I was grinning. "So once Teddy has the money, he arranges a funds transfer to Brazil while he's still in jail. Jonathan doesn't have anything to do with it. Then, if he's granted bail, he jumps. Teddy will have his freedom, and Green can deny any knowledge of Teddy's proposed flight."

Lucy nodded. "That would work. Plus, any communication between the two is privileged and not admissible in court."

Pike said, "Ain't justice grand."

I said, "Sonofagun," and held up my hand and Lucy gave me a high five. It felt like we'd done something.

But then Joe said, "And there's nothing we can do about it."

I blinked at him. "Man, are you ever Mr. Wet Blanket."

Joe watched me for a moment, then stood and went to Lucy. He towered over her. "You're going tomorrow."

"That's right. In the morning."

Pike looked at me, but he spoke to Lucy. "He's going to miss you. He's done nothing but pine since he got back from Louisiana."

I said, "Pine?"

Lucy smiled. "I like pining."

Joe frowned at me. "You must be out of your mind, talking about this stuff when it's her last night." He turned back to Lucy. "I'm going to miss you, too."

Lucy stood on her toes and gave him a quick kiss on the lips. "Joe, thank you."

Joe said, "Hey, Ben."

Ben rolled over the back of the couch and grinned at him. "Bye, Joe. I hope you come visit."

Joe pointed at him, then glanced again at Lucy and walked to the door. The cat saw that Joe was leaving, hurried down the stairs, and slipped out with him. Soulmates.

When Joe was gone Lucy wrapped her arms around me. "He's so nice."

"Nice isn't a word often used to describe him."

"He cares a very great deal for you."

"Joe's okay."

She said, "I care about you, too."

"I know." I put my arms around her then and hugged her. I lifted her off the floor and my heart filled, and in a strange moment I felt as if I were fading into a shadow and if I did not hang onto her tight enough I would disappear. I said, "Want to do something wild?" I think I whispered it.

"Yes."

"Want to do something crazy?" I said it louder.

"Oh, God, I can't wait."

Ben said, "Hey, can I do it, too?"

And I said, "You bet, bud."

I put her down, and then the three of us made hot

cocoa and sat in the cool night air on my deck and talked about our time together as the coyotes sang.

We talked until very late, and then Lucy put Ben to bed, and she and I sat up still longer, no longer talking, now simply holding each other in the safety of my home, pretending that tomorrow would not come.

31

I brought Lucy and Ben to LAX at just after nine the next morning. We returned her car to the rental agency, then sat together at the departure gate until the plane boarded, and then I stood with them in line until they entered the jetway and I could go no farther. I watched them until an efficent young woman in a neat airline uniform told me that I was blocking the door and asked me to move. I went to the great glass windows and watched the plane, hoping to see Lucy or Ben in one of the ports, but didn't. I guess they were seated on the other side. We had spent the morning speaking of innocuous things: *It's certainly cloudy this morning, isn't it? Yes, but it will burn off by ten. Oh, darn, I forgot to phone the airline and order the fruit plate.* I guess it was a way of minimizing our separation. I guess it was a way of somehow pretending that her getting on an airplane and both of us going back to our lives wasn't somehow painful and confusing.

When the little tractor pushed the airplane away from the dock and out to the taxiway, I said, "Damn."

An older gentleman was standing next to me. He was

stooped and balding, with a thin cotton shirt and baggy old-man pants pulled too high and a walking stick. He said, "It's never easy."

I nodded.

He said, "Your wife and son?"

"My friends."

"With me, it was my grandkids." He shook his head. "They come out twice a year from Cleveland. I put them on the plane, I always think that this could be the last time. The plane could crash. I could drop dead."

I stared at him.

"I'm not a young man anymore. Death is every-where."

I walked away. Too bad you couldn't get a restraining order against negativity.

Joe picked me up outside the terminal and we drove directly to Louise Earle's. We parked at the mouth of her drive, again went up to her door, and once more rang the bell and knocked. If we knocked much more we'd probably wear a groove in the wood. I was hoping that she might've returned home, but the drapes were still pulled and the house was still dark, and there was no sign that she had come back, then left again. While we were standing there, Mrs. Harris came out of her house and made a nervous wave at us. Pike said, "Looks wor-ried."

"Yeah."

We walked over to her. I could see that her face was pinched and frightened, and that she was cupping one hand with the other, over and over. She said, "That man came back this morning. I thought it was the milkman, they came so early."

"They."

"There were three men. They were walking all around Louise's house. They walked around the side. They went in the back."

Pike looked at me, and I showed her the photograph of Kerris. "Was this one of them?"

She squinted at the picture and then she nodded. "Oh, yes. That's the one who was here before." She bustled to the edge of the porch, wringing her hands, flustered by the dark thoughts. "They were in her house. The lights came on and I could see them moving."

"Did you see them leave?"

She nodded.

"Did Mrs. Earle leave with them?"

She looked at me with large, frightened eyes. "What do you mean by that? What are you saying to me?"

"Did she leave with them?"

Mrs. Eleanor Harris shook her head. Just once. Imperceptibly.

I said, "Had Mrs. Earle come home?"

She was looking at her friend's house, wringing the hands, shifting in a kind of encompassing agitation.

"Was Mrs. Earle at home?"

She looked back at me with big eyes. "I don't know. I don't think so, but she may have."

Pike and I trotted around the side of Louise Earle's house and into her backyard. I felt washed in a cold air, the hair along the back and sides of my head prickling, and scared of what we might find. Pike said, "The door."

Louise Earle's back door had been forced. We slipped out our guns and went in and moved through the house. It was a small home, just the kitchen and the dining room and the living room and two small bedrooms and a single bath. Papers had been pulled from drawers and furniture shoved out of place and closet doors left open, as if someone had searched the place more out of frustration than with a specific goal. I was worried that we might find Mrs. Earle, and that she might be dead, but there was nothing. I guess she hadn't come home, after all. Pike said, "First Lester, now her. Green's tying off the loose ends to protect himself."

"If she got scared, then she ran. If she ran, she might've bought tickets and they might show up on her credit cards. Also, she might've called a guy named Walter Lawrence."

Pike said, "I'll take the bedroom. You start in the kitchen."

We went through her house quickly and without speaking. She had two phones, one in her kitchen and one in her bedroom. The kitchen phone was an older dial-operated wall mount with a little corkboard next to it filled with notes and clippings and Prayers-for-the-Day and messages that she'd written to herself and probably not needed for years. I looked through them all, then checked the Post-its on her refrigerator door, and then I went through the papers that Kerris's people had left on the floor. I was looking for a personal phone book or notes or anything that might help me find Walter Lawrence or point to where she might've gone, but if there had been anything like that Kerris and his people had taken it. When I finished in the kitchen I went back through into the bedroom. Pike was working in the closet. He said, "Credit card bills by the phone."

I sat on the edge of the bed by the phone and looked at what he'd found. There were five past Visa and MasterCard bills, three Visas and two MasterCards. Charges were minimal, and nothing on the bills gave any indication of where Louise Earle might've gone, but then I didn't expect them to. Tickets purchased within the past few days would not yet have been billed to her, but I didn't expect that, either. I picked up her phone, called the toll free number on back of the Visa bill, and said, "Hi. I'm calling for my mom, Mrs. Louise Earle." I gave them the credit card number that showed on the bill and the billing address. "She charged a plane ticket yesterday, and we need to cancel, please."

The Visa woman said, "Let me punch up her account." She was very pleasant when she said it.

"Thanks. That'd be great."

Maybe three seconds later, she said, "I'm sorry, sir, but we're not showing an airline charge."

"Gosh, she told me she'd bought the tickets. She always flies United."

"I'm sorry, sir."

I said, "You know, maybe it wasn't an airline. Are you showing a bus or a train?"

"No, sir. I'm not."

I made a big deal out of sighing. "I'm terribly sorry.

She told me about this trip and I got concerned. She's a bit older, now." I let it trail off.

The Visa woman said, "I know how that is." Understanding.

I thanked her for her time, and then I called Master-Card and went through it again, and again I learned that Louise Earle had bought no tickets. Of course, she might've paid cash, but since I couldn't know that, it wasn't worth worrying about. Like most other things in life.

When I hung up from MasterCard, Pike was waiting. "Looks to be some missing clothes. No toothbrush."

"Great."

"She has to be somewhere."

I picked up the phone again, called my friend at Pacific Bell, gave her Louise Earle's phone number, and asked for every call that Louise Earle had made in the past five days. Her records would show only toll calls, so if she'd phoned someone the next street over I'd never know it. But, like paying cash for airline tickets, it wasn't worth worrying about.

My friend read off twelve numbers that I dutifully copied, nine of which were in local area codes (310, 213, or 818), and three of which were long distance. The long distance calls were all to the same number, the first two of which were collect calls that she'd accepted the charges on. The third time she'd dialed the number direct. I thanked her for the help, then hung up and started dialing. Minimum-wage detective work.

I called each number and got two answers out of the first five calls, one from a pharmacy and one from an elderly woman. I hung up on the pharmacy and asked the elderly woman if she knew where I could find Mrs. Earle. She didn't. The sixth number was long distance. The phone rang twice, and a male voice said, "Federal Correctional Facility, Terminal Island."

I didn't speak.

The voice said, "Hello?"

I told him I was sorry, then hung up and looked at Pike. "LeCedrick."

Pike said, "She probably didn't go to stay with him." Everyone's a comedian.

"She didn't call LeCedrick. LeCedrick called her. LeCedrick calls, and she changes her story. She wouldn't do it six years ago, but she does it now. What do you think he told her?"

Pike shrugged.

I tapped the phone, thinking about it, and then I called Angela Rossi at her home. Her machine answered, but again she picked up when she heard that it was me. I said, "At six this morning, Kerris and two other guys broke into Louise Earle's house, looking for her. They searched the place, and I don't know if they got a line on her or not."

"Why are you telling me this?"

"Because LeCedrick Earle might know where she's gone. When I spoke with Louise she told me that she hadn't spoken to LeCedrick since he was sent up. She said he wouldn't speak to her. But four days ago he called her twice. Three days ago she changed her story. She called him the day before yesterday. That's the day she disappeared. He might know where she's gone. Do you see?"

Angela Rossi didn't say anything.

"I saw him before, but the last time he agreed to see me. I'm pretty sure he won't this time, and I need a badge to get in without his permission. Maybe you could talk to Tomsic. Maybe he could get me in."

Angela Rossi said, "Pick me up."

"You're suspended, Rossi. You don't have a badge."

"I'll get one, goddammit. Pick me up and we'll go see him. I'll get it set up before you get here."

She hung up before I could say anything else.

32

Angela Rossi was waiting at the mouth of her cul-de-sac, looking professional in a dark blue business suit that'd she'd probably worn to work every other week for the past three years. She swayed back and forth the way cops do when they're anxious. It's an unconscious habit they pick up in their uniform days when they have to stand in a place for long hours with nothing to occupy themselves except their baton. It's called the nightstick rock.

We stopped at the curb, and she climbed into the back seat. She said, "It's set up. The guards think we're coming to interview him about a past association. That's what he thinks, too."

Pike said, "Did you get a badge?"

"Don't worry about it." Protecting someone, saying if you don't know you can't tell.

Pike pulled back in traffic without waiting for her to buckle in. I said, "You could give us the badge, then you wouldn't have to come in. Less chance of anyone finding out that you're violating your suspension."

She neither answered nor looked at me. Her mouth

was set and her eyes empty. Cop eyes. Just another day on the job walking the razor's edge.

We picked up the San Diego Freeway and headed south, and once more I was passing Inglewood and Hawthorne and Gardena and Torrance. Angela Rossi sat behind me in silence, hands in her lap, gazing out the window without seeing, dressed in her cop clothes, carrying a cop's badge, going on a cop's mission. She had given her all to it for a great long while, and I wondered if she was thinking that it might now be at an end. I wondered if she was thinking that the dream of being the first female chief of detectives had been a silly one. I wondered if she had regrets.

Forty minutes later we crossed the land bridge onto Terminal Island and passed through the gate, and then we were at the administration building. We parked, took off our guns, and then Angela Rossi and I went in. I said, "You okay?"

Rossi said, "Keep your mouth shut and try to look like an officer. I'll do the talking."

Yes, ma'am.

We went through the front door and up to the reception desk. I was worried that the reception guard would be the same guy, but he wasn't. This guy was paging through *Saltwater Fisherman* magazine, but looked up when we approached. He said, "May I help you?" He was a young guy, tall and athletic and looking as if he'd just mustered out of the military. He was wearing the blue blazer and tie.

Rossi showed the badge. "West L.A. robbery/homicide. I called to see an inmate named LeCedrick Earle."

The receptionist jotted down the badge number, then said, "Sure. Hold on." He flipped through the loose-leaf book until he found Earle's name, then told someone on the phone that he wanted prisoner number E2847 in the interview room. When he hung up he said, "Guns?"

Rossi said, "Left'm in the car."

"Great. Someone will be right out for you. Wait by the sally port."

Rossi said, "Would it be a problem to check your logs for the visitors that Mr. Earle has had over the past two weeks?"

"No sweat." He turned to a computer and typed something. "We enter the log into the computer at the end of each day for the record. You want a hard copy?"

"Yes."

It took maybe sixteen seconds, and then a laser printer spit out a single sheet. Modern crime fighting at its finest. He said, "Here you go."

Rossi took it and we looked at it as we went to the sally port. The only visitors that LeCedrick Earle had had in the past two weeks were Elliot Truly and Stan Kerris. How about that?

A second guy in a blue blazer opened the sally port for us and said, "This way, please."

We followed him through and turned right. He was a couple of years younger than Rossi and he looked her over. "You guys down from L.A.?"

Rossi said, "That's right."

"What kind of case?" Rossi was trying to ignore him, but the guard was giving her the grin.

"Don't know yet."

The guard grinned wider. "How long are you going to be down here? Maybe we could get together for a drink."

Rossi never looked at him. "Do yourself a favor, sport. I just tested positive for chlamydia."

The guard's grin faltered and he moved a half-step away. Talk about a conversation stopper.

He brought us to the same interview room that I had used before and opened the door. He stood kind of bent to the side so that Rossi wouldn't brush against him when she went by. "I've got to lock you in. Your guy will be here in a minute."

Rossi said, "Thanks."

He locked the door behind us and we were alone. I nodded at her. "Chlamydia. Nice."

Rossi shrugged. I guess it was something she'd had to do ten thousand times.

We had been there less than thirty seconds when the rear door opened and a third guard led in LeCedrick Earle. His eyes widened when he recognized us, and he shook his head at the guard. "Forget this shit. I don't wanna see'm."

The guard shoved LeCedrick toward the table without acknowledging him and said, "Just punch the buzzer when you're finished."

LeCedrick Earle said, "Hey, fuck this shit. Take me back to my cell."

Rossi said, "Thanks, officer."

The guard closed the door and locked it, and Rossi smiled. "It's my favorite perp. How're you doing, LeCedrick?"

LeCedrick Earle glowered at us and stood with his back to the door, as far from us as possible. He said, "I don't have anything to say to you." He wiggled a finger at me. "I said everything I had to say to you before. I ain't gotta see you without my lawyer."

I said, "Stan Kerris is trying to kill your mother."

He blinked twice, and then he laughed. "Oh, that's right. You drove all the way down here for that?" He laughed some more.

Rossi said, "Jonathan Green's scam is falling apart, LeCedrick. He's falsified evidence and suborned testimony, and now he's scared that it's coming out. We believe that he ordered the death of a man named James Lester, and we believe that he's after your mother, too. If he is, then he'll probably come after you as well."

"Bullshit. You just talkin' trash." He wiggled the finger at Rossi. "You just worried cause your ass is in a crack. You know I'm gonna get your ass for puttin' me in here." He went to the near chair, plopped down, and put up his feet. "I ain't sayin' nothing without my lawyer."

"You want Mr. Green?"

LeCedrick smiled wide. "I think you'll find that he represents me in all matters criminal and civil. Especially in the civil case where we whack your ass for every nickel in your pension fund for planting bullshit evidence on me."

I stepped past Rossi and slapped LeCedrick's feet from the table. He said, "Hey!"

I said, "We've got to get past that right now, LeCedrick." He tried to get up but I dug my thumb under his jawline beneath his right ear. He said, "Ow!" and tried to wiggle away, but I stayed with him.

Rossi pulled at me from behind. "Stop it. We can't do that."

I didn't stop it. I said, "You didn't call the hotline about this, they called you. That's the way it started, isn't it?"

He grabbed at my hand, but he couldn't pry it away.

Rossi said, "Stop it, dammit. That's over the line."

"Kerris and Truly came to see you and convinced you to speak with your mother, didn't they?"

He was finally listening.

"What did they say, LeCedrick? You hadn't spoken to the woman in years, but you called her and convinced her to change her story. They offer you money? They say they could get you an early release?"

He stopped trying to pull at my hand, and I relaxed the pressure. Rossi said, "Jesus Christ, they could arrest us for this."

I said, "Think about it, LeCedrick. Jonathan and Truly and all those guys went to see her and probably told her what to say and how to say it, and that means she could testify against them."

Now he was squinting at me, hearing the truth of it, even though it was masked by his suspicions.

"I uncovered a connection between Lester and Green, and two days later Lester went through his shower door and damn near cut off his head. You see that in the papers?"

He nodded.

"The day after that I went to your mother's house to

ask why she changed her story, and she was missing. You know Mrs. Harris next door? Mrs. Harris told me that Kerris had cruised your mother's house three times, that he'd walked around the place and tried to get in."

He said, "Mrs. Harris?"

"At six this morning Kerris and two other guys went back to her house and turned the place upside down. Why would they do that, LeCedrick?"

Now he was shaking his head. "This all bullshit."

"Would Mrs. Eleanor Harris bullshit you? You grew up next door to her. Would she bullshit you?"

He made a little headshake. One so tiny that it was hard to see. "Lady 'bout raised me. Like a second mama."

Rossi pushed the buzzer, and when the guard came she asked if we could have a phone. He said no problem, brought one, and when he was gone again I turned it toward LeCedrick Earle and said, "Call her. I've got the number, if you need it."

He stared at the phone.

"We have to find your mother, LeCedrick. If we don't find her before Kerris, he'll kill her. Do you see?"

He wet his lips.

Rossi said, "Goddammit, you piece of shit, call the woman."

LeCedrick Earle snatched up the phone and punched the number without asking for it, and spoke with Mrs. Eleanor Harris. When she answered his manner changed, and he hunched over the phone and spoke in a voice that was surprisingly young and considerate. I guess the lessons we learn when we're small stay with us, even as we harden with the years. They spoke for several minutes, and then LeCedrick Earle put down the phone and kept his eyes on it, as if the phone had taken on an importance that dwarfed everything else in the room. He crossed his arms and started rocking. He said, "Why they do that? Why they go there so early?"

Rossi said, "They want to kill her. And after they kill her, they will almost certainly arrange to have you killed, and then no one can implicate them in the manufacture of false evidence. Do you see that?"

He didn't say anything.

I said, "She left the house with a bag. She has a gentleman friend named Mr. Lawrence."

LeCedrick Earle nodded dumbly. "That old man been chasin' her for years."

"Would she go there?"

"Sure, she'd go there. She ain't got nobody else."

I felt something loosen in my chest. I felt like I could breathe again. "Okay, LeCedrick. That's great. Just great. Do you know where he lives?"

LeCedrick Earle slumped back in the chair with an emptiness that made him seem lost and forever alone. His eyes filled with tears, and the tears spilled down across his cheeks and dripped on his shirt. He said, "I can't believe this shit. I just can't believe it."

Rossi said, "What?"

He rubbed at the tears, then blew his nose. "I must be the stupidest muthuhfuckuh ever been born. That woman ain't never done nuthin' but what she try to do right, and this what she gets for it. A fool for a son. A goddamned stupid fool." He was sobbing.

Rossi said, "Goddammit, LeCedrick, what?"

LeCedrick Earle blinked through the tears at us. "Your man Kerris called me 'bout an hour ago and asked about old Mr. Lawrence, too. He say they need to get her story straight. He say they want her to do a news conference, and I told him where she was. I told him how to get there and now they gonna kill my momma. Ain't I a fool? Ain't I God's own stupid muthuhfuckin' fool?"

I was pressing the buzzer even before he was finished, and Angela Rossi was shaking him until he told us the address, and then we were running out to the Jeep. It was almost certain that Louise Earle was dead, but neither of us was yet willing to give up on her.

Maybe we were God's own fools, too.

33

Pike pushed the Jeep hard out of the parking lot and through the gate and across the land bridge. Angela Rossi used her cell phone to call Tomsic as we were climbing back onto the freeway. She told him about Kerris, and that Louise Earle was probably staying with a Mr. Walter Lawrence in Baldwin Hills. They spoke for about six minutes, and then Rossi turned off her phone. "He's on the way."

I said, "You sure you want to go to the scene?"

"Of course."

Pike glanced at her in the rearview. "It gets back to the brass that you're involved, it's over for you."

Rossi took her Browning from under the seat and clipped it onto her waistband. "I'm going."

We scorched up the Harbor Freeway to the San Diego, the speedometer pegged at a hundred ten, Pike gliding the Jeep between and around traffic that seemed frozen in space. We drove as much on the shoulder as the main road, and several times Pike stood on the brakes, bringing us to screaming, sliding stops before he would once more stomp the accelerator to rocket around lane-changers or people merging off an entrance ramp. I said, "We can't help anybody if we're piled up on the side of the road."

Pike went faster.

Hawthorne slipped past, then Inglewood, and then we were off the freeway and climbing through the southern edge of Baldwin Hills along clean, wide residential streets lined with spacious postwar houses. Baldwin Hills is at the southwestern edge of South Central Los Angeles, where it was developed in the late forties as a homesite for the affluent African-American doctors and dentists and lawyers who served the South-Central community. At one time it was called the black Beverly Hills, though in recent years the community has diversified with upwardly mobile Hispanic, Asian, and Anglo families. Rossi's phone beeped, and she answered, mumbling for maybe ten seconds before ending the call. "Dan just got off the freeway. They're three minutes behind us, and he's got a black-and-white behind him."

We used Pike's Thomas Brothers map to find our way through the streets, watching for turns and scoping the area. Mothers were pushing strollers and children were playing with dogs and everyone was enjoying a fine summer day. I said, "We're almost there."

We were two blocks from Walter Lawrence's home when a tan Aerostar van passed us going fast in the opposite direction and Pike said, "That's Kerris. Three others on board."

Rossi and I twisted around, trying to see. "Louise Earle's in the back. Looks like Lawrence and someone else, too." Louise Earle looked scared.

Rossi said, "The other guy is probably one of Kerris's security people."

Pike jerked the Jeep into a drive and did a fast reversal. I said, "Did they make us?"

Pike shook his head. The Aerostar turned a far corner, but it hadn't increased its speed, and its driving seemed even. We went after them, Pike hanging back. In cases like this there are always two choices: You can let them know that you're there, or you can hide from them. If they know that you're there they might get nutty and start shooting. As long as they're not shooting, you're better off. Louise Earle and Walter Lawrence would be better off, too. Rossi unfastened her seat belt and leaned forward between me and Joe, better to see. "Don't crowd them, Joseph. Let's give them room."

Pike pursed his lips. "I know, Angela." Nothing like a backseat driver in a pursuit situation.

Rossi got on her phone again and told Tomsic where we were and what we were doing. She didn't cut the circuit this time, but kept up a running flow of information so that Tomsic knew where we were at all times. I said, "Can he get in front of them?"

"No. He's west of the hills and behind us. He's calling in more black-and-whites."

I glanced at Rossi, but she seemed impassive. The brass would know now, for sure.

We followed the van down out of the residential area onto Stocker Boulevard, then started climbing again almost at once, leaving the residential area behind as we wound our way through dry, undeveloped hills dotted with oil pumpers and radio towers. I had hoped that they would turn into the city, but they didn't. They were heading into a barren place away from prying eyes.

We followed them deeper into the hills, staying well back, catching only glimpses of their dust trail so that we wouldn't be seen, and as the peaks rose around us Rossi's cell phone connection became garbled and our link to Tomsic was broken. She tossed the phone aside. "I lost him."

Pike said, "He knows about where we are."

"About."

Maybe a half mile ahead of us the van turned up the side of a hill along a gravel service road, making its way toward two great radio towers. We could see the towers, and what was probably a maintenance shed at their bases, and another car parked there. I said, "They're going to kill them. They couldn't kill them at the house with so many people on the street, but they're going to do them here."

Rossi craned her head out the window. "If we take the road up after them, they'll see us coming a mile away."

Pike slapped the Jeep into four-wheel drive, and we left the road, heading first down into a gully, then up. We lost sight of the towers and the van, but we watched the ridgeline and followed the slope of hills and we did what we could until we came to an elevated pipeline that we could not cross. Pike said, "Looks like we're on foot."

Pike and I were wearing running shoes, but Angela Rossi was wearing dress flats. I said, "Going to be a hard run."

She said, "Fuck it."

She threw her jacket into the backseat, took her

Browning from its holster, then kicked off her shoes and set out at a jog. Barefoot. The ground was rough and bristling with stiff dried grass and foxtails and must have hurt, but she gave no sign.

The hill was steep and the going was slow. The soil was loose and brittle, and the dessicated grass did not help bind it together. Our feet sunk deep and every step caused a minor landslide, but halfway up the hill we saw the tops of the towers, and pretty soon after that the roof of the shed. We went down to our hands and knees and eased our way to the ridge. The Aerostar was parked next to a bronze Jaguar. Kerris was already out of the van and moving toward the shed. He'd left the van's driver side door open. The same black security guard I'd seen at Green's party came out of the shed. The van's side door slid open and a younger guy with a very short crew cut pushed out. Walter Lawrence climbed out after him, but I guess he wasn't moving fast enough because the crew cut took his arm and yanked, and Mr. Lawrence stumbled sideways to fall in a little cloud of dust. The black guy ignored all of that and opened the Jag's trunk to lift out two shovels and a large roll of plastic. Rossi said, "They're going to execute these people."

Pike said, "Yes."

I edged higher on the ridge. "They'll bring them inside the building. Maybe we can work our way around to the backside of the slope and come up behind the building without being seen." I didn't think Kerris would just shoot them in the open, even out here in the middle of nowhere.

Pike started backwards with Rossi behind him when

the crew cut leaned into the van and said something to Louise Earle. I guess she didn't want to get out, because he reached in and pulled. He had her by the upper arm and it must've hurt. She tried swatting at him like you might a fly, but it did no good. That's when Walter Lawrence scrambled up out of the dust and grabbed the crew cut's jacket and tried pulling him away. Defending his woman. The crew cut guy put a hand on Walter Lawrence's face and pushed. Walter Lawrence flailed backwards and fell again, landing flat on his back, and the crew cut guy took a steel Smith & Wesson 9mm from beneath his left arm, pointed it at Walter Lawrence, and fired one shot.

The shot sounded hollow and faraway, and Mrs. Earle screamed just as Elliot Truly stepped out of the maintenance shed.

34

Pike worked the Python out of his waist holster and pushed it in front him, lining up on the crew cut.

Rossi said, "We're too far."

"If they point a gun at her, Joe." Ignoring Rossi.

"I'm on it."

Rossi said, "Can he make this shot?"

We were more than a hundred yards from them. It was a very long shot for a four-inch barrel, but Pike could brace his hand on the ground, and he was the finest pistol shot I've ever seen.

Truly waved his arms, raising hell with Kerris and the guy with the crew cut, and the guy with the crew cut put away his gun. Truly did some more waving, then went back into the maintenance shed. Kerris raised hell with the crew cut too, then he and the black guy lifted Mrs. Earle by the arms and dragged her past Walter Lawrence's body to the shed. The crew cut went over to the shovels and plastic, and didn't look happy about it.

I said, "We don't have much time."

We crabbed back down beneath the ridgeline and trotted around the side of the hill until we had the maintenance shed between us and the van. The shed was at the base of the north tower, and its structure formed a kind of latticework around the shed and would provide cover between the shed and the Jaguar. We moved fast, but with every passing second I was frightened that we'd hear the second shot. I guess we could've just started yelling and let them know we were here, but they had already committed murder; Mrs. Earle would probably catch the first shot.

When the shed was between us and the van, we crept up the hill to the rear of the base of the north radio tower. I said, "Rossi and I will take the shed. You take the guy at the van."

Pike slipped away to the edge of the shed, then disappeared among the girders at the base of the radio tower.

I looked at Rossi. "You ready?"

She nodded. Her stockings were shredded, her feet torn and bleeding and clotted with dirt and little bits of brown grass. Her nice suit pants were ripped.

The maintenance shed was a squat cinderblock and corrugated metal building built against the base of the north tower. Inside, there would be tools and parts and paint for maintaining the towers and adjusting the repeater antennas. There were no windows, but doors were built into the front and back. Truly had probably been here for a while and had opened the doors for the air. The door nearest the cars was wide and tall so you could move oversized parts and equipment in and out, but the rear door, the door by the tower, was a people door.

Rossi and I slipped up to the side of the shed, then crept toward the door. We listened, but all we could hear was Mrs. Earle crying. I touched Rossi, then pointed to myself, then the door, telling her that I was going to risk a look. She nodded. I went down onto my hands and knees, edged forward, and peeked inside. Mrs. Earle was on the floor, tied, and Kerris and Truly were standing together just inside the far door. Truly looked nervous, like he didn't want to be there. The black guy wasn't inside; he'd probably gone back to help the crew cut with the shovels. I was still looking at them when the guy with the crew cut walked past the side of the shed with the shovel and the plastic and a sour expression and saw us. He did a classic double take, said, "Hey!" then dropped the shovels and plastic to claw for his gun when I shot him two times in the chest. I said, "Get Mrs. Earle."

Rossi rolled past into the door with me behind her when we heard three shots from the front of the shed. Kerris grabbed Truly and pushed him in the way and fired fast four times. Rossi said, "Shit."

Truly was looking confused and Mrs. Earle was staring at us with wide, frightened eyes, and I was scared that if I tried to hit Kerris I would hit her. I fired high and Kerris fell back, scrambling through the door, firing as he went. Truly turned to run after him, and when he did he turned square into Kerris and was kicked backwards by one of the rounds, and then Kerris was gone. There was shouting out front, Kerris and the black guy, and more firing. The black guy was yelling, "I'm hit! Oh, Holy Jesus, I'm hit!"

Rossi went to Mrs. Earle and I went to Truly. Truly was trying to get up and not having a good time of it.

The bullet had hit him maybe three inches to the right of his sternum, and a flower of red was blooming on his shirt. He said, "I think I've been shot."

Rossi was untying Mrs. Earle. I said, "Are you all right?"

Mrs. Earle was still crying. "They shot Mr. Lawrence."

Rossi helped her up, telling her that she had to stand, that she had to move to the side, out of the way, telling her that everything was going to be okay. The lies you tell someone when you need them to cooperate because their life depends on it. Truly said, "Am I going to die?"

I tore off my shirt and bundled it and pressed it to his chest. "I don't know."

I pulled off his belt and wrapped it around his chest and the shirt and buckled it tight. He said, "Oh, God, that hurts."

There were more shots by the cars and running footsteps, and then Joe Pike slipped through the door. Maybe six shots slammed into the door and the walls and through the open doorway. Maybe seven. Pike said, "Those Glocks are something."

Rossi duck-walked over. "What's the deal out front?"

Joe said, "The black guy's punched out. Kerris is behind the Jaguar. I don't know about the crew cut."

Rossi nodded toward the rear. "Forget him."

I said, "Can we get to Kerris?"

Pike made a little shrug. "He's got a clean field of fire at us. We could go back the way we came, maybe, and work our way around." He glanced at Truly. "Take about twenty minutes to work around behind the Jag."

I turned Truly's face so that he looked at me. "You hear that, Elliot? You're bleeding and we're pinned down in here and Kerris is doing the pinning."

Truly opened his mouth, then closed it. He blinked at me, then shook his head. "Kerris kidnapped these people. He shot that old man. I didn't know anything about it."

Rossi said, "Bullshit."

I shook Truly's face. "Stop lying, you idiot. Stop worrying about incriminating yourself, and start worrying about dying."

He shook his head. His eyes filled with tears, and the tears tumbled out and ran down into his hair.

I said, "It's you and Kerris and the black guy and the guy with the crew cut. Is there anyone else up here?"

He shook his head again. "No." A whisper.

"Is anyone else supposed to come up here?"

The crying grew worse and became a cough. When he coughed, pink spittle blew out across his chin and the chest wound made a wheezing sound.

I said, "Tell Kerris to give it up. If Kerris gives it up, we can get you to a hospital."

Truly's face wrinkled from the pain and he yelled, "Kerris! Kerris, it's over. I need a doctor!" It wasn't much of a yell.

Kerris didn't answer.

Elliot Truly yelled, "Goddammit, Kerris, enough of this, would you, please?! I'm dying! I've got to get to a doctor!" He coughed again, and this time a great red bubble floated up from his mouth.

Rossi duck-walked over. She said, "You're fucked, Elliot. Your man outside is in for murder and he's looking to save himself. He's got to kill us and this woman to do that, and he doesn't give a damn if you live or die."

Truly moaned. "Oh, God."

Rossi leaned closer to him. "Maybe you'll make it, but maybe you won't. We still might get Kerris, though, and the sonofabitch who put you into this spot. Give him up, Elliot. Tell us what we want to hear."

Truly squeezed his eyes shut, but still the tears came out. "It was Jonathan."

Rossi smiled. It was small, and it was personal.

I said, "Everything that's happened, it's so Jonathan can take over Teddy's companies, isn't it?"

Truly tried to nod, but it didn't look like much. "Not at first. At first, Jonathan was just going to defend him, like anyone else."

"But Teddy got scared."

Truly coughed, and more bubbles came up. "Oh, God, it hurts. God, it hurts so bad."

I said, "Did Teddy kill his wife?"

Truly wet his lips to answer, and made his lips red. "Yes. He denied it at first, but Jonathan knew. You can always tell. You know when they did it."

Rossi frowned at me and nodded. You see?

Truly said, "Then he just admitted it. I'm not sure why, but he did, just out of the blue one night when we were going over his story. Jonathan and I were alone with him and he started to cry and he admitted that he killed her. That changed everything. Jonathan advised him to negotiate a plea, but Teddy wouldn't do that. He was scared of going to prison, and he begged Jonathan not to quit the case. He said that he'd do anything rather to go to prison."

"Even give away everything he owned."

Another nod. "That was Jonathan's price."

Rossi said, "All that stuff about Pritzik and Richards. That was bullshit?"

"Jonathan and Kerris and I put it together. Jonathan had the idea of a straw man, and Kerris came up with Pritzik and Richards, and I knew Lester. We just put it together." He started coughing again, and this time a great gout of blood bubbled up and he moaned. I put my hands on the compress and leaned on it. He said, "I don't want to die. Oh, God, please Jesus, I don't want to die. Please save me."

I wiped the blood off his face and forced open his eyes and said, "You're a piece of shit, Truly, but I'm going to save you, do you hear? Just hang on, and I will get you to a hospital. Do you hear me?"

He nodded. "Uh-hunh."

"Don't die on me, you sonofabitch."

He moaned, and his eyes rolled back.

I checked on Mrs. Earle, and made sure that she was behind as much metal as possible, and then Rossi and I went over to Pike. Pike was peering through a split in the door jamb. "He got a shotgun from the van. He's talking on his cell phone."

"Great. Probably calling for reinforcements."

Pike glanced at Rossi. "Be real nice if Tomsic happened to find us about now."

Rossi shrugged. "Let's all hold our breaths."

I edged past Pike and looked through the split. Kerris

was behind the Jaguar with the shotgun. The black guy was lying on his side between the Jag and the van, and Mr. Lawrence was on his back a few yards behind him. The black guy was probably unconscious, but he might've been dead. I yelled, "Come on, Kerris. There's three of us and one of you. Don't be stupid."

The shotgun boomed twice, slamming buckshot into the corrugated metal about eighteen inches above my head. Mrs. Earle made a kind of moaning wail, and Rossi dived across the doorway, popping off caps to force Kerris down.

Pike looked at me. "I don't think he's scared of the odds."

"Guess not."

Rossi edged toward the door and stopped just shy of the jamb, squinting out into the sun. She said, "Hey, the old man's still alive."

Mrs. Earle stopped wailing. "Walter?"

I went back to the split and saw Walter Lawrence slowly roll onto his belly, then push up to his knees before falling onto his face.

Mrs. Earle started for the door, but Pike pulled her down. "Stay back, ma'am. Please."

"But Walter needs help." She said it loudly, and Pike put his hand over her mouth.

"Don't draw attention to him. If Kerris sees him he's a dead man."

Her eyes were wide, but she nodded.

Walter Lawrence pushed up again, then looked around as if what he was seeing was new and strange. He saw the guy in the red knit shirt about ten feet in front of him and he saw the guy's pistol, a nice blue metal automatic, lying in the dust. He looked past the guy in the knit shirt and almost certainly saw Kerris hiding behind the Jaguar, pointing the shotgun at us. Walter Lawrence was behind Kerris, and since Kerris was looking at us, he wasn't looking at Walter Lawrence. Mr. Walter Lawrence began crawling for the pistol. I said, "Rossi."

"I see him."

I watched through the split jamb, and could see the hills and the pumpers and the rough service roads below, and as I watched a dark sedan appeared on the road between the pumpers, heading our way, kicking up a great gray roostertail of dust. Rossi saw it, too. I said, "Is that Tomsic?"

She ejected her Browning's clip, checked the number of bullets left, then put it back in her gun. "I can't tell."

I glanced at Pike and Pike shrugged. Guess it didn't matter to him. Guess he figured the more the merrier.

Walter Lawrence crept toward the gun like a drunken infant, weaving on his hands and knees, bloody shirt hanging loose and sodden between his arms. He reached the pistol and sat heavily, but he did not touch the gun. As if simply reaching it had taken all of his energy. Rossi said, "In a couple of seconds we're going to be able to hear the car. If Kerris looks that way, the old man's dead."

I looked at Pike and Pike nodded. I took a breath, and peered out the split again. Kerris had taken up a position behind the Jaguar's front end. You could see about a quarter of his face behind the left front tire. The tire was probably a steel-belted Pirelli. Might be able to shoot through it, but it wasn't much of a target. "Kerris? Truly's dying. He needs a doctor."

"It's the cost of doing business." All heart.

I stood. "Listen, Kerris! Maybe we can work something out." I sprinted past the open door to the other side of the shed. When I flashed past the door, the shotgun boomed again, but the buckshot hit the wall behind me.

Pike said, "Lucky."

I yelled, "I didn't sign on to this job to get killed, and neither did Pike. You want the old lady, we just want to go home. You hear what I'm saying?" I hopped past the door in the opposite direction. Kerris fired twice more, once behind me through the doorway and once high through the wall. Maybe I could just keep running back and forth until he ran out of ammo.

Kerris said, "Bullshit, Cole. I checked out you and your partner, remember? You aren't built that way."

Another boom, and this time the number four slammed through the wall just over Joe's back.

I crawled across him to the split again and looked out. Walter Lawrence had once more focused on the gun. He leaned forward from the waist, picked it up, then held it as if he had never held a gun before in his life. Maybe he hadn't. He cupped it in both hands and pointed it at Kerris, but the gun wavered wildly. He lowered the gun. I yelled, "I'm serious, Kerris. What's all this to me?"

"If you're so goddamned serious, throw out your guns and come out."

"Forget that."

"Then let's wait it out."

The car was close, now, and if I strained I thought that I might hear it. Walter Lawrence raised the gun again. Rossi said, "That's Tomsic!"

I yelled, "Okay, Kerris. Let's talk."

I stepped into the door, and as I did Mr. Walter Lawrence pulled the trigger. There was a loud BANG and his shot slammed into the Jaguar's rear fender and Kerris jumped back from the wheel, yelling, "Sonofabitch!"

Walter Lawrence fired again, and again the shot went wide, and Kerris swung the shotgun toward him but as he did Angela Rossi shouted, "No!" and she and Joe Pike and I launched out the door, firing as fast as we could.

Kerris brought the shotgun back, pulling the trigger *BOOM-BOOM-BOOM-BOOM* as our bullets caught him and lifted him, and then slammed him into the soft gray earth, and then the noise was gone and it was over and there was only the sound of Louise Earle crying.

r. Walter Lawrence fell onto his back and kept trying to right himself the way a turtle might, clawing at the air with his arms and legs. I took the gun from him and told him to lie still, but he wouldn't until Louise Earle hurried out from the shed and made him.

Linc Gibbs and Dan Tomsic pulled up in a cloud of dry gray dust, then ran over with their guns out. Tomsic said, "Who's this?"

"One of the good guys. Get an ambulance, for Christ's sake. We've got another wounded in the shed."

Linc Gibbs made the call while Tomsic ran for the first aid kit that every cop keeps in his trunk. The crew cut had put one high into the left side of Mr. Lawrence's chest. His shirt and jacket were soaked red, and he felt cold to the touch. The blood loss was extreme. When Tomsic came with the kit, we put a compress bandage over the wound and held it in place. Mrs. Earle held it. While Tomsic was working with the bandage he glanced at Angela Rossi. "You okay, Slick?"

She made an uncertain smile. "Yeah."

When Mr. Lawrence was bandaged we ran into the

shed, but Elliot Truly was dead. Tomsic looked close at Truly as if he wanted to be sure of what he was seeing. "Is this who I think it is?"

"Unh-huh."

"Sonofabitch."

Gibbs had them send a medivac helicopter, and while we waited, we secured the scene. There wasn't much to secure. Both the guy with the crew cut and the guy in the knit shirt were dead. Kerris was dead, too. Tomsic said, "Do all of these guys work for Green?"

"Kerris was his chief investigator. I think these other two worked for Kerris. I saw the black guy at Green's home."

Tomsic shook his head and stared at the bodies. "Man, you really wrack'm up."

I frowned at him. "Do you have a spare shirt in your car?" My shirt was still a bloody wad on Elliot Truly's chest.

"Think I might have something." Most cops keep a spare shirt for just such occasions.

He had a plain blue cotton dress shirt still in its original plastic bag stowed in his trunk. It had probably been there for years. "Thanks, Tomsic." When I put it on, it was like wearing a tent. Two sizes too big.

The medivac chopper came in from the north and settled to a rest well away from the radio towers. Two paramedics hustled out with a stretcher and loaded Mr. Lawrence into the helicopter's bay. They told us that they were going to lift him to Martin Luther King, Jr. Hospital, which would be a five-minute flight, and Mrs. Earle wanted to go. They refused to take her until Angela

Rossi volunteered to go with her. Lincoln Gibbs told Rossi that we would pick her up at the hospital.

When the helicopter had lifted away and disappeared over the hills, Gibbs looked at me and Pike, and said, "Well?" The first of the black-and-whites was just now kicking up dust on the roads below.

"Green's people got to LeCedrick Earle. They offered him money and an early out from prison if he could get his mother to change her story. He hadn't spoken to her in six years, but he called and told her that the guards and the other prisoners were beating him because she was defending the police. Green's people went to her also, and helped convince her that it was real, and that the only way they could save LeCedrick was if she changed her story so that they could get him away from the guards."

Gibbs nodded. "Figured it had to be something like that. Figured she wouldn't do it for money."

Tomsic said, "Will she say that on the record?"

"Yes. And we've got something else, too."

They looked at me.

"Truly made a dying declaration that Teddy Martin admitted murdering his wife, and that Jonathan Green conspired with Truly and Kerris to fabricate false evidence against Pritzik and Richards."

Tomsic smiled, and Lincoln Gibbs made a little whistle. Gibbs said, "Truly said that to you?"

"Pike and Rossi heard it, too. Mrs. Earle might've heard it, but I'm not certain that she did."

Gibbs went back to his car and spoke on his cell phone for a time. As the black-and-whites rolled up, Tomsic met them and told them to hang around. There wasn't anything for them to do until the detectives who would handle the scene arrived. Gibbs came back in a few minutes and said, "Is that your Jeep on the other side of the hills?"

Pike said, "Mine."

"Okay. We'll pick up Rossi and Mrs. Earle at MLK and go see Sherman."

I spread my arms. "Like this?"

Tomsic was already walking to his car. "The shirt looks great on you. What's your beef?"

"It looks like I'm wearing a tent."

Pike's mouth twitched.

I said, "Hey, Gibbs."

He looked back.

"How about I pick up Mrs. Earle? It might be easier for her."

He stared at me for a short moment, and then he nodded. "We'll meet you at Sherman's."

A black-and-white brought us to Pike's Jeep, and we drove directly to the MLK emergency trauma center. Mr. Lawrence was in surgery, and Rossi and Mrs. Earle were in the waiting room. I sat next to Mrs. Earle and took her hands. "We need to go see the district attorney. We need to tell her what we know about all of this. Do you see?"

She looked at me with clear eyes that were free of doubt or equivocation. "Of course. I knew that we would."

The four of us drove to Anna Sherman's office in Pike's Jeep. Mrs. Earle rode with her hands in her lap and her head up. I guess she was thinking about LeCedrick. We did not listen to the radio during this time, and perhaps we should have. Things might've worked out differently if we had.

It was just after three that afternoon when Louise Earle, Angela Rossi, and I were shown into Anna Sherman's office. The bald prosecutor, Warren Bidwell, was there, along with another man I hadn't seen before, and Gibbs and Tomsic.

Sherman greeted us, smiling politely at Louise Earle and giving me a kind of curious neutrality, as if the meeting in Greenblatt's parking lot had never happened. I guess that they had told her what to expect.

Sherman offered coffee, which everyone declined, and as we took our seats she passed close to me and whispered, "Great shirt."

I guess that they'd told her about the shirt, too.

Anna Sherman asked Mrs. Earle if she would mind being recorded, and if she would like to have an attorney present.

Mrs. Earle said, "Am I going to be arrested?"

Anna Sherman smiled and shook her head. "No, ma'am, but it's your right, and some people feel more comfortable."

Mrs. Earle raised her hands. "Oh, Lord, no. I don't care for all those lawyers."

Tomsic grinned big time at that one. Even Bidwell smiled. Sherman said, "Do you mind if we record?"

"You can record whatever you want. I don't care who hears what I have to say." Her jaw worked, and for a moment she looked as if she was going to cry again.

"You know, those things I said about LeCedrick and the officer wasn't true." She looked at Angela. "I want to apologize for that."

Angela Rossi said, "It's okay."

Mrs. Earle said, "No, it is not. I am so ashamed that I don't know what to do." She looked back at Sherman. "They said that the most horrible things were happening to my boy. They said that he would surely die in that place unless I helped get him out of there."

Anna Sherman turned on the recorder. "Who is 'they,' Mrs. Earle?"

Mrs. Louise Earle went through her part of it first, telling how she received the first phone call that she'd had from LeCedrick in six years, how he'd pleaded with her that his life was in danger there in the prison, that he'd called again, crying this time, begging her to help and saying that he'd hired an attorney named Elliot Truly who wanted to come speak with her. She told us how Truly and Kerris had come to the house, confirming the horror stories that LeCedrick had claimed, and convincing her that the fastest way to get LeCedrick moved from harm's way was to claim that the police had framed him those six years ago, just as LeCedrick had always said. She said that Truly helped her work out what to say.

Anna Sherman took notes on a yellow legal pad even though the recorder was running. Bidwell was taking notes, too. Sherman said, "Did Jonathan Green take part in any of these conversations?"

"No, ma'am."

Bidwell said, "I saw you and Green together at a news conference."

"That's right. When Mr. Truly said it was time to say my piece, he drove me over to meet Mr. Green."

"Did you and Mr. Green talk about what you were going to say?"

Louise Earle frowned. "I don't think so." She frowned harder, trying to remember. "I guess we didn't. I guess he knew from Mr. Truly. He just said to say it to the newspeople as direct and as honest as I could."

Gibbs leaned forward. "He said for you to be direct and honest?"

Sherman shook her head. "Green's smart." She drew a line across her pad. "Okay. Let's hear what you have."

I told them how Rossi and I had gone to see LeCedrick, and what we had learned from him, and how Kerris and his people had gotten to Mrs. Earle first and how we had followed them to the pumping fields west of Baldwin Hills, and what happened there. I told them what Truly had said as he lay dying. I said, "Truly confirmed everything that Mrs. Earle and LeCedrick said. He tied in Jonathan Green, and stated that it was Green who directed the fabricating of phony evidence implicating Pritzik and Richards."

Bidwell put down his pad. "Why would Green do that?"

I handed him the hard copy printout of the contracts between Jonathan Green and Theodore Martin. "These are copies of confidential retainer agreements between Green and Teddy Martin. They have an amended agreement that gives Jonathan Green ownership and control of most of Teddy's businesses." Anna Sherman stared at me without emotion as I said it.

Bidwell flipped through the sheets, frowning. "How in hell did you come by these?"

I shrugged. "You just find things sometimes."

Sherman smiled, still without emotion.

Bidwell passed the pages to her. "Inadmissable."

Anna Sherman took the pages but didn't look at them. The neutral smile stayed. She said, "You have a dying declaration from Elliot Truly implicating Jonathan Green in the falsification of evidence."

I nodded. "We do."

"Who heard it besides you?"

Rossi said, "I did. So did Joe Pike."

Sherman looked at Louise Earle. "Did you hear it, Mrs. Earle?"

Louise Earle looked uncertain. "I don't think so. They put me behind all this metal. There was shooting, and I thought Mr. Lawrence was dead."

Anna Sherman patted her hand. "That's all right."

Bidwell said, "So what we've got is a dying declaration witnessed by three people who have an interest in attacking Jonathan Green."

Rossi said, "What in hell does that mean?" She stood. "We're giving it to you on a plate, and you're saying it's not enough?"

Bidwell crossed his arms and rocked.

Anna Sherman looked at the third guy. He hadn't said anything, and now he was staring at her. She stood and said, "It's not the best, but I want to move on this. I am confident that these people are telling the truth, and that Jonathan Green is guilty of these crimes."

Rossi said, "Truly said something else, too."

Everyone looked at her.

"He said that Theodore Martin admitted killing his wife."

Anna Sherman smiled again, and Bidwell leaned forward.

"That's why the agreement was amended. Teddy said that he'd pay anything for Green to save him, and Green went for everything. Teddy put almost all of his personal and corporate holdings into escrow as payment to Green."

Bidwell snatched up the pages and flipped through them again.

I said, "There's also a second amendment that releases several million dollars in holdings back to Teddy Martin. I figure it's because Teddy thought he could get bail, and if he got it he was planning to skip."

Rossi said, "Truly confirmed that."

Anna Sherman leaned forward just like Bidwell now, but she wasn't smiling anymore. "Truly said Teddy was planning to skip?"

Rossi and I answered at the same time. "Yes."

Bidwell ran out of the room. The third guy angrily slapped his hands and said, "Sonofabitch!"

I said, "What?"

Anna Sherman slumped back in her chair and looked terribly tired. "Theodore Martin was granted bail this morning at ten o'clock."

heodore "Teddy" Martin was granted bail in the amount of five hundred thousand dollars at ten that morning under a nine-nine-five motion made by Jonathan Green on the defendant's behalf in the Los Angeles Superior Court. The nine-nine-five was granted, according to the presiding judge, due to the revelation of "evidence consistent with innocence." Namely, the evidence found by one Elvis Cole linking Pritzik and Richards to the kidnapping of Susan Martin. The same evidence that Elliot Truly declared to have falsified as he bled to death in a maintenance shed in the Baldwin Hills.

Lincoln Gibbs and Anna Sherman got on the phones in a mad scramble to ascertain Teddy's whereabouts. Calls were made to Green's office, Teddy's business manager, and Teddy's home. Radio cars were sent to all three locations. Both Green's office and the business manager denied any knowledge of Teddy's whereabouts, and there was no answer at his home. The radio car reported that his home appeared empty, and that a Hispanic housekeeper had responded to their knock and said that "Mr. Teddy" was not and had not been home. Sherman grew so angry that she slammed her phone and cursed, and Mrs. Earle said, "What's going on?"

I said, "Teddy jumped bail."

Sherman snapped, "We don't know that."

I picked up the amended retainer agreement and flipped to the list of Teddy's personal and corporate possessions. Teddy Jay Enterprises owned a Cessna Citation jet aircraft. It was listed among the properties transferred to Jonathan Green's control, but what does that matter when you're running for your life? Stealing jets isn't much when you compare it to killing people.

Anna Sherman was yelling into the phone at someone in Jonathan Green's office when I held the amendment in front of her with my finger pointing to the jet. She saw the listing, then said, "Call you back," and hung up. "Where does he keep it?"

"I don't know."

Sherman called Green's business manager again and demanded to know where Teddy housed the jet. She was yelling, and the business manager probably got his nose out of joint because of it, and he probably made the mistake of asking if she had a court order. Sherman went ballistic. Her face turned purple and a webwork of veins stood out on her forehead, and Gibbs said, "Lord, Anna. You'll have a stroke."

Anna Sherman shouted into the phone that if the business manager didn't cooperate she would have him arrested within the hour for accessory after the fact and conspiracy. It worked. The business manager told her, and Anna Sherman repeated the information as he gave it. "Van Nuys airport. Skyway Aviation." She also repeated a phone number, which Dan Tomsic copied.

Gibbs, Tomsic, Rossi, and I watched Anna Sherman dial Skyway, identify herself, and ask to speak with whoever was in charge. Mrs. Earle was watching, too, but you could tell that it wasn't as important to her. Bidwell was arranging a ride back to the hospital for her. The Skyway manager came on the line, and Anna Sherman identified herself again. She asked as to the status of Theodore Martin's Citation jet, then asked several follow-up questions. We knew the answers from her expression. Lincoln Gibbs yelled, "That sonofabitch," and kicked the couch. Tomsic sat and put his face in his hands, as if he'd played a long, close game and given it everything and lost in the end. After maybe six minutes Anna Sherman hung up and looked at us with an ashen, strained face. "Theodore Martin boarded his airplane at approximately eleven-forty this morning, and the jet departed at exactly eleven-fifty-five. His pilot filed a typical IFR flight plan to Rio de Janeiro." Anna Sherman sat in her chair with her hands in her lap and put her head back. "He's gone."

Mrs. Louise Earle looked as if she was about to cry. "Did I do something wrong?"

Angela Rossi stared at her for a moment, then put her arm around Mrs. Earle's shoulders. "No, ma'am. No, you didn't. He just left. It happens all the time."

Sherman took a deep breath, then sat forward and picked up the phone again. Only this time there wasn't any urgency to it. "I'll notify the FBI and ask them to speak to the State Department. He's still in the air. Maybe we can work something out with the Brazilians."

Bidwell said, "We don't have reciprocal extradition with Brazil."

Sherman snapped, "Maybe we can work something out."

I said, "You going to do anything about Green?"

Anna Sherman stared at me for maybe six seconds, then she put down the phone. "Oh, yes. Yes, I'm definitely going to do something about Mr. Green."

Bidwell said, "You want to file an arrest warrant?"

Anna Sherman was looking at Angela Rossi. "Yes, we'll file an arrest warrant. I saw Judge Kelton downstairs. Look him up and have it signed." Arrest warrants had to be signed by a judge.

Bidwell started toward the door. "I'll call Green's office and set it up. How much time do you want to give him to turn himself in?" Often in cases like this, the attorney is notified that a warrant has been issued and is allowed to turn himself in.

Anna Sherman shook her head, still looking at Angela Rossi. "To hell with that. We're going to go over there and arrest his ass."

Angela Rossi smiled. So did everyone else.

I said, "You guys mind if I tag along?"

Lincoln Gibbs was pacing now. Grinning and anxious to take action, sort of like a leopard sensing that a hunt was on. "No sweat."

Rossi wanted to come, too, but Lincoln Gibbs told her no. She was still suspended, and an administrative action could be taken against her for violating her suspension.

Sherman and Bidwell made their calls and drafted their documents, and one hour and ten minutes later they were ready to pay a visit to Mr. Jonathan Green, Attorney to the Stars. Mrs. Louise Earle had already been returned to the hospital. Rossi walked out with us, but in the lobby she had to go one way and we another. A radio car was going to take her home.

Rossi put out her hand and we shook. "I want to thank you."

"No problem."

"No, I mean it."

"I understand."

"I'll call Joe."

I said, "So long, Rossi."

We smiled at each other and then she walked away.

Gibbs and Tomsic and I crowded into Anna Sherman's car and drove to Jonathan Green's office on Sunset Boulevard. A couple of uniforms in a radio car followed us. A district attorney almost never accompanied the police on an arrest, but then neither did freelance private eyes. I guess this was just too good to pass up.

We double-parked in front of his building, jamming up the westbound flow on Sunset, and walked in past the receptionist and the security guys in their blazers. A blond security guy with a red face tried to make a deal about stopping us to see the warrant, but Dan Tomsic said, "You've gotta be kidding," and motioned at the uniforms to walk the guy out of the way.

We took the elevator up to the fourth floor and Sherman said, "You've been here before. Which way?"

I showed them to Green's office. Green had not been notified of Elliot Truly's death, nor of the deaths of his other people, nor had it yet hit the news. As we walked through the halls, lawyers and legal assistants and secretaries and clerks appeared in their doors. Jonathan Green's secretary stood as we approached, and I said, "Knock knock knock, Chicken Delight!"

She looked at Anna Sherman. "May I help you?"

Anna Sherman said, "No." We trooped past the secretary and through the door and into Green's office. Green and the two lesser attorneys and the videographer and three people I'd never seen before were seated around his conference table with their jackets off and their sleeves rolled. The videographer and his sound tech were seated in the background, the camera on the floor, sipping coffee and talking between themselves. Guess there's only so much you can do with endless footage of lawyers sitting around tables. Jonathan Green looked at us without a great deal of surprise and said, "Doors are made for knocking."

I said, "Not bad. I was kinda hoping you'd say, 'What's the meaning of this?'"

Anna Sherman smiled sweetly. "Sorry for the intrusion, Jonathan. But we're here to arrest you on the charges of tampering with evidence, obstruction of justice, conspiracy to commit murder, and murder."

The videographer's eyes got big and his jaw dropped. I waved at his camera. "Better turn it on. You don't want to miss this." The videographer jumped across the sound tech for his camera, spilling both his coffee and hers.

Anna Sherman turned to Lincoln Gibbs. "Lieutenant, please inform Mr. Green of his rights and take him into custody."

Lt. Lincoln Gibbs handed the warrant forms to Jonathan, then recited his rights. Jonathan didn't interupt, and didn't bother to examine the forms. He sat with a kind of half-smile, as if he had anticipated these events. Maybe he had. When Gibbs finished with the rights, he said, "Would you stand, sir? I have to handcuff you." Polite.

Jonathan submitted without complaint. He said, "Anna, this is the most flagrant case of judicial manipulation I've ever seen. I'll have you before the bar for this."

Anna Sherman said, "Teddy Martin has jumped bail and is on his way to Brazil. Elliot Truly, Stan Kerris, and two other men in your employ are dead. Elliot Truly supplied a dying declaration implicating you in the manufacture of false evidence, as well as the murder of James Lester and the kidnapping of Louise Earle."

Jonathan Green said, "That's absurd. I don't know what you're talking about." He angled his face toward the camera when he said it.

She said, "That's why we have trials, Jonathan. To determine the facts."

Lincoln Gibbs took Green by the arm and guided him to the door. Jonathan Green turned back just long enough to say, "We won't get to trial, Anna." He smiled when he said it, and his smile was confident and without fear. "I guess you believe you have reason to do this, but for the life of me I can't imagine what it might be." He angled toward the video camera again. "I look forward to seeing your proof, and I hope for your sake that this isn't some ugly form of harassment."

Gibbs and Tomsic escorted him out, the videographer scurrying ahead of them to capture every moment of the arrest and departure.

I stood with Sherman, watching them go, and wondered at Jonathan Green's lack of concern. I was thinking that maybe he was crazy, or arrogant, or brimming with the fatal flaw of hubris, but you never know.

Maybe he was just used to winning.

37

Theodore Martin's flight from the country was covered throughout the evening by every one of the local Los Angeles television stations, effectively eliminating regular programming. Live news remote teams assaulted Skyway Aviation, Angela Rossi's home, Jonathan Green's office, and spokespeople for both the LAPD and the District Attorney's office. Angela Rossi did not return home that night, and so was unavailable for comment. She picked up her boys and spent the night with a friend. The Skyway people were available, however, and were more than a little surprised by the army of microwave vans and news teams who invaded their otherwise quiet world.

The Skyway employees who were interviewed included the flight operations manager, a young female flight dispatcher, and an even younger male line attendant. The line attendant was a seventeen-year-old kid name Billy Galovich who washed the planes, pumped them full of jet fuel, and pushed them in and out of a hangar with a little tractor. The sum total of his involvement in Teddy Martin's escape was that he had towed out Teddy's Citation, fueled it, then greeted the pilot, a very nice Hispanic man who introduced himself as Mr. Garcia. I counted fourteen interviews with Billy Galovich that evening, and then I stopped counting.

The flight dispatcher's claim to fame was that she had taken the call from Teddy Martin, who personally ordered that his Citation be readied for flight. The dispatcher's name was Shannon Denleigh, and she related that Mr. Martin told her that his pilot would be a man named Mr. Roberto Garcia, and that Mr. Garcia would be along directly. She said that she informed the flight operations manager, a Mr. Dale Ellison, of the call and then she left the premises to have her nails done. I stopped counting her interviews at sixteen. Dale Ellison related that Mr. Garcia arrived moments later, preflighted the Citation, and filed his flight plan. He said that Mr. Garcia was an amiable, friendly man who identified himself as a flight officer with Air Argentina who picked up corporate charters to earn extra money. I didn't bother to count the number of times that Dale Ellison was interviewed, but it was plenty.

Reports of Jonathan Green's arrest and the charges against him were interspersed with the coverage of Teddy's flight, but when the newspeople discovered that the Citation was still in the air, the real show began. Reporters and cameras descended upon the FAA and the various Flight Operations Centers between Los Angeles and Rio. The Citation's path was charted, and its progress was depicted on a global map. It was kind of like watching the beginning of *Casablanca*. Every network put a little clock in the corner of their picture, counting down the time until the Citation landed. Crime and show business had merged.

Foreign bureau reporters flocked to the Rio de Janeiro airport, and Teddy Martin's landing was covered live even though it was after midnight in Rio and you really couldn't see anything. The Citation taxied to a private flight service facility for corporate jets where it was met by Brazilian authorities and a small army of newspeople. A spokesman for the Brazilian authorities said that Mr. Martin would be questioned as to his plans, but thereafter would be free to go. Teddy Martin pushed through the cameras with his face covered, ignoring the shouting reporters. He reached the flight service facility's door, then apparently changed his mind and paused to make a short statement. Teddy Martin said, "Please don't interpret my flight from California as indicative of guilt. I promise you, I swear to you all, that I did not murder my wife. I loved her. I left because I am convinced that I could not and would not get a fair and just hearing. I do not know why they are doing this to me." He disappeared into the building and must have slipped out by some prearranged and secret manner because he was not seen again.

I went to bed at twenty minutes after one that night, and still the networks were on the air, rehashing the landing, replaying the interviews, offering taped "live" coverage of something that was no more alive than a nightmare.

he phone rang several times throughout the night. I stopped answering and let the machine get the calls after I realized that they were reporters, looking for yet another comment. I finally unplugged the phone.

I slept late the next morning and woke to a quiet house. The cat was sleeping on the foot of my bed and the finches were waiting on the deck rail and no one was trying to shoot me, which was good, but for the first time in many days I felt the emptiness of Lucy's absence, which wasn't.

My involvement with Angela Rossi and Louise Earle and the events in their lives seemed to be at an end or, if not ended, then certainly diminished. Anna Sherman wanted to interview me in greater detail, but she would speak to Rossi first, then Gibbs and Tomsic. It might be days before we could get together.

I got out of bed, took a shower, then ate a bowl of granola and cottage cheese and sliced peaches. I drank a glass of nonfat milk. I phoned Martin Luther King Hospital, asked about Mr. Lawrence, and was told that he was doing well even though he was listed in critical condition. The nurse remembered me, and told me that Mrs. Earle was still there, asleep in the waiting room. She had been there throughout the night. I called a florist I know and sent flowers, addressing them to Mrs. Earle as well as to Mr. Lawrence. I hoped that they would brighten her day.

At twenty minutes after eleven my phone rang again, and this time I answered. Life in the fast lane. Joe Pike said, "Are you looking at this?"

"What?"

"Turn on your television."

I did.

Jonathan Green was surrounded by reporters on the steps of the Superior Court Building. The network legal analyst was saying that Green had been arraigned at ten A.M., had posted minimal bail, and was now about to make a statement. The two lesser attorneys were behind him, as was an older, gray-haired African-American attorney named Edwin Foss. Foss was a criminal defense attorney of Green's stature who had made his reputation defending a transient who had shot four people to death while robbing an AM-PM Minimart. The murders had been caught on videotape, but Foss had still managed to gain an acquittal. I guess he had convinced the jury that it was reasonable to doubt what they had seen.

Edwin Foss whispered in Jonathan's ear, then Jonathan stepped to the microphones and made his statement. His tone was somber and apologetic, and Foss kept a hand on Jonathan's shoulder as he spoke. Guidance. Green said, "No one is more surprised by Theodore Martin's actions than me. I have believed in his innocence from the beginning, and I still believe him to be an innocent man. I believed then, and believe now, that the evidence against Theodore Martin was planted by unscrupulous officers involved in the investigation. Teddy, if you can hear these words, I urge you to return. Justice will prevail."

Pike said, "You think Teddy's tuned in, down there in Rio?"

"Shh."

Green said, "I pledge my full cooperation to those investigating the charges that have been made against me. I will aid in uncovering whatever wrongdoing has occurred, if any, and in the prosecution of anyone in my employ who has conspired to breech the canon of ethics by which I have lived my life. I state now, publicly and for the record, that I have behaved honorably and within the law. I have done no wrong."

Green's attorney again whispered something in Green's ear and gently pulled him away from the microphones. The reporters shouted questions, but Green's attorney waved them off and said that there would be no questions.

I turned off the television and said, "This guy is something. He's already doctoring the spin."

Pike didn't respond.

"You don't think he can beat this, do you?"

There was a pause, then Pike hung up. Guess he didn't have an answer. Or maybe he didn't want to think that it was possible.

I made an early lunch for myself, then brought the phone out onto the deck and called Lucy Chenier at her office. She had heard about Jonathan's arrest and Teddy's flight on the national news, but she didn't seem particularly anxious to hear the inside dirt. When I described the events beneath the radio towers, she told me that she was late for a meeting. Great. Anna Sherman called later that afternoon and asked me to come to her office the following day to make a statement. I did, and spent three hours in the Criminal Courts Building being interviewed by Sherman, Bidwell, and three LAPD detectives whom I had not previously met. Pike came in as I was leaving. Sherman told me that Mrs. Earle had been interviewed the day before.

Two days after my interview, Mr. Walter Lawrence was taken off the critical list. His prognosis was excellent. I went to see him and brought more flowers. Mrs. Earle was still there, and told me that she planned to visit LeCedrick. It would be the first time that she'd seen him in the six years that he had been at Terminal Island. I offered to drive her.

Teddy's flight and Green's arrest stayed in the headlines. "Teddy Sightings" were a regular feature in the tabloids, which reported on various occasions that Teddy was now living in a palatial Brazilian mansion that had been built by a famous Nazi war criminal, that Teddy had been seen in the company of Princess Diana, and that Teddy was gone for good because he had been abducted by short gray aliens with large heads. The California State Bar Association announced that it was launching an investigation into Jonathan Green's conduct independent of that by the Los Angeles Police Department and the District Attorney's office. Green said that he welcomed the opportunity to clear his name and would cooperate fully.

Jonathan Green and his attorney appeared regularly on local television news, local radio talk shows, and in the L.A. *Times*. Reports from "unnamed sources" began surfacing that Elliot Truly had made a secret deal with Teddy, unknown to Mr. Green. Leaks "close to the prosecution" were quoted as saying that computer files found at Elliot Truly's home confirmed such an agreement. Other sources leaked that Truly had had several meetings with Teddy while Teddy was in jail to which Mr. Green was not privy. Carefully worded public opinion polls charted a swing in the belief of Jonathan Green's involvement from "absolutely" to "probably" to "uncertain."

Eleven days after the events beneath the radio tower, the LAPD Internal Affairs Division announced that it had completed its investigation of Detective Angela Rossi and had found there to be no evidence either in the LeCedrick Earle matter (LeCedrick Earle himself had recanted his claims against her) or that she had manufactured or planted evidence against Theodore Martin. The story was given two inches on page nineteen of the *Times*, and the same public opinion polls indicated that seventy-three percent of the public still believed that she was a corrupt cop who had framed LeCedrick Earle (even though he now denied it) and who had "probably" mishandled evidence against Teddy Martin. She was returned to active duty with her partner, Dan Tomsic.

I listened to the news and followed the investigations with a growing sense of unease. Jonathan Green signed a two-million-dollar contract with a major book publisher to publish his version of the story. He appeared on *Larry King Live* and *Rivera Live*, and each time he presented himself as a victim. I was offered many jobs, but I declined them. The press still called, though with less frequency, and I avoided them. I listened to talk radio and gained weight, as if I felt a hunger that I couldn't satisfy.

The days grew warm again, and I decided to refinish the deck. It had been almost eight years since I'd last stained and sealed the deck, and the wood was showing its age. Joe offered his help, and we spent the core of each day sanding and staining and sealing. We listened to music as we worked, but from time to time we turned to the news. Twenty-three days after the events beneath the radio tower, the California Bar quietly closed its investigation, saying that all evidence pointed to wrongdoing by Elliot Truly and not by Jonathan Green. Twenty-five days after the tower, the District Attorney's office dropped all charges against Jonathan Green save one count of tampering with evidence. I was on a ladder beneath the deck when we heard the news, and Pike said, "He's getting away with it."

I went inside and called Anna Sherman, who said, "It's the best we can do." Her voice was faraway and sounded lost.

I said, "This is crap. You *know* he was behind it."

"Of course."

"He set up Truly just like he set up Rossi and Pritzik and Richards. He ordered Lester's murder. They were going to kill Louise Earle. He did his best to destroy the life and career of a police officer who did nothing worse than do her job."

She didn't say anything for a time, and then she said, "He knows how to play the game, Elvis. What can I tell you?" Then she hung up.

Twenty-eight days after the towers, Pike and I finished sealing the deck. It was slick and gleaming and smelled of marine-grade varnish. After the varnish had cured, we put the deck chairs and the Weber and the little table back, and sat in the sun drinking cold Falstaff. We sat for awhile, and then Pike said, "Say something."

I looked at him.

"You haven't said anything for three days. You've said next to nothing for almost two weeks."

"Guess I'm getting like you."

I smiled at him, but he didn't smile back.

I finished my Falstaff, crimped the can, then put it carefully onto the shining deck. Little rings of condensation beaded on the thick varnish. I said, "I'm not sure that I want to do this anymore."

"Be an investigator?"

I nodded.

"What do you want to do?"

I shrugged.

"You want to stop being what you've been for almost fifteen years because Jonathan Green is getting away with murder?" He frowned when he said it. Like maybe he was disappointed.

I spread my hands. "I guess that's it. Elvis Cole, sore loser."

Pike shook his head.

I went inside, brought out two fresh Falstaffs, and gave him one. I said, "What would you say if I told you that I was thinking about moving to Louisiana to be closer to Lucy?"

Pike sipped some of the Falstaff, then gazed out at the canyon, then wet his lips and nodded. "I'd say that I'd miss you."

I nodded.

"I'd say that if that's what you needed to do, that I would help any way that I could."

I nodded again.

"You talk to her about it?"

"Not yet."

Pike shook his head. "You're something."

Four hours later Pike was gone and I was cooking a very nice *puttanesca* sauce when I decided to call Lucy Chenier. I was most of the way through a bottle of California merlot. In the course of my life I've been shot, sapped, slugged, stabbed with a broken beer bottle, and I've faced down any number of thugs and miscreants, but talking to Lucy about moving to Louisiana seemed to require fortification. She answered on the third ring, and I said, "Guess who?"

"Have you been drinking?" Don't you hate smart women?

"Absolutely not." Giving her affronted. Giving her shocked. Then I said, "Well, maybe a little."

She sighed. "I heard on the news that the charges against Green were reduced. How's Angela?"

"Not great, but not bad, either. The public still thinks that she's rotten, but IA cleared her."

"How nice for her children."

"Green kept himself insulated so that there was always plausible deniability."

"What about Truly's dying declaration?" I had told her about Truly weeks ago. "That's legitimate evidence."

"It is, but since it was witnessed only by me and Angela and Joe, the powers that be view it as questionable. Because I resigned from Green's employ, and because he accused Rossi, the powers that be feel that a jury would discount our version of events."

She didn't say anything for a time, and then she said, "Well, in this case the powers that be are probably right."

I nodded, but she probably couldn't see it. "I don't believe Truly had a secret agreement with Teddy Martin. Green fabricated that, just as he fabricated the business about Pritzik and Richards."

"I'm sure you're right."

"Truly was telling the truth."

"I'm sure of that, too."

I didn't say anything. I was staring at the bubbles rising in the sauce and my shoulders felt tight and I was wishing that I hadn't drunk all the wine.

Lucy said, "It hurts, doesn't it?"

I moved my tongue, trying to scrub away the wine's taste. "Oh, God, yes."

"You try so hard to make things right, and here's this man, and he's oozing through the system in a way that keeps things wrong."

"He is defiling justice." Defiling. That was probably the merlot talking.

She said, "Oh, Studly." I could see her smile. "The law is not about justice. You know that."

I finished the merlot and turned off the sauce. It was thick with chunks of tomatoes and black olives and raisins. I had cooked it without being hungry. Maybe I just wanted to give myself something worthwhile to do. "Of course I know, but it should be."

Lucy said, "The law is an adversarial contest that defines justice as staying within the rules and seeing the game to its conclusion. Justice is reaching a conclusion. It has very little to do with right and wrong. The law gives us order. Only men and women can give us what you want to call justice."

I took a deep breath and let it out. "God, Lucille, I wish you were here."

"I know." Her voice was soft and hard to hear. Then she said, "You're still the World's Greatest Detective, honey pie. They can't take that away from you."

It made me smile.

Neither of us spoke for a time, and then Lucy said, "Do you remember Tracy Mannos at Channel Eight? We met her at Green's party."

"Sure. The program manager."

"She called me last week. She arranged for the network affiliate here in Baton Rouge to shoot a test tape of me, and after she saw it she offered me a job as an on-air legal commentator."

I said, "In Baton Rouge?"

"No, Elvis. Out there. In Los Angeles."

I couldn't say anything. The merlot seemed to be rushing through my ears.

Lucy said, "It's more money, and we would be closer to you, but it's such a big move." You could hear her uncertainty.

I said, "You'd come to Los Angeles?"

"There's so much to think about. There's Ben. There's my house and my friends. I'm not sure what to do about Richard."

"Please say yes." It came out hoarse.

She didn't say anything for a time. "I don't know just yet. I need to think about it."

"I told Joe that I was thinking about moving to Baton Rouge."

Another pause. "Are you?"

"Yes."

"Would you?"

"Yes."

"Why?"

"You know why, Lucille. I love you."

She didn't speak for another moment, and when she did her voice seemed lighter, somehow more at ease. "I need to think."

"Call me tomorrow."

"I may not know tomorrow."

"Call me anyway."

She said, "I love you, Studly. Always remember that."

Lucille Chenier hung up, and I lay on my kitchen floor and smiled at the ceiling, and not very much later I knew that I had found the last and final way to bring Jonathan Green to justice.

Or, at least, a close approximation.

39

I called Eddie Ditko first. He came over that night, coughing and wheezing, but happy to eat spaghetti with the *puttanesca* sauce and listen to my account of the events in the maintenance shed while he recorded my every word. He grinned a lot while I talked, and said that he could guarantee a bottom half of the front-page position for the story. He said, "Man, the shit's gonna hit the fan when this comes out."

"That's the idea."

When Eddie was gone, I called Tracy Mannos, who put me in touch with Lyle Stodge at twenty minutes after ten. Lyle and Marcy anchored the eleven P.M. newscast as well as the five. Lyle was only too happy to talk to me, and only too happy to accept my offer of an interview. He said, "We've been hoping to get you for a comment on all of this! Can you make the eleven o'clock?"

"Nope."

"How about tomorrow at five?"

"I'll be there." The five o'clock newscast had the larger audience.

I phoned every person who had interviewed me in print or on radio or television, or who had wanted to interview me. I spent most of the night and part of the next morning on the phone, and everybody was happy to talk to me. I called both Peter Alan Nelsen and Jodi Taylor, and asked if they could put me in touch with any of the major network and cable news people, and of course they could. Even *Daily Variety* wanted an interview. Everybody wanted to know if I had been duped by Theodore Martin, and everybody wanted to know what had happened in the maintenance shed, and everyone still considered me the hero of the defense effort, just the way Jonathan had hoped when he had staged the news conferences with his hand on my shoulder. I told them that I would be happy to tell them exactly what happened, especially if we were on the air live.

By three the following afternoon, I had completed eleven interviews, and had provided each interviewer with a copy of Green's amended retainer agreement with Theodore Martin. Seven other interviews were scheduled, and more would be forthcoming. I had copies for them, too.

At twelve minutes after three, I parked in a red zone outside Jonathan Green's Sunset Boulevard building and went inside. I shoved past the receptionist and ran up the stairs and barged past the army of clerks and assistants and minions. There was a noticeable absence of blue-blazered security guards, but I guess those few who hadn't been killed in Baldwin Hills had been fired. All the better for Green to separate himself from Kerris.

The *Inside News* videographer and his sound technician were talking to a slim woman by the coffee machine when I went past. The videographer's eyes went wide when he saw me, and the sound tech dropped her coffee. The videographer said, "What are you doing here?"

I grabbed him by the arm and pulled him along. "Do you have tape in that thing?"

"Sure."

"You're going to love this."

The sound tech scrambled after us.

Jonathan Green's office occupied the entire east end of the fourth floor. An efficient-looking woman in her early forties tried to tell me that I couldn't go in, but I ducked around her and hit the door, only the door wouldn't open. The woman said, "You stop that! You stop that before I call the police!"

The sound tech said, "You have to buzz it open."

I said, "Where?"

The sound tech hurried to the woman's desk and pressed the buzzer. The sound tech was grinning.

I kicked open the door and stormed in and found Jonathan Green on the phone. The two lesser attorneys were with him, along with a younger man with a notepad. Somebody's secretary. The smaller of the lesser attorneys fell over a chair trying to get out of my way. Green said, "I'm calling the police!"

I pulled the phone out of his hands and tossed it aside. I said, "Here's the bad news, Jonathan: You've become my hobby. I know what Truly knew, and I am telling it to anyone who will listen."

Green maneuvered to keep his desk between us. His

face had grown white. "The police are on their way! I'm warning you!"

I threw a copy of the retainer agreement at him. "I'm also passing out copies of this. The *Examiner* is going to print it in this evening's edition."

Green looked at it without touching it and shook his head. "This means nothing. For all anyone knows you wrote it yourself. It isn't admissible."

"Not in a court of law, Jonathan. But we're going to try you in the court of public opinion." I shoved his desk, and Jonathan jumped backward. "I will hound you, and I will not stop. I will tell everyone that it was you who falsified the evidence, and you who ordered James Lester killed, and you who attempted to take the life of Louise Earle." I started around the end of the desk, and Jonathan scrambled in the opposite direction.

"You can't do that! I'll get a restraining order!"

"What's that to a tough guy like me?"

"No one will believe you!"

"Sure they will, Jonathan. I am the World's Greatest Detective, remember? Above reproach. Trustworthy."

Jonathan glared at the lesser attorneys and yelled, "Don't just stand there! Do something!"

The larger lesser attorney ran out the door.

"I will keep this alive until the DA can finally build a case or until you are driven out of business. I will haunt you like a bad dream. I will come to your house and follow you into restaurants and send videotapes of my interviews to your clients."

He drew himself up into a vision of outrage. "We have

laws against that, you idiot! That's libel! That's slander! You won't get away with it!"

I looked at the videographer. "Are you getting this?"

The videographer was all smiles. "Hell, yes! What an ending!"

I jumped across the desk and punched Jonathan Green hard in the mouth one time. He floundered backward and went over his chair and landed on his ass. The smaller lesser attorney shouted, "Oh, my God," and then he ran, too.

Jonathan Green said, "You hit me! You actually laid hands on me!" He felt his mouth, then looked at his red fingers and started crying. "You broke my teeth!"

I walked over to Jonathan Green, looked down at him, and said, "So sue me."

And then I walked out.

If you loved *Sunset Express*,
be sure to catch Robert Crais's
Indigo Slam coming in June 1997
from Hyperion.

Here's the first chapter.

Indigo Slam

PROLOGUE

At two-fourteen in the morning on the night they left one life to begin their next, the rain thundered down in a raging curtain that thrummed against the house and the porch and the plain white Econoline van that the United States Marshals had brought to whisk them away.

Charles said, "C'mere, Teri, and lookit this."

Her younger brother, Charles, was framed in the front window of their darkened house. The house was dark because the marshalls wanted it that way. No interior lights, they said. Candles and flashlights would be better, they said.

Teresa, whom everyone called Teri, joined her brother at the window, and together they looked at the van parked at the curb. Lightning snapped like a giant flash-bulb, illuminating the van and the narrow street of clapboard houses in the Ferengi Hills in the south part of Seattle, just up from Jessup Bay. The van's side and rear doors were open, and a man was squatting inside the van, arranging boxes. Two other men finished talking to the van's driver, and came up the walk toward the house. All four men were dressed identically in long black slickers and black hats that they held against the rain. It beat at them as if it wanted to punch right through the coats and the hats and hammer them into the earth. Teri thought that in a few minutes it would be beating at her. Charles said, "Lookit the size of that truck. That truck's big enough to bring my bike, isn't it? Why can't I bring my bike?"

Teri said, "That's not a truck, it's a van, and the men said we could only take the boxes." Charles was nine years old, three years younger than Teri, and didn't want to leave his bike. Teri didn't want to leave her things, either, but the men had said they could only take eight boxes. Four people at two boxes a person equals eight boxes. Simple math.

"They got plenty of room."

"We'll get you another bike. Daddy said."

Charles scowled. "I don't want another bike."

The first man to step in from the rain seemed ten feet tall, and the second seemed even taller. Water dripped from their coats onto the wooden floor, and Teri's first thought was to get a towel before the drips made spots, but, of course, the towels were packed and it wouldn't matter anyway. She would never see this house again. The first man smiled at her and said, "I'm Peterson. This is Jasper." They held out little leather wallets with gold and silver badges. The badges sparkled in the candlelight. "We're just about done. Where's your dad?"

Teri had been helping Winona say goodbye to the

room that they shared when the men arrived fifteen minutes ago. Winona was six, and the youngest of the three Hewitt children. Teri had had to be with her as Winona went around her room saying, "Goodbye, bed. Goodbye, closet. Goodbye, dresser." Beds and closets and dressers weren't things that you could put in eight boxes. Teri said, "He's in the bathroom. Would you like me to get him?" Teri's dad, Clark Hewitt, had what he called 'a weak constitution.' That meant he went to the bathroom whenever he was nervous, and tonight he was *very* nervous.

The tall man who was Jasper called, "Hey, Clark, whip it and flip it, bud! We're ready!"

Peterson smiled at Teri. "You kids ready?"

Teri thought, of course they were ready, couldn't he see that? She'd had Charles and Winona packed and dressed an hour ago. She said, "Winona!"

Winona came running into the living room. She was wearing her pink plastic *Beverly Hills 90210* raincoat and carrying her purple plastic toy suitcase. Winona's straw-colored hair was held back with a bright green scrunchie. Teri knew that there were dolls in the suitcase, because Teri had helped Winona pack. Charles had his blue school backpack and his yellow slicker together on the couch.

Jasper called again, "Hey, Clark, let's go! We're drowning out there, buddy!"

The toilet off the kitchen flushed and Teri's dad came into the living room. Clark Hewitt was a thin, nervous man whose eyes never seemed to stay in one place. "I'm ready."

"We won't be coming back, Clark. You're not forgetting anything, are you?"

Clark shook his head. "I don't think so."

"You got the place locked up?"

Clark frowned as if he couldn't quite remember, and looked at Teri. Teri said, "I locked the back door and the windows and the garage. They're going to turn off the gas and the phones and the electricity tomorrow." Someone with the Marshals had given her father a list of things to do, and Teri had gone down the list. The list had a title: *Steps to an Orderly Evacuation*. "I just have to blow out the candles and we can go."

Teri knew that Peterson was staring at her, but she wasn't sure why. Peterson shook his head, then made a little gesture to Jasper. "I'll take care of the candles, little miss. Jasper, get'm loaded."

Clark started to the front door, but Reed Jasper stopped him. "Your raincoat."

"Hunh?"

"Earth to Clark. It's raining like a bitch out there."

Clark said, "Raincoat? I just had it." He looked at Teri again.

Teri said, "I'll get it."

Teri hurried down the hall past the room that she used to share with Winona and into her father's bedroom. She blew out the candle there, then stood in the darkness and listened to the rain. Her father's raincoat was on the bed where she'd placed it. He'd been standing at the foot of the bed when she'd put it there, but that's the way he was—forgetful, always thinking about something else. Teri picked up the raincoat and held it close, smelling the cheap fabric and the man-smell she knew to be her father's. Maybe he'd been thinking about Salt Lake City, which is where they were going. Teri knew that her father was in trouble with some very bad men who wanted to hurt them. The Federal Marshals were here to bring them to Salt Lake City where they would change their names. Once they had a Fresh Start, her father had said, he would start a new business and they would all live happily ever after. She didn't know who the bad men were or why they were so mad at her father. Something about testifying in front of a jury. Her father had tried explaining it to her but it had come out jumbled and confused, the way most things her father tried to explain came out. Like when her mother had died. Teri had been Winona's age, and her father had told her that her Momma had gone home to see Jesus and then he'd started blubbering and nothing he'd said after that made any sense. Teri hugged him tight, and it was another four days before she'd learned that her mother, an assistant night manager for the Great Northwest Food Store chain, had died in an auto accident, hit by a drunk driver.

Teri looked around the room. This had been her mother's room, just as this house had been her mother's house, as it had been Teri's for as long as she could remember. There was one closet and two windows looking toward the alley at the back of the house and a queen bed and a dresser and a chest. Her mother had slept in this bed and kept her clothes in this chest and looked at herself in that dresser mirror. Her mother had breathed the air in this room, and her warmth had spread through the sheets and made them toasty and perfect for snuggling when Teri was little. Her mother would read to her. Her mother would sing "Edelweiss." Teri closed her eyes and tried to feel the warmth, but couldn't. Teri had a hard time remembering her mother as a living being; she remembered a face in pictures, and now they were leaving. Goodbye, Mama.

Teri hugged her father's raincoat tight, then turned to leave the room when she heard the thump in the back yard. It was a dull, heavy sound against the back wall of the house, distinct against the rain. She looked through the rear window and saw a black shadow move through the rain, and that's when Mr. Peterson stepped silently into the door. "Teri, I want you to go to the front door, now, please." His voice was low and urgent.

Teri said, "I saw something in the yard."

Peterson pulled her past a man in a still-dripping raincoat. The man who'd been loading the boxes. He held his right hand straight down along his leg and Teri saw that he had a gun.

Her father and Charles and Winona were standing with Mr. Jasper. Her father's eyes looked wild, as if at any moment they might pop right out onto the floor. Jasper said, "C'mon, Pete, it's probably nothing."

Her father clutched Jasper's arm. "I thought you said they didn't know. You said we were safe."

Jasper pried her father's hand away as Mr. Peterson said, "I'll check it out while you get'm in the van." He looked worried. "Jerry! Let's move!"

The third man reappeared and picked up Winona. "C'mon, honey. You're with me."

Jasper said, "I'll check it with you." Jasper was breathing fast.

Mr. Peterson pushed Jasper toward the door. "Get'm in the van. Now!"

Jasper said, "It's probably nothing."

Charles said, "What's happening?"

A loud cracking came from the kitchen, as if the back door was being pried open, and then Peterson was pushing them hard through the door, yelling, "Do it, Jasper! Take'm!" and her father moaned, a kind of faraway wail that made Winona start crying. Jerry bolted toward the street, carrying Winona in one arm and pulling Teri's father with the other, shouting something that Teri could not understand. Jasper said, "Oh, holy shit!" and tossed Charles across his shoulder like a laundry bag. He grabbed Teri *HARD* by the arm, so hard that she had never felt such pain and thought her flesh and bone would surely be crushed into a mealy red pulp like you see in those Freddie Kruger movies, and then Jasper was pulling her out into the rain as, somewhere in the back of the house, she heard Mr. Peterson shout, very clearly, "Federal Marshals!" and then there were three sharp BOOMS that didn't sound anything like thunder, not anything at all.

The rain felt like a heavy cloak across Teri's shoulders and splattered up from the sidewalk to wet her legs as they ran for the van. Charles was kicking his legs, screaming, "I don't have my raincoat! I left it inside!"

The driver had the window down, oblivious to the

rain, eyes wide and darting as Jerry pushed first Winona and then Clark into the side door. The van's engine screamed to life.

Jasper ran to the rear of the van and shoved Teri inside. Clark was holding Winona, huddled together between the boxes and the driver's seat. Winona was still crying, her father bug-eyed and panting. Two more BOOMS came from the house, loud and distinct even with the rain hammering in through the open doors and windows. The driver twisted toward them, screaming, "What the fuck's happening?!"

Jerry yanked a short black shotgun from behind the seat. "I'm with Pete! Get'm outta here!"

Japser clawed out his gun, trying to scramble back out into the rain, saying, "I'm with you!"

Jerry pushed Jasper back into the van. "You get these people outta here, goddamnit! You get'm out NOW!" Jerry slammed the door in Jasper's face and the driver was screaming, "What happened?! Where's Peterson?"

Jasper seemed torn, but then he screamed back, "Drive! Get the hell outta here!" He crushed past the cardboard boxes to the van's rear window, cursing over and over, "Always some shit! Always some goddamn bullshit!"

The van slid sideways from the curb as it crabbed for traction. The drive shouted into some kind of radio and Jasper cursed and Teri's father started crying like Winona, and Charles was crying, too. Teri thought that maybe even Federal Marshal Jasper was crying, but she couldn't be sure because he was watching out the van's square rear window.

Teri felt her eyes well with tears, but then, very clearly, she told herself: *No, you will not cry.* And she didn't. The tears went away, and Teri felt very calm. She was soaked under her raincoat, and she realized that the floor was wet from rain blown in when the doors were open. The eight cardboard boxes that held the sum total of their lives were wet, too.

Her father said, "What happened back there? You said we were safe! You said they wouldn't know!"

Jasper glanced back at her father. Jasper looked scared, too. "I don't know. Somehow they found out."

Teri's father shouted, "Well, that's just great! That's wonderful!" His voice was very high. "Now they're gonna kill us!"

Jasper went back to staring out the window. "They're not going to kill you."

"That's what you people said before!" Her father's voice was a shriek.

Jasper turned again and stared at Teri's father for the longest time before he said, "Peterson is still back there, Mr. Hewitt."

Teri watched her brother and sister and father, huddled together and crying, and then she knew what she must do. She crawled across the wet, tumbled boxes and along the van's gritty bed and went to her family. She found a place for herself between Winona and her father, and looked up into her father's frightened eyes. His face was pale and drawn, and the thin wet hair matted across his forehead made him look lost. She said, "Don't be scared, Daddy."

Clark Hewitt whimpered, and Teri could feel him

shivering. It was July, and the rain was warm, but maybe he wasn't shivering because he was cold. Teri said, "I won't let anyone hurt us, and I won't let anything happen to you. I promise."

Clark Hewitt nodded without looking at her. She held onto him tightly, and felt his shaking ease.

The van careened through the night, hidden by the darkness and rain.

THREE YEARS LATER

1

It was plant day in the City of Angels. On plant day I gather the plants that I keep in my office and bring them out onto the little balcony I have overlooking West Los Angeles where I clean and water and feed them, and then spend the remainder of the afternoon wondering why my plants are more yellow than green. A friend who knows plants once told me that I was giving them too much water, so I cut their rations in half. When the plants turned soft as well as yellow, another friend said that I was still overwatering, so I cut their water in half again. The plants died. I bought new plants and stopped asking other people's advice. Yellow plants are my curse.

I was sneering at all the yellow when Lucy Chenier said, "I don't think I'll be able to get away until much later, Elvis. I'm afraid we've lost the afternoon."

"Oh?" I was using a new cordless phone to talk to Lucille Chenier from the balcony as I worked on the plants. It was in the low eighties, the air quality was good, and a cool breeze rolled up Santa Monica Boulevard to swirl through the open French doors into my office. Cindy, the woman in the office next to mine, saw me on the balcony and made a little finger wave. Cindy was wearing a bright white dress shirt tied at the belly and a full-length sarong skirt. I was wearing Gap jeans, a silk Tommy Bahama shirt, and a Bianchi shoulder holster replete with Dan Wesson .38 caliber revolver. The shoulder holster was new, so I was wearing it around the office to break in the leather. I wondered if Cindy found it odd.

Lucy said, "Tracy wants me to meet the vice-president of business affairs, but he's tied up with the sales department until five." Tracy was Tracy Mannos, the news director of KTAY television. Lucy Chenier was an attorney in Baton Rouge, Louisiana, but had been offered a job by KTAY here in Los Angeles. She had come out for three days to discuss job possibilities and contract particulars, and tonight was her last night. We had planned to spend the afternoon at the Mexican marketplace on Olvera Street in downtown LA. Los Angeles was founded there, and the marketplace is ideal for strolling and holding hands.

"Don't worry about it, Luce. Take all the time you need." She hadn't yet decided if she would take the job, but I very much wanted it to happen.

"Are you sure?"

"Sure, I'm sure. How about I pick you up at six? We can go for an early dinner at Border Grill, then back to the house to pack." Border Grill was Lucy's favorite.

"You're a dream, kiddo. Thanks."

"Or, I could drive over and pull the veep out of his meeting at gun point. That might work."

"True, but he might hold it against me in the negotiation."

"You lawyers. All you think about is money."

I was telling Lucy how rotten my plants looked when my outer door opened and three children stepped into my office. I cupped the receiver and called, "Out here."

The oldest was a girl with long dark hair and pale skin and little oval glasses. I made her for fifteen, but she might have been older. A younger boy trailed in behind her, pulling a much smaller girl. The boy was wearing oversized baggy shorts, and Air Nike sneakers. He looked sullen. The younger girl was wearing an X-Files tee-shirt. I said, "I'm being invaded."

Lucy said, "Tracy just looked in. I have to go."

The older girl came to the French doors. "Are you Mr. Cole?"

I held up a finger, and the girl nodded. I said, "Luce, don't worry about how long it takes. If you run late, it's okay."

"You're such a doll."

"I know."

"Meetcha in the lobby at six."

Lucy made kissy sounds and I made kissy sounds back. The girl pretended not to hear, but the boy muttered something to the younger girl. She giggled. I have never thought of myself as the kissy-sound type of person, but since I've known Lucy I've been doing and saying all manner of silly things. That's love for you.

When I turned off the phone, the older girl was

frowning at my plants. "When they're yellow it means they get too much sun."

Everyone's an expert.

"Maybe you should consider cactus. They're hard to kill."

"Thanks for the advice."

I brought the phone back into my office and the girl followed. The younger girl was sitting on the couch, but the boy was inspecting the photographs and the little figurines of Jiminy Cricket that I keep on my desk. He squinted at everything with disdain, and he carried himself with a kind of round-shouldered skulk. I wanted to tell him to stand up straight. I said, "What's up, guys? How can I help you?" Maybe they were selling magazine subscriptions.

The older girl said, "Are you Elvis Cole, the private investigator?"

"Yes. I am." The boy snuck a glance at the Dan Wesson, then eyed the Pinocchio clock that hangs on the wall above the file cabinet. The clock has eyes that move from side to side as it tocks and is a helluva thing to watch.

She said, "Your ad in the Yellow Pages said you find missing people."

"That's right. I'm having a special this week. I'll find two missing people for the price of one." Maybe she was writing a class report. *A Day in the Life of the World's Greatest Detective.*

She stared at me. Blank.

"I'm kidding. That's what we in the trade call private eye humor."

"Oh."

The boy coughed once, but he wasn't really coughing. He was saying, "Asshole," and masking it with the cough. The younger girl giggled again.

I looked at him hard. "How's that?"

The boy went sullen and floated back to my desk. He looked like he wanted to steal something. I said, "Come away from there."

"I didn't do anything."

"I want you on this side of the desk."

The older girl said, "Charles." Warning him. I guess he was like this a lot.

"Jeez." He skulked back toward the file cabinet, and snuck another glance at the Dan Wesson. "What kind of gun is that?"

"It's a Dan Wesson .38 caliber revolver."

"How many guys you kill?"

"I'm thinking about adding another notch right now."

The older girl said, "Charles, *please*." She looked back at me. "Mr. Cole, my name is Teresa Haines. This is my brother, Charles, and our sister, Winona. Our father has been missing for eleven days, and we'd like you to find him."

I stared at her. I thought that it might be a joke, but she didn't look like she was joking. I looked at the boy, and then at the younger girl, and they didn't appear to be joking, either. The boy was watching me from the corner of his eye, and there was a kind of expectancy under the attitude. Winona was all big saucer eyes and unabashed hope. No. They weren't kidding. I went behind my desk, then thought better of it and came around to sit in one of the leather director's chairs opposite the couch. Mr. Informal. Mr. Unthreatening. "How old are you, Ms. Haines?"

"I'm fifteen, but I'll be sixteen in two months. Charles is twelve, and Winona is nine. Our father travels often, so we're used to being on our own, but he's never been gone this long before and we're concerned."

Charles made the coughing sound again, and this time he said, "Prick." Only this time he wasn't talking about me.

I nodded. "What does your father do?"

"He's in the printing business."

"Unh-hunh. And where's your mother?"

"She died five and a half years ago in an automobile accident."

Charles said, "A friggin' drunk driver." He was scowling at the picture of Lucy Chenier on my file cabinet, and he didn't bother to look over at me when he said it. He drifted from Lucy back to the desk and now he was sniffing around the Mickey Mouse phone.

I said, "So your father's been gone for eleven days, and he hasn't called, and you don't know when he's coming back."

"That's right."

"Do you know where he went?"

Charles smirked. "If we knew that, he wouldn't be missing, would he?"

I looked at him, but this time I didn't say anything. "Tell me, Ms. Haines. How did you happen to choose me?"

"You worked on the Teddy Martin murder." Theodore Martin was a rich man who had murdered his wife. I was hired by his defense attorneys to work on his behalf, but it hadn't gone quite the way Teddy had hoped. I'd been on local television and in the *Times* because of it. "I looked up the newspapers in the library and read about you, and then I found your ad in the Yellow Pages."

"Resourceful." My friend Patty Bell was a licensed Social Worker with the county. I was thinking that I could call her.

Teri Haines took a plain legal envelope from her back pocket and showed it to me. "I wrote down his birth date and a description and some things like that." She put it on the coffee table between us. "Will you find him for us?"

I looked at the envelope, but did not touch it. It was two-fifteen on a weekday afternoon, but these kids weren't in school. Maybe I would call Dale Miller. Miller was a lieutenant with the LAPD Juvenile Division and would know what to do.

Teresa Haines leaned toward me, arched her eyebrows, and suddenly looked forty years old. "I know what you're thinking. You're thinking that we're just kids, but we have the money to pay you." She pulled a cheap red wallet from her front pocket, then fanned a deck of twenties and fifties and hundreds that was thick enough to stop a 9mm Parabellum. There had to be two thousand dollars. Maybe three. "You see? All you have to do is name your price."

Charles said, "Jeezis Christ, Teri, don't tell'm that!

He'll clean us out!" Charles had moved from the Mickey phone and now he was fingering the Jiminys again. Maybe I could handcuff him to the couch.

Teri was looking at me. "Well?"

"Where'd you get the money?"

Her right eye flickered, but she did not look away. "Daddy leaves it for us. It's what we live on."

Teresa Haines had long dark hair that hung loosely below her shoulders. Her hair appeared clean and well-kept. Her face was heart-shaped, and a couple of pimples had sprouted on her chin, but she didn't seem self-conscious about them. She appeared well-nourished and in good health, as did her brother and sister. Maybe she was making all of this up. Maybe the whole thing was their idea of a joke. I said, "Have you called the police?"

"Oh, no." She said it quickly.

"If my father was missing, I would."

She shook her head.

"It's what they do, and they won't charge you. I usually get around two grand."

Charles yelled, "Ripoff!" A small framed picture fell when he said it, and knocked over three Jiminy figurines. I glanced at him again, and he scuttled toward the door. "I didn't do anything. Jeezis."

Teresa straightened herself and calmly said, "We'd rather not involve the police, Mr. Cole." You could tell she was struggling to be calm. You could see that it was an effort.

"If your father has been gone for eleven days and you haven't heard from him, you should call the police. They will help you. You don't have to be afraid of them."

She shook her head. "The police will call Children's Services, and they'll take us away."

I tried to look reassuring. "They'll just make sure that you guys are safe, that's all." I spread my hands and smiled. Mr. Nothing-to-be-Afraid-of-Here. "I may have to call them, myself."

Teresa Haines did not move for maybe ten thousand years. She did not breathe. Then she shook her head and slowly stood. Winona stood with her. "Your ad said confidential." Like an accusation.

Charles said, "He's not gonna do frig. You see?" Like they'd had this discussion before they came, and now Charles had been proven right.

I said, "Look, you guys are children. You shouldn't be by yourselves."

Teresa Haines put the money back in the wallet and the wallet back in her pocket. She put the envelope in her pocket, too. "Maybe this was a mistake. We should be going."

I said, "C'mon, Teresa. It's the right way to play it."

Charles was already skulking toward the door. He said, "Eat me," and this time he didn't bother to cough.

There was a flurry of fast steps, and then Teresa and Charles and Winona were gone. They didn't bother to close the door.

I looked at my desk. One of the little Jiminys was gone, too.

I could hear Cindy's radio, drifting in from the balcony. The Red Hot Chili Peppers were singing "Music Is My Aeroplane." I pressed my lips together and let my breath sigh from the corners of my mouth, and stared at the desk.

"Well, moron, are you just going to let them walk out of here?" Maybe I said it, or maybe it was Pinocchio.

I pulled off the Dan Wesson, ran down four flights to the lobby, then out to the street just in time to see them pull away from the curb in a metallic green Saturn. The legal driving age in the state of California is sixteen, but Teresa was driving. It didn't surprise me.

I ran back through the lobby and down to the parking level and drove hard up out of the building, trying to spot their car. A guy in a six-wheel truck that said LEON'S FISH almost broadsided me as I swung out onto Santa Monica Boulevard, and sat on his horn.

I was so focused on trying to spot the Saturn that I didn't yet see the man who was following me, but I would before long.